He saw her . . .

Phoebe Malleson lay reclining on a chaise, the light striking garnet glints from her red hair falling on the pages of the book she was engrossed in. A plate of fruits sat on a low table. As Deverell watched, her eyes never leaving the page, Phoebe extended one slender arm, deftly plucked a grape, then carried it to her mouth, slowly easing the plump grape between her luscious lips.

He watched it slide into her mouth.

He shifted his weight.

She sensed the movement and looked up.

She quickly swallowed her grape.

"Good afternoon. I don't believe we've met."

"I fear I have the advantage of you, Miss Malleson. I'm Deverell."

He drew near and offered his hand.

Surrendering her hand, she rose.

"Were you after a book?"

"No."

He hadn't let go of her hand.

"I came for you."

STEPHANIE LAURENS

To Distraction

A BASTION CLUB NOVEL

AVON BOOKS

An Imprint of HarperCollins*Publishers*

AVON BOOKS
An Imprint of HarperCollins*Publishers*
10 East 53rd Street
New York, New York 10022-5299

To Distraction

The Bastion Club

"a last bastion against the matchmakers of the ton"

MEMBERS

Christian Allardyce,
Marquess of Dearne

#2 ~~Anthony Blake,~~   Alicia
~~Viscount Torrington~~   "Carrington"
Pevensey

Jocelyn Deverell,
Viscount Paignton

*Please see page ii for a list of previous

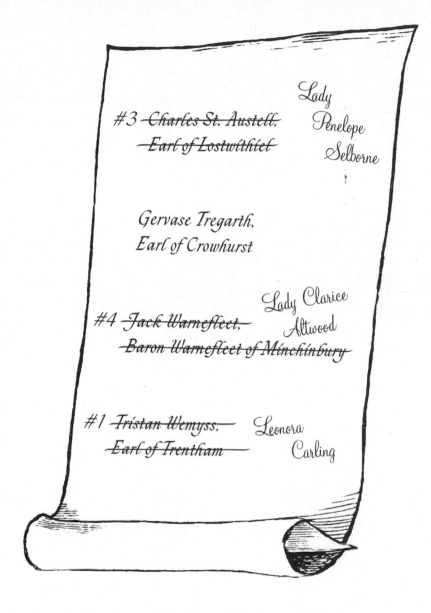

#3 ~~Charles St. Austell,~~
~~Earl of Lostwithiel~~ Lady Penelope Selborne

Gervase Tregarth,
Earl of Crowhurst

#4 ~~Jack Warnefleet,~~
~~Baron Warnefleet of Minchinbury~~ Lady Clarice Altwood

#1 ~~Tristan Wemyss,~~
~~Earl of Trentham~~ Leonora Carling

titles in the Bastion Club series.

Chapter 1

London
Late April, 1816

"**D**ear Deverell, of *course* I know exactly the right lady for you." Head high, Audrey Deverell swayed back on the stool on which she was perched, narrowed her eyes at the canvas she was daubing, then delicately touched the tip of her brush to one spot. Apparently satisfied, she regained her equilibrium and looked down at the palette balanced on her arm. "I'm only surprised it's taken you so long to ask."

Seated in a well-cushioned wicker armchair beside the wide windows through which the afternoon sun washed across his aunt's "studio," Jocelyn Hubert Deverell, 7th Viscount Paignton, known to all as simply Deverell, watched Audrey select another hue to add to her creation—a landscape featuring what he thought was supposed to be a single large oak.

The last time he'd visited, a mere few months ago, this room had been devoted to basket weaving. When he'd been shown in and had discovered Audrey sitting on a high stool before a canvas on an easel, her long, thin frame swathed in a dun-colored smock with a black beret atop her brassy curls, he'd had to fight a grin, one she, who took each of her outlandish pursuits absolutely seriously, would not have appreciated.

His only paternal aunt, much younger than her three brothers, of whom his father had been the eldest, Audrey was in her late forties. A determinedly confirmed spinster, she frequently pursued the outrageous. Nevertheless, being a Deverell and comfortably well-to-do, she remained an accepted member of the haut ton. Even though her more conventional friends, all long married, often displayed a certain jealousy over Audrey's flamboyant freedom, she was much sought after, if nothing else to add color and verve to said matrons' entertainments.

Audrey's audacious unconventionality had from his earliest years drawn Deverell to her; he felt infinitely closer to her than to any of his other aunts—three maternal and two by marriage. Consequently, now that he quite clearly needed the sort of assistance aunts provided gentlemen such as he, it was Audrey to whom he'd turned.

He hadn't, however, expected quite such a definite answer. Caution made him hesitate, but recollection of his state made him ask, "This lady—"

"Is quite perfect in *every* way. She's of excellent family, attractive and lively, suffers from no affliction, physical or mental, is well dowered, correctly and appropriately educated, and I can personally vouch for her understanding."

That last had him arching a brow. "A connection?"

Audrey flashed him a smile. "She's one of my goddaughters. I have a small platoon of them." She refocused on her painting. "Goodness knows why, but a multitude of my friends named me godparent to their offspring. I often wondered if they thought, childless as I am, that I shouldn't be allowed to escape the nurturing role entirely."

Deverell thought that only too likely. "This lady—"

"Will make you an outstanding wife. Trust me, I've seen your predicament coming for months, so of course I've given the matter due thought. You're thirty-two, and what with the title as well as the estates, you really must marry. Admittedly there are your uncles who could inherit after you, but as neither George nor Gisborne have sons of their own, that really isn't an acceptable alternative." Pausing in her daubing, Audrey shot him a severe glance. "And the last thing any of us would wish is to see the estate revert to Prinny!"

"Indeed not." The idea of the estates that, courtesy of the unexpected death of a cousin twice removed, had fallen into his lap reverting on his death to the Crown, and its licentious bearer, was one Deverell viewed with intense disfavor. He might not have expected to have to care for entailed estates, but now they were his, he'd be damned if he let Prinny, or whoever succeeded him, get their greedy hands on them.

Especially not now he'd visited his new holdings, the houses, farms and fields, and met those who tended them. Along with a title came responsibilities, and he'd never been one to shirk such obligations, even if unlooked for.

He was now Viscount Paignton; as such he had to marry. "Quite aside from the matter of an heir—"

"There's the social obligations, of course." Audrey nodded sagely, her gaze still on her canvas. "Your wife must be able to manage your houses, and even more importantly manage the dinners, parties, balls, and so on that as Paignton you will have to attend."

He didn't try to hide his grimace. "If she could *minimize* the latter—"

"Don't even think it, not until you've been married for years. Then, perhaps, you might be allowed to slink off and hide in your library. Until that time, you'll have to grit your teeth and stand by her side at all necessary functions." Audrey threw him another strait glance. "Along with managing your appearances, your wife's duties will include keeping you up to the mark—ensuring you appear at all the functions you ought."

Deverell met Audrey's glance levelly and inwardly wished his wife-to-be good luck. She'd need it. "You seem to have a very clear vision of the qualities my wife should possess."

"Well, of course, dear. I've known you from birth, and despite what you think, you are *very* like your father—you have little time for artifice and none at all for fools. And after spending the last ten and more years being a spy in France, I imagine your prejudices have only become more fixed. Consequently the notion of you finding any degree of marital satisfaction with the general run of young ladies is utterly untenable." She arched a brow at him. "I understand you've been casting your eye over the herd."

"The 'herd' appear to be henwitted flibbertigibbets with less sense than my horse."

Audrey grinned. "Quite. Well, there you are—it's clearly necessary to look elsewhere for your bride." Laying aside her palette, she reached for a rag; sitting back, she started cleaning her brush.

He frowned. "Are you saying there's some other place— some other field—in which I should have been searching? That the marriage mart isn't the place to look?"

Audrey cast him a droll look. "Really, dear, I can't believe you'd be so obtuse. The ladies who would suit you are no more enamored of the marriage mart than you. You won't find *them* eating stale cakes at Almack's."

He blinked. Hope welled. After a moment he asked, "This

paragon you believe would be the perfect wife for me—who is she?"

Eyes on her brush, Audrey smiled. "Phoebe Malleson."

He could place neither lady nor name. "Have I met her?"

"If you can't remember her, the answer is no. But I doubt you would have crossed Phoebe's path, not if you've been doing the pretty by the matchmaking mamas and considering their latest offerings. Phoebe turned twenty-five just last week, but she's been avoiding matrimonially inclined gatherings for years."

He had to wonder. "Twenty-five and yet unwed." He caught Audrey's eye. "Why is it you think this lady is the perfect bride for me?"

The fond feminine smile, full of patronizing solicitude, that Audrey bent on him made him feel six years old. "Really, Deverell dear, do use your head—the very reasons Phoebe is unwed are precisely the reasons that make her perfect for you."

He knew better than to quiz Audrey on the meaning of that conundrum; her answers would make his head ache. She had at least said the lady was attractive. Besides, there was clearly a more direct route to learning all he needed to know about Phoebe Malleson. "I take it Miss Malleson is not in town. Where, then, might I find her?"

"Oh, she's often in town." Audrey waved her brush. "Just not where you'd think to look. She's an only child, and her mother died years ago. Phoebe has a small army of aunts and is usually to be found with one of them, either at their houses or visiting others in their train."

Dropping her brush into a jar, Audrey swung to face him. "As it happens, I know Phoebe is presently with her aunt Mrs. Edith Balmain, and they'll be attending a house party at Cranbrook Manor—it starts the day after tomorrow."

He kept his eyes steady on Audrey's face. "Lady Cranbrook's a friend of yours, isn't she?"

Audrey grinned. "Indeed. I'll be traveling down tomorrow." She let her gaze slide appreciatively over him, taking in his broad shoulders encased in Bath superfine, his neatly tied cravat, pristine linen, fashionable waistcoat, and his long legs, stretched out before him, defined muscles apparent beneath tight-fitting buckskin breeches tucked into glossy black Hessians. Her grin widened. "And if I tell Maria I've persuaded you to attend, she'll kiss my feet."

He grimaced. "And when will Miss Malleson be arriving?"

"Oh, Edith won't want to miss a day—and you'd be well advised to take advantage of every moment available. If you arrive in the afternoon the day after tomorrow, then I'm sure Phoebe will be there. The party is only for four days, so you'll want to make use of every minute."

He frowned. "I will?"

"Well, of course! You surely can't imagine your campaign will be easy?"

His campaign? "How long can it take to look Miss Malleson over and decide to offer for her hand? You've already assured me she's suitable on all counts bar the personal."

Audrey sobered. She regarded him directly for a long minute, then slowly shook her head. "Dear boy, you have the matter entirely by the tail. It's not a case of Phoebe meeting with your approval, but of *you* meeting with *hers*. And that won't be readily forthcoming. It's not a question of whether she's the perfect bride for you—you may rest assured she is—but of you convincing her that *you* are the perfect husband *for her*."

He blinked.

Audrey smiled, fondly patronizing again. "You surely didn't think securing the perfect bride would be easy."

Reading the truth in her eyes, Deverell swallowed a groan.

* * *

He could think of ten activities he'd much rather be engaged in than setting out to persuade some difficult-to-please lady she should entrust her hand to him. Nevertheless, riven by mixed feelings, two days later he duly tooled his curricle out of town and down the newly macadamized roads into Surrey.

At least the day was fine, the breeze light, scented with grass and earthy growing things. His pair of matched grays leaned into their harness, glad to be stretching their legs beyond the confines of London's crowded streets.

He was of two minds about following Audrey's direction, yet he had asked, and she'd given her aid—her opinions and her advice. To not follow said advice might well rate as flying in the face of fate, and he'd long ago learned to bow when necessary. As his need of a bride was acute, the present situation qualified; that need was what had driven him to swallow his pride and ask for Audrey's help in the first place.

Besides, underneath it all he trusted Audrey; he had confidence in her ability to read him. Consequently he was more than a little curious to meet the paragon she'd deemed perfect for him. God knew his own reconnaissance had signally failed to uncover any lady close to that ideal.

Until Audrey had mentioned it, he hadn't considered the more than ten years he'd spent as a secret operative in Paris throughout the latter years of the war, when he'd kept a close eye on the commercial links crucial to the operation of the French state—the contracts, the connections—and, when wise or necessary, disrupting those links, to have had any material bearing on his requirements in a bride. No matter how deeply he delved into his own character, he couldn't see that those years, and all he'd done and been forced to do, had changed him, not the true him, the real him behind his polished exterior.

He was the same man he'd always been destined to be . . . but, on reflection, he could see that Audrey might be correct in one sense: The years had entrenched his traits. The experience had made him harder, more definite and defined, more ruthless and impatient; he'd been forced to face questions many men went most if not all their lives without facing—the sort of questions that, once answered, disallowed self-delusion.

Consequently he knew and accepted that he wouldn't be an easygoing husband, the sort of mild-mannered gentleman fashionable ladies married and thereafter took for granted. He was demanding, and not just as a lover; if a lady was his, he would expect to be the central focus of her life. And in such matters he had very little tolerance; his temper was such that he could bend just so far, and no further.

Indeed, his temper was one aspect ladies rarely read aright. The persona he showed to the world was one of fashionably languid laissez-faire. The reality was that he was ruthless and determined, and in the main insisted and ensured that he got his own way; he might smile and charm while he did it, but the result was the same.

A comfortable gentleman he was not, nor would he ever be.

And that was the root cause behind his rejection of all the bright young things he'd had paraded before him in recent months. If a magic wand had been waved and they'd been allowed to see the real man behind his glamor, the majority would have fainted. The rest would have fled.

He wasn't the sort of man who would fit their mold, regardless of the ambitions too many of them, and even more of their mamas, fondly nursed.

Which was why from the first—the opening of the Season a month or so ago—he'd been careful. As until recently he'd been unencumbered by large estates, London had always been his favored haunt; although previously he'd known it only as a well-heeled gentleman of twenty-one, he'd learned the ton's ropes well enough. Enough to exercise all due caution. Enough to reconnoiter from the sidelines, appearing at balls at the last moment decency allowed and escaping half an hour later, as soon as he'd assessed the young ladies present.

Such guerrilla tactics, often executed in the company of Christian Allardyce, Marquess of Dearne, had caused consternation among the matchmaking ranks, but had kept everyone safe. Christian was a close comrade, one of the other six gentlemen of similar ilk—ex-secret operatives now retired from His Majesty's service, all wealthy, titled, and needing to return to the world of the ton, and thus all requiring a wife—who had the previous year banded together to form the Bastion Club, their bolthole and stronghold against the marauding mamas who prowled the ton.

All of them had been determined not to fall victim to any leg-shackling trap but rather to choose their own brides, and while he had doubts that rational choice had been quite the way matters had transpired, four of their number were now happily married. Three days ago he'd returned from Jack Warnefleet's wedding in Somerset even more set on finding his own bride.

He could admit, if only to himself, that seeing the others find their mates had increased his own restlessness, had escalated his need to find his bride—his salvation. The thought of returning to his new castle, Paignton Hall in Devon, alone, to face a summer of being hunted by every local mama with a daughter to settle, to have to attend innumerable functions and smile, chat, dance, all the while forever remaining on guard was for him a working description of hell.

During all the years he'd spent in France—every minute of every day of every month of every year—he'd been on guard. Alert, watchful, never resting. He was tired of the tension and increasingly impatient over the continuing need; although now home, he still needed to be on guard.

He'd had enough of it.

He wanted—*needed*—surcease. He wanted to relax, to enjoy a woman again—her company, her laughter, her body, her sighs of pleasure—without having the specter of her likely motives hanging over his head.

He wanted a wife. A lady who would happily be his, who would share his life and remove him from the ranks of the eligible.

Marriage was, for him, a necessary escape.

The regular reverberating thuds of the grays' hooves underscored his thoughts, and his determination.

The green fields of Surrey flew past. Ten minutes later, he spotted the signpost for Cranbrook Ford. Checking the grays, he turned them south; less than a mile down the lane, stone gateposts appeared, a brass plaque proclaiming them the entrance to Cranbrook Manor.

He swept through and set the grays briskly trotting. A light breeze rippled through the leafy canopies of the oaks bordering the drive. The manor appeared ahead, a low, wide house in gray stone, its façade whimsically crenellated.

"Be that where we're going then?"

Deverell glanced around at Grainger, his groom-cum-tiger. "Yes." Deverell faced forward. He'd known Grainger, about nineteen years old, a lanky, good-hearted lad with a quick laugh, for less than a year. He'd discovered him on his first visit to Paignton; a natural with horses, Grainger had nevertheless been something of an outcast—a lowly orphan with no known family, tolerated because of his unusual skill. Deverell had changed that; he'd made Grainger his groom, taking him out of the routine of the larger stables and giving him his prize cattle to tend.

When it came to horses he had complete faith in Grainger. In other spheres . . .

"While we're here, you'll behave as if you were at Paignton Hall, under Mallard and Mrs. Mottram's thumbs. Mind what everyone says and do nothing untoward."

He felt Grainger's gaze.

"Be n't I to help you then? Ain't there nothing I'm supposed to do—beyond the grays, I mean?"

Deverell was about to disavow any need, but recollection of Audrey's words had him temporizing. "There may be something I need you for later, but the first thing you must do is be quiet and friendly, helpful and undisruptive with all the other staff. Keep your eyes and ears open so that when I need information, you'll know who to ask—or more rightly who to encourage to talk to you." He glanced at Grainger. "Do you understand?"

The light in Grainger's eyes assured him that horses weren't his groom's only interest. "Oh, aye—I can do that."

Looking forward, hiding his grin—his understanding that Grainger was now fantasizing about the maids he might meet and how to encourage them to talk to him—Deverell steered the curricle onto the gravel forecourt before the manor's wide stone steps.

A groom came running; Grainger greeted him jovially.

Halting the horses and handing over the reins, Deverell stepped down and started up the steps. Before he reached the porch, the door swung wide; a large and stately butler waited to bow him in.

He was shown into the drawing room, a long room with French doors along one side, presently open to the terrace and the manicured lawns beyond. As Audrey had prophesized, Maria, Lady Cranbrook, was delighted—no, *aux anges*—to welcome him to her home, informing him without a blink that his presence would assuredly cause a considerable stir among her female guests.

In the face of her enthusiasm he smiled charmingly and

cast a sharp glance at Audrey; seated beside her ladyship, his aunt merely smiled back, fondly smug, and nodded her encouragement when Lady Cranbrook directed him to the lawn, on which the bulk of her guests were strolling.

Stepping out onto the terrace, he cast a quick, searching look around—and very nearly stepped back. There was a small army of young ladies present, and he'd omitted to ask for a description of Audrey's paragon.

But most of the guests, both ladies and gentlemen, had noticed him; to retreat would make him appear ludicrously high in the instep, as if he thought himself above their company.

"Besides," he muttered to himself as, nonchalant smile in place, he stepped down to the lawn, "how hard can it be to identify one female and run her to earth?"

Fatal words. By the time he'd done the rounds, been introduced and spoken politely with every female, both young and old, gracing the wide lawn and drifting beneath the trees, and discovered that Miss Phoebe Malleson was simply not there, his patience—always limited—had worn distinctly thin. Spying Audrey descending from the terrace, he excused himself from the matron who, along with her two daughters, had corraled him, and strolled to intercept his aunt.

One look into his eyes and Audrey's lips twitched.

His own lips thinning, he hung on to his temper. "Your paragon is playing least in sight."

"Well of course she is, dear—I did warn you." Audrey patted his arm, leaned closer, and murmured, "Now she's twenty-five, she's determined to go her own way and waste no more time even pretending an interest in gentlemen and marriage. So she's here at the house, but elsewhere."

He frowned. "If she has no interest in gentlemen and marriage, why am I here?"

"To teach her the error of her ways, of course." Taking his arm, Audrey drew him around. "Have you met Edith Balmain, Phoebe's aunt?"

"Yes." He glanced to where the sprightly, white-haired widow sat, bright blue eyes drinking everything in, interested and alert. At first glance she appeared the epitome of a little old lady, tiny, slightly stooped, with a soft lined face and a retiring manner, but once he'd met those eyes he'd reassigned her to quite a different category. She was an astute observer—one who saw, detected, and consequently knew everything, including all those private matters people thought they'd concealed.

Even without the connection to his paragon he would have been drawn to, and interested in learning more of, Edith Balmain. However . . . "She didn't know where her niece might be skulking, either."

"Well, Deverell dear, if there's one gentleman in all this gathering with the right skills to hunt Phoebe down, it's you." Audrey caught his eye, smugly smiled. "And when you do I'm sure your persuasive talents will be up to the challenge of making her rethink her rejection of matrimony."

He let his frown deepen. "One point continues to elude me—why do you think she's so unquestionably the right lady for me?"

Audrey's smile took on an edge—one of understanding and determination. "You'll have your answer when you find her."

He wasn't going to get any more from her; with a sigh he let her hear, he bowed over her hand and headed for the house.

In one respect, Audrey was right—tracking down people was one of his fortes. By dint of asking the butler, Stripes, he learned first that Miss Malleson had not called for a carriage or a horse and was consequently somewhere in the house or within walking distance of it but was not in her chamber, and, secondly, where all the places a lady might seek solitude were located.

He ranked those places in order of the most likely—the conservatory, the orangery, the shrubbery, the maze, the chapel, the billiard room, and the library—and set out on his search.

When he opened the paneled door of the library, stepped silently inside, and instantly, instinctively, knew she was there, he realized that when dealing with Phoebe Malleson he was going to have to adjust his thinking.

She wasn't the average young lady.

He couldn't see her from where he stood, but instincts honed through years of constant danger informed him he wasn't the sole human in the room. That, indeed, there was a female in the room.

Closing the door silently, he walked forward, smoothly, barely disturbing the air. And saw her.

He halted.

Head and shoulders comfortably supported by a large fringed cushion, Phoebe Malleson—he had no doubt it was she—lay reclining on a chaise angled away from a long window. The light streamed in, striking garnet glints from her neatly coiled coronet of dark red hair before falling on the pages of the book she was engrossed in.

So engrossed she hadn't yet noticed him; he seized the moment to take stock.

She was, he estimated as he eyed the length of leg demurely concealed beneath filmy pale blue skirts, a trifle taller than the average. Her figure was slender, yet, as far as he could judge given her pose, her hips were nicely rounded. Her breasts were too, not large yet promising a firm handful. Her throat was long, her skin pale and fine. Her jaw . . .

Even in respose, her jaw suggested determination.

Indeed, all her features—broad brow, straight nose, wide eyes—he couldn't tell their color—set beneath finely arched dark brows and framed by lush lashes, and her fractionally too large mouth with its full, red lips, all neatly set in the pale oval of her face—held a hint of the dramatic. The whole projected a sense of aliveness, of vitality and purpose—attributes he'd failed to discern in other young ladies.

Audrey had been right. Just setting eyes on Phoebe Malleson awoke a compelling curiosity—a wish to know more, to learn what made such an unusual lady tick.

A plate of fruits sat on a low table before the chaise; it had clearly been sampled at length. As he watched, her eyes never leaving the page, Phoebe Malleson extended one slender arm, searched, located a bunch of grapes, deftly plucked one, then carried it to her mouth, hesitated while she finished a section, then slowly eased the plump grape between her luscious lips.

Deverell watched it slide into her mouth.

Inwardly grimacing, he shifted his weight.

She looked up.

Phoebe Mary Malleson glanced across the room and quite unexpectedly found herself gazing at a nattily striped waistcoat. She blinked, then lifted her gaze . . . slowly.

The man—gentleman—was tall. And large.

How had he got so close?

He had the most gorgeous green eyes she'd ever seen.

Fascinating green eyes . . . and a direct gaze that was, even more to her surprise, frankly disconcerting. She wanted to look away, to break the contact, yet some part of her didn't dare. . . .

Who the devil was he?

More to the point, her inner self whispered, *what* was he?

A peculiar little shiver slithered down her spine. She continued to stare, mesmerized, hypnotized—caught, trapped, within his green gaze. Alarmed, and not a little disgusted at such ridiculous and newfound susceptibility, she forced herself to blink and succeeded in wrenching her eyes from his.

Lying all but supine in the presence of a dangerous man wasn't wise; clearing her throat, she swung her legs over the side of the chaise and sat up.

She quickly swallowed her grape. "Good afternoon." Her voice, at least, was her own, firm and even. Reassuringly steady. "I don't believe we've met."

Her last sentence carried commendable hauteur—polite but coolly distant. A trifle censorious. Encouraged, she risked lifting her eyes to his again, only to find the mesmerizing green screened by long dark lashes. She should have been relieved, only she could feel his gaze still on her, still watchful, assessing, in a distinctly predatory way.

He was indeed tall, and large, but his broad shoulders and chest were entirely in proportion with the long, lean lines of his legs. Her brain registered his fashionable, quietly elegant attire—expensive and select—and the aura of leashed power that hung about him even as her gaze, without conscious direction, rapidly scanned his face.

Clean, well-defined angles and planes, his features stamped him as one of her kind, her class, but there was a hardness there she didn't miss or mistake, a strength in his well-shaped nose and squared chin, and a certain cynicism in the set of his mobile lips.

As her gaze settled on those lips, they lightly curved.

"I fear I have the advantage of you, Miss Malleson." His lids rose; startled, she met his gaze again. "I'm Deverell."

The amusement she glimpsed in his distracting eyes was more than enough to prick her temper. She frowned lightly, shifting her gaze from him. "Deverell . . ." She tapped one fingernail on her book, then quickly looked back at him as he came forward. "You must be Audrey's nephew."

He drew near and offered his hand. She glanced at it, sorely tempted to remain seated, but having him towering over her wasn't worth the minor victory. Surrendering her hand, she rose.

Clasping her fingers firmly, he assisted her to her feet, then bowed, the action smooth and graceful. "Indeed. I'm Paignton."

She bobbed the obligatory curtsy; far too conscious of his largeness, the strangely overwhelming—strangely impressive—wall of masculinity a mere foot away, she refused to again meet his eyes. "Ah, yes—I heard that you had come into the title."

Why was he there disrupting her peace? Intending to dismiss him, she glanced pointedly at the shelves. "Were you after a book?"

"No."

He hadn't let go of her hand. Forced to it, steeling herself, she lifted her gaze and met his eyes. Now much closer, more alluring, even more mesmerizing.

She was staring again.

Into the fascinating emerald depths.

At the edge of her vision, the curve of his lips deepened. "I came for you."

It took a moment or three for his words to reach her brain. Even when they did, they made no sense—not when matched with the tenor of his voice. Deep, reverberating, it seemed to suggest . . . a meaning far more primitive than could possibly be the case.

With an effort, Phoebe harried her brain into action. "Is my aunt asking after me?"

His brows, dark, slightly winged, rose. "Not that I know of."

She blinked, and glanced through the French doors at the lawns beyond. "I take it it's time for tea?" She eased her fingers from his firm grip.

Allowing her digits to slide from his clasp, he glanced over her head at the clock on the mantelpiece beyond the chaise. "Soon, I daresay."

Phoebe suppressed a frown. If he hadn't come searching for her because of her aunt, or to summon her for afternoon tea . . .

Sudden suspicion bloomed. Narrowing her eyes, she fixed them on his. "*Why* did you come looking for me?"

His light smile was charming; behind it, she sensed, he thought quickly.

"Audrey suggested I do so."

She frowned, hard, at him. "Audrey?" She hoped she conveyed her disbelief that he was so malleable that his aunt could direct him.

His lips quirked. "Indeed."

"Why?"

"I gather she believed I would benefit from making your acquaintance."

She raised her brows haughtily. "And have you?"

His smile deepened, genuine, warm—and subtly teasing. "Time will no doubt tell."

Her instincts flickered. She held his gaze while thoughts milled in her head, recollections of what she'd heard of him—little by way of specifics, nothing that had prepared her for the impact of his physical presence, yet of his station speculation had been rife. He was wealthy, titled—and undeniably required a wife.

His aunt Audrey was her godmother, and a close friend of her aunt; it didn't require much mental effort to discern why he'd been pointed in her direction. Yet despite her aunt's and her godmother's fond hopes, she wasn't interested in filling the position he had vacant.

She refocused on his eyes and noted the intensity, the acuity behind his green gaze. How best to get rid of him? Tell him plainly to go away? In her experience such tactics rarely worked, especially not with men like him. He would either not believe she was serious, or worse, decide to interpret her refusal as a challenge.

No. In their current location there was a much more effective way of dealing with him.

"Perhaps," she said, very conscious of his nearness and more, of his attention being completely focused on her, "we should join the others for afternoon tea?"

His lids flickered, then he searched her eyes. A moment passed, then he inclined his head. "If you wish."

Before he could offer his arm and leave her compelled to take it—and thus be far closer to him than she needed to be—she flashed him a smile and turned to the French doors. "We can go this way."

With determined brightness, she led the way outside.

Chapter 2

*B*emused, surprised, Deverell followed his quarry from the library, stepping out through the French doors she'd set swinging wide onto a narrow terrace.

He'd sensed the connection, that indefinable spark that had flared between them the instant their eyes had met. He knew she'd felt it, too, but she'd merely blinked and ignored it. And him.

He wasn't accustomed to being ignored, let alone having a lady so dismissively resist an attraction of that degree. Indeed, he couldn't recall any female who had so focused his attention at first glance.

Without looking back, she descended to the lawn.

"You haven't visited here before, have you? Maria—Lady Cranbrook—always gathers a lively crowd."

She set out along one side of the large house; stepping down from the terrace in her wake, Deverell looked about, noting the line of mature trees that faded into woodland on the opposite side of the lawn. The other guests were congregated on the lawn at the rear of the house; Phoebe led him in that direction, determinedly blithe and gay.

"I'm sure you'll find plenty to interest you during the next few days. Maria usually organizes a picnic on the downs, and there's some lovely rides."

She spoke over her shoulder as she walked briskly on, as if she saw him as something not quite civilized, certainly not safe—the sort of companion that made returning to the herd seem a good idea. A sufficiently compelling idea to make her forget her book; she'd dropped the tome on the chaise without a glance.

Despite her clear hope, he wasn't about to let her slip from his sights.

She prattled on, extolling the pleasures of the gardens and a nearby folly. Unhurriedly lengthening his stride, he closed the distance between them, enjoying the view as he did. His earlier estimation of her figure had been pleasingly exceeded by the reality; she was a touch taller than he'd imagined—no Long Meg, yet the top of her head was level with his chin. Most of the unexpected length was in her legs, and while she was indeed slender, the curves beneath her muslin skirt held definite allure. As did those that more than adequately filled her bodice.

Her blue gown, with its rounded neckline, was neither prim nor precocious. It was ladylike, of the sort that declared the owner aware of her femininity yet not absorbed by it, deeming it unnecessary to make any point of it.

One of his peculiar, now finely honed talents was being able to read people—their characters, their traits—rapidly, with just a glance and a few words. His initial reading of Phoebe mirrored what Audrey had said of her: She had no interest whatever in gentlemen, nor did she expect to develop any such interest in the near future.

Well enough; he clearly had a challenge on his hands, but that spark of attraction held definite promise. And given what he now realized had been the wellspring of his recent restlessness—his lack of anything to actively pursue—he was not at all averse to viewing Phoebe Malleson, and her hand, as a prize to be fought for and won.

Especially as, in just a few minutes, she'd managed to intrigue him.

She rounded the corner of the house. Drawing alongside, he glanced at her face; expression determined, she was looking ahead to where the other guests were gathering about tables set for afternoon tea.

He couldn't recall when a lady had so piqued his curiosity, or his fickle and long-jaded interest. Her refusal to acknowledge their mutual attraction only drove the spur deeper.

She felt his gaze but resisted meeting it; instead, she gestured at the guests. "I expect you've done the rounds and met everyone. Peter Mellors visits here regularly—he'll be able to answer any questions you might have."

He'd much rather ask her. He ambled beside her, interested to see where she was leading him—what she thought she was going to do with him.

How she thought she was going to lose him.

His lips curved. His expectations of the next four days soared; his entertainment appeared assured. He made a mental note to remember to thank Audrey.

Phoebe Malleson marched into the clustered guests much like a general visiting his troops; others gave way before her, reminiscent of the parting of the Red Sea. Deverell followed close behind, smiling genially on everyone yet making no attempt to disguise his intent; he preferred all to see him as he was—an experienced gentleman in fixed pursuit of Phoebe Malleson.

She headed for the table behind which Stripes stood, magisterially manning an ornate silver samovar.

Deverell drew level; reaching the table, he nodded to Stripes. "A cup for Miss Malleson."

She threw him a glance, but when he handed her the delicate cup, she accepted prettily enough.

"And you, sir?"

Deverell met Stripes's gaze. The man knew perfectly well that he was not the type to coddle his innards with tea. However . . . "Indeed."

Taking the cup Stripes offered, Deverell was aware of Phoebe's frowning gaze as she sipped and studied him over the rim of her cup.

He turned to her, and she turned away. Her gaze raced over the guests, then she shifted and drifted to a nearby group. Not the closest group; one she'd selected. He followed, wondering why.

"Mrs. Hildebrand. Leonora, Tabitha. Mr. Hinckley." Phoebe glanced at Deverell as he halted beside her. "I believe you've met Viscount Paignton?"

The ladies smiled brightly, gazes already locked on him; Mr. Hinckley inclined his head.

"I was just describing to his lordship the many activities we usually indulge in whilst here." Phoebe smiled at Leonora Hildebrand, a dashing blond. "You're such an excellent rider, Leonora—did you intend to go riding this afternoon?"

Leonora hadn't, but as she lifted her blue eyes to his face, Deverell was perfectly sure Phoebe had known that. Just as she'd known Leonora would breathily gush, "I had thought of it. Perhaps we could get up a party?"

Leonora's eyes remained on his face. He smiled vaguely, as if thinking of other things, and took a sip of tea, apparently unaware that Leonora's general question had in fact been addressed primarily to him.

When he didn't respond, Leonora was forced to look to Mr. Hinckley.

Who was only too ready to leap into the breach. "We could ride to the ford. It's not that far away. We'd be back in plenty of time to change for dinner." Eager, enthused, he appealed to Mrs. Hildebrand.

Having taken shrewd stock of Deverell's immobility, Leonora's mama deigned to smile on Mr. Hinckley. "Indeed— fresh air and exercise. That's precisely what the doctor prescribed for blowing away the megrims poor Leonora has suffered over these last weeks. I declare, London has been overrun by encroaching cits and halfpay officers."

Mr. Hinckley contrived to look sympathetic.

Deverell didn't bother; he'd already taken stock of Leonora and Mrs. Hildebrand.

Hinckley turned to him. "Can we interest you in joining us, Paignton?"

Setting his cup on its saucer, he used the moment to appear to be considering. "It's tempting, but I think not. I've only just arrived, and I need to get my bearings."

Hinckley disguised his relief well. He turned to Phoebe. "Miss Malleson?"

Phoebe shot a glance at Deverell; instinct pushed her to accept simply to ensure she was somewhere he wouldn't be . . . but she didn't trust him not to change his mind. "Thank you, but no. However, you might speak with Mr. Manning and Miss Pilborough. They're both keen riders."

Mr. Hinckley and Mrs. Hildebrand turned eagerly to scan the guests. Leonora looked distinctly less keen.

Before she could initiate any conversational gambit to try to hold Deverell, Phoebe took charge. "I believe you wished to speak with Mr. Mellors, Paignton. He's just over there." She smiled brightly at the other three. "If you'll excuse us?"

Everyone murmured politely. Parting from them, she steered Deverell toward the group that included Peter Mellors—along with his ravishingly beautiful sister, Deidre.

Obviously, Leonora didn't suit; she'd have to find some other young lady to catch Deverell's eye.

And deflect it from her.

She had far too much going on in her life to have a potential suitor dogging her heels. Especially one like him.

She'd recalled he was, or had been, involved with the military, or the army—the authorities in some guise. A number of her regular activities were of debatable legality; having Deverell peering over her shoulder . . . just the thought made her shiver.

With apprehension. She was sure it was that.

Deidre had been keeping a surreptitious eye on Deverell; she turned and smiled delightedly as they neared, and quickly shifted to make space for them beside her.

Phoebe adjusted her approach so that Deverell had no option but to stand next to Deidre. She waited until everyone had finished exchanging greetings, then caught Peter Mellors's eye. "Peter dear, I've been extolling your knowledge of the house and surrounds to Viscount Paignton. He hasn't visited here before and needs to find his way about."

Peter grinned good-naturedly. He nodded to Deverell. "Just ask away, old man. Happy to help."

Deverell smiled easily. "I've already found the billiard room."

"Ah, well. Most important room in the house." Peter winked. "We—well, most of the gentlemen—usually gather after dinner for a few rounds."

"After doing your duty in the drawing room, I hope!" Mrs. Morrison, a formidable matron, eyed Peter with mock censure, sure to become real if he didn't respond appropriately.

Peter's grin was irrepressible. "Of course," he vowed. "That's understood."

"It better be." Mrs. Morrison faced Deverell. "The last thing we want is to find you gentlemen deserting us."

"With such a coterie of fascinating ladies, I can't imagine you'll endure such a fate." His glib answer, delivered with a charming smile and a hand over his heart, had Mrs. Morrison's lips twitching.

"We'll see." After an instant's hesitation, she inquired, "Are you intending to remain for the entire four days?"

"That is my intention."

"Unless you're called away, of course." Deidre Mellors, an exquisitely beautiful young lady with glossy brown hair, shifted to draw his attention her way.

He obliged, but remained more aware of Phoebe on his other side, quietly observing, than of Miss Mellors's lovely hazel eyes.

Eyes she deployed shamelessly. "I understand your new estates are in Devon. It must be quite fatiguing, learning all the ropes when you hadn't expected to inherit."

"It hasn't been as difficult as it might have been. There were excellent staff in place—they helped me pick up the reins."

"I expect you'll be spending the summer down there."

"I hadn't really thought." Although conscious of Deidre's eager expression, registering it and smiling in response, his attention had locked on Phoebe as she turned to speak with Mrs. Morrison; he couldn't hear what she was saying. "There's a few matters I need to settle before I retire for the summer."

"Indeed?" Deidre's eyes lit.

With an easy, yet noncommittal, faintly vague smile in place, he glanced at Peter Mellors. "Is there much shooting in the vicinity?"

Peter pulled a face. "Not much game at this time of year, but"—he glanced at Edgar Thomas, standing beside him— "we could set up a tournament."

"Not pistols," Deidre immediately said. "Archery. That way we ladies can join in."

Deverell smiled—genuinely. The others took the altered expression to signify encouragement; they immediately fell to discussing plans for an archery tournament. In reality, that smile was for himself; as he'd expected, thinking him drawn in, Phoebe was making her move.

She'd already turned from him to chat with Mrs. Morrison; quietly taking her leave of that lady, she continued turning away and slipped from his side.

"Will you join us with bow and arrow, my lord?" Deidre gazed up at him, hazel eyes openly inviting.

He raised his brows. "I certainly plan to take aim at a target."

His intended target was out of earshot.

Deidre beamed and turned to her brother. Deverell seized the moment to nod to Peter and Edgar. "Put my name down. If you'll excuse me?"

A rhetorical question. Deidre swung to him, disappointment in her eyes, but she quickly concealed it. She bobbed a curtsy; Mrs. Morrison nodded approvingly and let him escape.

Finding Phoebe wasn't hard; she was skirting the knots of guests, clearly intending to slip away.

Amiably smiling, he set out in pursuit.

Phoebe saw him coming. She stifled an irritated sigh and turned to face him, mentally canvassing who else was present, what other young ladies might interest him. Neither Leonora nor Deidre had managed to hold his interest; perhaps he liked *young* young ladies?

Twenty minutes later, her frustration had reached new

heights. *Young* young ladies made him cling even more tightly to her skirts. More, it had belatedly occurred to her that he was being far too amenable—too malleable—in allowing her to guide him around. He wasn't the malleable sort.

He had no intention whatever of letting her distract him; no matter how pleasant and sociable his interaction with others, his real attention—his focus—had never shifted from her.

The realization sent a most peculiar ripple through her usually unimpressionable nerves.

Exasperated, both with him and that ripple, that he'd been able to make her feel such a thing, she marched away from the last knot of guests to which she'd introduced him— Heather Jenkings was a perfectly sweet chit—ridiculously aware that, if anything, he now prowled even closer beside her; all her senses, all her skin on that side, were flickering at his nearness.

Halting beneath the branches of a nearby tree, out of earshot of any others, she swung to face him. And fixed him with a narrow-eyed glare. "Audrey told me you were a major in the Guards, and that you fought at Waterloo. Is that correct?"

His green eyes met hers; the glint of amusement she caught in their depths sent her temper soaring. He nodded. "Along with an army of others."

"Indeed. But having faced down Boney's finest, I can't see why a quiet chit like Heather Jenkings should have the power to render you witless."

His dark brows shot up. "Witless?"

"Well, *speechless* at any rate." She waved back at the group about Heather. "You stood there like a sphinx— beyond a hello and a good-bye, and the curtest of replies, you uttered not one word."

His expression remained mild, still faintly amused. "Remaining silent seemed wisest. Better than allowing my boredom to show."

She frowned at him. "Heather bored you?"

He glanced at the other guests. "All young ladies bore me."

Eyeing his face—a study in masculine impassivity—Phoebe pressed her lips tightly together, reminding herself that *she* was no longer classed as a young lady. She made herself think twice, then said, "I understand . . . well, we've all heard that you need a wife."

His attention shifted back to her; once more she was treated to the full intensity of his gaze.

She lifted her chin. "It's common knowledge, and here you are, looking over the field."

His mobile lips quirked. "Not quite. But you're right in that I need a wife, and I am here."

She nodded, and forced herself to hold his gaze. "And if you have any thought of me filling that position, you may put it out of your head—I have no interest in marriage. However, I realize Audrey and Edith have probably hatched some scheme and might well have got you down here under false pretenses. The least I can do is assist you in your search."

His eyes widened; the curve of his lips deepened. "Assist me?"

"Yes. You clearly need help." Folding her arms, she swung so that she could survey the assembled guests. He stood beside her, facing in the same direction, yet his gaze remained on her face. "Now, have you any physical preferences regarding your bride?"

He didn't immediately answer. She waited, eyes fixed on the crowd.

Eventually, he said, voice deep and low, "Tall—she should be taller than the average."

Phoebe glanced over the heads, studying all the females. Other than old Lady Althorpe, she was the tallest lady present. None of the unmarried young ladies stood taller than the average, but perhaps Monica Simmons or Georgina Riley might do; heaven knew they were pretty enough. "Blond or brunette?"

After a moment, his deep drawl reached her. "I've a penchant for a certain shade of dark red."

The color of her hair.

Lips compressing, she kept her gaze on the crowd, then demanded, crisply, "Eye color?"

"A curious blend of violet and blue."

She narrowed her eyes; slowly turning her head, she pinned him with a violet-blue stare. "This is not going to work. There is no point whatever in you fixing your attention on me."

His lips curved. "Too late." He glanced at the others. "Introducing me to the others did nothing more than confirm that in pointing me in your direction, Audrey understood my needs remarkably well."

She drew a deep breath; lowering her arms, she turned to face the crowd. "Be that as it may, my lord, as I've already informed you, I have no interest in marriage."

"Yes, I know. I heard you the first time."

"Well, then you'll realize that there is no benefit in spending any further time with me." She made shooing motions toward the rest of the gathering. "Even if none here meet your requirements, I'd strongly suggest you use the opportunity to polish your approach. Permit me to inform you that you could use the practice."

It was an impertinent speech, but she meant every word—every insult. The damned man got under her skin as no other ever had. Eyes on the crowd, she waited for him to take his leave of her.

A full minute ticked by.

"I have a better idea."

Five simple words, but his tone, dark and infinitely dangerous, had her whipping her gaze back to his face.

Her eyes, wide, locked with his. Her heart leapt; her lungs stilled. They stood at the edge of a crowd, yet in that moment she could have sworn they were alone, isolated, the two of them standing in some world out of time.

His green gaze, sharp and hot, lazily, indolently, insolently roamed her face, lingered on her lips, then returned to her eyes.

Her every pore registered his nearness—as heat, power, a threat she couldn't name. His next words, when they came, seemed to wrap about her, a potent, flagrant seduction in sound.

"Have you ever thought of changing your mind?"

She looked into his eyes and saw, behind the charm and the lurking amusement, a hardness, a ruthlessness, a power that reminded her of a time, a place, an incident she had no wish to recall.

Cold raced over her skin. "No." Holding his gaze, she fought to quell a shiver. "That will never happen."

She had to get away. Folding her arms, tightening them, she inclined her head, then turned and left him.

"What the devil's the matter?"

Phoebe lifted her gaze to the mirror before her and met her maid, Skinner's, dark eyes. Gowned for the evening, she sat before the dressing table in the bedchamber she'd been assigned; it was nearly time to go down for dinner. Skinner, thin and wiry, her steel gray hair pulled back in a tight bun, stood behind her, brushing and twisting her hair into a knot atop her head.

Hands busy, Skinner nodded to the jeweled comb Phoebe

had been fiddling with. "You'd best give that here before you break it—you've been scowling at the thing ever since you sat down."

Phoebe grimaced and raised the comb; Skinner reached over her shoulder, took it, then set it into her hair. Skinner had been her maid for years. Phoebe had no closer confidante. "A gentleman arrived this afternoon—Deverell, Viscount Paignton. He's Audrey's nephew, has recently unexpectedly inherited the title, and thus is now in need of a wife."

"Aha." Skinner slipped in a last hairpin and threw her a shrewd glance. "Got his eye on you, has he?"

"So it seems, but he'll have to take his intentions elsewhere. I've far too much to do with this rescue we've arranged to have a man of his ilk dogging my heels, wanting to monopolize my attention."

"Hmm." Skinner busied herself with Phoebe's jewel box. "From what I heard in the servants' hall, he sounded like a swell." She handed a pair of pearl earrings to Phoebe.

Swiveling to look directly at Skinner, Phoebe took them. "How do you know? Did he bring a gentleman's gentleman?"

She wouldn't have classed Deverell as the sort to have a valet.

Skinner snorted. "No. He brought a groom-cum-tiger, a young lad from the west country who can't say a bad word about his new lord. Seems he's top of the trees, and our Fergus and the other coachmen were saying his lordship has a great eye for cattle—seems his pair are prime 'uns. But the lad's a nice boy. He's minding his p's and q's and tripping over his feet to be helpful. If his master's got half as good a heart, he won't be a bad 'un."

"Regardless"—turning back to the mirror, Phoebe attached one earring—"we can't have him watching me, attaching himself to my skirts and dogging my footsteps, particularly not here, not now." She picked up the second pearl drop. "Speaking of which, have you heard when Lady Moffat is expected?"

"Tomorrow morning. She's been staying just over at Leatherhead with her sister, so she's liable to arrive not long after breakfast."

"Excellent. That should give us plenty of time to get everything in place to make our move after the ball on the third night."

Skinner fastened Phoebe's single strand of pearls about her throat. "I'd have thought you'd want to wait 'til the last night."

Phoebe shook her head. "No, the small hours of the morning after the ball will be perfect. Everyone will be guaranteed to be snoring, and with any luck Lady Moffat won't miss her maid until noon or later the next day. That way, even if something untoward occurs, the others will have plenty of time to overcome any hurdle and disappear into London."

"Aye, well—there is that."

"Indeed. But the first thing I must do is convince Deverell that when it comes to marriage, he has no chance whatever of changing my mind—that's the only thing that will make him stop looking my way."

Skinner snorted.

Interpreting that as a comment on the temerity of the man, Phoebe patted her pearls into place and considered her reflection.

The amber silk of her gown deepened the dark red of her hair and lent a subtle glow to her complexion, underscored by the sheen of the pearls about her throat. Her eyes appeared more violet in candlelight, her lips a deeper red.

She looked well enough, she supposed, although if looks were all, then he should have fastened on Deidre or Leonora.

Regardless, his comment that introducing him to the best of the eligible ladies had only confirmed him in his pursuit of her, while doubtless complimentary in its way, suggested that any further attempts in that direction would be doomed to continuing failure.

She narrowed her eyes. "If I can't distract him with any other lady, how else can I make him stop focusing on me?"

She'd muttered the words to herself, but Skinner had heard.

"Tell him the truth." Skinner spoke from the wardrobe, where she was hanging Phoebe's day gown. "If the man is anything like the master, then straight-talking will serve you best."

"I've already told him I'm not interested in marriage."

"No doubt, but did you tell him why? Men, logical creatures that they are, like reasons. I'm thinking you might have greater success if you give him a reason or two for why you're unlikely to change your mind."

Phoebe met her own eyes in the mirror and wrinkled her nose.

In the distance a gong sounded, summoning all downstairs. She was as ready as she'd ever be; with a sigh, she rose. "I'd better go."

She was waiting for him when he walked into the drawing room.

Deverell saw her instantly, standing to one side with Peter Mellors and two others. Her gaze equally instantly locked on him. Given the way they had parted, he wondered what new tack she had in mind to discourage him from pursuing her; if the set of her jaw was any guide, she was impatient to try it.

He nodded to Lady Cranbrook and Audrey, then moved into the growing crowd of guests standing and talking in small groups. He didn't head directly for Phoebe; instead, he took a circuitous route, stopping here and there to exchange a few words, simultaneously assessing his target.

She was well gowned, but not in the latest style. In her style, once again feminine yet aloof. Even as he studied her, he was aware other gentlemen did too; regardless of her disinterest in the opposite sex, she had that indefinable something that caught men's eyes.

Making her an even more attractive target; the notion of succeeding where others had failed greatly appealed to his competitive nature.

He steadily circled the room toward her. Unfortunately Lady Cranbrook had been correct in predicting that he, his presence, would create a stir; regardless of his already demonstrated fixation with Phoebe, various matrons couldn't resist trying their—or, more precisely, their daughters' or nieces'—hands with him. He dealt with them with courtesy and patience, that last aided by the observation that their interference was irritating Phoebe, feeding her impatience.

In the end, she left those she'd been chatting with and strolled his way.

Glibly excusing himself from Lady Riley and her daughter, Georgina, he turned and, in a few long steps, intercepted Phoebe before a pair of long windows.

"Miss Malleson." He reached for her hand.

For one second she considered not letting him have it, but then she surrendered it. He bowed easily; he held onto her slim fingers as he straightened, lightly caressing her knuckles with his thumb before, with clear reluctance, releasing her.

She shifted to fully face him, her back to the rest of the gathering. Her narrowed, violet-blue eyes met his. "I had hoped you would take the hint—the *large* hint I dropped this afternoon—and turn your attention to other ladies, but you haven't, have you?"

He smiled at her. "Of course not." He studied her eyes, then more quietly said,"You didn't really believe I would."

No, she hadn't. Still battling the effects of that gentle, far too seductive touch on her fingers, Phoebe drew a deep breath and carefully enunciated, "This has to stop. There is no point. I am not interested in marrying, not you or any gentleman, because, put simply, I have no inclination whatever in that direction."

He held her gaze, seemingly not the least put out by her declaration. "Why?"

Skinner had been right. "Because there are only three reasons any female contemplates matrimony. One, because she needs financial security. Two, because she wishes for a family to fill her time. Or three, because she desires that degree of male . . . companionship that marriage affords."

She'd tried hard to come up with a better phrasing for her third reason; she wasn't surprised to see amusement flash through his eyes.

"Male companionship?"

She narrowed her eyes to slits. "You know perfectly well what I mean."

He had the gall to smile. "Indeed."

For definable seconds, she was trapped in his eyes, his gaze warm, inviting . . .

Frowning, she snapped free. She was quite sure he more than understood her allusion; indeed, he no doubt knew to what she referred far better than she. Reordering her thoughts, she harried her wits to action. "In my case, as my father's heiress I stand in no need of a husband to keep me. Likewise, I have interests and concerns that more than adequately fill my time and engage my attention. My *full* attention. And lastly, when it comes to any desire for male companionship, I've never felt the slightest need to indulge.

There is, consequently, no benefit whatever for me in taking a stroll to the altar."

He searched her eyes; his lips remained lightly curved, not so much indicating amusement or dismissal of her words as the fact that she hadn't—yet—succeeded in convincing him, in shaking his confidence that he could win and wed her. "Not being privy to your financial state, I'll concede that as your father's heiress you won't need a husband to support you. However, I wonder—have you considered that in terms of you being an attractive parti from a gentleman's point of view, your fortune elevates rather than decreases your eligibility?"

She frowned "My eligibility is not the issue here—rather, it's marriage's attraction for me."

His smile took on an edge, as if she'd walked into a trap. "Indeed." His tone deepened, becoming more private. "Leaving aside your second reason—one I'm not persuaded, given your third reason, that you as yet have had either opportunity or necessity to properly evaluate—then to address your third reason . . ." His eyes held hers, trapping her attention, drawing it all to him, to them. Focusing it entirely on their interaction. "How many gentlemen have courted you?"

She blinked, distantly aware that Stripes had appeared and was announcing dinner. "None. I've . . ." She broke off.

An instant passed as he waited for her to continue, then one dark brow arched. "Never permitted any to attempt it?"

"Well, no. Why would I?" Gathering her shawl, she turned to join the company; Lady Cranbrook was moving through the guests, pairing them for the table. "I've never been interested—"

"How can you tell if you've never let any gentleman close enough to . . . find out?"

The words fell by her ear and sent a shiver spiraling down

her spine. He'd moved closer, behind and to her side; she glanced up, over her shoulder, and met his eyes.

He'd been going to say "seduce you" but had deigned to spare her, not that she hadn't heard his meaning in the tenor of his voice, couldn't read it, clear and unclouded, in his eyes.

She forced herself to hold his gaze. "I have no interest in 'finding out.'" In *being seduced.*

They could hear Lady Cranbrook approaching, blithely directing this gentleman to partner that lady.

Deverell held Phoebe's gaze. "You're not such a coward."

On the last word, he looked up—to smile at their hostess.

"There you are, my lord—your organization is quite perfect. Please do lead Miss Malleson in."

He smiled and inclined his head. "It will be my pleasure, ma'am."

With a light pat on Phoebe's arm, Lady Cranbrook fluttered on.

Very conscious of Phoebe's sudden stiffness, Deverell elegantly offered his arm and waited. Only when she slid her hand onto his sleeve did he lift his gaze to her face and lightly smile. "I promise not to bite."

Her eyes flashed, briefly meeting his, then she faced forward. "I don't."

Deeming it wiser not to utter an assurance that he wouldn't mind if she felt so inclined, he led her to join the exodus heading for the dining room.

Phoebe escaped from the dining room with the other ladies, leaving the gentlemen to pass the port.

Entering the drawing room, she glided to where a pair of French doors set open to the pleasant evening gave her some excuse to stand alone and contemplate.

Not that she was contemplating anything so bucolic as the view.

Deverell had . . . seduced her, at least in one way. Much as she shied from the word, it was the most applicable.

She'd entered the dining room on his arm, stiff, on guard, determined to preserve an aloof distance; Maria had doubtless imagined she was being helpful in seating them side by side. But from the moment he'd taken his seat beside her, he'd undermined her stance with questions and comments, following those with observations so acute she'd been drawn into replying against her better judgment, indeed, against her will.

Before she'd properly comprehended his direction, she'd been absorbed.

She *knew* that gentlemen like him, arrogantly powerful and not just used to getting their own way but strong enough to insist on it, should never be trusted. Yet somehow she'd fallen under the spell of conversing with a gentleman—of her class, of her generation—whose mind was as incisive, if not more so, than hers, whose tongue was just as sharp, whose vision of their society was as clear and as cynical as her own.

If she was honest, it had been refreshing; she couldn't recall ever enjoying a dinner—being entertained by her partner over dinner—more.

Unfortunately she was fairly sure he knew that; when he'd stood and drawn back her chair for her to rise, she'd met his eyes and noted a certain calculation in the green. He hadn't tried to hide it, as a lesser man—one less confident of his ability to sway her—seduce her—would have. He'd let her see, let her know, which only confirmed her view that men like him were not to be trusted. They had a deeply ingrained tendency to expect to win.

Much as she'd enjoyed Deverell's company, much as she'd

delighted in crossing verbal swords with him, in measuring her wits against his, he was definitely one man with whom she had no need to play.

Restating that goal forcefully in her mind, she swung around and took stock of the company. A trio of young ladies stood nearby; she smiled at Leonora Hildebrand. "Did you and Mr. Hinckley enjoy your ride?"

In short order she'd surrounded herself with six highly eligible young ladies. They clustered before her as she stood by the French doors; they appealed to her, as one older and clearly embracing her unwed state, for advice and information. She knew the house, the grounds, and most of the eligible gentlemen present better than they; when the gentlemen strolled in, they were engrossed in a discussion of the relative merits of nearby rides.

As she'd anticipated, Deverell was not among the first through the door, allowing the more eager gentlemen to join their group and swell its numbers. She smiled and chatted, encouraging all to remain as one large group—protecting her.

She kept her gaze from the drawing room door, but somewhat to her surprise she knew the instant Deverell stepped into the room; she felt his gaze on her—on her face, her throat, her shoulders. She had to fight to quell a reactive shiver—then fight to suppress her resultant frown. What on earth was it, this effect he had on her? No other gentleman had ever plucked her nerves as he seemed so effortlessly to do.

Increasingly tense, she tracked his movements more by sense than sight. He moved into the room, but not directly to her. She risked one glance and saw him bowing over Edith's hand, then chatting to Audrey, seated beside her aunt on a chaise across the room.

She looked back at those about her, momentarily deaf to

the conversation. Perhaps, seeing her so bulwarked, Deverell would spend the evening learning what he could from Edith, pursuing her from a different quarter. . . .

The thought should have brought relief. She told herself that's what she felt, but couldn't quite make herself believe it.

She mentally set her teeth. Irritated, annoyed, and not a little dismayed, she kept a smile on her lips and forced her mind back to the discussions around her—and forced it to remain there. May the saints preserve her if she was so easily seduced by a man's glib tongue that in just an hour or two she'd come to crave his company.

As matters transpired, she needn't have worried about disturbing any celestial host; leaving Edith and Audrey, Deverell crossed the room to her side.

Directly to her side.

She felt his gaze on her, steady, unwavering, and growing in intensity as he neared, and then he was there; as if by magic, a space opened up, allowing him to stand beside her. She continued to smile, but when she glanced his way, the gesture grew somewhat thin.

His eyes met hers, amusement lurking, but then he turned to the others.

And in a matter of minutes, with a few well-placed comments, a few artful suggestions, dispersed the group.

She fought to keep her jaw from dropping. His questions over the dinner table hadn't been idle, the information he'd encouraged her to impart far from random. She'd told him all he needed to know to distract every other eligible gentleman or lady there.

The realization left her momentarily dumbfounded, unable to bludgeon her wits into thinking of any clever way of circumventing his strategy. When Peter Mellors and Georgina Riley, the last of her unwitting defenders, flashed her parting smiles and left to ask Lady Cranbrook about the croquet equipment, leaving her deserted, entirely alone with her nemesis by the side of the room, she drew in a long breath and turned to face him, unable to keep her eyes from narrowing.

He met her gaze and merely raised a brow.

"My lord—"

"Call me Deverell. Everyone does."

"You appear to be laboring under a misapprehension. No matter how set on the outcome you are, I am not going to be swayed—"

"Perhaps"—his green gaze remained steady on her face— "we should adjourn to the terrace? While I am, of course, eager to hear whatever you wish to say to me, I see no reason for the numerous interested others populating this room to be privy to our discussion—do you?"

She didn't. He'd shifted so his shoulders effectively screened her from the room, but she had little doubt a certain amount of prurient interest was, nevertheless, focused on them.

"If the propriety troubles you, your aunt can see us."

"Propriety be damned—I'm twenty-five!" Turning on her heel, she led the way through the French doors onto the paved terrace.

Hiding a smile, Deverell followed at her heels.

So close that when she abruptly halted halfway across the wide terrace and swung to face him, he nearly mowed her down.

He stopped just in time, with no more than an inch between them, a bare inch separating her silk-clad breasts and his chest.

Looking down, he watched as the ivory mounds revealed by her low-cut bodice swelled and rose. But she didn't step back. Raising his gaze, first to her lips, fractionally parted, then to her eyes, wide, her gaze disoriented, he realized she'd stopped breathing.

Dazedly, she blinked, then her gaze drifted to his lips.

Every instinct he possessed urged him to slide an arm about her, draw her against him, bend his head, and taste those luscious lips.

And counter her arguments with one of his own.

Chapter 3

But...
Her pulse was racing; he sensed it—a primal knowledge he didn't think to question. She'd never been this close
to a man, any man intent on wooing her. Seducing her. He'd
already accepted that the latter would precede the former; as
she'd so stridently stated, she was twenty-five.

And highly, extremely—more than he'd ever known any
woman to be—sensually aware of him. A highly passionate woman unawakened, she'd fallen into his grasp, and
she would be his.

She was all but quivering; he felt an overwhelming urge
to soothe as well as seize her.

Slamming a mental door on such distracting feelings, he
forced himself to take her hand, suspended in midair to one
side, and gently ease her back; stepping back from her was
beyond him. His body was screening her from the drawing

room. She was still dazed. He closed his fingers more firmly about hers. "Phoebe? What was it you wished to say to me?"

Years of dissembling allowed him to keep his tone even, to eradicate all trace of the primitive emotions riding him.

She blinked, then blinked again. Then she blushed and took another step back. He retained his hold on her hand, preventing her from moving too far away.

"I, ah . . ." She drew in a huge breath and fixed her eyes on his. "I wanted to inform you that . . . that I truly have no ambition whatever to be any man's wife, and if you have any sensitivity whatever, you won't press me further on that score."

Phoebe stared into his eyes and wondered where those words had come from; they certainly hadn't been the tirade she'd intended to heap on his head. But that had been before she'd turned and found him so close, looked up and discovered his lips so near . . . felt him near, felt his heat down the entire front of her body, sensed the maleness of his hard frame as a beckoning temptation.

Her heart was still thudding in her throat.

She'd wanted him to kiss her.

The realization was so stunning she wasn't the least surprised it had frozen her mind. But . . .

She had to get away, escape . . . somehow break free of the mesmerizing spell he and his eyes and his fascinating lips had cast over her. Blinking, she realized her gaze had once more lowered to those disturbingly sensual lips. Jerking her eyes up, she discovered he seemed to have a similar fascination; his gaze had settled on her lips.

They throbbed. Instinctively, she licked them.

His eyes briefly closed, then opened and trapped hers.

"If that's the case . . ." His voice was a dark whisper in the night. "If you truly feel no inclination to be any man's wife, then perhaps . . ."

She couldn't see the color of his eyes, but she could tell they'd darkened. Mesmerized, she watched as he lifted the hand he still held, turning her fingers. His eyes locked with hers, he lowered his head, raised her wrist to his lips, and pressed a kiss—hot and shockingly ardent—to the sensitive inner face.

His lips burned like a brand. She sucked in a breath, felt the world spin, then settle as he lifted his head.

"Don't answer—not now." His voice was deep, dark, rippling through her. "Think about it."

Her brain wasn't functioning, not at all. As if sensing that, his lips twisted, then he turned and, setting her hand on his sleeve, guided her toward the drawing room. "We should go in."

They had; Deverell had returned her to Edith as the tea trolley had been wheeled in, then he'd remained by her side while the cups had been dispensed and the customary ritual observed. Between him, Edith, Audrey, and Mr. Philips, the conversation had flowed; she hadn't had to do more than nod.

As usual, Edith had elected to retire in the wake of the tea trolley. Phoebe had insisted on seeing her aunt to her bedchamber, then she'd cravenly slipped away to her own.

Skinner had been waiting to help her undress. Beyond confirming she'd done what she could to discourage Deverell—including offering him reasons for her disinterest in marriage—she'd said nothing more, nothing of that disconcerting moment on the terrace or the confusion in her mind.

Only when she blew out her candle and snuggled down in the dark did that confusion clear enough for her to review what had happened, to relive those moments, what she'd felt, what he'd done, what that meant. . . .

Cocooned in darkness, she blinked, then sat up, stunned

by the conclusion now shining brightly, with absolute clarity, in her brain.

If that's the case . . . then perhaps . . .

Try as she might, she could think of no other interpretation, not when his tone and actions were combined with those words.

If she wasn't interested in marriage . . . he was suggesting a liaison.

A little voice scoffed, reminding her he was her godmother's nephew and wouldn't do such a thing, that he had to be pulling her leg, that he hadn't finished his sentence and stated his proposition in plain words because he hadn't truly meant it, but that voice was weak.

And weakened even more by her memories of him, of the sheer weight of the sensual aura that clung to him.

She sat for a full ten minutes, stunned, shocked—not by his suggestion but by her reaction. Not just puzzled but astonished—at herself, not him.

He, after all, was a gentleman of a type she recognized well enough.

The cold reached through her nightgown. With a sudden scowl for her susceptibility—for her unexpected weakness—she lay down and pulled the covers to her chin.

And fought to keep the insidious idea that he truly had suggested a liaison from intruding on her dreams.

She woke the next morning determined to focus on the important things in life—on the task she had to accomplish while at the manor. With that goal in mind, avoiding Deverell seemed wise; rising, she sent Skinner to retrieve the book she'd completely forgotten from the library and fetch her breakfast on a tray, then she washed and dressed.

Sitting before the window, she broke her fast and tried to

rediscover her interest in the novel. Skinner had reported that Deverell had been at the breakfast table with the others, and that the consensus for the morning's activities had been a long ride to the ruins of an Iron Age fort.

Through the open window, Phoebe heard the clatter of booted feet, then laughter and chatter as the riding group assembled on the terrace; the voices faded as they headed for the stables. She waited for ten more minutes, then pushed aside her tray, rose, and, taking the novel with her, headed downstairs.

The front hall was cool, dim, and empty. Stepping onto the tiled floor, she listened but could hear no young voices— no young ladies gaily chattering, no deeper rumble from any gentlemen. The older ladies were all late risers; those few who had come down to preside over the breakfast table would have retired once more to their rooms.

All was as it should have been. Phoebe headed for the morning room at the back of the hall. As she'd expected, the room was empty. Slipping inside, she left the door ajar and settled to wait.

According to the mantelpiece clock, half an hour had passed when the sounds of an arrival drifted to her ears. Setting aside the book, she went to the door but remained behind it, screened from the hall as she listened.

Stripes went bustling past; footmen were already in attendance. An imperious female voice added to the cacophony, then Lady Cranbrook came hurrying down the stairs, her face beaming.

"Aurelia! Welcome, my dear."

Smiling, Phoebe opened the door and made her entrance, gliding forward to join Lady Cranbrook and Lady Moffat, embracing amid the pile of her ladyship's luggage.

Lady Moffat saw her. "Phoebe, how lovely to see you. I take it Edith's here?"

Phoebe smiled and touched fingers with Lady Moffat. "Indeed, ma'am. She's looking forward to chatting with you."

"As I am with her. I declare no one knows more of what's going on in the ton than Edith."

Still smiling, Phoebe stood back, only very briefly meeting the eyes of the maid hovering protectively over her ladyship's boxes. With the faintest nod to the girl, unseen by any other, Phoebe turned and glided away.

She went into the empty drawing room; crossing to the long windows already set open to the brilliant day, she folded her arms and looked out.

Really! What had Aurelia Moffat been thinking? One glance had been enough to confirm the problem; the maid was quite lovely, short perhaps, but a pocket Venus, the sort gentlemen described as a ripe armful. With Lord Moffat's propensities, hiring such a maid was simply asking for trouble.

Irritated, Phoebe wondered whether, later, it might be prudent for her, or better still Edith, to drop a word in Lady Moffat's ear. Now she'd seen the girl . . .

Regardless, she'd done all she could for the moment, despite her impatience to get on and make things happen. The bright sunshine outside beckoned. Her gown was suitable for walking; the sun wasn't strong enough to make a hat or parasol necessary.

A sound came from behind her; she turned as Stripes came into the room.

"Oh—I'm sorry, miss. I didn't know you were in here."

"That's perfectly all right, Stripes—I'm about to go out. If my aunt inquires, please tell her I've gone for a walk to the folly." Phoebe hesitated, then asked, "Did all the gentlemen go riding?"

"I'm not sure, miss, but there's no one in the library or the other downstairs rooms."

Phoebe smiled. "Thank you, Stripes." Turning, she walked to the open French doors and confidently stepped through.

From his seat under the apple trees close by the stream, Deverell watched Phoebe walk toward him. Safe at this distance, he let his gaze roam, over her curves and the long lines of her legs, the evocative sweep of her thighs clearly outlined beneath her light skirts as, looking down, she steadily crossed the lawn.

Crying off from the riding party, he'd taken refuge there; the rustic bench set near the bridge over the stream gave an unimpeded view of the back of the house and the walks leading to the stables and shrubbery on one side, and to the woods on the other. It was the perfect spot to lie in wait.

His quarry looked pensive, absorbed; while he might hope her thoughts were of him, of them, he doubted that was so. Her revelations last night had brought one puzzling aspect of her to the forefront of his brain.

She'd stated unequivocally that she had some occupation that demanded her full attention, something that absorbed the energies normally devoted to a husband and family. Yet when he'd later interrogated Audrey, she'd had no idea of Phoebe's consuming interest; both she and Edith had given him the impression Phoebe was largely at loose ends—reading, writing, visiting, in general living the customary life of a fashionable lady with no commitments.

But that wasn't how Phoebe had painted herself, and he would swear she hadn't been lying. Moreover the existence of some absorbing occupation fitted better with her character; she was vibrant, vital, and actively alive—doing nothing was not an option. Just as he'd been chafing at the bit because he'd had no finite goal to pursue, so, too, with her; she couldn't possibly *not* be actively involved in something, some scheme, some project, some real activity to engage her mind and absorb her considerable energies.

The more he thought of it—her secret occupation—the more convinced of its existence he became. Whatever it was, she was, at least in part, concealing it. He'd seen enough of her to suspect it wouldn't be anything mundane.

He needed to know what it was—what interested and absorbed her, what endeavor filled her time and occupied her mind. There might be something in it he could use in pursuing her. He also needed to confirm that said occupation would prove no hurdle to her being his bride.

Phoebe didn't see him until she stepped into the cool shade beneath the trees, and by then it was too late to retreat. Inwardly cursing, she halted, watching him swing his long legs to the ground and slowly stand.

He met her eyes. He didn't grin wolfishly but simply said, "Not even a twenty-five-year-old lady should go walking alone."

Her first impulse was to sniff and at least *try* to dismiss him, but insisting she was in no danger with him standing before her was patently absurd. Elevating her nose, she airily informed him, "I'm going to the folly on the hill. It's quite a way."

He did smile then and stepped closer. "I'll come with you—you can show me the sights you described yesterday."

She narrowed her eyes fractionally, trying to penetrate his amiable mask. He knew perfectly well she didn't want him with her, but he wanted to walk with her and she had no grounds on which to deny him. She could read nothing of his intentions in his face; what reached her was his determination. Arguing would be futile.

With a gesture, she turned to the bridge. "It's this way."

He walked beside her in the sunshine. She kept her lips

firmly shut. Somewhat to her surprise, he made no effort to fill—disrupt—the pleasant silence. Beyond the gurgling stream, the path slowly wended its way up the hill; the grade was gentle enough for her not to need his arm, for which she was devoutly thankful.

He was matching her stride, a good two feet between them, yet to her irritation that wasn't separation enough. Enough to deaden his impact on her witless senses.

That fraught moment on the terrace the previous night, along with his suggestion of a liaison, seemed to have exacerbated the effect of his nearness, leaving her nerves twitching, her senses ruffled, and her distracted.

Somehow, he'd stirred to life a side of her she hadn't known existed, not until she'd clapped eyes on him. To her immense annoyance, she was exhibiting all the symptoms of a schoolgirl afflicted with her first infatuation; what truly stung was that she'd never in truth fallen victim in that way, even in the schoolroom. It was lowering to acknowledge that she was infatuated now, at the ripe old age of twenty-five, yet she could hardly ignore the disturbing sensations, the way her nerves skittered and her thoughts scattered. . . . She felt a horrible urge to start babbling just to distract herself— and wouldn't that make him smile?

Lifting her head, she coolly said, "Audrey didn't say much about your time in the army, other than that you were in the Guards. In which theaters did you see action?"

When he didn't immediately reply, she glanced at him. Pacing by her side, he was looking down; she couldn't read his expression.

"Initially I was with the Guards, but within a month I was seconded to another arm of the services." He looked up and met her eyes. "I spent most of the last ten years of the war in Paris."

She stared at him. *"Paris?* But . . ."

Deverell watched her face blank, watched her work out the implications, then she blinked and refocused.

"You were a *spy?"*

He grimaced, but if she was going to marry him, she needed to know. "The official term is 'covert operative.'"

To his relief, far from being horrified, she seemed thoroughly intrigued. "What did you do? Did you ferret out secrets and smuggle them to Whitehall?"

His lips quirked. "Not often—that wasn't my brief." He hesitated, then went on, "Prior to enlisting, quite aside from the usual education—Eton and Oxford—courtesy of my father I had an excellent grounding in business affairs. It was his forte—supply and demand on a national scale. Knowing how to influence transport, and the logistics of moving large quantities of commodities from one side of the world to the other. The family fortune derived from such enterprises."

They continued along the path; he grasped her elbow to steady her over an exposed root. "Because of my peculiar knowledge and the fact that I speak fluent French and could pass myself off as, if not French, then from one of France's far-flung colonies, I was a natural to infiltrate that arm of French business crucially involved in keeping France—the state—afloat."

He glanced at her and saw she was truly interested. "For instance, it's difficult to keep an army supplied with rifles if pig iron doesn't arrive at the ports that serve the foundries. Disrupting vital cargoes at critical times can cause significant damage to any war effort."

"How . . . enthralling. It must have been so—" She broke off, a frown tangling her brows. After a moment, she said, "I was going to say it must have been exciting, and I suspect in one way it was, but it must also have been very dangerous." She looked at him. "Ten years is a long time."

Nodding, he looked down, remembering every one of those years. "One had to be very careful, always on guard against giving yourself away."

The path curved around and up the hill, spiraling about the nearly conical mound. Here and there clumps of trees shaded the way, providing cool spots in which to linger and appreciate the vistas that opened up as they climbed ever higher.

Phoebe paused in one such spot, looking out across the patchwork of fields dappling the downs; he halted beside her. At this elevation, a light breeze skipped and swooped, flirting with tendrils of her hair that had slid from the knot on the top of her head to caress her exposed nape.

His gaze rested on that sensitive skin; as if she felt it, she turned and met his eyes. Her own had widened; once again, he knew she'd stopped breathing.

After a moment, she said, "I've heard that your cattle are prime 'uns, from which I infer that now you're back on this side of the Channel, you've taken up the reins of the life you would have led had the war not intervened."

He laughed, shortly, as they started walking again. "Would that that were so, but the unexpected acquisition of both title and large estate changed my destiny." He thought, then shrugged. "Truth be known, even if my distant cousin hadn't unexpectedly died, I doubt I could have settled back to fashionable life. Ten years of tension and action tend to alter one's tastes."

Even without looking, he sensed he'd puzzled her, that he wasn't fitting the mold she'd imagined he would.

"What do you think of the Regent? Have you met him?"

"Prinny? Yes. I can't say I'm enamored."

That made her smile. She continued peppering him with questions, outwardly random, yet he sensed she was searching for some level of understanding, of comprehension, some framework within which she could place, measure and judge him. Nothing loath, he played her game, admitting, when she pressed him on what other horses he owned, that collecting prime horseflesh was one of the fashionable vices in which he indulged.

He waited for her to ask which other fashionable vices he was prey to, but while the thought definitely occurred, she shied from being quite so impertinently direct.

A pity. He'd had an excellent answer prepared.

Despite outward appearances, he wasn't like others of his kind. Phoebe couldn't escape that conclusion, or the fact that learning more about him had done nothing to lessen her infuriating infatuation. Quite the opposite. She now felt an entirely unhelpful curiosity about him—about what was important to a man like him, one with his peculiar history, about what drove him.

At least curiosity was a great deal more managcable than infatuation, and much easier to own to and excuse.

By the time they reached the folly, a small circular lookout perched on the hilltop, she'd learned enough to accept that she'd do well to wipe her mental slate clean of all preconceived notions where he was concerned. That, of course, left her wondering about his words on the terrace—had he meant them as she'd interpreted them? If so . . .

Deverell followed her onto the circular wooden platform beneath the fanciful carousel-like roof. Painted white, the structure was in good repair. Phoebe walked to one side; gripping the railing, she looked out.

Halting in the center of the floor, he grasped the moment to observe her—her stance, the way she moved—and what that told him. In one way, she was easy to read; characteristically direct and decisive, she projected her intentions clearly. Yet her motives, the reasons behind her decisions and the actions that flowed from them, remained largely hidden. Despite his facility for reading others, what Phoebe was thinking remained a mystery.

And she was sufficiently unusual to make relying on extrapolating from his extensive experience of other ladies unwise.

For one of his ilk, that was a trifle disconcerting. Managing—manipulating—a woman whose thought processes were screened from him was a significantly more difficult task. One fraught with the potential for failure, yet with Phoebe he didn't intend to fail.

But with her he was reduced to guessing. He didn't *think* she'd changed her mind over entertaining any marriage proposal. He didn't *think* she'd yet decided to take up his alternative approach to persuading her into matrimony, his suggestion of an informal relationship, but he thought—*hoped*—she was considering it.

He stirred and walked to her, halting with just a foot between them, behind her and to one side. The view before them was magnificent; they looked down on the manor in its grounds, and far beyond to field and river, to gently undulating hills that stretched away to the purple-tinged horizon.

Dipping his head, he glanced at her face. He hid a smile at the light frown etched between her brows; she wasn't thinking of the fields and river.

They were very much alone yet theoretically in public, the perfect setting in which to indulge in a little persuasion.

His lips curved; straightening, he gave in to temptation. Lifting one hand, with one finger he touched—just touched—the fine curls caressing her nape. The silky curls brushed her skin; he didn't.

She shuddered. Her hands gripped the rail more tightly, then she dragged in a breath and shot him an irritated glance. "Stop that!"

He met her gaze only briefly, then returned his attention to her nape. "Why?" Before she could answer, he looked back and trapped her gaze. "Didn't you like it?"

For a telltale moment, honesty held her tongue, but then she freed it and her blue eyes snapped. "No!"

He grinned but lowered his hand. And shifted fractionally closer, tilting his head so their gazes were closer to level, so he could study her face and she could study his.

She eyed him warily, her grip on the rail rigid.

He smiled genuinely. "Breathe."

She blinked, and did. Rather tightly.

"If you faint, I'll have to catch you, hold you—perhaps even carry you back to the house."

Her eyes widened and locked with his. "I don't faint."

He didn't answer; instead, he slowly lifted his hand and cupped her nape. Lightly, not forcefully, but that was all it took. She shivered again, unable not to, unable to quell her reaction to his touch.

The realization sent a shaft of unadulterated lust spearing through him.

She closed her eyes, tried to stiffen her spine; as his fingers and palm firmed, she dragged in a breath and held it.

Every instinct he possessed urged him to tighten his grasp and draw her to him, draw her lips to his and simply take possession.

His muscles tensed to do so; he shifted a fraction nearer.

Her lids flew up; her eyes locked with his.

He froze. Confusion tinged with a species of fear ran riot in her lovely eyes, swamping her burgeoning desire.

The sight stopped him as nothing else could have; he instantly eased his hold, forced the muscles in his arm to relax. He didn't take his palm from her nape; instead, he lightly, soothingly stroked, as he would a skittish horse.

The analogy was apt; studying her eyes, he knew—could see—that he was going too fast. She was barely breathing; once again she was inwardly quivering. She was unawakened, untouched; she was immobilized by his nearness—if she'd been free, she would have bolted.

She was twenty-five; he couldn't believe she'd never been kissed. Yet this degree of reaction, of panic . . .

Her reaction to him was unusually intense, as was his reaction to her. While that attracted him even more, perhaps to her it was too much, too soon. They'd only set eyes on each other yesterday.

He wasn't a patient man, but she wasn't just any woman.

Reining in his impulses, he leaned closer. She tried to stiffen, to pull back, but that only made her feel his restraining hand at her nape all the more. She tensed, but he didn't try to kiss her. Instead, he touched his lips to the sleek hair above her ear.

"Stop fighting this." He waited while the whispered words sank into her mind, until the realization he wasn't going to force a kiss on her allowed her to ease her locked muscles. "Stop fighting me. I can teach you more about pleasure than you can imagine."

She frowned as he drew back. She opened her mouth.

"And don't bother telling me you're not interested in pleasure." He caught her eyes. "With the type of pleasure we're discussing, everyone is."

They walked back to the house; Phoebe's heart pounded the entire way. She felt as if she'd escaped being devoured by a dangerous beast, only to have that same dangerous beast dog her heels every step of the way back to safety.

The beast wasn't him; it was what flared between them.

As they crossed the lawn and the house rose before them, she was perfectly clear about that.

She didn't know what to make of him, but what flared between them was more unnerving than he was.

Much more disconcerting than he was. For reasons she couldn't elucidate, she—her female mind—increasingly viewed him as . . . interesting. He'd proved to be other than she'd thought, and her curiosity was piqued. And while what flared between them was beyond unsettling, when he'd seen she hadn't wanted to be kissed, he'd stopped.

And hadn't.

What shook her to the core was that at the time, at the precise instant he'd drawn back, she—some wild, incomprehensible, self-destructive part of her—hadn't wanted him to stop. Had wanted him to disregard her leaping fear, brush aside her instinctive panic and . . .

And metaphorically take her hand and teach her all she didn't know.

All he'd offered, quite specifically, to teach her.

Which was surely madness. A dreadfully tempting madness.

She marched up the steps to the terrace, then, dragging in as large a breath as she could past the constriction banding her chest, swung to face him. "Thank you for your company, my lord."

He met her eyes, his gaze direct, a certain cynicism in the green.

Before she could incline her head and leave him, a bell sounded from inside.

His lips twitched. With a graceful gesture, he waved to the French doors. "That will be luncheon. Shall we join the others?"

She inwardly cursed, nodded, still tense, and swept through the door.

* * *

If asked, she would have said that the last thing she needed at that moment was to be surrounded by a chattering horde. As it transpired, pretending to listen to the gay outpourings of the others back from their ride to the ruins gave her time to regain her equilibrium. Many of said outpourings were directed at Deverell, their aim to make clear how much excitement he'd missed. She quelled a snort and kept her eyes on her plate; he was, of course, seated next to her.

As before, his nearness ruffled her senses, but the effect wasn't actually distressing. It was . . . not calming, certainly not soothing . . . pleasant, insidious, unrelenting temptation was the best description she could muster. She might be able to ignore it, if she put her mind to it, but her mind seemed to have other ideas.

Among them dwelling on the intriguing fact that in that fraught moment at the lookout, even though he hadn't needed to, he had indeed stopped. He'd had absolute control and had exercised it; she found that infinitely fascinating.

Unfortunately once lunch ended, it was impossible to escape. The others had organized their archery contest; everyone adjourned to the back lawn, sitting in the shade under the trees while the butts were set up under Peter Mellors's and Edgar Thomas's direction.

More chairs had been brought out; all the ladies had seats. Deverell lounged on the lawn between Audrey's chair and the one Phoebe occupied. She pretended to be attending to Georgina and Leonora chatting on her other side, while she listened to Deverell tell Audrey about the view from the folly. To her relief, Audrey didn't ask who had gone there with him, and he omitted to volunteer that information.

Then Edgar clapped his hands, drawing their attention.

"Right now, everyone!" He grinned around at the assembled company. "We've divided you into groups of four, the winner of each heat to progress to the next." He proceeded to read out the rules they'd decided on, then the names in each group. "We'll have the ladies' heats first, then the gentlemen's, then follow with the final rounds."

Those who had put their names forward rose. Deverell stood. He glanced down at her. "Not competing?"

She looked up at him. "No interest."

He grinned, then, inclining his head in parting, sauntered away to where the other gentlemen were gathering.

The ladies' heats eventually got underway. Phoebe glanced around; if she wanted to slip away, now was the time. The older ladies were either deep in gossip or watching their charges. The few older gentlemen had gathered to one side; they were engrossed in talk of hunting. Deverell was standing with the other eligible gentlemen, a longbow held in one hand; like the others, he was watching the younger ladies' efforts.

Some, like Peter and Edgar and Charlie Wickham, occasionally called comments or encouragement. There was much laughter and good humor at the shooting line; no one was taking the contest all that seriously.

They were shooting parallel to the line of trees under which the ladies were sitting, far enough away from the shade so that anyone shifting within it wouldn't distract the archers.

Phoebe told herself to get up and quietly slip away under the trees. She kept meaning to, yet the afternoon was so pleasant, the breeze warm and summer-scented, the atmosphere so lazy that she couldn't summon the will.

And although she had no interest in archery herself, the antics about the shooting line were entertaining, as was the gradual increase in competitiveness that slowly permeated the air. She found herself smiling, sometimes cynically, sometimes simply in amused understanding.

Somewhat to everyone's surprise, the ladies' final was hotly contested by Leonora and Deidre. One blond, one brown-haired, they made an attractive pair of modern-day Dianas. In the end, Deidre prevailed; delighted, she looked around, inviting acknowledgment, gaily and charmingly accepting when it was duly tendered.

Phoebe noted Deidre's eyes resting on Deverell, noted the way she clung to his words of congratulation.

But it was now time for the gentlemen's final, and Deverell was one of the three finalists. Like the others, he had to open his coat to draw the bowstring; watching, Phoebe inwardly admitted that the width of chest thus revealed was impressive.

He was a few years older than the other two finalists— Carlton Philips and Charlie. He was also taller and heavier and, Phoebe was quite sure, stronger. She wasn't the least surprised when he was clearly in the lead after the first round.

In accordance with the rules, the other two then shot before him. Watching not them but Deverell, Phoebe saw him eyeing not the other finalists but the knot of young ladies who had remained, eager and excited, behind the shooting line, patently waiting to congratulate the winner, to hang on his arm and claim his attention.

Then it was Deverell's turn at the line. He took his place; Phoebe watched as he sent his three arrows flying toward the target in quick succession. They all struck, but none were anywhere near as close to the eye as his previous shots.

Even more telling, when the points were tallied, he was no longer in first place. Charlie was declared the winner, and laughingly insisted on the adoration of the assembled young ladies as his due. They laughed and obliged, but more than one pair of eyes followed Deverell as, after shaking Charlie's hand and clapping him on the back, he handed Edgar his bow and made his way across the lawn—directly back to Phoebe.

"Damn!" Seeing his direction, even at that distance feeling the weight of his gaze, she realized her time to escape him had passed.

Assuming she had wanted to escape him.

Deverell reached the shade; ducking under a low-hanging branch, he halted before Audrey. She'd been watching the contest through a pair of lorgnettes, which now lay in her lap.

She looked up at him and blandly observed, "I had no idea Charlie was such an excellent shot—even better than you."

He shrugged. "He was the better man on the day."

Audrey raised her brows but said no more.

He turned to Phoebe—just as Stripes arrived on the lawn, heralding afternoon tea. Suppressing a grimace, he looked at Edith and Audrey. "Tea?"

"Yes, please." They both nodded.

He turned to Phoebe and raised a brow.

She held out a hand. "I'll come and help."

Grasping her hand, he drew her to her feet. Side by side, they crossed to the trestle, where tea and cakes were being dispensed; he quizzed her on her lack of interest in archery, extending his interrogation to her childhood, anything to fill the time while he swiftly herded her past the urn and the cake plates and had them both on their way back to Audrey and Edith, avoiding all the other young ladies casting inviting glances his way.

They reached their aunts and handed around the cups. The two were engrossed in remembering some long-ago event and barely paused to nod their thanks; he and Phoebe stood beside their chairs and sipped.

Over the rim of her cup, Phoebe's eyes met his.

He held her gaze for an instant, then drained half his cup in one swallow.

His back to the others, he looked toward the surrounding trees. Nothing more than distantly aware of other ladies' glances, he was highly sensitive to Phoebe's. Ever since they'd left the folly, she'd been casting surreptitious looks his way; for the past hour, she'd all but constantly been watching him.

She and her glances were starting to distract him in a way in which he hadn't been distracted for years—no, decades. Not since he'd been at Eton and the maids had cast covetous eyes over him. To his surprise, his reaction now wasn't all that different from his reaction then, a lowering thought considering all the experience he'd accumulated in between.

It was clear that Phoebe was seriously considering his suggestion. That fact, combined with the effect of her glances, was steadily inflating his desire for her, a lust that, after that moment in the folly, he was all too well aware he couldn't yet slake. Indeed, that it might be some time before he could slake it.

He'd been going to kiss her but hadn't. While prudence and wisdom had dictated he pull back, his own needs were anything but appeased. And after the last hour of those considering looks, which strongly suggested she was at the very least of two minds over continuing to resist him, all he wanted was to get her alone and reassess their situation.

As Audrey had guessed, he'd deliberately lost the archery contest so he could pursue Phoebe without distraction.

And hopefully convince her to surrender the kiss he hadn't taken earlier. If he didn't kiss her soon, didn't at least taste her, he was going to go insane.

He drained his cup. Deciding the level in hers had dropped sufficiently, he caught her eye. "There'll be nothing but talk for the next hour or so." He kept his voice low, beneath the level of Audrey's and Edith's conversation. "I wonder if you'd care for a walk. There's a pretty spot along the stream."

He'd discovered it that morning and had taken due note.

She held his gaze for an instant, then nodded. She moved to set down her cup on the small table beside Audrey. Audrey paused and glanced at her.

"We're going for a walk by the stream." Phoebe met Edith's eyes as her aunt looked up; she waited, the defense that she was twenty-five hovering on the tip of her tongue. But both Edith and Audrey merely smiled.

"Yes, of course, dear." Edith waved her away. "It's such a glorious afternoon."

"A pity not to enjoy it to the full," Audrey added. Then they resumed their discussion.

Phoebe narrowed her eyes at the pair. Admittedly they would have had to swivel to glance at Deverell, as he was standing behind their chairs, but they should at least have looked at him in the way chaperones always did—warning him to behave himself.

She was twenty-five and they weren't going far, but still.

Inwardly shaking her head, she turned to Deverell and promptly forgot about her godmother and her aunt. There was something in his face—a hardness edging the lines of cheek and jaw—that seemed somehow different.

He stepped back and waved her along the line of trees. "It's this way."

Luckily, they'd been at the end of the line of chairs; they slipped away beneath the branches without drawing the attention, or the company, of any of the other young people. She saw his watchful glance over her head and knew he didn't want any others to join them.

Neither did she.

Chapter 4

*T*hey strolled through sunlight and shade, wending their way between the old trees that bordered the lawn and dotted the gentle slope leading away from the house. The stream burbled along the bottom of its own narrow valley formed by more steeply sloping banks; Deverell took her hand, steadying her as they made their way down, climbing over gnarled roots to the narrow path that edged the rippling water.

Still swollen by spring rains, the stream was running high, splashing and gurgling over large rocks and boulders. The sound was a pleasant song; the zip of dragonflies and the high-pitched call of finches punctuated the bright melody. The lazy warmth of the afternoon had gathered in the valley; it wrapped around them, sinking to their bones. They walked along without words; she'd visited the manor many times but had never strolled this way.

Then they rounded a curve, and she saw what he'd meant

by "a pretty spot." The stream widened into a large pool; the music of its passing fell away, muted as the babbling rush spread with a sigh into deeper water. The path, which had been hugging the stream's edge, diverted inland a little way; between it and the water a group of trees clustered, their spreading branches overhanging the pool.

Deverell led her beneath the green canopy. After walking in the sun, the cool air beneath the arching branches was refreshing. She followed him to where an old tree grew just a few yards back from the bank. Halting by the smooth bole, she leaned against it and watched as he stooped, picked up a flat stone, and with one flick of his wrist sent it skipping over the still surface.

The stone sank just before the opposite bank. A flash of turquoise marked a kingfisher, disturbed enough to dart away downstream.

He stood, hands on hips, looking out over the pool. She leaned more heavily against the bole and wondered what she was doing there.

Tempting fate.

As if he'd heard her thoughts, he turned and looked at her. Then, arms lowering, he walked back to her.

He stopped a foot away. He looked into her eyes, searched them, then without a word raised his large hands, gently framed her face, tipped it up, and kissed her.

It happened so smoothly, so easily, she had no time to panic. There'd been no hint of a threat in his movements or his touch; her lips had softened beneath his before she'd had time to think.

Then she did, and mentally froze, waited, ready to tense and push him away. But nothing happened, nothing changed; his lips remained warm and pliant against hers, beguiling as they caressed, seductively tempting.

But he made no move to press her. He didn't shift closer,

didn't crowd her with his large, hard body; there were only his hands, his lips.

And the pleasure.

Pleasure that insidiously bloomed, that slid through her like warmed honey and slowly heated her.

Slowly, step by step, made her want more.

Hunger for more.

Until she followed his direction and parted her lips, did something she'd never done with any man and welcomed him into her mouth.

Even then he was gentle, unhurried, unthreatening.

There was nothing but pleasure in the heavy stroke of his tongue against hers, in the artful, skillful caresses he fed her, in the gentling of his hands about her face as she responded.

Deverell fought down the instinct to reach for her, to draw her into his arms and take things further; she might be kissing him back, but he'd felt her hesitation, could sense just how wary she was, how ready to take flight. Innocence, inexperience, and wariness; with such a combination, he had to tread carefully.

Had to go slowly, slower than he'd ever gone with any woman.

The knowledge clashed with a burgeoning primitive urge to seize her, to make her his—to at least take steps to set that in train. He could overwhelm her so easily, let loose the passion he held reined and sweep her into intimacy, there in the grass by the stream, but everything he knew of her told him he'd never win her that way.

But if he couldn't have her yet, he was determined to take the first step at least, to make her crave his kiss. So he kept his hands still, gentle about her face, and bent his mind, his will, and his considerable expertise to capturing her with just a kiss.

Raising one hand, Phoebe touched the back of his, still so

gently cradling her face. The muscles and tendons were hard, rigid, yet his touch was almost reverent. So careful, so reassuring. So not what she'd expected.

Even while she indulged and let him beguile her into more, into long, slow exchanges that all but curled her toes, some part of her mind puzzled at the implicit contradiction.

His kiss remained gentle and beguiling, yet he wasn't a gentle and beguiling man.

He was ruthless, hard, determined beyond measure, and comprehensively used to getting his own way.

She might have avoided such exchanges as far as she'd been able, yet she knew enough not to be deceived. Closing her hand over his only confirmed that he, his body, was locked, held immobile beneath his steely will.

He was holding back all that she feared. It wasn't that he didn't wish to sweep her into his arms, that he didn't want to crush her to him, to touch her body, her breasts, her bottom; he wanted all those things, but had sensed she didn't, and he was strong enough—and for whatever reason had decided to be gallant enough—to check his own desires.

In pursuit of hers?

The thought drifted through her mind, a seduction all its own.

But the passion she sensed through her touch on his hand, while not a threat, was proof a threat could yet exist. She didn't yet know if she was safe with him.

Reluctantly—she was surprised by how reluctantly—she drew back from the kiss. He hesitated, then let her break it, but he didn't release her face.

She opened her eyes, blinking back into the world. Focusing on the darkened green of his eyes, she watched him search hers—and mentally scoffed at her earlier thought. Safe? With him? He was the epitome of *un*safe, the type of man she *knew* could never be "safe," not for her or any woman.

Yet . . . try as she might, she could sense no threat from him.

She frowned, sensing the question in his mind. "I don't know . . ." He confused her as no man ever had.

His gaze sharpened. "Why don't we take this one step at a time, and see where the path leads us?"

He was, quite clearly, speaking of indulging in an affair, but was indicating he was willing to accommodate her as to the pace. . . .

She would never, ever, get a better offer—a chance more to her taste, or more responsive to her needs.

From a man like him, it was a generous suggestion, one that would cost him far more than it would her, assuming he adhered to it. She knew in her heart she would regret saying no, could not say no—not yet.

"I . . ." She drew in a breath and took the plunge. "Yes. All right—but just one step at a time, and let's see."

His gaze remained steady on hers, then his features softened in a smile. One that took on an almost rueful edge as he lowered his hands from her face, lightly stroking one cheek as he did.

"I've been waiting to kiss you since I first laid eyes on you."

"In the library?" She wasn't overly surprised.

"Yes." He closed a hand about one of hers, engulfing it in warmth and hardness. "But if I'd acted then, I wouldn't have stopped at just a kiss, not with the chaise there and no one else in the room."

She tilted her head, greatly daring said, "There's no one else here now."

His gaze sharpened; he hesitated but then shook his head. "No, there isn't, but there's a time and place for all things, and this isn't it."

Deverell stepped back and drew her away from the tree.

"Come—we should return. You'll need to dress for dinner."

And after turning down that last invitation—which had been no invitation but a test in disguise—he needed to take another walk.

To cool his ardor.

"Tell Jessica to meet me in the music room once everyone settles for the night." Sitting before her dressing table, Phoebe glanced at Skinner in the mirror. "Tonight's our musical evening. It will no doubt be boring in the extreme, but we may as well capitalize on it. If anyone sees Jessica downstairs later tonight, she can say Lady Moffat left her fan in the music room and she's looking for it."

"Aye, I'll tell her. Though if the evening's to be as boring as you say, I'm wondering why you're insisting on wearing this." Skinner lifted Phoebe's peacock green silk gown from her second trunk and shook it out, then looked at Phoebe, her brows raised high.

Phoebe met her eyes briefly, then reached for her perfume. "Because I live in hope that the company will be more interesting than the entertainment."

"Company, heh? Tall, dark, and handsome as sin—*that* company?"

"*Any* company," Phoebe repressively replied, although Skinner was, of course, correct. She was dressing with more care because she knew Deverell would be present.

More, because she knew he would spend time with her, and she was looking forward to those moments, to see what he would make of them, and what she might learn. In terms of teaching her about the pleasure to be gained from a liaison, she doubted any man was better qualified.

"Should I tell Jessica that it'll be tomorrow night?"

Finishing dabbing perfume behind her ears and on her

wrists, Phoebe stoppered the bottle. "Yes. Has Fergus sent word to Birtles?"

"He has. He's expecting to hear back tomorrow morning."

"Good. Let me know when everything's in place." She rose and let Skinner slide the striking blue-green gown over her head. She wriggled, settling it, then looked in the mirror and was pleased. The unusual hue wasn't one many ladies could successfully wear, but it complemented her coloring; most importantly, the vivid hue attracted and held the eye.

Anyone's eye.

She stood while Skinner laced the gown, then sat again to let Skinner attend to her hair. She always wore it up, so Skinner had to unravel the topknot that had seen her through the day, then brush out her long hair and refashion a more stylish knot for the evening.

While Skinner worked, Phoebe donned aquamarine earrings and a matching bracelet and pendant. Skinner helped her clip the chain around her neck.

"Damn!" Skinner muttered, poking at the curls that brushed her nape. "These strands are too short to reach the knot. I'll pin them up."

Phoebe blinked. In that instant felt again the sensation of Deverell touching those strands, cupping her nape. "No. Leave them."

Skinner looked at her in surprise; she usually insisted that her hair be perfectly tidy.

Phoebe lightly shrugged and reached for her figured shawl. "I've grown used to them."

And if they weren't there, Deverell might not touch her in quite that way again . . . and he'd been right. She'd liked it.

After dinner, the company adjourned to the music room. By then, Phoebe's view of the evening had grown distinctly jaundiced. She walked into the ornate room with no expectations beyond being bored to tears.

She'd gone down to the drawing room buoyed by an eagerness she hadn't felt in years, only to be waylaid by Peter and Edgar the instant she'd crossed the threshold. They'd kept her chatting about the croquet tournament they were arranging for the following afternoon; every time she'd opened her mouth to excuse herself, they'd asked her another question.

Exasperated, she'd glanced about the room, hoping to locate Deverell and move him to rescue her, only to discover him trapped before a window with Deidre and her friends, Heather and Millicent, who formed a frilly wall before him.

Between her and him.

She'd looked at Peter—Deidre's brother—and all had become clear.

Just as she'd started to narrow her eyes, her mind evaluating various less polite means of escape, a stir beside her had resolved itself into Stripes, who had announced that dinner was served.

Unfortunately, Maria had a habit of juggling her guests about the dinner table. Tonight, Phoebe had been seated at the other end of the table from Deverell. He had been flanked by Georgina and Deidre, while she'd had Charlie and a Mr. Combes to entertain her.

They'd tried but hadn't succeeded.

She'd endured, but with not even any time in the drawing room, she now had nothing more ahead of her than a few hours of listening to weak musical performances with the entire company gathered around.

She enjoyed music, but it had to be well performed. As she glided toward the pianoforte, she couldn't drum up the slightest iota of enthusiasm.

Maria had already whispered in her ear; being the eldest unmarried young lady, Phoebe would be the first to perform. She'd nearly declined; the aim of such evenings was to display to the assembled—captive—eligible gentlemen the accomplishments of the marriageable young ladies. The underlying purpose was matchmaking, and she was no longer in the market. However, if she was going to be forced to sit and listen to others mangle rhythms and chords, then they could first listen to her demonstrate how it should be done.

Raising the pianoforte's lid, she ran her fingers experimentally over the keys, confirming that the instrument was adequately tuned, then she reached for the pile of music sheets left in readiness.

She was flicking through the pile, evaluating possibilities, when her senses stirred, then focused. Looking up and around, she found Deverell approaching, his gaze on her. She glanced at the others, now settling into seats spread about the room. Deidre and her friends had been summoned by their mothers and were now in earnest consultation over what piece would best demonstrate their talents.

Deverell halted beside her. He held her gaze for an instant, then looked at the sheets in her hands. "What were you thinking of playing?"

She shrugged. "An air, a sonata—something soothing."

She glanced up in time to see his lips quirk.

His eyes met hers. "Do you sing?"

"Yes."

"In that case, what about a ballad? If you can find something suitable, I'll sing with you."

She blinked, but she certainly wasn't about to turn away such an offer. "Baritone?"

He nodded.

She'd seen something in the pile; she hunted, found the

sheet, and drew it free. "What about this? Two parts—first in alternate verses, then combined."

He scanned the sheet, then nodded. "I remember it."

"Excellent."

He took the other sheets from her; while he set them aside, she adjusted the seat, then settled on it. As she set their selected piece on the stand, Maria bustled up, her face wreathed in smiles.

Phoebe smiled and made her even happier. "Paignton and I are going to perform a ballad."

Maria glowed. She clapped in delight. "How wonderful!" She turned to Deverell, who had taken up his position by Phoebe's right shoulder. "Thank you, my lord. This is *quite* the most perfect way to encourage the other gentlemen, and the other young ladies, too, to get into the spirit of things."

Turning, she clapped loudly, calling the gathering to order, then announced them, and that they had elected to entertain the group with a ballad.

Cynically amused, Phoebe placed her fingers on the keys. "I'm not normally cast as an example to be followed."

She looked up at Deverell. He met her eyes and dryly replied, "I imagine not."

He understood what she meant, yet there was something in his tone, in his green eyes . . . then he nodded at the pianoforte. "When you're ready."

She turned back to the instrument and the music.

What followed was unlike any performance she'd given before. The notes flowed from her fingers as they always did, all but effortlessly, perfectly gauged in both rhythm and force; her voice rose, an unusually sweet contralto, strong enough to fill the room yet never strident. She sang the first verse alone, but even then she felt a difference, a subtle reshaping of her senses and thus how she delivered the notes and lyrics, because he stood so near.

And then he sang, and she lost all touch with the room in which they stood, forgot that there were others watching. His voice, effortlessly strong yet amazingly controlled, perfectly in tune, wove a web of sound around her—a web that only grew stronger, more mesmerizing, when she added her voice to his.

It was no contest, but a sensual interweaving; her voice rose when his fell and vice versa, first one dominating, then the other, not so much testing each other's strengths as discovering how to interact, how to support, how to elicit the best from each other—the most from each other.

Never before had she participated in such an exchange, where her partner's voice stretched hers, and hers demanded more from his.

The ballad had twelve verses. The music and their voices led them on, deeper into the ever twining harmony, until at the last they reached the final note—two perfectly held tones riding over two chords creating a single, perfectly blended sound.

It ended, died, and she returned to the world. To that instant of complete silence that follows a great performance, when the listeners have to draw breath and blink before they can applaud.

They did applaud. She smiled, acknowledged the accolades with a gracious nod, then allowed Deverell to take her hand and draw her to her feet.

They moved away so the next young lady, looking decidedly nervous, could take her place at the instrument. Deverell led her to the side of the room, where Audrey and Edith, smiling delightedly, were settled on a chaise.

"Lovely." Edith beamed.

Audrey simply looked smug.

Standing beside the chaise, they turned to face the room. Deverell spoke softly. "I enjoyed that."

"So did I." She glanced up at his face. "I admit I didn't expect it of you. Such talent isn't all that common."

He met her gaze; his lips curved. "One of the benefits of spending so much time in Parisian salons."

"Ah." She looked back at the pianoforte as the next young lady started to play.

The rest of the musical offerings were as boring as she'd expected. Worse, after their performance and with Deverell so near, her restlessness and impatience did nothing but grow. But there was nothing to be done, no way to escape, nothing to do but endure. Two young ladies gave creditable performances, but too many had demonstrably no real flair.

She glanced at Deverell. Stoic, he gave no sign whatever of impatience, but when he met her eyes, she sensed he was finding the evening as frustrating as she.

They'd stepped onto a new path that afternoon, one she wished to further explore. While their shared ballad had whetted her appetite, it hadn't satisfied her craving to learn more. She positively itched with impatience but could think of no way to advance her cause.

By the time the tea trolley was wheeled in, later than usual to accommodate the performances, she was resigned to making no headway that night.

As soon as she'd finished her tea, Edith rose to retire. Setting aside her cup, Phoebe was about to go to her when Deverell laid a hand on her arm.

She turned to him.

He took her hand, briefly scanned the room, then met her eyes. "Later—the temple by the lake?"

She hesitated. He arched a brow and lifted her hand to lightly touch his lips to the backs of her fingers.

The light caress was enough to bring her nerves alive. Through his grip on her fingers, she sensed that, if anything, he was even more determined than she to forge ahead.

"Yes. All right," she whispered back. "When all's quiet."

With a nod, he released her. She turned and went to Edith, then assisted her from the room, all the while conscious of Deverell's gaze on her back, equally conscious of her focus on him.

It was close to midnight when she left the house by the side door near the music room. She'd had to wait until all the guests had been abed before meeting with Jessica, Lady Moffat's recently hired lady's maid.

Phoebe had explained to Jessica how they planned to rescue her, and how their little business operated; Jessica had all but fallen on her neck in gratitude. The poor girl was frantic at the prospect of returning to the Moffats' country house, where lecherous Lord Moffat lurked.

After reassuring Jessica that she would be whisked away after the ball the following night, Phoebe parted from her and slipped outside. Rounding the house, she made for the small classical temple that stood by the side of the ornamental lake.

Lounging against one of the temple's marble pillars, Deverell saw her coming, but not from the direction he'd expected. After parting from her that afternoon, he'd gone to the stables to look in on his grays and instruct Grainger to find out what he could about Miss Phoebe Malleson, only to discover the lad had acted on his own initiative. Deverell now knew that Phoebe had a maid called Skinner, a strict and severe sort but with a kind heart, who had been with her since childhood, that Edith's coachman, a Scotsman by name Mc-Kenna, was also Phoebe's groom, and that the chamber Phoebe had been given was beside Edith's in the central wing overlooking the terrace at the rear of the house.

His room was above the library, facing the front of the house. If Phoebe had left from her room, the most direct route to the temple would have been the way he'd come, via the library.

He'd discovered the temple after leaving the stables, while he'd been walking off the frustration caused by instincts he knew he couldn't indulge. He'd noted the structure but hadn't had any plans for it—not until the evening had unfolded and his frustration had reached new heights.

After their duet, he'd known he'd get no sleep, not unless he kissed Phoebe again, not until he'd taken advantage of the impatience he'd sensed in her to steer her through at least one more step.

One more step on her long road to seduction.

She slowed as she neared, peering through the shadows; the temple was screened from the house by a stand of trees. Pushing away from the column, he moved to stand in the archway closest to her. She saw him; even through the dimness he caught her quick smile. Lifting her skirts, she came on more quickly.

Looking down, she climbed the steps. "I didn't know if you were here—"

He reached for her and stepped back, pulling her into the temple's shadows. His impulse was to haul her fully against him; her small gasp reminded him—he stopped before he did.

Instead, he caught her face, tipped it up, and kissed her.

But this time, he wasn't stopping there.

He drew her into the kiss; she followed willingly. Her hands came to rest, first one palm, then the other, on his chest. Her touch was light, yet he felt it to his bones.

Gently, slowly, he eased one hand from her face. She'd given him her mouth freely; her tongue flirted with his, innocent, inexperienced, yet learning. Learning to give and take, to receive pleasure, and return pleasure to him.

It was a heady sensation and a simple, yet real, sign of her interest. But it wasn't enough.

Slowly, he slid his arm around her waist. He let it rest there, let her feel the weight, let her grow accustomed to it, to being within his control. Only gradually, oh-so-gradually as he continued to kiss her, continued to lead her, to show her what more a kiss could be, did he draw her to him, ease her inch by inch closer, until at last the silk of her bodice brushed his coat.

And she noticed.

Phoebe felt that first contact like a spear of sensation striking through her, tightening the peaks of her breasts. She hesitated, wondering, but with his lips on hers, his tongue languidly stroking hers, no panic awoke, no fear raised its head. She knew his arm was around her, knew it would feel like steel if she stepped back, but it—he—wasn't forcing her forward, wasn't seizing or trapping. His hand, resting lightly at the side of her back, wasn't even grasping.

Yet she could feel him all around her. The more they kissed, the longer she stood there, she could feel the hard heat of him sinking into her bones.

Weakening them.

There came a moment when the temptation to lean into him simply became too much. Refusing to let herself think, she took that last half step and let their bodies meet. Let her breasts press against his chest, let her thighs touch the hard lengths of his.

A shiver of sheer pleasure swept through her; she welcomed it, wallowed in the sensation. But it was his reaction that enthralled her, that focused her mind even as they both instinctively readjusted the angle of their heads, continuing the kiss, continuing to taste and explore—even while she wondered, amazed at his restraint.

Fascinated by it.

His kisses remained unhurried, lazy and inviting, yet his body felt as if he had a devouring demon trapped within, a demon he held chained by sheer force of will. She pushed her hands, trapped against his chest, up and over his broad shoulders, savoring, assessing, marveling at the tension locked in every muscle of his large frame.

Behind the veil of his kisses lurked heat and fire, and hunger. A hunger she wondered if she could sate, could satisfy.

He was keeping her protected, shielded from it all—from his desire, his passion, all he wanted from her.

A certain sultriness slid through her mind. She kissed him back, more definite, more demanding; he took all she offered, gave all she wanted in return, but his control—steely and absolute—didn't quake. It didn't so much as quiver.

Temptation welled, stronger, more assured, more compelling, but even in her hazy, pleasured state, she knew it was too dangerous.

Far too dangerous to tempt him to drop his shields, and let her experience the full force of his desire.

It was he who eventually pulled back and lifted his head. He looked down at her; shadows wreathed his face—she couldn't see his eyes.

But she could feel him all around her.

She stood within his arms, held gently against him, and not one nerve was shrieking in warning.

All her nerves were pleasured, warm, all but purring with content.

He searched her face, his own hard-edged planes sharpened by restraint. "You taste like fine wine. You're addictive, intoxicating even in small sips."

"You taste . . . dangerous." Dangerously male.

"I am dangerous. But not to you."

She looked into his eyes and found she believed him.

His arms fell from her and he stepped back. "Come—I'll walk you to the house."

She acquiesced with a nod. They walked back side by side, through the trees and across the lawns. He showed her how to walk across the gravel drive without making a sound, then led her to one of the French doors of the library.

He opened it and stood back.

As she moved to pass him, he reached out and drew her to him. She was surprised, but permitted it—permitted him to kiss her, one last, long, lingering time.

Raising his head, he murmured against her lips, "One small step at a time."

Hands braced against his chest, she looked into his dark eyes and nodded. Then she stepped back.

He released her and guided her through the door. "Good night."

She turned to look at him. "Aren't you coming?"

He shook his head. "I'll walk for a while."

She frowned; he looked at her, then shut the door.

She stared, through the glass saw him move to the steps, go down onto the lawn, then stride away. Puzzled, she turned and headed upstairs.

Chapter 5

"Do you think we could take a wrong turn?"

"Easily." Deverell considered the carriages ahead of his curricle. Another line followed behind. "Unfortunately, I doubt that we'd be allowed to get lost."

A delightful picture in magenta-sprigged muslin, Phoebe sighed and adjusted the angle of her parasol. "Picnics are all very well in their way, but to have to listen to so much silly chatter—that invariably ruins my appetite."

"Don't expect any argument from me." After a moment, he asked, "How did we get roped into this?"

"I don't know." Phoebe shot him a darkling glance. "But if you'd been rather less pointed in your attentions to me, I, at least, could have claimed ape-leader status and retired to the library with my book. I still haven't finished it."

He hid a smile; he knew what she'd been doing instead. "But such craven behavior on your part would leave me exposed to the likes of Deidre and Leonora—you couldn't be so cruel."

She sniffed. "A gentleman has to be prepared to contend with such difficulties when he attends a house party to look over the field."

"I didn't. I came to look at you." He congratulated himself on his decision to leave Grainger at the manor.

She blinked, then turned her head to study him. "Did you?"

"I told you so the first time we met."

Phoebe faced forward. *I came for you.*

She remembered his words clearly; replaying them in her mind, in his deep, decisive voice, sent the same peculiar shiver through her. "So you did. I should have paid more attention. . . ."

He glanced at her, a frown in his eyes, as if he couldn't follow her thoughts and felt uneasy that he couldn't. But then the carriages ahead turned off the main lane onto a narrow rutted track and he had to concentrate on his horses.

Prime 'uns, as she'd been warned.

By the time he drew the curricle to a halt and came to hand her down, she'd formulated and rejected three different scenarios whereby he and she and his fabulous horses managed to free themselves of the surrounding throng. He'd been right; it wouldn't be allowed.

Apparently all the other eligibles, male and female, had determined not to allow them any private time together. He, she, or both of them were constantly in demand; even during the picnic at a spot high on the downs, she was frequently applied to for information on the landmarks dotting the wide view.

"You're very knowledgeable about the surrounding countryside." Deverell lay stretched beside her on the grass, looking out to the distant horizon. She was seated on a rug likewise looking out, the fresh breeze flirting with her hair. They were temporarily alone, surrounded by the chattering horde.

"I grew up not far from here. My father's Lord Martindale—Martindale Hall is about twenty miles away, over there." She pointed to the east.

He looked, then asked, "Do you spend much time there?"

Her lips twisted wryly. "Not since I was eight. My mother died when I was seven. My father became a recluse—he rarely leaves the hall. When I came out of mourning, I was sent to stay with my aunts—I have eleven of them. I moved around between them, but I've spent most time with Edith. Her husband had died and she was alone, and so was I."

He said nothing. After a moment, she glanced at him. "Do you have any brothers and sisters?"

He shook his head. "Like you, my mother died when I was young. My father passed away while I was overseas. I've uncles and aunts, but no cousins on the paternal side."

"Thus your need to marry."

He nodded.

Before she could probe further—although she wasn't at all sure why she wanted to know more—Georgina and Heather joined them.

"We're going to stage the croquet tournament when we get back. Both of you must play, of course."

Phoebe raised her brows; Georgina's comment had been couched far too dictatorially. "I fear that after the exigencies of this picnic, I won't have sufficient energy to make an adequate showing. You must count me out."

"Oh." Georgina blinked at her, considered, then patently decided they didn't need her anyway. She turned her bright eyes on Deverell. "But you'll play, won't you, my lord? You certainly won't be too fatigued."

Phoebe looked too, only to find Deverell's green eyes, slightly narrowed, fixed on her face.

Without shifting his gaze, he said, "I'll play only on one condition—that Miss Malleson be my partner."

She looked into his eyes and had to struggle not to laugh. They'd pushed too far; he'd retaliated with a demand that left Georgina no choice but to turn to her and plead, "Phoebe? You will play, won't you?"

She held his gaze—he was a devil, no doubt, for he'd trapped her, too. "If Lord Paignton will lend me his undoubted expertise, then yes, very well, I'll marshal enough energy to compete."

Thus it was that three hours later they found themselves standing side by side at the edge of the croquet lawn.

"I haven't played in years," Deverell informed her.

Despite that, Phoebe quickly discovered he hadn't forgotten how, but the game as he played it differed subtly from the one she knew.

In his version, there was a great deal more touching between partners, at least between them. She hadn't previously considered croquet a sport with much, if any, contact, but his version was filled with little touches, brushes, the gentle pressure of his hand at the back of her waist, the tantalizing glide of his leg clad in tight buckskin breeches and glossy boot against her skirts.

The lightest brush of his fingers over the bright curls caressing her warm nape.

She knew from the first that he was doing it deliberately; oddly, from the first, she didn't truly mind. To her continuing surprise, she didn't mind being touched by him; indeed, she quite enjoyed the occasional *frisson* when supposedly unintentionally skin met skin.

Or when his hand passed lightly over a curve he really shouldn't touch.

At least not in public. No one saw, of course.

Those fleeting, private touches added another dimension to their play. Although defeated in the final round by Peter and Heather, both keen players who concentrated fiercely, she was prepared to wager that of them all, she and Deverell had gained the most enjoyment from the tournament.

She parted from him, leaving him with the other men to tidy the hoops and mallets away. Trooping inside with the other ladies to get ready for the ball, she decided the afternoon hadn't, after all, been entirely wasted.

Except . . .

It didn't strike her until she was in her room that all those little touches had had a cumulative, inevitable effect. By the time she climbed into her garnet-colored ball gown, she felt as if she were ready to jump out of her skin.

It . . . *flickered*. Her nerves were tight, sensitive to even the lightest touch, eager for even the slightest caress, and desperately hungry for more.

"Damn him." She muttered that and various other injunctions as she hurried to get ready, hoping against hope that he had something planned to ease her sudden need, although how he might accomplish that within the confines of a ballroom, she had no clue.

Sinking onto the stool before her dressing table, she reached for her favorite perfume. Skinner came to stand behind her and started to unpin her hair.

"Is everything set for tonight?"

Reaching for her brush, Skinner nodded. "They'll be waiting with the carriage in the lane like you wanted. Jessica knows to meet you in the library. Poor mite, she's that desperate I'm sure she'd run away if we weren't about to get her away."

"Hmm. Keep an eye on her if you can. We don't want her to do anything silly and make Stripes or anyone else suspicious."

"I'll mother-hen her. Are you going to change after the ball?"

Phoebe reviewed what she planned to do later, then shook her head. "The way's clear enough. I shouldn't need to."

"In that case, I'll stick with Jessica. I'll stay with her once she's settled her ladyship for the night, keep her company until it's time to meet you."

"Yes, I think that would be wise."

A light tap fell on the door. Phoebe and Skinner exchanged a glance, then Skinner crossed to open it.

With a breezy smile, Audrey glided through. "There you are, dear. I hoped I'd catch you."

Clad in ivory and black silk draped much like a toga, a gold-and-black silk turban swathing her head, Audrey crossed to the armchair to one side of the dressing table, her shrewd gaze taking in Phoebe's gown. "That color becomes you, dear. What are you going to wear with it—your garnets and pearls?"

In the mirror, Phoebe glanced at Skinner, who had returned to work on her hair. "That's what I'd planned."

"Excellent." Audrey sank elegantly into the armchair. "Both Edith and I are . . . well, heartened, and very pleased to see you making an effort."

Phoebe wanted to turn and look at Audrey, but a hiss from Skinner and a tap with the comb warned her to keep her head straight.

Before she could formulate any sensible response, Audrey continued, "I thought perhaps I should mention that the Deverells, all the males that is, while being quite . . . well, not to put too fine a point on it, *rakehellish* through their formative years, all of them—every last one throughout the family's history—have become quite *staid* once they wed."

From the corner of her eye, Phoebe saw Audrey tilt her head, considering, then she added, "I've never been sure that the two states weren't connected. That the latter wasn't a direct consequence of the experience of the former, if you take my meaning."

Audrey fell silent; Phoebe wasn't sure what to say. Then Audrey spoke again.

"Your mother and I were very close. We shared all our hopes and dreams. I've told you that before, but there's one story I haven't mentioned, and I feel now is the time. When I was young—younger than you, about twenty-two—I had a beau and thought I was in love. For all I know I was, but my father was quite sure my suitor was a wastrel and he forbade the match. In those days I wasn't quite so independent as I've since become, and while I sulked, I can't say I fought all that hard. But . . ." Audrey shrugged lightly.

Phoebe frowned. "You've never stopped loving him?"

Audrey blinked her eyes wide. "Oh, no—it wasn't like that. My father was quite right—poor Hubert was a wastrel. No, it's not that I've been carrying a torch for him all these years. But what I have often wondered was, What might have been?

"You see, dear, we never do know." Straightening, Audrey resettled her shawl. "I should hope, knowing me as you do, that you realize I regret very little in my life, that indeed I enjoy my life and am quite content with matters as they are. Or so I believe, but I do wonder, from time to time, whether my life would have been even better, even happier, if I'd grasped the chance that fate once offered and fought for what I wanted. I did want him at the time, but now I'll never know what might have been—would he have been a wastrel if I'd married him? Would I have been even more content than I am?"

Audrey paused, then, with a rustle of silk, rose. "What I wished to say to you, dear, poised as you are at this moment in your life, is that while I regret nothing I've done in my life, I do sometimes regret what I didn't do—those opportunities fate sent me that I didn't grasp."

Skinner finished Phoebe's hair and moved aside. Audrey took her place, meeting Phoebe's eyes in the mirror, laying a beringed hand lightly on her shoulder. "I just wanted to suggest, dear, that when opportunity knocks, you think of *what might be* before you turn it away."

Phoebe looked into Audrey's hazel eyes. Lifting one hand, she touched Audrey's where it rested on her shoulder. "Thank you. I will think carefully."

Audrey's smile lit her face. "Good." She turned to the door. "Now I'd better go and roust out Edith. We'll see you in the drawing room."

Skinner moved to hold the door for Audrey. Closing it behind her, Skinner returned to pick up and shake out Phoebe's fringed shawl. "She's still a devilishly handsome lady—no reason for her to think she's past it. She's not that old."

"No, she's not." Phoebe rose so Skinner could drape the shawl over her shoulders. "Where's my reticule?"

While she put on her garnet and pearl earrings, and looped her pearls about her neck, she thought over what Audrey had said. She had, of course, been speaking of marriage, but . . .

Phoebe let herself out of her room and headed for the stairs, confident that in her case, the same dictum applied to indulging in a liaison.

How would she know what might be if she didn't?

Audrey's revelation about Deverell males continued to play in Phoebe's brain. He entered the drawing room late, dark and devilishly handsome in black evening coat and crisp white linen; he came straight to her side, but there was little time for any but the mildest observations before Stripes arrived and the company went in to dinner.

Once again, she and he weren't side by side. They were, however, seated opposite each other, which in some respects suited her better. In between chatting with Milton Cromwell and Peter, she grasped moments to observe Deverell, to evaluate and assess, and ponder. *Rakehellish* Audrey had said; it was an apt description. He didn't exhibit the behavior of a true rakehell, but he definitely had a propensity for the role, as well as all the qualifications.

It wasn't just his handsomeness, not just his glib tongue. There was something in his gaze, some hint of . . . not wildness, but something untamed and untameable, something not quite civilized, that set him apart.

Very definitely apart from the other gentlemen present. Which was no doubt the reason that all the young ladies continued to cast interested—willing to be infatuated—glances his way.

She inwardly sniffed; they would have to stand in line.

By the end of the meal, she'd decided it was those elements that made it so clear he would run in no woman's harness that most attracted women to him. That, after all, was the essential danger in him.

It was what most fascinated her.

That defined, she would have given a great deal to know what attracted him to her—what brought him directly to her side as the company filed into the ballroom.

Halting beside her, he reached for her left hand and raised it, looking for the dance card that wasn't there.

When he looked at her, brows rising, she explained, "I'm twenty-five."

He grinned and lowered their hands, letting his fingers slide over hers. "Good. Then you can waltz every waltz with me."

"Nonsense." She retrieved her hand and primly clasped both before her. "Two waltzes is the maximum—well, perhaps three."

"You being twenty-five?"

"Exactly. But you'll have to dance with others, too."

He didn't look impressed, but there wasn't a matron present who would allow it to be otherwise. He might be focused on her, but the chance to waltz with him was nevertheless an opportunity, one the matchmaking mamas wouldn't allow their charges to miss.

Which thought had her dwelling on opportunities again.

Georgina came up on Milton's arm, then Deidre appeared with Peter and Charlie.

"We were thinking of taking some guns out tomorrow." Peter looked at Deverell. "Will you join us?"

He glanced at Phoebe, and declined, but then asked what sport Peter expected to find. It took a moment before Phoebe realized he'd chosen a topic guaranteed to bore the ladies present. Georgina shifted, as did Deidre, but neither gave any sign of moving on.

Phoebe took pity on them. "That's a lovely comb, Deidre— where did you find it?"

The three of them were soon engaged in a comparison of London's milliners and haberdashers.

Then the musicians at the end of the large ballroom started the prelude to a waltz. Deverell's hand closed strongly about hers before the first chord faded.

He raised their linked hands, boldly raised her fingers to his lips, and kissed. "My dance, I believe."

She wasn't about to argue, but as she let him lead her to

the floor, she glimpsed the chagrined look Deidre sent Peter, and his helpless grimace.

"You upset their plan," she said as Deverell swung her into his arms.

He caught her eyes as he drew her to him. "My plan comes first."

That was instantly apparent; he set them revolving with consummate grace, all powerful strength and ineffable control. Throughout their first circuit of the large room she was fully engaged in growing accustomed to the sensation of being so utterly in his control. And in letting her starved senses soak in his seductive nearness, and the promise therein.

Having him close seemed to subtly ease her flickering nerves—not so much soothing them as reassuring them that satisfaction was nigh. In that respect, a waltz with him was a flagrant exercise in sensual promise.

His strength surrounded her; she was even more aware of it than when she'd stood in his arms and let him kiss her. As they revolved and precessed, she was totally in his control, and he managed her effortlessly, guiding her where he willed, drawing her a fraction too close as they whirled through a tight turn, and later not easing his hold.

And all the while, his eyes held hers; she felt trapped in his green gaze. She wondered what he could see, what he was reading as he searched her eyes.

Deverell doubted she knew how transparent she was, at least to him, at least in this. Since he'd parted from her that afternoon, she'd reached a decision; she wasn't seeking to be seduced but she was willing to be seduced. By him. Her altered stance did not extend to any other gentleman, only him. He was the one who had evoked the change, and he was the only one she had any interest in allowing to attempt her seduction.

That last calmed a primitive part of him, one he wasn't well acquainted with and didn't understand, that had been stirring—that hadn't entirely liked the way Milton Cromwell had looked at Phoebe, or the glances other gentlemen had cast her undeniably appealing figure.

She'd been paying more attention to how she dressed, an indication of her interest that hadn't escaped him. Her subtle transformation had focused his attention even more strongly, feeding his desire.

And now she'd decided to put her hand in his and allow him to lead her along the path to intimacy.

The scent of victory set a spur to his desire; he ruthlessly tamped it down. Her decision was a triumph, yes, but only in the sense his way forward was now clear—to the next step.

He put his mind to the task. Bringing them out of a turn, he set them revolving up the long room. "Why is it that chits like Deidre Mellors think that revealing as much of their charms as possible without precipitating a scandal is alluring?"

Phoebe's brows rose. "I don't know." After a moment, she asked, "Isn't it? Don't gentlemen prefer that?"

He smiled into her eyes. "It's not so much what we prefer as what we find most fascinating." While Deidre had thought to capture interest with her daringly low-cut bodice, Phoebe had fixed his attention, and others', much more effectively with her gown that hinted at what lay beneath but didn't reveal enough to satisfy even their imaginations.

"We're simple creatures," he murmured. "You need to tease us."

She laughed. "I'll remember that."

"Do." He caught her eyes as they revolved, and let his voice deepen. "The mind is the most powerful target for seduction, and the most potent weapon."

She raised her brows. "A point you'd know."

"Indeed."

The music ended; he whirled her to a flourishing halt, then bowed.

Laughing, a touch breathless, Phoebe curtsied, then let him take her hand and lead her to where Audrey and Edith had commandeered a chaise. He didn't need to return her to her aunt's side; at her age that was no longer necessary. It was on the tip of her tongue to remind him, but the combination of his words and him being near was a powerful distraction.

The mind is the most powerful target . . . and the most potent weapon.

Was it her imagination, or had there been a warning—an indication of what direction he intended to take—in those words?

She spent the next hour on tenterhooks, waiting—hoping—to find out.

He didn't disappoint her. But . . .

"The morning room?"

"Strange to tell, it's the one room in any house almost always overlooked, and never ventured into by anyone during a ball."

He spoke with authority distilled, she presumed, from extensive experience, but as he ushered her through the door, she discovered he was right; the room was empty.

The curtains hadn't been drawn. Moonlight washed through the long windows, providing enough light to navigate by, but not enough to see subtle variations in colors or fine detail. As the room hadn't been prepared for use that evening, no lamps were lit.

Phoebe was relieved. Dealing with Deverell on this plane was difficult enough in the dark; she didn't need to see him, didn't need any visual reminder of his strength, that hers was so much less.

That, as usual, she was in his control.

Behind her, he closed the door. She heard the lock snib. A moment passed in which he studied her—she could feel his gaze on her back—then he pushed away from the door; she sensed him approaching.

She whirled. "I wanted to ask—"

Her breath suspended. He looked into her eyes from a distance of mere inches.

Then he reached for her; his arms slowly, gently surrounded her, and he eased her toward him. "What?"

She blinked and struggled to remember. "Ah . . ."

Above their heads, music played; the ball was in full swing, the dancers whirling to the strains of the first waltz after supper. On leaving the supper room, together and briefly alone, he'd led her into the house rather than back to the ball; no one had seen them disappear; no one knew where they were.

Her gaze had fixed on his lips.

They curved. One hand rising to cradle her face, he murmured, "Is it urgent?"

Amusement laced his tone; it, and his touch, made her shiver.

She lifted her gaze to his eyes. "What are you thinking of?" Perhaps that would give her some clue as to what he intended.

He held her gaze for an instant, then replied, "You."

The arm about her waist tightened; he drew her fractionally closer. She spread her palms on his chest, fought down an urge to slide them further. She cleared her throat, hurriedly asked, "What about me?"

His devilish smile deepened. He leaned nearer; his lips

brushed the corner of hers. "About what I want to do to you. With you."

Her lips throbbed, hungry for his, but she swallowed and whispered, "What?"

"This." His tone suggested she'd teased him far enough, that he'd reached the end of his patience. He kissed her, took her mouth, not forcefully, yet she couldn't have resisted, couldn't have denied him had she so wished.

Luckily, she hadn't any intention of denying him, or herself. She let him take, then, emboldened, encouraged him to take more.

He did, but not as she'd expected. He lifted his head, breaking the kiss.

She caught the glint of his eyes beneath his heavy lids.

"This." He murmured the word against her lips, his voice gravelly and deep. Then the arm about her tightened still more, a steely band locking her against him.

She tensed. He hesitated, but then bent his head and kissed her more deeply, more persuasively, more urgently, until she responded, until she slid her hands up and wound them about his neck and kissed him back.

Deverell battled to keep his mind on her lips, her mouth, on the heated tangle of their tongues. Fought to keep his senses enmeshed in the increasingly sensual play, away from the sensation of her svelte body plastered the length of his.

Away from the warm pressure of her breasts against his chest, from the provocative weight of her hips and thighs caressing his.

She was pliant, willing, to that point at least, yet there remained within her a core of flighty, skittering resistance.

Of rearguard defiance—that was how the more primitive side of him chose to interpret it, that side of him few women had ever drawn forth but which she evoked so effortlessly.

The side of him that wasn't all that safe, that was in many ways dangerous.

That side of him he couldn't, with her, forever hold back.

It was that aspect of him that deliberately stoked the kiss into a conflagration, into a building firestorm of need so that she gasped and clung, then melted.

So that she sank against him, so that it seemed her wish that he send one hand sliding down, palm spread, sculpting her hips, then swooping lower to cup her bottom and knead provocatively, her wish that he give in to temptation and flagrantly mold her to him.

Phoebe gasped, overwhelmed by sensation. By the depth and searing heat of their kiss, by the steady, unrelenting temptation of his lips and tongue, of his questing hand, of her own needs and wants flaring in response. Then his hand firmed; he pressed her to him—and everything within her stilled.

Her heart, her pulse, her wits, her mind.

Her fears.

He shifted against her; there was no mistaking the hard ridge of his erection pressing against her belly.

The last time she'd been this close to a man—

She blocked off the thought surprisingly easily; this was so unlike that other time. This time, desire warmed her veins; this time, passion and lust lapped about her—hers as well as his.

This time she was willing; this time she had some say, some influence.

She might not have control, but he did.

Nerve by nerve, tendon by tendon she let her fears slide away, let their grip on her unravel. Felt them fall away as his hand firmed again; he'd known she'd tensed, known she was close to pushing him away, and had waited.

He hadn't backed away, but he hadn't tried to press her on.

When the last vestige of her tension evaporated and she sank willingly against him again, Deverell mentally sighed with relief. They were, thank heaven, over that hurdle. If she'd panicked . . .

He would have stopped, but the cost would have been more than he wished to contemplate. He'd taken a risk leading her this far, but the angels had smiled and she was still with him.

But he knew his limits, and they'd reached them. He didn't dare tempt himself more by dallying with her for much longer.

Gradually, moment by moment, he eased them back from the brink of the next step. She wasn't any great help; her lips clung and tempted, demanded, then pouted when he insisted on lifting his head.

He looked down at her slumbrous eyes and inwardly gloated. Raising one hand, he brushed the pad of his thumb over her full, lower lip and watched passion swim through her lovely, dazed eyes.

He wanted her more than he'd imagined possible.

Dragging in a tight breath, he eased his arms from her; making sure she was steady on her feet, he stepped back, putting space and safe air between them.

She sighed, then looked down and shook out her skirts. "I suppose we should get back."

Her tone suggested she wasn't convinced. Through the waning moonlight, he stared at her. It was go back, or . . .

His body felt wooden, but he forced one arm up and waved her to the door. "Yes. We should. We need to be seen again."

She passed by him on her way to the door, head tilting, a slight frown on her face as she tried to see his eyes well enough to gauge the reason behind his terse tone.

He broke; as she passed, he swung behind her and slipped an arm about her waist. He drew her back against him, one hand splayed over her waist, the other palm stroking her upper arm—his fingertips quite deliberately lightly caressing the side of her breast.

She sucked in a breath but didn't freeze.

Bending his head, he pressed his lips to the warm, scented hair above her ear, and whispered, "I want you, Phoebe, and you will be mine. Soon."

A second ticked by, then he straightened. And released her.

She didn't immediately move forward. Instead, she turned her head and over her shoulder met his eyes. Then she looked at his lips, and nodded. "Soon."

With that, head high, she swept to the door.

He blinked, mentally shook his head free of his lust, and, his expression studiously impassive, followed.

She was going to do it—she was going to have an affair. With Deverell.

Later that night, a full hour after the last guest retired to his chamber and the house at last fell silent, Phoebe started down the main stairs on her way to take care of the last outstanding item on her immediate agenda. Once she'd dealt with Jessica, she would be free to devote her mind entirely to Deverell and his seductive abilities.

Not least of those was the ability to stir her, to excite her as no man ever had. Just by looking at her. One touch, and her skin came alive; one darkly whispered word, and her desire took flight.

If she was ever to learn of passion, he was the one to teach her.

He was obviously godsent, for the most impressive of his

abilities, the one she valued most, one she knew was rare among men of his type, was not so much his control but his willingness to exercise it on her behalf.

That was impressive. It was also comforting and reassuring, especially to her. Time and again, he'd drawn a line and stuck to it. He could have gone further tonight—she wouldn't have minded taking one step more—but no. They'd agreed on one step at a time, so one step at a time was what she'd got.

She might be impatient, but she wasn't about to argue with that. Instead, she was fantasizing about what their next step would entail.

But first . . .

The front hall was wreathed in deep shadows. Stepping off the last stair, she listened, but everyone, including the exhausted staff, was slumbering deeply; no sound of any human reached her ears. Reassured, she walked across the hall to the library.

This part of their rescues always fell to her; if anyone saw her walking about at night, they wouldn't question her. If any servants chanced to happen by, she could easily dismiss them.

Opening the library door, she walked in and shut it behind her. The room lay in darkness; the curtains weren't drawn, but the moon had waned. She searched the dense shadows but saw nothing. Walking forward, she halted in the center of the room. "Jessica?"

The girl audibly gulped. "H-here, ma'am." She rose and came forward from the nook beside the fireplace where she'd been crouched. She was clutching a small satchel and a bundle in her arms and was wearing a thick coat over a plain gown.

"Good." Phoebe nodded approvingly. She spoke quietly and clearly as she turned to the French doors. "Not long now and you'll be safe away. Come along."

She'd arranged to meet Jessica in the library because it gave onto the side lawn, which in turn gave ready access to the wood. Unlocking the French doors, she led Jessica through, then closed the doors, leaving them unlocked. Turning, she crossed the terrace, beckoning Jessica to follow, then went down the steps to the lawn.

"This way." She kept her voice down, as whispering only increased the tension unnecessarily. She led the way directly across the side lawn. "The carriage will be waiting in the lane on the other side of the wood. There's a break in the wall, so we won't need to climb over."

When she glanced at Jessica, scurrying, huddled, beside her, the maid nodded, but her eyes were wide, and her pallor owed little to the poor light.

Mentally cursing Lord Moffat, Phoebe faced forward and walked steadily on.

They reached the wood and marched into the dense shadows beneath the trees. The way was dark, but Phoebe knew it well enough. She'd exchanged her fringed silk shawl for a more serviceable woolen one, but the wood was kept well-thinned; there was no undergrowth on which to snag her skirts.

She unerringly led Jessica between the trees to the spot where the stone wall circling the manor's park had crumbled, leaving a gap large enough to easily climb through.

Scatcher was waiting, silhouetted in the gap.

"Don't worry," Phoebe told Jessica. "He's a friend."

A friend who looked like a disreputable shopkeeper, but then that was what Scatcher was.

When they reached the gap, he held out mittened hands to help her through. "There you be. We was starting to wonder."

She wasn't late, but she knew they would have started "to wonder" the instant they'd arrived. Phoebe waited until

Jessica joined her in the lane, then turned and led the way to the waiting carriage.

It was old and unremarkable, but ran exceedingly well. Birtles and Fergus made sure of that; tonight it was Birtles up on the box, saluting her with his whip.

She smiled and waved back, then Scatcher opened the carriage door. Smile deepening, Phoebe exchanged a glance with the carriage's occupant—Emmeline Birtles, the first woman she'd helped—then turned to Jessica. "Emmeline here and her husband—he's Birtles, the driver—will take you to the agency in London. You'll be safe with them. I'll come to see you once you're settled, and we can talk about your next position."

Jessica peered into the carriage; the worst of her tension dissolved. She looked up at Phoebe. "Thank you, miss. I don't know as how I can ever thank you enough."

Hearing the catch in the girl's voice, Phoebe smiled and stepped back. "Just do as Emmeline tells you, and we'll count ourselves repaid."

Then Scatcher was there, helping Jessica into the carriage. Emmeline, a warm, motherly woman, welcomed her and settled her beside her on the seat. Emmeline nodded to Phoebe, then Scatcher shut the door.

He turned to her, eyeing her frowningly from beneath wildly overhanging brows. "You sure you don't need me to see you back to the house? It's dark in that wood."

Phoebe grinned at him. "No—I'd much rather you climbed up and let Birtles get you all back to London without more ado."

Scatcher muttered something, but knew better than to argue. He climbed up to sit beside Birtles.

Phoebe stood back. Birtles gave the horses the office, then flourished his whip in farewell. Phoebe raised her hand, then lowered it. She waited until the carriage had rumbled quietly around the first bend in the lane before she turned and climbed back through the gap in the wall.

There was a ditch just inside the wall. She clambered down and then up the other side, lifting her skirts as she toiled up the short slope and back under the trees. Reaching level ground, she released her skirts; marching on, she glanced at her elbow, tugging her shawl into place.

She looked ahead—and walked into a wall.

Of muscle and bone.

Chapter 6

*T*he breath she sucked in stuck in her windpipe; she almost panicked, but in the instant before she would have lost her head and screamed, he caught her arms and steadied her, and she knew who he was.

She let out her strangled breath with a whoosh. "Deverell."

A second ticked by in complete and utter silence.

It was then she noticed that his grip on her arms was tight, that instead of the comforting sense she usually derived from his strength, what was reaching her was the scarifying aura of an angry male.

A powerful, strong, highly irate male.

In whose control she was.

She jerked her gaze up to his face; not enough light reached it for her to read his expression or his eyes, but she could feel them on her—burning.

Then he spoke; his voice cracked like a whip.

"What the devil are you about?"

She stiffened, then lifted her head. "Unhand me."

He stared at her. He didn't immediately do as she asked.

Phoebe waited, breath bated, but then his jaw clenched and, finger by finger, he peeled his hands from her arms.

His compliance should have reassured her, but her nerves were leaping, alarmed beyond being easily allayed. It was difficult to breathe. They faced each other in the darkness; he was blocking the path to the house.

"What were you doing?"

His tone was more measured, his words even, but the steel running beneath reminded her of what, over her recent interludes with him, she'd forgotten. His background, his links with the authorities.

She couldn't tell him anything. Elevating her chin, she fixed him with a look that, darkness or not, should have had a duke stepping back. "What I do is none of your concern."

He studied her for a long moment, then simply said, "Think again."

His tone sent cold sluicing through her; the man facing her was the dangerous male she'd always sensed lurking behind his languid façade.

He scared her, yet . . . she knew it was him, that no matter the situation he wouldn't harm her.

His gaze didn't waver from her face; his attention was locked entirely on her. "I saw you leave the house with another woman. I saw you lead her through the wood and give her over to some men waiting with a coach—they knew you, and you knew them. You put the woman into the coach, then watched it leave. Who was the woman? What's going on? And what's your role in it?"

If she'd entertained any doubt over how effective he'd been as an "operative," that speech would have slayed it. His tone was clipped, his diction precise, rendering every word an indictment, imbuing each phrase with authority and un-relenting pressure. More, with the promise of *infinite* unrelenting pressure until she surrendered and told him all.

Bad enough; simmering beneath his outward, clearly professional detachment was something not detached at all.

Something that set her senses clamoring, but as she stood in the dark, her gaze locked with his, her logical mind repeated what she'd already learned—that with him she was safe—and more forcefully reiterated that her business was none of his affair, had no bearing on their affair, or vice versa.

Regardless of any liaison that might or might not develop between them, telling him of her "business" was a risk too great to take.

"I have nothing to say to you, my lord." Her words matched his in evenness, in underlying determination. "Regardless of what you may think, I see no reason, no justification, no relationship that necessitates my answering to you."

Head high, she held his gaze for an instant, then inclined her head. She started to step around him. "If you'll excuse—"

"No relationship?"

The words were soft, quiet . . . dangerous. His tone sent a dark shiver down her spine. Halting, she lifted her head. He hadn't moved an inch; her step had brought her closer to him. She met his eyes across the inches; her gaze stony, she enunciated, equally quietly, equally clearly, "None."

His brows rose.

Then he moved.

One second she was standing on the path, in the next she was backed against a tree. A hard hand at her waist pinned her there; before she could blink he caught her chin and tipped it up—and his lips came down on hers.

No relationship?

She knew what he was trying to prove; hands fisting on his shoulders, she tried to hold firm, to deny—but he'd invaded her mouth in that first instant and immediately set about plundering. Her senses, her wits—her strength. The strength she needed to stand against him.

Tightening her fingers in his coat, she tried to push back, but the tree was behind her, and he was immovable.

She gasped through the kiss, desperately searching for some way to end it.

Abruptly his lips lifted from hers.

Eyes closed, she dragged in a breath.

"Tell me."

An outright order. She hauled in another breath, bolstered her courage. Opening her eyes, she met his—an inch away. "No." She pushed at his shoulders. "Let me—"

Again he moved so fast her mind was too slow following; he plucked her hands from his shoulders, raised them above her head, and locked them against the trunk, manacled in one of his.

Fear leapt to life inside her, then he leaned into her—and panic *roared.*

Exploded as his mouth came down, hard, crushing, on hers.

Deverell fully intended to kiss her witless, to distract and overwhelm her, lay waste to her resistance until she softened and told him what he needed to know.

He fully expected to succeed.

Fully expected her to melt under the primitive onslaught and give in.

Instead, she started to fight him.

Which seemed ridiculous. She couldn't . . .

But she was.

His mind locked on sensual conquest, it took him a good minute to realize, then accept that she was indeed struggling, albeit ineffectively.

That she was trying to escape, not simply resist.

That she was growing increasingly frantic.

He immediately lifted his head. Her breath sawed in, one step from hysterical panic. He eased his body back from hers but didn't let her go.

Her eyes, open and wide, had locked on his face.

He couldn't read their expression, but he saw enough— she was frightened, panicked. *Afraid.*

Of him.

To his intense surprise, his heart constricted and abruptly felt like lead.

But . . . confused, he frowned at her. His hand was still locked at her waist; the other held both of hers, but not hard enough to bruise.

And he hadn't, even in those most forceful moments, gone as far as they had earlier that evening.

She sucked in a tight breath. Her wide-eyed gaze, that of prey trapped by a predator, never shifted from his face. "Let me go. Now."

Her voice quavered; gone was her earlier confidence—all hint of defiance.

It was very nearly a plea.

He complied instantly, releasing her hands and stepping back.

His heart sank further, but he remained nonplussed. Through the shrouding shadows he stared, trying from her face to get some hint of what was happening, trying to make sense of her fraught reaction.

Her hands fell to her sides, grasping the tree trunk. Her chest heaved as she dragged in another breath. He waited, unmoving, silent—not daring to do or say anything in case it was the wrong thing.

A minute ticked by.

On the surface she'd calmed, but he sensed she remained one small step from senseless panic. Slowly, carefully, her gaze trained on him the entire time, she pushed away from the tree.

He couldn't bear that look. He'd never intended . . . she couldn't think . . . He put out a hand to steady her. "Phoebe?"

She stepped quickly sideways, avoiding his hand as if he were a leper. "Stay away from me."

The words were low, pained. They struck him like a blow.

He let his hand fall. Stood and watched, unmoving and silent, as she edged around him onto the path. Then she abruptly swung around and started for the house, her steps rushed and not quite steady.

"Stay far, *far* away from me." Her words drifted back to him, a fading whisper as she put space between them. "Don't *ever* come near me again."

Jaw set, he waited until she was far enough ahead, then trailed her; stopping within the shadows of the wood, he watched until she disappeared into the library.

And then there was just him and the night, and an abject sense of failure. Of a mistake he'd inadvertently made, a misstep he'd unwittingly taken. He stood in the dark, replaying the scene in the wood again, and tried to understand what had happened.

He was down early for breakfast the following morning, but she, along with the majority of other guests, didn't appear.

Accepting a copy of the latest London news sheet from Stripes, he retreated to the peace and quiet of the library.

He sat in an armchair at the other end of the room from the chaise on which he'd first sighted Miss Phoebe Malleson reclining and eating grapes. Flicking out the news sheet, he held it before his face and pretended to read; the last thing he wanted was for some other guest to engage him in cheery conversation.

After untold hours reviewing all that had passed between them, he was feeling unrepentant, and just a trifle sour. Last night—that unsettling interlude in the wood—had been her fault first to last. It had been her fault that, rather than sleeping, he'd once again been pacing the darkened gardens, walking off the effects of the lust she'd evoked.

That was why he'd been there to see her slipping so suspiciously away from the house with another female in train. Of course he'd followed. The only thought in his brain had been to ensure she was safe.

Until he'd seen her hand the girl over to the unknown men.

Then he hadn't known what to think.

So he'd asked her.

All that had followed had been a direct result, as far as he could see, of her refusal to explain and set his mind at rest.

A simple explanation, that was all he'd asked for—surely not too much to ask of the lady who, just hours before, had unequivocally indicated that she was willing to let him seduce her, ultimately into marriage. Her acceptance had been implicit in all they'd said and done.

She'd made her decision, but then, when faced with the need to explain her suspicious actions, she'd changed her mind.

His reaction to that was so sharp, so intense, he paused and turned over a page of the news sheet just to give the feeling a moment to subside.

For her, he'd ridden his desires more strongly, more

rigidly than he had with any woman before; the previous evening, he'd exercised restraint he hadn't known he possessed. She'd appreciated that at the time, but later how had she repaid him?

By refusing to trust him and, to his mind even worse, refusing to take adequate care.

Why that last aspect should head his list of grievances he didn't know, but the danger inherent in her flitting through a dark wood, without any protection, to meet with rough and uncouth men in a lane after midnight, was the point that did most violence to his soul.

If anything had happened to her . . .

He inwardly snorted and told himself that the reason her safety mattered so much was because if anything happened to her, he wouldn't be able to marry her, which would leave him where he'd started. . . .

Even in his present mood, the argument wasn't convincing.

The damned woman had got under his skin in a way he didn't understand. Regardless, she was now there, and he would have to cope with the ramifications.

So would she.

On that, he was unalterably determined.

He checked on and off through the morning, but none of the ladies came downstairs.

Stripes informed him that that was often the case after a ball. "Getting their beauty sleep, my lord."

He suppressed a snort, but as Stripes had prophesized, it wasn't until after the luncheon gong sounded that he heard the tap of female footsteps on the stairs. Folding the news sheet—in desperation he'd read every word—he laid it aside and rose.

When he reached the dining room, where a cold collation had been laid out upon the sideboard, he discovered Phoebe already at the table—surrounded by the other young ladies. She knew he'd walked into the room, but while the others—Deidre and Leonora especially—looked up and smiled brightly in welcome, Phoebe avoided his eye.

Preserving his urbane mask, he returned the others' smiles with one merely polite, then walked to the sideboard.

After heaping his plate, he retired to the other end of the table where Lord Cranbrook and Lord Craven, one of the few older male guests, sat chatting. They welcomed him, and the talk turned to horseflesh.

More gentlemen drifted in, followed by the older ladies in twos and threes. Audrey glided in; she paused and considered the table, then glided to the sideboard.

A few minutes later, he looked up to see her approaching. He rose to hold a chair for her.

Instead of immediately sitting, she paused beside him and laid a hand on his sleeve. "What have you done?"

Her tone was long-suffering. He fought back a scowl. "Nothing." Before she could scoff, he added, "Something's going on."

She'd always been able to read him well; she didn't make the mistake of thinking he was inventing something to distract her. Concern crept into her eyes. "What do you mean?"

Grim, he drew out the chair. "If I knew . . ."

She hesitated, patently thinking, then patted his arm and finally sat. As he resumed his seat beside her, she murmured, "Edith and I have every confidence in you, dear, so do get whatever it is sorted out."

Feeling as if he were twelve again, he gave his attention to his plate.

At least outwardly; most of his senses were focused on Phoebe.

The older ladies continued to arrive in trickles. Luncheon

was almost over when Lady Moffat, a female he'd labeled a tartar with a liking for histrionics, swept into the room, out of breath and transparently out of temper.

"Maria—*Gordon!*" Her hair straggling wildly, her gown obviously hastily donned, Lady Moffat appealed to Lady and Lord Cranbrook. "It really is *insupportable!* My maid has up and disappeared, and no one seems to have any idea where the ungrateful chit's gone!"

"Good heavens!" Lady Cranbrook looked stunned, as did most others.

"What am I to *do?*" Lady Moffat wailed.

Deverell looked down the table at Phoebe. Displaying her customary calm, she was watching Lady Moffat with a detached, even critical, eye; she was certainly not surprised.

Not a hint of astonishment showed as she observed the reactions of the others—Lady Cranbrook, who had risen and gone to calm Lady Moffat, the other older ladies who were gathering around, Lord Cranbrook, who was ponderously getting to his feet.

She didn't look at Deverell, but then she knew he was watching her.

Despite now knowing the identity of the female Phoebe had led into the wood, he still couldn't fathom why.

One part of his mind had been following the exclamations and expostulations of the bevy of older ladies gathered about Lady Moffat. To his surprise, Lady Cranbrook, with Audrey beside her, turned to him.

"My lord, I wonder if we might prevail upon you to lend us your expertise." Maria wrung her hands. "It's really quite unsettling. This is the third female servant to go missing at a house party in recent months." She paused, blinked, then hurried to assure him, "Not all here, of course. But among our circle." She gestured to the other ladies, crowding behind her to bend appealing gazes on him.

It was hardly the sort of thing he had any experience of.

Lord Cranbrook came to stand beside his wife. "I'm the local magistrate, Paignton, but I have to say I'm not up to snuff with this sort of thing. Servants disappearing—well!" His lordship puffed out his cheeks. "I'd take it very kindly if you would lend me your assistance and look into the matter."

What could he say? He met Audrey's eyes and saw nothing but calm certainty that he'd accept Lord Cranbrook's commission. Rising, he took Lady Cranbrook's hand and bowed. "If it will set your mind at rest, ma'am, I'll do whatever I can."

With his lordship, he retreated to Lord Cranbrook's study. There they interviewed the redoubtable Stripes and the housekeeper, an upright female, neither of whom could add anything to the tale that when Lady Moffat had summoned her maid at one o'clock, the girl, Jessica, had been nowhere to be found.

"Have you searched her room?" Deverell asked.

Stripes understood. "Her bed was slept in, my lord, and some of her things are still there."

"Some?"

"Her uniforms and the like," the housekeeper put in, "but not her brush or personal things, and there's no bag. She had a bag with her things in it when she arrived."

Deverell nodded and stood. "I'd like to see her room."

Aside from his own ever-increasing curiosity, there was Phoebe and her reputation to consider. He wanted to make sure there was nothing in the girl's room that might link her to Phoebe or one of her servants.

Lord Cranbrook accompanied him into the attics. Deverell searched, far more thoroughly than the housekeeper had, but found nothing. He did, however, note that the girl's bed hadn't been slept in; it had been deliberately disarranged. There was no adequate indentation or appropriate creases in the thin sheet.

Together with Lord Cranbrook, he returned downstairs. The description Lady Moffat had given of the maid tallied with what he'd glimpsed of the female Phoebe had spirited away.

In the front hall, he turned to his host. "With your permission, my lord, I'll look around and see what other information I can gather."

The implication was "alone." Lord Cranbrook nodded readily. "Very good. I'd best get back to the others."

Deverell watched his lordship head for the library. After a moment, he turned and headed for the back lawn.

As he'd expected, the older ladies were seated beneath the trees, still exclaiming over the latest happening while keeping their charges, ambling about the lawns, some playing a desultory round of croquet, others simply chatting, under their watchful eyes.

He avoided most; pretending not to notice the gazes trained on him, he went to Audrey's side.

She turned from Mrs. Hildebrand as he neared; she raised her brows as he hunkered beside her chair.

"Lady Cranbrook mentioned two other disappearances at house parties—did you attend both those events?" he asked.

Audrey blinked. "No, but Edith did. She could tell you about the second, at Winchelsea Park, but I was at the first, at Lady Alberstoke's in March. It was their governess who went missing." Audrey frowned. "Mind you, there was no reason to believe the woman's disappearance was *connected* with the house party. It seemed obvious she'd simply had enough and run away." She caught Deverell's eye. "If you knew Lady Alberstoke, that would come as no surprise—no truer harridan was ever birthed."

Deverell grimaced and nodded. "I'll speak with Edith."

He rose, his gaze going to Edith, who was sitting beneath a tree chatting with Lady Cranbrook. Phoebe sat in a chair beside her aunt, ostensibly reading her novel.

Perfectly aware she'd been surreptitiously watching him, he walked to the group, mentally listing the information he intended to let fall.

Smiling, he greeted Lady Cranbrook and Edith. Crouching between their chairs, with glib charm he elicited their help, and received breathless assurances that he could rely on them. He turned to Edith. "Audrey told me you were present at both the earlier house parties from which female staff disappeared. Is that correct?"

"Yes, indeed!" Edith nodded decisively.

Deverell let his gaze travel past Edith to Phoebe on her other side. Mildly, he asked, "And Miss Malleson, too?"

Edith flicked a smile Phoebe's way. "Phoebe's been with me since last Christmas. She accompanies me to all these events. Such a comfort."

Phoebe lifted her gaze from her book and returned a fond smile; only he saw it as a fraction too tight. Only he knew how carefully she avoided his eyes.

"I've already heard about the event at Lady Alberstoke's— Audrey suggested it was simply coincidence that her ladyship's governess reached the end of her tether and fled at the time the party was underway."

Edith nodded. "I would have to agree. No female of any sensitivity could have endured Lady Alberstoke for long, and my memory of the young woman was that she was . . . genteel."

"Actually," Lady Cranbrook put in, "she was quite lovely, as I recall."

Deverell waited, but no further recollections were forthcoming. "What was the second incident, the one at Winchelsea Park?"

"That," Edith replied, "was Mrs. Bonham-Cartwright's new French dresser. A very strange affair. One minute, Mrs. Bonham-Cartwright was singing the girl's praises, and the next, the girl had vanished. No one had any idea what had happened."

"Well," Lady Cranbrook said, "while we could imagine well enough that the Alberstokes' governess might have absconded with some man—any man, really, who might have offered her a decent escape—no one could imagine where the French dresser had gone to, much less why. Mrs. Bonham-Cartwright is a kind woman, no Lady Alberstoke, but what really had us puzzled was that the dresser had only recently arrived in the country and supposedly had no friends or family here."

"It was," Edith gently said, "a trifle distressing imagining what might have happened to the girl, which is why this latest happening is so exercising everyone."

Deverell met her eyes and nodded. Quickly shifting his gaze, he trapped Phoebe's and nodded again—much less benignly. "I see."

With that he stood; when he looked down at Edith and Lady Cranbrook, all trace of grimness had been erased from his face and his usual languid charm shone through to reassure them.

Lady Cranbrook looked up at him. "You will see what you can learn, won't you, and tell us?"

He bowed. "That is my intention, ma'am." Then he left.

He summoned Grainger. Together they walked out to check on his grays, currently kicking their heels in one of Lord Cranbrook's paddocks.

Grainger was as mystified as everyone else. "A sweet little thing, she was. A bit timid, but I thought as that was just starry eyes, her being newly hired an' all."

"Newly hired?" Leaning on the paddock fence, Deverell glanced at his groom. "Are you sure?"

"Aye. Not six weeks. Told me so herself." After a moment, Grainger asked, "Why? Is that important?"

"It might be." Deverell described the two earlier disappearances.

Grainger nodded. "Makes you wonder if that governess was new to the place, don't it?"

"Indeed." Deverell hesitated, then more diffidently asked, "How did Miss Malleson's people take the news? Skinner, and her coachman-cum-groom—what's his name?"

"McKenna." Grainger frowned, clearly replaying the moment in his mind. "Clear as I can remember, they were both shocked—same as everyone else." Puzzled, he looked at Deverell. "Why do you ask?"

It was reassuring that her staff were better actors than Phoebe.

He hesitated, his gaze on his horses, inwardly debating, but Grainger had proved himself not just useful but also discreet. Briefly, he outlined what he knew, and what he'd deduced. "Miss Malleson's involved, but her involvement with anything illegal won't be by choice."

Grainger's brow had furrowed. "You mean some blackguard is . . . well, *blackmailing* her into helping them snatch women away?"

"I don't know, but that's one possibility. Because of that, we need to tread warily." He straightened. "Keep a close eye on Miss Malleson's people. Miss Malleson had to have help in whisking Jessica away. Skinner most likely was the one who disarranged the girl's bed. But remember"—he caught Grainger's eye—"if Miss Malleson is in this type of trouble, we can expect her people to go to great lengths to protect her. Don't alert them, don't do anything to draw their attention. In defending their mistress, they could prove dangerous."

Like him.

Grainger swore he'd be careful.

Together they returned to the house.

Everything he'd learned suggested that the incident the previous night was the tip of a large iceberg, something dangerous and illicit, and Phoebe was involved up to her pretty neck.

Deverell prowled the house, then stood at the drawing room windows and studied his target, still seated in the shade reading her damned novel. She was doing her utmost to avoid him, to cut herself off from him. Regardless, he was going to learn the truth—if nothing else to ensure that she wasn't hurt. To ensure that he could protect her.

The *why* wasn't something he needed to dwell on; his aim was clear in his mind.

So he lay in wait for her.

Phoebe stayed outside, safe with the others, for as long as possible. She kept her nose buried in her novel, turning pages now and then, but read not a word.

She hadn't expected Deverell to see her with Jessica last night, but after she'd escaped him, her mind had been in too great a turmoil to think things through. Not "business" things. Instead, she'd spent the hours until dawn castigating herself over other things entirely.

At first she'd paced, driven by shaky fury and a crushing sense of betrayal, railing against her foolishness in ever imagining that he might be different from others of his kind, for being taken in by him. For being *stupid* enough to imagine that if denied, he wouldn't resort to force and simply take.

He'd charmed and seduced her, gained her confidence—and *then* . . .

She'd tripped over her hem and stopped to wrestle it clear . . . then remained stationary as her fury, held close for too long, had abruptly leached from her. She'd lifted her head, drawn in a deep breath—calmed.

And sanity, honesty, and rationality had poured back into her mind.

Standing stock-still in the middle of her bedchamber, she'd relived those moments in the wood . . . and her heart had sunk.

She'd panicked not over what had happened but over what she had, in a moment of evoked memory, thought had been happening.

With a quiet groan, she'd slumped onto her bed and stared blindly at the floor as the veils of panic dissipated, revealing the interlude, his actions and hers, in a cold and unforgiving light. Yes, he'd done what he'd done, reacted as he had, but it hadn't been his actions that had panicked her. That had all been a sleight of memory—a memory she'd assumed she'd put behind her long ago.

The implication had left her feeling numb and quietly aghast. Since that long-ago incident, she'd been extra careful, as any woman would be, especially vigilant over large, strong, and powerful men, but as no man had interested her in the slightest, keeping all gentlemen at a nonthreatening, non-memory-evoking distance had been easy. She'd told Deverell the truth—she'd allowed no man to woo her; she'd never been interested enough to even consider it.

He, however, had breached her guards—and, apparently, stirred that awful memory. He'd been so successful in easing her into his arms, easing her past all those moments when she'd frozen, poised on the brink of uncertainty, that she hadn't seen the danger. She'd long ago assumed that the memory and its effect on her had died; she'd had no inkling it could rise up and ambush her as it had last night.

She'd spent the following hours wallowing in disappointment and mortification. Disappointment because she'd allowed herself to hope that with Deverell she could experience all she'd never had a chance to know. He was the only one who had ever raised her interest, let alone her desire. She was shatteringly disappointed that their affair was not to be.

And last but by no means least, the more she thought of those moments in the wood, the more she cringed in mortification. He'd witnessed her weakness, her silly, irrational, ungovernable panic; she truly didn't want to face him again. If he'd guessed what lay behind her reaction, he'd doubtless pity her; if he hadn't, he'd think she was touched.

Luckily, Skinner hadn't come to rouse her until late. She'd gone down to luncheon feeling dismal and morose but able to keep an adequate mask in place. She'd sat at the table, not allowing herself to look at him, waiting for the day to end, and considering how early tomorrow morning she and Edith could depart.

Lady Moffat's sweeping in and protesting her loss had abruptly refocused Phoebe's mind—she'd instantly seen that Deverell would guess the connection. And matters had gone downhill from there. The last thing she'd expected was for him to be asked to investigate, and through that learn of the two earlier rescues.

He was learning far too much, yet although she'd racked her brain, she couldn't see how he might learn any more. Not unless she told him, and that she'd never do.

Unfortunately, he now knew enough to cause her serious problems. If he revealed what he'd seen last night, if at the conclusion of his investigation he pointed his finger her way . . .

She'd wasted no further time on her personal woes. As the sleepy afternoon had dragged on, she'd assessed the situation from every angle, imagining what he might do, evaluating the ways in which she might react. In the end, only one tack would work. Blank denial, complete and absolute, was her only possible defense.

She would simply say he was mistaken, that the woman he'd seen certainly hadn't been her. His word against hers. Not a strong defense; it would inevitably raise questions in people's minds and make future rescues more difficult.

But not impossible. Most importantly, simply staring down any accusations Deverell might make would keep all the others, and her enterprise itself, safe. Still functioning.

Finally the sun sank low and everyone headed indoors to dress for dinner. She went in surrounded by others, but as she and Edith planned to leave early the following morning, she detoured via the library to return the novel she'd lost all interest in.

Cautiously slipping through the library door, she was immensely relieved to see no dark, handsome ex-major lounging about, waiting to pounce on her. Under Lord Cranbrook's and Lord Craven's benign gazes, she returned the volume to the shelves, then left.

She'd just pulled the library door closed when she sensed him.

Before she could whirl, a hard hand settled at the back of her waist and propelled her forward. She took an involuntary step, then dug in her heels.

He drew close, beside and behind her. His breath brushed her ear. "Don't struggle. Don't make a scene—or I'll pick you up and carry you."

The thought of calling his bluff occurred only to be dismissed. It wasn't a bluff.

Obedient to the pressure at her back, she walked stiffly forward. He steered her across to the morning room, opened the door, and guided her inside.

He paused to close the door; she walked quickly forward and turned to face him over a small table.

Quitting the door, he strolled up. He eyed the table, then looked at her. And raised both brows.

To her intense annoyance, every nerve she possessed leapt and skittered, reacting to his nearness in a thoroughly distracting way. Her spark of anger felt like salvation; she embraced it, clung to it, fed it. Unable to help herself, she quickly searched his eyes, but his expression was impassive; she could see no hint of pity, nor yet any sign he thought her demented.

Folding her arms, she lifted her chin and imperiously demanded, "What do you want? I've nothing whatever to say to you."

Eyes slightly narrowed, he studied hers. To her relief, he made no move to come around the table. A minute ticked by, then he said, quietly and evenly, "You're going to have to tell me sometime."

He was speaking of the rescue. She held his green gaze, kept her anger close, and tipped her chin higher. "When hell freezes."

To her surprise, he didn't react, or at least not with the immediate arrogant response she'd expected.

He stood there, watching her, considering, thinking . . . letting the silence and, she belatedly realized, her nerves stretch. And stretch.

She tightened her arms and reminded herself that her cause was too important to risk, not in any circumstance.

That she would resist him, that he couldn't force her to tell him anything, no matter what he thought, that . . .

When he spoke, she nearly sighed with relief.

"I think you'll discover it will be much sooner than that."

She blinked. Waited. But that was, it seemed, all he wished to say.

With a slow nod, he turned, walked to the door, opened it and left.

The door shut with a click. Puzzled, she stared at the panels.

Wondering what he intended to do. Realizing she had no idea.

Wondering why, even now, she didn't fear him as much as she suspected she should.

He'd intended to press her a great deal harder, but seeing her standing there, arms crossed defensively, determined to resist yet with all manner of emotions coloring her eyes, he'd remembered that learning her secret was only one step along what was proving a difficult road.

A more challenging road than he'd foreseen, but in that moment when he'd studied her across that silly table—he could have pushed it aside with one finger—he'd remembered his true goal. And adjusted his strategy accordingly.

Pressuring her would only increase her resistance and, it seemed likely, her strange, underlying fear. He was going to have to find some different route to her secret, preferably one that didn't involve her; he was too old a hand at strategy and tactics to let his push to learn her secret put his ultimate goal out of reach.

That evening, throughout their time in the drawing room before dinner, which he spent with Audrey and Lady Cranbrook, then during dinner itself, when he was flanked by

Georgina and Heather, Phoebe watched him, puzzled and wary.

When the company regathered in the drawing room, he made no move to join her. Which only puzzled her more.

As he'd anticipated, Lord Cranbrook called the company to order, then turned to him. "Perhaps, my lord, we should share our conclusions with all here."

Even though she stood across the room, he sensed the tension that gripped Phoebe.

He nodded and faced the company, who fell obediently—expectantly—silent. "As requested by his lordship, I've spent the day investigating the disappearance of Lady Moffat's maid." He nodded to her ladyship, still florid and inclined to take umbrage; frowning, she nodded curtly in return.

"After questioning all those likely to have information"—he let his gaze roam the wide circle, coming to rest on Phoebe's white face—"all I can conclude is that the maid ran away, or perhaps was lured away, sometime during the night, after she'd seen Lady Moffat to bed."

Phoebe's hand clenched tightly on her fan.

Deverell inclined his head, apparently to the company, in reality to her.

"Beyond that, all else is conjecture."

A murmur rose; people turned to their neighbors. Speculation filled the air.

Phoebe stood with Deidre, Peter, and Edgar and let the talk wash over her. She felt dizzy, giddy with relief that Deverell hadn't revealed what he knew, but with trepidation dawning, slowly gaining ground.

He hadn't given her away. Why? The one thing she felt sure of was that there would be a reason.

She shifted and glanced around Edgar's shoulders to where Deverell stood talking with Lord Cranbrook and Lord

Craven. The events of the day had somehow drawn a line between him and the younger gentlemen; no one could any longer see him as one of them.

He was not just older, but other. Not just more experienced but an altogether different sort of man. Which brought her back to the confusion she felt every time she looked at him, every time she was near him.

As if he felt her gaze, he half turned; across the room, his eyes met hers.

Their gazes locked, held. And she could almost hear his promise, in his deep, dark, dangerous voice, sensed beyond question his resolution, his implacability.

A heartbeat passed, then two.

Then, as if confirming her understanding, he inclined his head. He held her gaze for one last pregnant moment, then turned back to their lordships.

Phoebe shivered. Shaken, rattled, it was a full minute before she breathed freely again. She turned back to the others, focused her attention on them, forced herself to respond to their comments about what entertainments they expected to attend when they returned to London.

Inside, she grew increasingly concerned.

Deverell had concealed her part in the disappearance. Did he, would he, expect some . . . recompense for his restraint?

Until that moment when she'd met his eyes and known he wasn't finished with her, she hadn't considered that his silence had in a very real way placed her in his debt.

The very last place she would have chosen to be.

That night, sleep was difficult to find, and when it came, she dreamt of him.

Not the him she'd known through the first three days of their acquaintance, he who had tempted her to believe that an affair between them was possible—more, had taught her that it was something she desired.

Not the him with whom she'd spent the picnic afternoon, different from others, yes, but entertaining and relaxing, his company very much to her taste.

The man who invaded her dreams stalked her, caught her—spun her, helpless, back against a tree. Hot green eyes seared her, then he bent his head and ravaged her mouth, took, seized yet more, then his hard body pressed flush against hers—and sent a flash of excitement unlike anything she'd ever known spearing through her—

She woke with a gasp and a thudding heart, and a body oddly aching, heated and restless, nerves flickering and tight.

Wrapped in darkness, she lay still, listening to her breathing slow, her racing heart gradually subside.

And wondered.

Chapter 7

*T*he next evening, ensconced in one of the large armchairs in the library at Number 12 Montrose Place,
Deverell sat in blessed silence, sipped a postprandial brandy,
and contemplated the ceiling on which shadows, thrown by
the fire leaping in the grate, flickered.

It would, at this juncture, be easy to step back—to simply
wash his hands of Phoebe Malleson and walk away.

His life would undoubtedly be simpler, less stressful, if he
did. She wasn't in any way a restful female, and the likelihood of what she was involved in held the promise of untold
difficulties.

Unfortunately, no matter how hard one part of his mind
tried to convince him to look elsewhere, he didn't want to;
he couldn't imagine not pursuing Phoebe, irritating female
though she was. She made him feel emotions he'd never
truly felt, edged those emotions with which he was familiar

with a fresh, strange, and compelling urgency. Her peculiar panicky fear was, to his mind, just another challenge, another hurdle to be overcome in wooing and winning her.

He thought back to all that had occurred at Cranbrook Manor, heard again Audrey's voice calmly pointing out that of all the men present, he was the one with the right skills to hunt down Phoebe. They'd been talking of locating her, but after all that had passed, he sensed he was, in many ways, still hunting Phoebe.

Regardless of his uncertain success thus far, he knew in his bones that Audrey had been right. He was the man with the best chance of capturing Phoebe; no other would succeed. Unless he missed his guess, even Phoebe sensed that.

More, Audrey had been right in reciprocal vein; Phoebe was the right lady for him. He was going to marry her; his resolution on that score had if anything hardened.

That being so, letting her secret, whatever it was, slide back into the obscurity she would no doubt prefer wasn't an option.

Idly sipping, he considered all he knew, searching for some lever to force the issue—some fact he could use to prise the lid from her secret.

Time and again his mind circled back to the two men he'd glimpsed in the lane with the carriage. For years, his life had depended on his visual acuity, among other skills his ability to recognize men from just a glimpse. He was sure he would recognize both men.

But where should he look for them? Logically, the answer would account for how Phoebe had met them and come to know them.

Draining his glass, he rose, then stretched.

Then he headed for his bed.

Tomorrow he'd go hunting.

*   *   *

The following evening, he strolled into Lady Loxley's ballroom. Pausing at the head of her ladyship's ballroom steps, he looked over the sea of heads, searching for the one he wanted.

A flash of glossy dark red, garnet beneath the light of the chandeliers, drew his eye. He located Phoebe across the room. Gowned in a creation of amber silk, she stood beside a chaise on which Edith was sitting; she was in earnest conversation with two ladies he didn't recognize. Lips curving, he started down the steps.

Although she was committed elsewhere, Audrey had been certain Edith, and therefore Phoebe, would attend the Loxleys' ball. She'd been right; certain she would be, she'd demanded in return that he "do something to the point."

He fully intended to do just that.

Phoebe sensed him before she saw him. Her head suddenly lifted; her gaze rose and locked with his. He was near enough to see the flash of surprise that lit her violet-blue eyes, then she veiled them and returned her attention to the ladies—one a matron, the other clearly her daughter—with whom she'd been conversing.

Deverell bowed before Edith and exchanged greetings with her and Mrs. Delauney, then moved on to Phoebe's little circle. She offered her hand; one brief glance into his eyes and she'd known if she hadn't, he would have commandeered it. He clasped her fingers but refrained from lifting them to his lips; he could feel the tremor running through them. Standing by her side, he could sense the tension permeating her slender frame; she was on edge, poised to react.

The matron and her daughter hovered, obviously hoping for an introduction. Phoebe obliged, but with a noticeable lack of enthusiasm. "Lady Cartwell, Miss Emily Cartwell— Lord Paignton."

He smiled urbanely and did his best to discourage Lady Cartwell from lingering. His best was excellent; taking the hint, Lady Cartwell excused herself and her daughter and moved on.

Phoebe shifted. "If you'll excuse me, my lord—"

"No."

She blinked as he turned his head and looked down at her. Between them, hidden by her skirts, he closed his hand around hers. "If you entertain any notion that I'm here because I enjoy doing the pretty by dozens of matrons and their insipid charges, allow me to disabuse you of it." He held her gaze. "Once again, I came for you."

She stiffened. Her head rose. "If you imagine—"

"At the moment, I don't imagine anything. I came to inform you of a number of facts that, no doubt, will be of interest to you."

She hesitated. He'd spoken in his customary social drawl, a tone he suspected she would find less threatening. Less frightening, especially in this arena. The social accents also made his comments less noticeable amidst the chatter around them.

Her gaze searched his face. "What facts?"

"I'm focusing on identifying the two men in the lane—the ones you handed the maid over to. My memory is excellent— I only caught a glimpse, but I'm confident that will prove enough. You should also probably know that I'm not at all averse to adopting a disguise and going out on the streets in search of information."

He caught and held her gaze. "I've already established that those men are not part of your aunt's household. The question that immediately arises, of course, is where it was that you, a gently reared lady, came into contact with rough men of significantly lower station."

Her violet-blue gaze held steady. A moment passed, then

she swallowed and said, with commendable coolness if not sense, "Nothing about those two men is any concern of yours."

"Much as it pains me to contradict a lady, that isn't how I view the matter." He let his gaze harden. "Do I need to remind you that I didn't expose your role in the incident at Cranbrook Manor?"

Her chin rose. "No. But—"

"Because of that"—he continued to speak mildly—"I naturally consider myself in some part responsible for your safety, given I didn't sound the alarm when—or so most would consider—I should have."

Her eyes widened. She stared at him. Then she stated clearly, as if the notion horrified her, "You are not in any way responsible for me—or my safety. If the question should ever arise, I absolve you entirely from all such responsibility, now and in the future."

He smiled, but she was well aware the gesture didn't reach his eyes. "How kind of you. However, be that as it may, I can't absolve myself." Abruptly he dropped every shield he possessed and told her, "That's never going to happen."

The unvarnished truth.

She didn't take it well. Her chin firmed; she drew in a breath.

The musicans set bows to strings.

He glanced in their direction. "How useful. You will waltz with me, won't you?"

A rhetorical question; he already had hold of her hand.

Was already leading her to the floor. Phoebe bit her tongue and went with him. This was not a good idea, but she needed to learn—

He swung her into his arms and her thoughts shattered, scattered, fled. He whirled her down the room, and once again she was reduced to battling sensation, trying to subdue the effect he had on her nerves, on her unruly senses. On her wits; they seemed to deflect—defect—to considering him and his fascinating maleness rather than obeying her will.

To focusing instead on savoring the power with which he danced, the exhilaration she found in matching his long stride, in whirling across the floor in his arms.

It was worse, more difficult, than the last time they'd waltzed. Her nerves seemed to have grown more sensitized and the dance floor was crowded; he could and was holding her closer than propriety allowed—but who was there to see?

Who was there to rescue her witless senses from his grasp?

He looked down at her and arched one dark brow. "I don't suppose you'd like to explain where you met those two men?"

She bludgeoned her wits into order, reminded herself that when it came to him there was only one word she need remember. "No."

Stick to her plan—deny everything, volunteer nothing; that was all she could do, all she could hope to do.

That, and pray he didn't . . . she couldn't even bring herself to think the words. Let alone imagine how she might react.

That, of it all, was the most frightening prospect.

Deverell saw trepidation dull her eyes, sensed in the sudden tensing of her spine the first stirrings of fear. He would have frowned and inwardly cursed, even brought their waltz to a premature halt, except . . . beneath the fear—no, *along* with the fear—he sensed something else.

Something that stopped his breath in his chest, that scattered his thoughts and momentarily left him foundering.

A flash of insight into her, into her peculiar fear, into her responses to him, even into her secret and how all might interact, how all might be part of the one whole.

He searched her violet eyes, trained on his face; she was wary, watchful . . . and battling an unwilling fascination.

By instinct he understood, but his mind couldn't grapple with the revelation, not on such short notice. But his reaction—

Looking up, he steered her to the edge of the floor. He halted them and smoothly stepped out of the stream of dancers, guiding her to the side of the room, stopping a little way from where Edith still chatted.

His face like hewn granite, he swung Phoebe to face him. "Enough." He paused to get his emotions under control. "Understand this: I won't rest until I learn all that you're hiding—your involvement with those men, and your reasons. Regardless, believe this—I will never, *ever* harm you in any way, and I won't allow anyone else to even attempt it."

He held her wide-eyed gaze, stunned, faintly shocked, for a fraught second, then demanded, "Do you understand?"

A frown formed in her eyes. "Yes—and no."

At least that was the truth. He hissed out a breath and glanced at the horde of guests before them, reminding himself of where they were. "I have to go." Before he did something to truly shock her—and half the ton. He glanced at her and trapped her gaze. "If you come to your senses and wish to confide in me, send word to Number 12, Montrose Place. If not . . ."

Beyond his control, his gaze dropped to her lips. He moved his thumb caressingly across the knuckles of the hand he still held. He lifted his gaze to her eyes in time to detect the sensual shiver she couldn't suppress. Stifling a curse, he released her hand, stepped back, and gracefully bowed. "I'll meet you tomorrow night and we can continue this discussion."

Turning, he left her, striding directly across the room and climbing the steps without glancing back.

*   *   *

He'd unnerved her—more than she'd thought possible.

Finally gaining the privacy of her bedchamber, Phoebe accepted Skinner's help in undressing, all the while struggling to slow her whirling thoughts enough to focus on what she had to do.

Skinner shot her a concerned look. "Off with the woolly ones, you are. Did something happen?"

She grimaced. "Deverell. He was there."

"Ah." Skinner said no more but busied herself rehanging Phoebe's gown.

Swathed in her nightgown, Phoebe sank onto her dressing stool and started pulling pins from her hair. "That night at Cranbrook Manor—he saw me take Jessica to the carriage."

"What?" Skinner stared at her, openmouthed. Then she snapped her lips shut. "You never said."

"No. I didn't know what he would do, not even how much he knows, and I didn't want any of you, Fergus for instance, doing anything to catch his eye. Regardless of anything else he might be, Deverell is not slow-witted."

"He didn't strike me as such, and if that lad of his was even half right, his lordship's not one to muck about with."

"Indeed." Phoebe unraveled her hair, then picked up her brush. "This evening he told me he'd seen Scatcher and Birtles enough to identify them, and he knows they're not part of this household. He wants to know where I met them."

Skinner frowned and folded Phoebe's chemise. "Why's he want to know that? He's not . . . well, pressuring you, is he?"

"No, not in the way you mean." Phoebe dragged in a long breath, then admitted, "He told me he would never do anything to harm me, but he wants to know what's going on."

Moving around the room tidying this and that, Skinner continued to frown. "You know, it's not like what we do is anything to be ashamed of—not to any right-thinking person. Perhaps you should tell him? From what his lad let fall, he sounds like the sort that might help."

"No. I can't take the risk. Gentlemen like him—worse, peers like him—have their own way of looking at our world. What seems right to us . . . he probably won't agree."

Setting down her brush, Phoebe rose. "Tomorrow morning, slip out and take a message to Scatcher and Birtles. Tell them to lie low—to keep to the backs of the shops, and above all else not to come here. If they need to send a message, use a boy or send Emmeline. Deverell didn't see her."

She climbed into bed, then looked across at Skinner, waiting by the door. "Go out via the mews—Deverell might be watching the house."

Skinner's brows rose high, but she nodded. "I'll do that. But I still say you should think about telling him."

With that, she left. Phoebe slumped back on the pillows and pulled the covers to her chin.

And let her whirling thoughts fill her mind.

The rational, logical part of her had firmly prayed he'd leave her alone, and was petulantly annoyed that he hadn't. Regardless, his words had slayed any hope that he would disappear from her orbit anytime soon.

That he wouldn't pursue her.

Her mind drifted back forty-eight hours. That night he'd uncovered far more than just Scatcher and Birtles and her association with fleeing maids. He'd seen her panic, and by some ungodly act of fate he might be intelligent enough to guess what it meant, experienced enough to see it for what it was.

She sincerely hoped he hadn't, that he didn't.

Lying on her back, she stared up at the ceiling and wondered if that was a lie.

She wasn't sure, couldn't tell—and therein lay her biggest problem.

He made her *feel* so much, even now. Even still. Even though she knew he had the strength to overwhelm her, subdue her, subjugate her. Even though he possessed every one of the physical and social attributes she'd spent the last eight years avoiding.

He was a gentleman of her class, in his prime, infinitely stronger than she, and powerful—not just physically but socially. Able to do much as he pleased, with ladies as with all other things.

She should avoid him, totally and completely, yet he clearly wasn't going to allow that. She wasn't going to be able to avoid what he made her feel—and that, beneath it all, was what scared her the most.

That, and the change she'd sensed in him tonight. She didn't know what he'd seen in her eyes that had turned his features so hard, his gaze so penetrating. For an instant, she'd felt as transparent as crystal, as if she hadn't been hiding anything at all from him . . . and then he'd declared that he would learn her secret *but* would never harm her and abruptly left.

What was she supposed to make of that? What did it portend—what did he intend it to presage?

She wrestled with those questions for untold minutes; unresolved, they followed her into her dreams.

The next morning, Deverell sat down before an array of breakfast platters in the club's dining room and glanced at Gasthorpe. "Send Grainger in."

Gasthorpe bowed and withdrew.

A few minutes later, Deverell heard Grainger's jaunty footsteps coming along the corridor.

"You wanted me, m'lord?" Grainger stood just inside the door, hair neat, boots polished.

Deverell nodded. "I want you to watch a house in Park

Street. Number 28. Mrs. Edith Balmain's residence."

Grainger's brow creased. "Balmain? She was at the manor, wasn't she? She's Miss Malleson's aunt."

Deverell nodded and sipped his coffee. Over the rim of the cup, he met Grainger's eager eyes. Lowering the cup, he said, "I want you to watch the house and take note of whoever goes in or out, and if Miss Malleson goes out, follow her."

Grainger straightened. "Right then—I follow her, but just watch everyone else."

"Precisely." Deverell nodded a dismissal, and Grainger, happy as a clam, took himself off.

Inwardly shaking his head in benign amusement, Deverell gave his attention to ham and eggs, and his mind to organizing his own investigations.

"Phoebe's financial state?" Audrey turned from her latest masterpiece to view him as he stood a few paces away. "Good heavens, Deverell dear, why ever do you need to know?"

He smiled cynically. "Humor me, dear Audrey—and do remember that it was at your behest that I went looking for Phoebe."

"Hmm . . . yes. Well, I suppose, seeing your mind is, thank heaven, heading in the right direction, I should do all I can to encourage you." Setting down her brush and palette, she swiveled to face him and happily told him all she knew.

Early afternoon found Deverell in the city.

"Miss Phoebe Malleson, Lord Martindale's daughter, and his heiress, at least as far as any unentailed property." Heathcote Montague, as ever neat, precise, and unshakably calm, carefully transcribed the information onto a fresh sheet of paper. "Very good."

He looked up; across his desk, he met Deverell's gaze.

"You want to know all the usual, I take it—current income, such as it might be, expectations?"

Sitting comfortably in the leather chair before the desk, Deverell nodded. "In the circumstances I'd like you to be as thorough as you can. You should remember I haven't done this before."

Montague's round face creased in a smile. "Of course, my lord. And might I say it's a pleasure and indeed an honor to be called on to assist you in such a matter."

Deverell acknowledged Montague's smile with his usual charm; like Audrey, Montague had assumed that his interest in Phoebe's financial affairs stemmed from matrimonial intent. As part of arranging an appropriate marriage settlement, learning of his intended's financial situation was a sensible move.

As he did, indeed, ultimately intend to marry Phoebe, he felt no qualms in allowing Audrey and Montague, his and his family's man-of-business, to believe that prospective marriage settlements were the reason behind his query. "I understand she's already inherited significant wealth from a great-aunt."

Montague scribbled some more. "That would most likely be held in trust."

"No, I believe Miss Malleson's great-aunt was a strong advocate of females taking responsibility for their own lives and, by extension, their own funds. As I understand it, Miss Malleson has been in control of her inheritance since the age of twenty-one. She's now twenty-five."

"Hmm." Montague frowned. "It's possible there may not be much left in that account." Over the pince-nez perched on his nose, he glanced at Deverell. "I gather she moves among the haut ton?"

"She does, but . . . Miss Malleson is not the average

tonnish young lady." She certainly hadn't spent a fortune on gowns or jewels, although from what Audrey had divulged, she could probably afford to. "Look closely at her expenditures as well as her income."

"Indeed, my lord." Head down, taking notes, Montague nodded portentiously. "I could wish all my clients were as wise. It never does to be surprised by habits one might have learned of prior to an offer, simply by exercising due caution."

Deverell suppressed an unexpected urge to correct Montague's misperception, to defend Phoebe's financial honor. Regardless of what she might be involved in, she was certainly no profligate.

Uncrossing his legs, he rose. "Send word to Montrose Place as soon as you have anything substantial to report."

"Indeed." Setting down his pen, Montague rose. "I expect you'll want to end the lease on the Mayfair house when it comes up for renewal?"

Deverell raised his brows. "I haven't considered." The Paignton estate included a large house in Mayfair; he'd lived in it for a few weeks early in the year, but it was far too large for a single gentleman; he'd rented it out for the Season. "Alert me when the lease nears its end, and I'll consult with Miss Malleson."

The thought of him and Phoebe rattling around the huge house wasn't attractive, but the thought of him, Phoebe, and their children filling the space held considerable appeal.

Imagining it, he shook hands with Montague and departed, leaving his man-of-business and his clerks in absolutely no doubt that wedding bells would shortly be ringing.

He returned to the Bastion Club in time to spend a quiet half hour in the library sunk in an armchair reviewing all he knew, and all he'd set in train. And all he was starting to suspect.

Grainger returned. He came to the library to report that Phoebe had attended various social engagements both before and after lunch, then returned to the Park Street town house. "I figure she'll be dressing for dinner about now, so I thought I'd come back and see if you wanted me to watch during the night."

"No. That won't be necessary." Lying back in the armchair, Deverell instructed, "Get a good night's sleep and you can watch again tomorrow—start at nine o'clock. She won't venture out before that."

Living up to her role of matrimonial facilitator—she would be offended to be labeled a matchmaker—Audrey had supplied him with a list of the three balls Phoebe was expected to attend that evening. After meeting with him at the last, he doubted she would be up at dawn.

With a jaunty nod, Grainger turned and left.

Deverell let the pleasant silence wrap around him once more. He was glad he was presently the only member living at the club; as matters stood, he wouldn't have wished to confide in even his colleagues. When the facts, his observations of Phoebe's actions, were simply stated, the obvious explanations—the ones most minds would leap to—were distinctly unpleasant and nefarious.

He knew, absolutely and without question, that in this case, given Phoebe's involvement, the obvious didn't apply. The notion of her being embroiled in schemes linked to prostitution or worse was simply untenable.

Especially given her reaction to him in the wood.

Especially given what was coloring their interaction still.

When he combined everything he knew, he still had no clue what she was up to, not specifically. However, the one thing he felt confident in concluding was that she would never, ever, place another female in a position of fear.

From what he already knew of her, such an act would go

entirely against her grain. Whatever she was doing with the female staff he felt certain she and her helpers, whoever they were, had spirited away, she would be helping the women, not harming them.

Phoebe was an agent for good, not evil.

He'd dealt with enough of the other sort over the years to be absolutely sure.

Unfortunately, being an agent for good could be a dangerous occupation, especially in the arena she'd chosen.

He turned over the possibilities and his options for learning more while the mantelpiece clock ticked on. When it chimed the hour, he glanced up, drained his glass, then headed upstairs to dress for the evening.

Chapter 8

*D*everell ran Phoebe to earth in Lady Camberley's ball-room. Rather than standing near where Edith sat chatting with a group of older ladies, she was strolling through the crowd, stopping here and there to exchange greetings and observations, but rarely lingering.

As she quit Lady Fitzmartin's side, she swiftly scanned her surroundings before deciding on her direction. Deverell hid a smile. He'd told her he'd see her tonight, and this was the last event on her evening's schedule.

She was watching for him—whether to avoid him or gird her loins before he got too near he didn't know. But if he knew anything of her, by now she would have grown impatient. As he'd planned.

Just as he planned his approach.

She was skirting the edge of the crowd when he came up behind her. She didn't sense him until he was too near, and then it was too late.

Too late to prevent him placing a palm on her back, to one side of her waist, through two thin layers of silk, feeling the warmth of her skin.

Letting her feel the weight of his hand.

As he'd expected, she didn't jump at his touch—she froze. Smoothly turning her at right angles to him, halting them both so her back was to the wall and no one could detect his impropriety, he met her wide eyes as they lifted to his.

Reaching across her, he took her hand, enfolded it in his; raising it, holding her violet gaze, he brushed his lips across the sensitive backs of her fingers. "I said I would come for you."

His tone was deep, dark—private. Phoebe dragged in a too-tight breath and struggled to focus her wits on him—on his eyes and the message therein, on his words and their meaning. Tried to wrench her senses free of his hold, of their immediate lock on the strength and heat of the hard male hand at the back of her waist. He wasn't touching her any more intimately than he would in a waltz. Why, then, was that simple touch registering as so much more?

It took effort to tilt her chin and coolly state, "I had hoped you'd find something else to amuse you."

His lips curved. He was standing close; he hadn't moved his hand. His eyes, a heated green, continued to hold hers, watching. "Learning your secrets—*all* your secrets—consumes me."

Studying his eyes, she felt her own widen. *All?*

As if she'd uttered the word, his gaze dropped to her lips and he reiterated, "All." His low tone sent the word resonating through her, a verbal caress as well as a promise.

A promise of what, she didn't want to imagine.

Her lips felt hot and dry; under his gaze, she licked them, and was instantly aware of the flare of heat in his eyes.

She'd noticed before how long and lush his dark lashes

were, but when they veiled his eyes, they were a distracting screen. One she could do without; she wanted to see his eyes, wanted to examine that reaction—

No, she didn't.

With an effort she mentally jerked her wits back and remembered what she'd been about to say. "My secrets are my own, and no concern of yours."

The curve of his lips only deepened. "On the contrary, every secret you have commands my attention."

"Why?"

His lids rose; his eyes met hers. Trapped hers, held hers. Then the hand on her back shifted, sliding slowly, heavily, over the silk, down to unhurriedly caress her bottom.

She sucked in a sharp breath, then couldn't breathe out. His gaze sharpened.

Without pause, let alone hesitation, he continued his artful stroking, every move languidly explicit, invested with an absolute cold-blooded certainty not only that he could do as he was, but of what his touch was doing to her.

Inwardly she shuddered, but forced herself to hold his eyes and not lower hers. Forced herself to let the sensations his touch evoked roll through her, sending a flush spreading under her skin, warming and weakening. She continued to meet his heated gaze, continued to witness that indefinable hardening of his features without wavering.

Without breaking and running, something she knew he wouldn't permit.

Then his hand left her curves and rose, smoothly, unhurriedly, up her spine. His fingers brushed the curls screening her nape, slid beneath and caressed, then the pads of his fingertips lightly gripped.

The caress made her shiver; the evocative grip made her shudder.

Her lips had parted; her gaze had fallen to his lips.

Realizing, she stifled a weak gasp and looked up—into his eyes.

"Why I intend to learn *all* your secrets should be clear enough." His voice reached her, soft yet infinitely danger-ous, the words slow, uninflected, yet all the more potent for that. His grip on her nape released; his hand slid down to the back of her waist.

"Tell me . . . or show me. It matters not which you choose. But one way or another, I intend to learn every last secret you possess."

She'd fallen into the green well of his eyes and couldn't find her way out. Couldn't, for the life of her, break free of his hold.

"I'm going to seduce you, as we agreed at the manor. One step at a time—do you recall?"

She almost nodded, stopped herself just in time. "No. That was then, this is now, and—"

"Nothing whatever has changed. I still want you—I still intend to have you. And along the way I intend to learn everything—every last little aspect you hide from the world. From me, you'll hide nothing." His gaze held hers, then he softly added, "You won't be able to. I intend to strip you naked in every way."

Deverell watched each word sink into her mind, watched her reactions darken her eyes—shock, yes, but that wasn't her dominant response. Fear, yes, but that, too, was overrid-den, not wiped away but rechanneled by the rush of some stronger, more elemental and primitive emotion.

There was nothing simple about her response to him and to what he was suggesting; it was complex and complicated. Fascination was a part of it, along with sexual need and a flaring, darker hunger.

He'd been with enough women to recognize its like, but

such responses were strongly individual. And with Phoebe, he sensed he'd be walking a tightrope—it would be crucial to get the balance right.

Tonight, he was feeling his way. Cautiously.

Lifting her hand, he raised it to his lips and once again kissed, breaking the spell. She blinked, then refocused on his face.

"Tonight, I want to waltz with you—just a waltz, nothing more." He'd pitched his voice to a cadence he knew ladies found soothing.

The suspicion in her eyes told him she wasn't fooled, but the musicians had started the prelude to a waltz.

"Come." He urged her forward.

Unable to deny him without creating a scene, she allowed him to lead her to the floor. Allowed him to take her into his arms and set them whirling.

Gradually, revolution by revolution, the frown in her eyes faded, the stiffness in her spine eased. But she remained puzzled, confounded, unsure whether or not she wished to flee. Whether or not she wanted to escape him.

Mildly he arched a brow at her. "I'm sure you'll be pleased to know I didn't learn anything of substance today. I did, however, set various lines of inquiry underway."

Her lips thinned; she studied him, then said, "You're not going to go away, are you?"

He let his mask slip for a moment, let her see the truth, then whirled her to a halt as the music ended.

He bowed over her hand, then straightened; raising her from her curtsy, he met her eyes. "Until tomorrow night—and our next step."

Without waiting for an answer, with a nod he left her—and left the Camberleys' ballroom before temptation, and she, got the better of him.

* * *

Phoebe didn't let her emotions surface until Skinner had left her alone in her bedchamber. Clad in her fine nightgown, her hair brushed and rippling over her shoulders, she paced before the dying fire in the hearth and tried to focus her mind.

Tried to deal with her feelings, to put them into some frame of reference so that she could manage them—or at least understand them.

When she couldn't do that, she turned her frustrated attention to their cause.

Deverell.

While she would have liked to heap full blame on his head, indeed, was sorely tempted, there was no point in self-delusion. It was her reaction to him that lay at the root of her problem.

Flinging out her hands, she addressed the room. "Why *him*?"

Indeed. Him kissing her was bad enough, but when he touched her *like that*—as he had that evening—while every sense she possessed knew enough to be afraid, while fear definitely leapt and coursed her veins, it was instantly, in the same breath, submerged beneath a tide of almost ravenous longing.

Her fear didn't drown, didn't evaporate, but became a part of that scintillating, surging sea of need. Merged with it, into it, lending a certain edge, a frankly primitive thrill that only added to the excitement.

The anticipation of excitement. And more.

No other man had affected her as Deverell did.

One part of her rational, logical mind unreservedly labeled him as dangerous—to be avoided. An equally assertive part of that same rational mind pointed out, quite tartly, that she knew perfectly well that with him she was safe.

Not only had he told her—*sworn* to her—that he would never harm her, she believed him.

Oddly enough, to her soul.

He was driving her demented.

He wasn't going to go away, and her chances of avoiding him were slim to none. If he wanted to whisk her away alone—for instance, tomorrow night—he would. There was precious little she could do to stop a man of his ilk from doing as he pleased, especially not one as experienced as he.

And then . . .

Her mind halted. Simply refused to go further. Didn't need to go further and imagine what would follow.

"I have to get control of this." She muttered the words through clenched teeth; the instant she heard them, she knew they were right.

The right—possibly the only—way forward.

She halted. Glancing at the clock, she grimaced at the hour. She had "business" to attend to tomorrow; determinedly she headed for her bed.

At least she now knew what she had to do.

The one remaining mystery was how.

Phoebe was waiting for Edith in the front hall, ready to leave for their morning engagements, when Fergus McKenna, her longtime groom, who also acted as the household's coachman, appeared at the open front door.

Alerted by the large shadow he cast, Phoebe looked up from buttoning her gloves and smiled. "What is it, Fergus?"

Fergus beckoned. Henderson, Edith's butler, was hovering; Fergus rarely ventured into the front hall, Henderson's domain.

Phoebe joined Fergus by the door, her eyes repeating her question.

"Thought as I should warn you," Fergus rumbled, his Scots burr smothering his words. "Paignton's young lad's skulking about in the street, keeping an eye on the house. D'you want something done about him?"

Lips thinning, Phoebe considered, then shook her head. "As long as he's only watching the front of the house, he won't see anything useful."

"I think he's been following us about town."

Phoebe raised her brows, then smiled. "In that case, we'll certainly keep him busy today—we've two morning visits, and three afternoon teas. Let him follow by all means—he won't learn anything."

Fergus shuffled. "Skinner said as how Paignton—Deverell as he's called—saw enough to become suspicious."

"Indeed." Phoebe turned as Edith came slowly down the stairs; she lowered her voice. "Which is why I want his lad let be. If you run him off, Deverell will know we've something to hide in where we go, and he'll set someone else to watch, from the mews, for instance. I'd much rather his lad was following us." She met Fergus's eyes. "That way, we'll control what he sees."

"Aye." Pulling one earlobe, Fergus nodded. "There is that." He smiled at Edith, then stepped back onto the porch. "Let's be off, then."

Phoebe waited for Edith to join her, then, arm in arm with her aunt, went down the front steps to the waiting carriage.

Phoebe spent the day interviewing prospective employers. Not, of course, that the ladies she spoke with had any inkling she was assessing them and their households; over the four years since she'd established her business, she'd grown adept at conducting such interviews without the interviewees suspecting.

"Lady Lancaster." Beside Edith, Phoebe curtsied to her

ladyship, the last of the hostesses they planned to call on that afternoon. After exchanging greetings and the usual small talk about the Lancaster children—Phoebe made a mental note that Annabelle, the eldest daughter, now married with her own household, was increasing and would thus, at some not too distant time, require a nursemaid and later a governess—she and Edith moved into her ladyship's drawing room.

The Lancaster events were always well attended. Despite her lack of success thus far that day, Phoebe remained optimistic that somewhere among the ladies gathered to chat over the teacups, she would find one with the right credentials.

After settling Edith with her cronies, all of whom Phoebe knew well, she started quartering the room, moving easily from one group to the next, all but unremarked.

All her aunts were godsent, but Edith most of all; she was widely regarded as one of those unusual people who always knew the latest news, not by actively searching for it but because the latest news somehow made its way to them. Edith was thus invited everywhere; Phoebe had long realized that becoming her shadow—literally viewed as just another facet of her aunt and therefore unremarkable—was the perfect entree into the circles she needed to assess.

The established households of the wealthy and well-to-do, those presided over by sensible ladies with appropriate sensibility who kept firm hands on the reins and who were looking for female staff were her principal targets.

From Mrs. Gilmore and Mrs. Hardcastle she heard that old Lady Pelham was considering moving to the country.

"Well," Mrs. Gilmore confided, "now her son's brought his new wife home, there's no reason she needs to remain in London, looking after that drafty old house. And being in the capital never suited her health."

Phoebe made the right noises, then left the ladies discussing how it must feel to hand over the reins of a house one had come to as a bride to one's son's bride.

She didn't go straight to Lady Pelham's side. She circled, waiting until the two ladies the old lady was chatting with stood to leave; as they moved away, she moved in.

With a smile, she sat beside her ladyship, who knew her and greeted her warmly.

"I hear you and Edith have been gadding down in Surrey with Maria."

Phoebe chuckled and told Lady Pelham what she wanted to know—who else had been there, and whether any matches might have been made during the house party.

At the end of her report, she fixed Lady Pelham with a quizzical look. "But I hear you're thinking of leaving us?"

Lady Pelham sighed. "Not just thinking of it, my dear— I'm *fixed* on it. The dower house at Craxley's waiting for me, and there's no longer anything to keep me here—at least not permanently. Craxley's not so far I can't venture up to town whenever I pine for company, but my health isn't what it was—I'll do much better in the country."

Phoebe soothingly agreed. "Will you be leaving soon?"

Lady Pelham snorted. "I would be there now, but I'm missing a maid. Just last week, my old Carson—she's been with me for years—had to leave me. Her brother's taken ill, so she's gone home to Devon to nurse him. It was a blow to both of us. We'd imagined growing old together. But now . . . well, really, my dear, where am I going to find a maid willing to spend the next years in the peace of the countryside? While there are plenty of young things with training enough who desperately want to be a lady's maid, unfortunately by that they mean a lady swanning about town, going to balls and parties, one who needs their skills and talents, and where they'll earn trinkets and tips for turning her out in style."

Lady Pelham grimaced. "I'm nearing sixty, my dear, and my swanning days are over. And the purpose of moving to Craxley is to get away from London."

"Hmm." Phoebe frowned; inside, she was jubilant. This was even better than she'd dared hope. "I have heard," she said musingly, "of an agency—an employment agency for maids and such like—that prides itself on closely matching ladies' requirements with that of the girls on their books, the intention being to promote a happier situation from the first." She opened her eyes wide. "Perhaps they could help you."

Lady Pelham was looking at her in dawning hope. "Do you know where this agency is?"

Phoebe frowned harder. "I know it's in town—Henrietta Willesden used their services not long ago, and I know she was pleased. Now where . . ." Her face cleared. "Oh, that's right—the Athena Agency in Kensington Church Street." She met Lady Pelham's eyes. "Why don't you try there? They might have just the girl you need."

Lady Pelham had brightened. She tapped her cane on the floor. "I'll call there tomorrow. If they have someone suitable, I'll take her on, and then I'll be off to the country."

Phoebe beamed, as delighted as her ladyship at the prospect. Rising, she helped Lady Pelham to her feet. "The Athena Agency. Kensington Church Street."

On returning to Edith's house in Park Street, Phoebe retired to her bedchamber to bathe and dress for the evening—and to advise Skinner of her success.

"I know we have other lady's maids who would be suitable, but I think we should seize the chance to get Jessica out of town. Both the Moffats are currently here. I knew Lady Moffat would return after the house party, but I met her this morning and she told me that when Lord Moffat heard about her maid going missing, he came tearing up to

London, irascible, insisting she was to blame, and generally being an overbearing ass." Climbing out of her petticoats, Phoebe met Skinner's eyes. "Her ladyship has no idea why."

Skinner made a rude noise.

"Precisely—but that's what we have to deal with. The blindness, willful or otherwise, of the Lady Moffats of this world, and the propensities of the Lord Moffats, who, after all, are the real villains."

Stripping off her chemise, Phoebe dropped it on a stool and climbed into the steaming bath Skinner had prepared. "I know it's unlikely that if hired by some tonnish matron, Jessica would inadvertently come under Lord Moffat's eye, but it's not impossible. Letting her take a position in any tonnish London-based household is too risky—for her and for us."

"Aye, well, you'll get no argument from me on that score." Skinner handed Phoebe her sponge, then moved to the wardrobe.

Phoebe leaned back against the tub's edge and closed her eyes. "I'll need you to take a message to Emmeline. While Deverell's keeping watch on the house, I daren't slip away. Tell Em that Lady Pelham's perfect for our purpose—she's one of the old school, quite strict but kind. She won't put up with anything untoward in her household, on that we can rely. Jessica should suit her perfectly—she's well trained, of sensible disposition and good temperament, and she has excellent references. Or at least she will have by the time we're finished with them."

Phoebe paused, imagining. "Lady Pelham said she'd call in Church Street tomorrow morning. Tell Em not to fall on her ladyship's neck, but to adhere to the usual procedures— Lady Pelham's old, but not dim-witted."

"Should hope not," Skinner replied. "No dim-witted ladies allowed on our books."

Phoebe smiled. "Tell Em to set up a meeting between

Lady Pelham and Jessica for . . . perhaps two days from today. That'll give us time to get her references done, and give
her an extra day to prepare . . ."

Eyes still closed, enjoying the soothing warmth of the
water, Phoebe grimaced. She would have preferred to speak
with Jessica herself, to prepare the girl for her interview, to
tell her what Lady Pelham was like and soothe the girl's
nervousness.

With all the women she'd rescued, that lingering fear and
the nervousness it inspired had always affected her most
keenly, always moved her to do whatever she could to as
swiftly as possible eradicate it.

Not an easy task, as she well knew.

Behind her, she heard Skinner head for the door.

"I'm going to take this skirt down to brush. You all right
until I get back?"

Phoebe raised a dripping hand and waved her on.

Skinner paused by the door. "Once you're out this evening, and his viscountship's watching you, I'll pop around to
Church Street and give Em the news."

"Yes, do—just be careful. Deverell seems to be concen-
trating on just me, but let's not take any chances."

On a humph, Skinner left. Phoebe heard the door close.

With a sigh, she opened her eyes and sat up. Lifting the
sponge, she squeezed and watched the droplets trickle down
her hand and drip into the cooling water. "Damn Deverell."

He and his actions were starting to interfere with the
safe and effective running of the agency. She didn't ap-
prove at all.

She wondered what "lines of inquiry" he'd set in train.

The longer he remained focused on learning her secret—
the one of her involvement in making maids disappear—the
more he would disrupt the agency's work, potentially even
exposing it and bringing the whole to ruin.

All she'd worked for for the past four and more years he now threatened. And it wasn't just herself involved; there were her people—both of her small household and those she employed at the agency, and others like Loftus and, albeit at a distance, Edith—who lent their aid in various ways.

And, of course, there were the girls and women the agency helped.

The water was growing cold. She put the sponge to her skin, slowly bathed her limbs . . . felt the gentle stroking, remembered his hand stroking, the sensations, the excitement . . .

She stared across the room. She couldn't let him continue to push ahead with his inquiries and threaten the agency and its work. She was going to have to act, to *do* something about him; she couldn't simply hope she'd be able to cope with whatever disaster he brought down on their heads.

Which meant she was going to have to distract him.

Give him something else—let him think he might learn something else by turning his attention away from the agency.

To her. To her other secret.

It was the only distraction she could imagine that might work.

The door opened; Skinner whisked in. "You nearly done there?"

Phoebe straightened and applied the sponge more vigorously. "Nearly." After a moment, she said, "I've changed my mind. Not the blue gown—the dark ruby red."

Skinner paused to bend a puzzled look on her, then shrugged and headed for the wardrobe. "You know best, but if it's discouraging his viscountship you're set on, the ruby red's not going to help."

Chapter 9

The last of the day's light was fading from the sky above the city's rooftops. Deverell sat in the chair before Montague's desk, steadily working his way through a list of dates and figures written in Montague's neat, precise hand.

He'd been at the club when Montague's message had reached him. When he'd arrived, Montague had said nothing, simply handed him the list and indicated he should read.

He'd now read enough to understand his man-of-business's tactful silence. The evidence before him strongly suggested that Phoebe Malleson was being blackmailed.

Only he'd take an oath that wasn't the case. Despite his earlier hypothesis, she didn't have the right temperament for a target—a blackmailee.

He looked up, across the expanse of the desk met Montague's impassive gaze. "Trace the money."

Stoic, still under the impression his sole interest stemmed

from matrimonial considerations, Montague studied him, then quietly asked, "You're sure?"

Deverell nodded and tossed the list on the desk. "I appreciate your tact, but of one thing I'm one hundred percent certain—these payments aren't what they look like. Indeed, if you were a betting man I'd lay you odds that the answer will be something you—or I—would never guess."

Whatever Phoebe was doing—he was fairly certain secretively—with her funds, it was sure to be out of the ordinary.

Montague pursed his lips and picked up the list. Through his pince-nez, he perused it. "I daresay some will be dressmakers' bills."

Deverell had noted the sums drawn in cash, as distinct from the large, regular bank drafts. "I suspect not. Given the amounts and more tellingly the timing of her cash withdrawals, coupled with the state of her wardrobe, I'd hazard she pays her modiste and other such accounts in cash. Consider—she lives with her aunt, doesn't gamble, has a groom and maid provided by her father. It's difficult to conjure what other significant calls she would have on her purse."

His frown deepening, Montague continued to study the figures.

Deverell rose. "It's the drafts I'm interested in—find out who those were paid to."

Still scanning, Montague nodded. "I'll get my people onto it right away." He looked up.

His hand on the doorknob, Deverell met his gaze. "Let me know the instant you learn anything to the point."

Montague nodded; returning his attention to his list, he drew a fresh sheet of paper toward him.

Deverell went out. Montague's head clerk leapt up from his stool and hurried to open the outer door. As he went through, Deverell heard a bell jangling, summoning Montague's people to their master's presence.

Pondering what he'd seen of Phoebe's finances, he stepped down to the street and turned toward the club.

Later that evening, once again assisted by Audrey, clearly relishing her role as matrimonial facilitator, he tracked Phoebe down in Lady Fenshaw's ballroom. Her ladyship's ball was the premier entertainment that evening; a few minutes spent charming Edith yielded the information that she and Phoebe were not gallivanting on elsewhere that night.

Perfect. Parting from Edith, Deverell checked Phoebe's progress down the line of the country dance currently demanding her attention. Physical and conversational, or so it appeared. Halting by the side of the room, he frowned; if Phoebe was so intent on claiming her status as ape-leader, why was she dancing with some eligible sprig?

Eyes narrowing, he studied the glimpses he caught of her face as she and her partner whirled through the figures. She looked animated. His gaze shifted to the gentleman, wondering who it was who was so engaging her interest . . . then he amended the thought: why was she intent on interrogating the man?

To his immense irritation, before he could better focus on Phoebe and her questioning, Lady Charters swept up, daughter and niece in tow, and claimed his attention.

"Now you simply *must* tell us if the gossip is correct—is Paignton Hall really a castle?" Lady Charters's eyes, magnified by her lorgnettes, were fixed, gimletlike, on his face.

"It seems so fanciful," her daughter Melissa cooed.

"So romantic!" the niece sighed.

He mentally goggled. "The hall itself isn't a castle but is built within the shell of an earlier structure."

"Do you mean some of the walls are truly from a castle— the original stones?" Miss Charters clasped her hands to her bosom, as if that were the most romantic notion of all.

"It must be dreadfully cold," Lady Charters opined. "How do your aunts find it?"

"Actually . . ." To his horror, he found he'd been trapped, boxed in by a discussion of his new principal residence. Despite his best endeavors, as soon as he civilly answered one question, one of the three ladies hemming him in leapt in with another.

His back was to the wall, literally and figuratively; he was feeling increasingly desperate when, to his utter surprise, Phoebe swept up. He'd been so distracted by Lady Charters's ambush he hadn't even noticed the music had ceased.

Phoebe beamed on Lady Charters, greeted her and both young ladies breezily, then brazenly twined her arm with his. "I fear I must drag Deverell away—a summons from his aunt."

She delivered the words with such deadpan assurance that, with no more than a murmur of regret and a wish that they might continue their fascinating discussion at some later time, Lady Charters and her assistant harpies stood back and let him escape.

The instant they were out of earshot, he exhaled. "That was . . . appalling." Puzzled, he looked at Phoebe, realizing she was steering him down the room rather than the other way around.

As if she truly were leading him somewhere.

"Audrey isn't here."

"I know—she had to attend the Deveraux event. But I didn't say which of your aunts—you have several, do you not?"

"Three—but none of them are here."

"Lady Charters won't know that." She slowed.

Studying her face, he got the impression that she was mentally casting about for something. She'd led him toward the end of the ballroom, away from the entrance.

He halted; laying his hand over hers on his sleeve, he held

her beside him. "As grateful as I am for your timely intervention, what's this in aid of?"

"There's something I wish to discuss with you. Can you find us somewhere private?"

He trapped her gaze. "What do you want to discuss?"

Her chin firmed. "I'll tell you—when we're private. Someplace where no one will interrupt."

A certain nervy tension had crept into her; she glanced around at the crowd milling about the ballroom. Deverell thought of Montague's list of dates and amounts, and wondered if, perhaps, he had it wrong. Now she knew he wouldn't rest until he knew her secret, had she decided that she might as well confess and enlist his aid in ridding herself of a blackmailer?

Instinctive reaction swept through him. Lifting his head, he swiftly scanned the room, swiftly dredged up from long-ago memory the amenities of Fenshaw House. "This way."

He led her on. The French doors at the end of the ballroom stood open to the terrace, but instead of conducting her through the flimsy billowing draperies, he led her to the side, into the corner.

When she frowned at him, as if to indicate that if this was his idea of private it fell woefully short of her need, he merely said, "Wait."

Other couples were passing back and forth from the terrace to the ballroom, often getting caught in the long curtains, having to stop and, with much laughter, disentangle themselves.

A party of four got trapped, their difficulties compounded as one couple was going out, the other in, and both had got tangled in the same pair of curtains.

The giggles and exclamations drew everyone's attention.

Deverell turned and opened the door concealed in the paneling before which they'd been standing.

Phoebe blinked, then scurried through; he followed, closing the panel behind them.

The narrow service corridor had no lamps burning; it ran halfway back alongside the ballroom, then turned to the right. A muted glow came from around the corner, evidence of a distant lamp. He waved Phoebe on.

She reached the corner and peeked around it; joining her, he took her arm and guided her on along the wider connecting corridor. Behind them, the sound of the ball faded. He went past three doors, then stopped before the next on their right. Opening it, he glanced in, then stood back and bowed Phoebe in. "As you commanded."

Moving past him, she entered the room; walking to its center, she halted, looking around at what was clearly a small parlor sited between two bedchambers. No lamps were lit in any of the rooms; they were not in use.

Crossing to a table on which a lamp sat, Deverell looked for a tinder box.

Phoebe cleared her throat. "That won't be necessary."

Lifting his gaze, through the shadows he studied her. What moonlight reached into the room was more illusion than illumination. Without light, he wouldn't be able to see her eyes. Read her thoughts.

"Ah . . ." Apparently growing nervous under his scrutiny, she gestured to the windows. "If you light a lamp, someone strolling in the gardens might see us."

Unlikely—they were too far from the terrace—but not impossible. Regardless, he couldn't find tinder or match.

"So." Rounding the table, he strolled to her. "Cut line— what did you want to tell me?"

Her head rose as he neared; it might have been a trick of the poor light, but he thought her eyes widened.

She waited until he halted before her, then slowly moistened her lips.

He realized her gaze had dropped to his, but then she raised her eyes—and stepped into him.

Lifted her arms, wound them about his neck, stretched up—and whispered against his lips, "I wanted to discuss . . . this."

Then she kissed him.

It was his evening for being ambushed.

The instant her body had made contact with his, his hands had instinctively risen to grasp her waist—to seize her, hold her, trap her. The unexpected pressure of her soft, beguilingly feminine lips on his, offering a blatant invitation in a language he knew well, sent a surge of reaction crashing through him. Lust, desire, passion erupted, had him raising one hand to her nape, locking her head so he could kiss her back, so he could ravage her mouth and take all she offered—all he desired.

Sliding his other arm around her, he locked her svelte form against him, crushing her to him, her breasts to his chest, her thighs riding against his.

Savoring the promise of all he yearned to possess.

All she'd invited him to take.

Or had she?

Her mouth was open beneath his, a soft, utterly fascinating landscape he could explore for years without growing bored; her body was pliant against his, unresisting . . . it was a battle to free any part of his mind enough to think—to even accept that he needed to do so.

To realize that this wasn't a logical extension of what had gone before.

He'd come here tonight fully intending to steer her through another step on her path to seduction; he'd expected to have to pursue her, herd her, to expend effort to even get her that far . . .

Her tongue touched his, in bold innocence stroked, then

tangled, lured . . . his body heated. Temptation burgeoned and grew; desire welled.

Secrets. He'd let her lead him there thinking she wanted to discuss the secret of her involvement with missing maids and payments of large sums of money. Instead . . .

Wrong secret. It was the other one she wanted to address.

Which seemed strange.

He had to battle her hold as well as his inclinations to break the kiss and lift his head enough to see her face. "Phoebe . . ."

She stared up at him for a second, then her gaze dropped to his lips. "I want more . . ."

The whisper was laden with discovery, with surprise.

Before he could remember what he'd been about to ask, she boldly stretched up, deliberately pressed her body more definitely to his, and drew his lips to hers again.

Pressed her lips to his again.

Effectively cindered his thoughts, effectively slayed his resistance.

His reaction was instinctive; she touched some primitive part of him no other ever had. A part of him he wasn't so experienced in controlling.

Before any part of his mind had engaged, he'd taken charge of the kiss, pressing her lips wide, plundering her soft mouth in a heated, explicit invasion from which, to his surprise, she didn't retreat.

Without conscious direction, his hands had spread over her back, poised to sweep lower and mold her hips to his, fingers testing the supple muscles framing her spine.

So he knew when she hesitated, when she paused, when she suddenly wasn't sure. . . .

Too much, too soon.

She didn't retreat, yet he sensed the shiver that raced through her, evocative, wholly sensual. His fingers firmed on her back in response, but he managed to keep them there, if not unthreatening, then at least not immediately threatening more, while he continued to feed from her mouth, continued to dally, lips and tongues caressing . . . it seemed she'd only just realized where her impulsive behavior had landed her.

The suspicion that he still wasn't reading all her motives, all her intentions clearly gained purchase in his mind. After the blatant invitation she'd issued, had she been any other lady he would have felt no compunction in accepting unreservedly, in laying her on the sofa or across the table and taking her there, in the deserted parlor, enjoying all she'd offered, her body, her pleasure, fully expecting her to be with him every inch of the way.

But this was Phoebe, and despite that invitation matters were nowhere near clear.

It took effort, yet once again he drew back from the kiss. Held back and watched her face until she lifted lids now heavy to reveal eyes now dazed.

"Do you have any idea what you're doing?" The words sounded harsher than he'd intended. She hadn't yet panicked, but recollection of that moment in the wood when she had remained a potent image in his mind. He didn't, ever, want to see such a look in her eyes again—especially not when she was looking at him.

She moistened her lips, breathed, "Yes."

Disguising his cynicism was beyond him. "Do you know what you're inviting?"

"Ye-es." Less certain, less sure. But then her voice firmed; her eyes flashed, briefly meeting his, and she pressed closer again. "*Yes*. Stop arguing."

Her body shifted against his; the flagrant incitement was enough to achieve her purpose—to have him jettisoning all resistance, urging her flush against him, bending his head and recapturing her mouth, plunging them back into a heated engagement. . . .

She met him—as boldly as she dared, still not completely sure, but unquestionably determined.

His mind was reeling. Not good.

Regardless of what she thought, she had no idea of what she was dealing with—of what, with him, she held the power to evoke. Provoke. Even he wasn't sure he'd yet glimpsed the full picture, but what he'd seen so far was enough to shake him; he didn't want to learn what being confronted by such raw sexual force might do to her.

Yet her lips were hot and swollen beneath his, her mouth yielded, her body wantonly tempting . . . he was a man, not a eunuch.

A stray thought slid over the surface of his dazed mind; he recognized it, remembered, caught it and clung.

Step by step.

That's what they'd agreed to. Slow, slow, *slow*—that had to be his credo.

He firmed his hands on her silk-clad back, then swept them to her sides, then up—and felt her pause, felt her hesitate in her headlong rush to cinder his control and learn all.

He shifted his hands, with his thumbs lightly grazed the sides of her breasts, traced the full curves. . . .

She'd stopped breathing. Totally focused on that simple evocative touch, on each slow, suggestive caress, she halted, waited, let him lead.

He continued to kiss her, continued to lightly caress.

It was the only way he was going to be able to control her, slow her, hold her back, by finding, each time—for clearly there would be other times, more times—the next point of her inexperience, and force her to follow as he educated her senses and her mind.

That was the only way he would—could—retain control. Of her, and himself.

Letting the kiss grow light, less distracting, he slid his hands forward so he cupped her breasts. They filled his palms; he cradled them, weighed them, alert to the tension that had risen within her, the racking of her nerves to the next level of sensual awareness.

Phoebe struggled to cope with the myriad sensations cascading through her, the instincts, the emotions, her nebulous fear. The latter added a sharp edge but didn't dominate; the pleasurable sensations did.

His touch, hands hard, fingers strong yet gentle—prepared to be gentle—had mesmerized her, her senses, her wits, her mind. Her breasts seemed firmer, swollen, heavier; the heat of his palms sank through her silk bodice and warmed her.

She stood before him, anchored by his kiss, by the continuing supping of his lips and tongue, steadied by the steely columns of his thighs against which hers were propped. She felt safe, supported; she didn't need to worry about standing erect but could simply concentrate . . . on her breasts.

On what he was making her feel.

His hands shifted again. She waited . . . then his thumbs cruised over the straining mounds, flirting about the tightened peaks, then settling to circle them, slowly, hypnotically.

Her flesh tightened, constricted until her nipples were furled buds, pinching and hot. Her senses reveled, wholly caught, nerves leaping. Anticipation rode them with a silver spur.

Sharp, promising excitement untold, pleasure unimagined.

And she wanted.

Her hands had fallen to grip his shoulders; she shifted one to cup his nape, to press in encouragement, to let him know . . .

He knew. His hands firmed; his fingers came into play, firming about her nipples, gently rolling them, gently tweaking.

Sensation streaked through her, shards of sharp delight; she gasped through their kiss, and sensed in him, in his response, a dark satisfaction.

Yet his touch didn't alter. Slow, unhurried—frustratingly languid. She wanted to rush on, yet . . . even as the thought formed, it was seduced from her mind by another, more evocative realization.

He was doing with her what he wished. As he wished.

The knowledge blossomed in her mind, washed through her on a heightened wave of pleasure as his fingers artfully, skillfully played.

She'd instigated this interlude deliberately, with unwavering determination. It was the only lure that held any chance of distracting him from his pursuit of her business secrets—encouraging his pursuit of her, and her private secrets.

When it came down to brass tacks, her private secrets were much less vital than the secret of the agency.

Although it was tempting to think of herself as some romantic heroine sacrificing her virtue to protect others, she couldn't so delude herself; she was there in his arms, inviting him to seduce her because she hoped he would. He was the only man she'd ever been attracted to, and if he wished, and if she managed to keep her old memories at bay, he was richly qualified to teach her all she had thought she would never know; distracting him in this way hadn't been that difficult a decision to make.

That was also why she'd been so determined—but she hadn't, as he'd so rightly guessed, known quite what it was she'd been inviting.

She'd deliberately propelled them along this path, yet she wasn't in control of this—he was. He wasn't dancing to her tune; she was dancing to his. She'd placed herself in his arms and now couldn't go back—couldn't pull away, and didn't want to.

He would teach her what she wished to learn, but there would be a price. His price.

It would be his way—his unhurried, languid way, a sensual demonstration of the control he could and would exercise over her.

The knowledge shivered through her, insidious and compelling, evoking a touch of fear and a wholly wanton anticipation. The expectation of experiencing pleasures she wouldn't be able to escape, let alone deny, all at his command, sent illicit excitement streaking through her.

The mind is the most powerful target for seduction.

Clearly he knew of what he spoke.

Practiced it, too. That was implicit in the way he held her back, somehow managed the reins so that she couldn't, no matter how she might wish, any longer rush ahead, push him or waltz them further, faster.

His hands on her breasts, his lips on hers, the net of pleasure he so skillfully wove held her—safe, but also secure.

Protected, but ultimately his.

When he finally drew his hands from her breasts, drew her once more flush against him and kissed her, long, deep, and lingeringly but with a finality impossible to mistake, then lifted his head, she sighed and accepted it when he eased her from him, letting her hands slide from about his neck.

His hands beneath her elbows steadying her, he studied her face, her eyes, then said, "Step by step. That's the way it will be."

A dictate, with a warning running beneath.

Tilting her head, she studied him in return, then inclined her head, turned, and led the way to the door.

* * *

The following evening, Deverell joined Phoebe at Lady Joinville's rout. He accompanied Audrey; as he turned from greeting Lord and Lady Joinville and offered her his arm, he prayed she wouldn't cramp his style.

It would take Montague some days at least to trace the recipient or recipients of Phoebe's drafts. He knew better than to try to hurry the process; Montague was painstakingly thorough, which was why he retained him.

Meanwhile, neither he nor Grainger had succeeded in discovering anything out of the ordinary in the movements of either Phoebe, her maid, or her groom-cum-coachman, at least not during daylight hours. Tonight, he'd extended Grainger's watch-duty to include the evening.

He led Audrey down the ballroom steps; the feather in her turban bobbed majestically by his ear. When they reached the floor, Edith, seated with a group of her cronies, waved and beckoned; with some relief, he delivered Audrey to them.

After greeting Audrey, Edith turned to him and smiled sweetly. "Phoebe's here somewhere—she's in fuschia, so she should be easy to spot."

He smiled, inwardly wondering what fuschia was. A color, or a material? He would have asked Audrey, but she was already engrossed in swapping the latest *on-dits*. With a general bow encompassing all four ladies, he left them and started quartering the crowd.

Fuschia proved to be a color—a brilliant hue midway between pink and purple. When he spotted Phoebe thus gloriously garbed, chatting amid a group of ladies and gentlemen, he stood back for a moment and drank in the sight.

If asked, he would have thought that the bright hue would clash with the color of her hair; instead, the combination was the epitome of dramatic. With the pale, flawless skin of her shoulders and arms exposed by the gown's tiny, off-the-shoulder sleeves, with the scooped neckline of the bodice closed with tiny pearls showcasing her ample charms, and the fall of the lush silk skirts revealing, then concealing, the lithe limbs beneath, she was a sight to fix the interest of any man.

Recalling Lady Charters's ambush of the previous night, he kept a wary eye out for potential attackers, but noting that Phoebe was once again animatedly questioning a gentleman, he hung back and watched. With the eye of a master interrogator analyzed.

Did the gentleman she'd cornered know he was being interrogated?

A moot point, but then, her curiosity apparently appeased, Phoebe drew back. And felt his gaze.

She turned her head, saw him, and smiled.

He found himself smiling back, surprised by the warmth he felt at her response. He was about to go to her; instead, she quickly made her adieus, swung around, and came to him.

It was difficult to temper his smile.

The musicians struck up a waltz as she neared. Taking her hand, he smoothly bowed, then immediately led her to the floor.

Turning her into his arms, he felt compelled to murmur, "It might be wise not to appear quite so eager."

She blinked at him. "Eager?"

Even the way she moved into the revolutions with him, without the faintest hesitation or even thought, bore witness to her fixed direction.

"Next time, wait for me to come to you. I promise not to be offended if you act a trifle haughtily"—he caught her eye—"in public."

A moment passed, then she elevated her nose. "I'll bear that in mind."

He hid his smile and steered her down the floor. And plotted their next step.

It might try his patience—and hers, come to that—but step by step was the only viable way forward, embracing her lack of experience and nascent fears while tempering his already too heightened passion with more sophisticated play. That tack would doubtless prove a tightrope he'd have to steady her along, but the long-drawn-out wait would heighten the ultimate pleasure, for both of them increasing the anticipation and priming their senses.

Such an approach would also allow him to ensure he in no way hurt or harmed her, that he didn't again evoke any real panic. That instead he allayed any fear that might rise in her mind, that might cloud and dim her senses.

When the music ended and he whirled her to a halt, they were at the end of the room, near the doors open to the terrace and the moonlit gardens beyond.

Raising her from her curtsy, he drew her arm through his and steered her to the doors.

"Where are we going?" Phoebe glanced at him, at his face, currently wearing what she mentally termed his social mask; a charmingly urbane expression he seemed able to assume at will, it veiled his ruthless edges.

"The garden, to begin with."

Those last three words made her hold her tongue; clearly, his direction was the same as hers. He'd said—to her mind, promised—a step-by-step progress; it was time for their next advance.

On the terrace, he turned her to walk along the flags; there were steps leading down to the lawn at each end. A number of other couples were strolling in the fresher air, both on the terrace and on the silvery lawn below.

As they neared one set of steps, she grew increasingly aware of being alone with him, of his body so close, of its warmth, its strength, its hardness. A shiver ran through her.

Instantly, he glanced at her. "Are you cold?"

She considered lying, but he might insist on returning inside. "No." It was anticipation, not the cool air, that had affected her.

The upward kick of his mobile lips as he looked ahead assured her he'd understood her perfectly. "Let's go down."

Once on the gravel walk bordering the lawn, rather than leading her to where other couples were ambling in full view, he steered her to the left, into the dark shadows beneath the large trees separating the lawn from various garden beds.

She cleared her throat. "You mentioned before that morning rooms frequently proved useful."

Through the darkness, he glanced at her. "Do you know where the morning room is?"

She pointed deeper under the trees to a minor path wending its way between herbaceous borders. "It's in that wing— the French doors look out on the next section of lawn."

He glanced at her, lips curving, then looked ahead and obediently led her down the narrower path.

To the next section of lawn and the morning room French doors. Which were locked.

She hissed, and glared at the lock. "Now wh—" She broke off as a blade glinted in his fingers where before no blade had been. He applied it to the lock, which immediately clicked. Smoothly sliding the penknife back into a pocket, he grasped the handle and opened the door.

Brows rising, she went in.

The room was much the same as the last time she'd seen it, some weeks before when she and Edith had last visited. As per his dictum, it was empty, helpfully deserted.

Behind her, she heard the door close. She turned to him—Directly into a kiss.

A demanding one, one she felt she immediately had to appease, had to give him her mouth and engage with him, lift her arms and grasp his shoulders as his hands seized her waist and he backed her.

Until the edge of the sofa table standing along the rear of the sofa hit the very tops of her thighs.

He held her there while he pressed the kiss on, drove her deeper into the seductive exchange, deeper into heat laced with toe-curling pleasure.

Then he drew back and lifted her.

Hoisted her up so she sat on the edge of the sofa table. She only just managed to swallow a weak shriek.

Eyes glinting under heavy lids, lips curved—was that what lust looked like?—he edged her knees apart and moved between. His hands slid from her waist, over her hips and down the outsides of her thighs.

And she froze. Caught her breath. Remembered.

She sucked in another breath, tighter than before. She blinked, and refocused on his face. Eyes narrowed, no longer sensually amused, he was studying her.

Before she could react, even think, he lifted both hands, slowly, gently framed her face, tipped it and held it steady as he leaned close and kissed her.

Gently, beguilingly.

Gradually, he drew her back into the heat, into the pleasure. As she had once before, she raised a hand and cradled the back of one of his.

Felt the tension in him, the passion, the desire, sensed how utterly, ruthlessly reined it was.

This was him, not that other. Her fears subsided and she relaxed, returning his caress, languid as ever, with increasing impatience.

At last he drew back, just enough for their eyes to meet. He looked into hers, then glanced at her lips. "I have a suggestion—a game we should play."

"A game?" She was sure he didn't mean pick-up-sticks.

"A mind game." He swooped in and took her lips, lingeringly held them, then drew back to whisper, "An imaginary situation where you choose how you'll respond."

The waft of his breath over her lips made them hungry. She tried to follow his, but his hands firmed; he held her immobile and drew back a fraction further.

Enough to meet her eyes.

"Imagine this—you're the daughter of a Spanish grandee. You've been dispatched to the Indies, there to marry a much older man as part of an arranged marriage. You're untouched, of course, but not by choice. Then, far out at sea, your ship is attacked by pirates."

Releasing her face, he placed his hands on the table on either side of her, caging her; she barely noticed, caught by the picture he was painting. "Every man on your ship is killed or dispatched. All the treasure on board is collected and transferred to the pirate vessel—yourself included. You're locked in the captain's cabin, then your ship is sunk. You see it going down out of the porthole. You also hear the men on the deck above muttering. They're superstitious and don't want a woman on board. They want to toss you into the briny deep."

Trapped in his eyes, she caught her breath, could feel— imagine—as if she were there, in that imaginary cabin.

His eyes held hers, searching, then he continued. "You hear the captain tell his men not to be fools, but you know he's facing a difficult situation. Then you hear his footsteps coming down the companionway, boots swiftly striding down the corridor to the door—then it opens and he's there.

"He's tall, dark, and handsome, everything a pirate captain should be. He explains what you've just heard—and asks what you'll give him in order to persuade him to overrule his men."

He straightened a fraction so her hands fell from his shoulders and his eyes were no longer level with hers; she had to look up to meet them.

And his wolfish smile. "I'm the pirate captain. What are you going to offer me to save your life?"

She blinked, then realized this was the point where she could choose how to react. She remembered her pearl necklace, the pearl drops at her ears. Lifting one hand to her throat, she touched the milky strand. "My pearls?"

He gave her a disgusted look. "I'm a pirate captain—I've just looted a Spanish brig. I have chests full of jewels."

She frowned at him. "What then?"

"Well . . ." His gaze lowered. First to her lips, where it lingered until they throbbed, then lower still. After a moment, after her breasts had swollen and peaked under his gaze, he murmured, "I might be amenable if you offered me . . . pearls of a different sort."

She drew in a breath, faintly scandalized, wholly fascinated, while her mind skittered and raced. "You want me to . . . ?"

He lightly shrugged, his eyes lifting to meet hers. "You have to offer. You have to decide."

He held her gaze, his unwavering, waiting. She could read nothing in his eyes; in the darkened room, he quite easily could have been the pirate he'd described . . . and she couldn't think of any alternative but to offer him what he'd suggested.

She exhaled, her breath tight and shaky, and looked down. Raising both hands, she set her fingers to the tiny pearl closures running down the center of her bodice.

As she slipped them free, the bodice gaped, then slid lower; the tiny fragments of sleeves set off the shoulder provided no anchorage.

Her character in this play was untouched . . . as she was. The haughty Spanish lady baring her breasts to a pirate captain was her.

A thrill, insidious, illicit, shot through her as her sleeves sank to her elbows and her gown slithered to her waist. Her hands were shaking as she tugged the bow securing her chemise undone, then she loosened the gathered neckline and drew the fine fabric down.

Leaving her breasts exposed, nipples already furled in the cool night air. In the weak light, her skin shone, pale, pearlescent.

She glanced at his face, but he wasn't looking at hers. She glanced down as he raised first one hand to brush, then cup one mound, thumb cruising the fine skin; her nerves leapt and tingled, her skin heated and flushed as her breast firmed and grew heavier. Then he repeated the gesture with her other breast, as if he truly were a pirate captain assessing captured treasure.

"Very nice." His voice was deep and gravelly, low enough to make her shiver. His eyes lifted to hers. He caught her gaze and slowly said, "These are mine, now, to do with as I please." His hands firmed, his thumbs caressed. "To enjoy as I please."

Trapped in his gaze, his hands hard and hot on her naked flesh, she swallowed, her throat constricted, and nodded.

Chapter 10

*H*e moved closer, nudging her thighs wider as he did. His hands firm about her breasts, he ducked his head, found her lips, and drew her into a long, increasingly ardent kiss.

She caught his shoulders and leaned back, tipped her head back the better to engage with him.

He broke the kiss briefly to say, his voice a dark murmur, "Lean back on your hands."

She did, and instantly felt steadier—instantly felt more exposed as his fingers closed about her nipples, and tightened . . . with a gasp she arched her spine, pressing her breasts more firmly into his hands, blatantly offering them up to him, to his artful ministrations.

It was the pirate who chuckled through the kiss, then drew back to look down at his hands, freely possessing, stroking, lightly kneading.

She didn't dare look; it was all she could do to watch his

face, to see the familiar planes grow more angular, more hard-edged. More ruthless.

"Now let's see . . ."

The low words shivered through her, then she gasped again, arched again, head tipping back, eyes closing as his fingers tightened, the pressure on her nipples increased, and sensation streaked like lightning through her veins.

Her lips parted; she was panting, then he covered her lips with his, filled her mouth with his tongue, and settled to plunder her senses.

Her wits were reeling, her senses giddily spinning, her nerves heated and alive when he drew back from her mouth. He didn't lift his head but trailed nipping, hungry kisses over her jaw, then down the taut line of her throat.

Arms braced, head back, eyes closed, as if from a distance she heard her own gasp as his lips touched, then cruised the flushed, taut skin of the upper curves of her breasts. Then his hand firmed about one heavy mound, raising it. She cried out when his mouth closed over her aching nipple.

Whimpered as he stroked his tongue across the peak.

Then he settled to feast, and she shuddered.

Burned as he turned his attention to her other breast— burned to lift a hand and bury it in his hair and hold his clever, ravenous mouth to her, but she needed both hands to lean on. She had to simply sit there, her spine arched, her breasts surrendered to him, and let him take as he willed, let him devour as he wished.

And he did.

As he drew one tight peak deep, Deverell thanked God and all the saints that she'd been susceptible to the game.

Where had her fears come from? Either a too-enthusiastic would-be lover or . . . he preferred not to dwell on the alternative. Knowing that some man had forced her, or tried to, or threatened to, wouldn't help; unless she told him who, he wouldn't be able to relieve his fury in any satisfactory way.

No, best to imagine some cowhanded stripling had tried to sweep her away and failed. Regardless of the cause, the effect was the same—not just one hurdle but a series of hurdles he'd have to work to overcome.

Tonight at least he'd triumphed. When he raised his head and gloatingly surveyed all he'd claimed, he felt not just a bone-deep satisfaction but also a sense of vindication.

Even though he was at some distant level conscious that his body ached for hers, that some more primitive part of him longed to stroke between her thighs, even through the silk of her gown to touch her there and lay claim to that most intimate place, his control had never once wavered, and courtesy of her fears, his control was vital, the bulwark, the cornerstone on which he could build her confidence, on which he would convince her to rely.

Without that, seducing Phoebe to wife would be anything but easy.

Even now it wouldn't be easy, but it was, definitely, going to be.

He stroked the pads of his fingers across the taut satin skin of her breasts, savoring the texture and the telltale heat. He assessed, examined; he'd been careful not to mark her anywhere that would show, yet her skin was so fine, so white, and now so evocatively flushed, that they would definitely be returning to the house via the gardens.

A long walk in the cool night air would let that flush fade, but first, he'd have to stop touching her, caressing her, possessing her.

He lifted his gaze to her face, noted the lack of any hint of tension in her fine features. A light frown bisected her brows; eyes closed, she was tracking the movements of his fingers, wholly absorbed with each caress, each sensation.

He smiled, for long moments continued to play with her

and her senses, then he inwardly sighed and drew his hands from her breasts. Sliding his palms up over her collarbones, up on either side of her long throat, he framed her face, bent and kissed her parted lips, then slid one arm around her and drew her upright.

Then he broke the kiss and whispered against her lips, "I've tasted enough for tonight, *querida*. It's time to return to the ball."

"One point continues to elude me." It was the following evening, and Grainger had learned nothing of note. Deverell had likewise heard nothing yet from Montague; he was feeling increasingly impatient.

Impatient enough to attend Lady Griswald's musicale, an act of desperation that had delighted Audrey, Edith, and their cronies.

He slanted a glance at Phoebe, standing beside him. "Perhaps you can enlighten me?"

She met his eyes, briefly searched, then arched a brow. "What is it you wish to know?"

He glanced at the crowd milling and shifting between the rows of chairs filling her ladyship's music room. The assembled audience had yet to take their seats. There were few eligible gentlemen among them; when he'd arrived ten minutes before, he'd found Phoebe chatting in her usual animated fashion with two youthful, highly fashionable matrons, both somewhat younger than she.

Aware she'd followed his gaze and was surveying the crowd, he asked, "Why is it, given you have no interest in marriage, that you continue to attend events such as these?"

Her gaze whipped back to his face; he met it, held it.

She blinked and tried to conceal her frown by assuming a surprised, near blank expression. "Why? Well, the truth is, I suppose, that I feel I owe it to Edith to accompany her to 'events such as these.' She's been very good to me over the years."

"I see. So your attendance here is more in the nature of a companion?"

Looking back at the crowd, she nodded. "Indeed, a companion of sorts. That's an excellent description."

Only if he were blind. Anything less companionlike than Phoebe and the way she swanned through the fashionable hordes was difficult to imagine. Regardless of any intentions, she still treated Edith much as a chaperone, a totally redundant chaperone, perhaps, but that was closer to the mark than any notion of a companion.

Edith certainly didn't regard her in that light; her aunt smiled encouragingly his way at every opportunity.

The musicians appeared and started tuning their instruments, the traditional signal for the audience to be seated.

"Come." He took her elbow. "Let's find some seats."

She glanced at him, the frown in her eyes more definite, then looked ahead as he steered her toward a line of chairs. When he paused to allow her to precede him into the row, she leaned closer and murmured, "I *thought . . . ?*"

She looked up and caught his eyes.

He suppressed an urge to smile wolfishly. "Not now. After the intermission."

Her eyes opened wider, her lips parted on an "Oh." Then she nodded and consented to sit.

Settling beside her, he fixed his gaze on the Italian soprano who had joined the musicians at the front of the room, listened to Lady Griswald's gushing introduction, then gave his mind not to the music but to the vexed question of how he was going to manage, at a musicale of all events, to live up to Phoebe's expectations.

Beside him, Phoebe stared unseeing at the buxom Italian diva and fought to keep a frown from her face.

If Deverell had noticed enough to question her presence at such events, what more had he seen? Had his watchers reported something she'd assumed they hadn't noticed? More importantly, had he deduced anything from whatever observations had prompted his question—she was quite sure it hadn't been idle.

Until now, she'd only considered him, the potential danger of his presence in ballrooms, from the moment he hove into her view. What if before approaching her, he'd been watching her?

She knew what he would have seen—her interviewing various gentlemen, and tonight two ladies. The older ladies she met at morning and afternoon teas weren't her sole source of information on the families of the ton. The younger generation were in many ways easier to elicit relevant information from; they spoke more readily, more openly and with far less discretion of the shortcomings of others, especially their relatives.

Since the age of twenty-one, she'd attended balls and parties and all the other varied gatherings of the ton with only one aim in mind—to identify the suitable, acceptable households and learn of any potential vacancies therein that the girls and women her agency represented might fill.

She slanted a sideways glance at Deverell; his expression impassive, he was watching the singer with an unwavering regard. Returning her own gaze to the woman, she wondered if she dared simply continue as she had been, and trust to luck that he wouldn't—couldn't—guess the truth. Or anything even close.

This time of year was the busiest for the agency in terms of rescued females they needed to resettle; with the prospect of summer looming ever nearer, heralding long months spent in close quarters with their employers on country estates, girls under pressure started looking for escape.

Once she and the agency had helped them "disappear," they had to then find them somewhere else to go. That had from its inception been the primary purpose behind the agency.

During these months, her own contribution was crucial; while they had other avenues for learning of vacancies, she was the prime gatherer of information on the relative safety of households. Without her input, the agency wouldn't be able to function properly.

But now she'd encouraged Deverell to join her in the ton's ballrooms, and unfortunately he saw too much. Worse, with his watch on the house and her movements, he'd reduced her ability to assist in other ways, such as coaching Jessica for her interview with Lady Pelham.

She frowned, unseeing, at the singer.

Matters were getting complicated. When she'd instigated a liaison in order to distract him from the rest of her life, she'd assumed, naïvely it now seemed, that their interaction would quickly progress to intimacy, which, after a few interludes, would be enough for them both—he would lose interest, and she would have learned enough—and then they would part.

Initially, she'd thought a week would be enough, maybe two.

She stifled a humph. At their current rate of progress—the rate he was holding them to—it would take at least that long to reach their first intimate interlude. And it was already clear that she had much more to learn, that there was much more he could teach her than she'd supposed.

Regardless of any fond hopes on her part, she wasn't going to be able to bid him farewell and cut all ties with him anytime soon.

Bad enough. But now it seemed as if her two separate pursuits—to distract him and seize the opportunity he offered to educate herself about passion on the one hand, and her indispensable role in vetting suitable households for the agency on the other—were getting tangled.

She sat and stared at the singer, hearing not a note. Her natural habit was to plan carefully and avoid potential pitfalls; unfortunately, no matter how she racked her brain, there was nothing she could think of that would result in the disappearance of the gentleman beside her.

"I take it you disapproved of the performance?"

His languid drawl jolted her back to the present, back to Lady Griswald's music room, and him. Head turned her way, his green gaze was on her face; his lips were lightly curved.

Seeing her bemusement, he added, "You looked like you'd swallowed something disagreeable. I assumed it was your reaction to the music."

Blinking, she sat straighter and looked around. The singer had finished; the audience was still applauding. She quickly put her hands together and clapped, too, ignoring his cynically arching brow.

Lady Griswald stood and informed her guests that Madame Grimaldi would return after supper to regale them with a further demonstration of her talents.

"Come." His hand at her elbow, Deverell drew her to her feet. "Let's head for the supper room."

Phoebe hesitated, wondering if she should join Edith and help her through supper to lend credence to her role as companion—then rejected the notion as laughable. She wouldn't fool him, but she'd certainly confuse Edith.

Deverell led her to join the stream of other guests exiting the room. According to Lady Griswald, supper had been laid out in a salon down the hall to the left. When they cleared the music room doors, he drew Phoebe out of the throng, moving to the right as if politely allowing the many older guests, or those with young ladies in tow, to precede them into supper.

Phoebe shot him a questioning glance.

Guiding her further along, then stopping near the wall beside a corridor leading deeper into the house, he met her gaze. "Are you hungry?"

She blinked. "No . . ." Her gaze dropped to his lips. She licked hers and softly said, "At least not for what Lady Griswald will be serving."

She was an innocent, yet that action and her words could have been delivered by the most gifted of courtesans.

They certainly had the requisite effect on him.

His hand tightened over hers where it rested on his sleeve. He cast a quick glance at those still filing out of the music room. Those who had seen them separate from the crowd had already moved on. Those just coming out didn't glance their way but instead turned left, following those ahead of them.

One step to the side, and he drew Phoebe around the corner and into the deserted corridor. She blinked, but said nothing; she kept pace as, her hand locked in his, he led her quickly on.

Where to, he wasn't sure; he didn't know this house. They passed the opening to another corridor on their right; he glanced down it as he strode past—and saw the perfect spot. Halting, he tugged Phoebe around and led her into the darkness of the narrower corridor. "This way."

He made for the alcove at the end.

It was perfect—not for intimacy but for seduction. The corridor ended in a bow window, glass panes set in wooden frames curving from one side to the other. The windows started at knee height and reached nearly to the ceiling; the twin panels in the center of the bow had been left open to the mild night. But what rendered the semicircular alcove absolutely perfect were the thick velvet curtains that hung suspended from brass rings at either end of a polished pole that stretched from wall to wall.

Halting within the alcove, Deverell released Phoebe.

Reaching to either side, he pulled the heavy curtains across, sealing them in, concealing them, creating a quiet, private space where no one would find them.

The curtains cut them off from the world.

Turning, he saw Phoebe standing before the open windows, hands grasping the frames on either side, head tilted. He drew closer, then heard it, too—the distant playing of the musicians in the music room.

They played in fits and starts, clearly using the time to practice. Like the alcove, the music room looked over the side garden filled with trees, large shrubs, and dense shadows. Some of the music room windows were open; they'd be able to hear the rest of the performance.

The spot couldn't have been more perfect for their needs.

Sensing him near, Phoebe started to turn; swiftly he stepped closer, eliminating the gap between them. Sliding a hand across her waist, he smoothly drew her against him, her back to his chest, her bottom against his thighs. Not tightly, but enough to let her know that that was where he wanted her. "Leave your hands where they are."

She stilled within his hold but didn't freeze. Twisting her head, she glanced back and up, caught his eyes.

The question in hers was easy to read even though the soft wash of moonlight pouring through the windows did little to illuminate the blue-violet depths.

"No kissing," he told her. "At least, not lips to lips." Raising his free hand, he brushed aside the bobbing strands screening her nape, bent and pressed his lips to the soft skin beneath. And felt her melt.

She breathed in; he felt her lungs swell. Felt her hold the breath as he moved his lips lightly over her sensitive nape.

"This time," he murmured, "you don't have to do anything . . . except feel."

Lids falling, Phoebe heard the words, a dark whisper

sliding through her mind. She felt herself relax against him as his lips trailed across her shoulder, then he nudged her head aside and pressed a hot kiss at the junction where her shoulder met her neck.

He seemed to know all the places where just a light touch made her inwardly shiver, where the brush of his lips seemed a subtle intimacy.

He shifted, and his other hand joined the first at her waist. Then in concert they rose. Closed over her breasts, but gently, kneaded but lightly—just enough to make the heat well beneath her skin, make her breasts swell and warm and tighten.

Then his fingers moved to the tiny gold buttons closing her bodice. In anticipation, she'd worn another gown with a bodice that opened fully at the front, rather than a gown with back laces. From beneath her lids, she peeked down, and watched as he peeled away the cornflower blue silk, then her chemise, exposing her breasts, already peaked and firm, to the night.

To the cool breeze that laid sensory fingers across her already flushed skin. To the faint moonlight that turned her skin pearly white, framed by the blue of her gown, by his darker, lightly tanned hands as they cradled, then closed.

Her lids fell; her head lolled back against his shoulder, her spine arching as his hands and fingers worked, and pleasure bloomed and spread beneath her skin, then heightened and coursed through her, tightening nerves, heating, melting . . . and still he continued, languid, unhurried, until a nameless longing rose within her, making her restless under his hands.

Unbidden, her hips moved against him.

He bent and set his lips to cruise her nape and bare shoulder, lightly nipping, then soothing.

Then one hand left her breast; the other remained, pandering to her aching nipples, caressing the hot heated mounds, holding her wits, her senses captive. So she had no chance of thinking of anything else.

Until she felt the cool touch of air on her calves and realized his hand at her thigh was slowly, unhurriedly, lifting her skirt.

She didn't just freeze—her entire body went rigid. Every muscle locked; she fought down and swallowed the urge to scream *No!*, battled to keep her hands where they were, gripping the sides of the open windows, rather than flailing and batting his away. Breaking free and running.

Blinking, mentally gasping, she struggled to subdue her reaction, tried to reorient her wits and her senses. Her breasts were rising and falling rapidly; her pulse was tripping and racing, not pleasantly.

He'd stopped. Simply stopped. His hands didn't move, either to press on or retreat. His body was still there, warm and hard against her back, his fingers still wrapped about one breast. His masculine strength was all around her, surrounding her, but not holding her, not restraining her.

He was waiting, patiently, to see what she would do.

Beat by shaky beat her heart slowed; her skittering wits calmed.

Slowly, his head lowered beside hers; gently he placed a hot kiss on her naked shoulder. "What do you want to do?"

The words whispered through her mind, uninflected, undemanding.

She closed her eyes, once more leaned her head back against his shoulder. "I . . ." She swallowed. "I want to go on." She did. Desperately. She licked her dry lips, whispered, "But I don't know if I can."

His lips grazed her earlobe. "You can. We can." His fingers

at her breast shifted, resuming their lazy caressing. Somewhat to her surprise, she didn't stiffen; after a few moments, that insidious heat started to stir and rise within her again.

"Here's how we're going to manage this."

His voice, although still low, had regained its dictatorial tones, but she sensed that in this, if she wished to argue he would listen.

"I desire you—you know that." His words drifted past her ear, darkly seductive. "I'm going to touch you as a man touches a woman he desires."

The statement elicited a sharp thrill—to her surprise not an unpleasant one; the thought of being touched by him in desire didn't repulse her.

His voice continued, his drawl languid and deep, "If you want me to stop, all you have to do is say 'no.' But think hard before you do, for if you say the word, I will."

Eyes closed, held within his arms, she thought about that. "What if . . . ?"

He seemed to follow her panicky thoughts easily, in itself a blessed relief. "If you want me to pause, to linger to give you more time to catch up, say 'wait.' "

His lips cruised her shoulder, then he whispered, "If you want me to go more slowly, say 'slow.' "

After a moment, he murmured, "Do you understand?"

She drew in a breath, conscious of his artful fingers at her breast stirring her senses to life again, setting pleasure once more coursing her veins, pooling within her. She nodded.

"Good." He hesitated, then said, "I'm going to touch you, but it will only happen if you desire it. You have control. It's mine, but I'll make it yours."

He couldn't have said anything more reassuring. She was glad he was behind her and so couldn't see the silly tears that filled her eyes.

She felt his hand at her thigh flex, tense, but he didn't

resume drawing up her skirt. Instead, she felt his gaze on the side of her face.

"Can I touch you, Phoebe?"

She held her breath and nodded.

His hand shifted, lifted.

She kept her eyes closed, the better to concentrate on her sensory perceptions, on her feelings.

Music reached her ears; the soprano's voice floated sweet on the night air. The other guests would have returned to the music room. Yards away, she stood in the darkened alcove at the open window, her heated breasts bared to the night and him, an anticipation more definite than any she'd ever known infusing and driving her.

Holding her as her hems reached midthigh, then he flicked his hand and slid it beneath her skirts. His fingers trailed boldly over her garter and found bare skin. He touched, stroked, and she shivered.

With delight.

He was watching her face, and he knew. His fingertips slid to her inner thigh and trailed upward.

When they lightly brushed the curls at the apex of her thighs, her entire body reacted; she gasped as her skittering senses tensed with scintillating expectation.

In the music room, the soprano trilled.

His fingers slowed.

She nodded, moistened her lips, and managed to whisper, "Slow."

His lips brushed her temple. "We can go as slow as you like."

He did; she didn't have to say the word again—not even think it. He seemed to know, to sense when she needed him to almost stop.

But he didn't stop.

He brushed her curls increasingly definitely, then let his

fingers tangle gently in them. Then they sought out the soft flesh beneath and caressed.

Slowly, deliberately.

The music welled, swelled, the crescendo of sound mimicking the steady rise of her passion, an emotion she'd never encountered before, one she grasped the building moments to absorb.

Until she wanted more. Her dazed wits were trying to decide what word to use for that when he reached further, parted her folds, and touched her. More intimately, more possessively.

She shuddered and let her legs part a little further to allow him to caress her. The building pleasure radiating from where he touched spread throughout her body; she let it fill her, take her, overwhelm her worries, her fears.

Let it drown them.

Then he found a spot, swirled, then pressed—and she gasped.

He caressed and she arched against him, eyes closing tight, wits scrambling, feeling very much as if she were losing her sensual footing, as if a tide of fiery delight had swept her into a surging sea of uninhibited, wanton pleasure.

The golden sensation spread through her, with every deliberate flex of his fingers burgeoned and welled. It surrounded her, lapped about her, filled and buoyed her as in the distance the soprano's voice soared.

Deverell knew they were running out of time, but there was nothing he could do. She was too new to this, too untouched, and he'd had to go too slowly; there simply wasn't enough time left to bring her to release at a pace she could handle.

Even with his own desires ruthlessly held in check—largely ignored—he couldn't bring himself to push her too fast, not even to alleviate the frustration she would later feel.

As for his frustration, he didn't want to think of that. Any other lady and he would have lifted the back of her skirts and eased his throbbing staff into the hot haven of her body. He tortured himself with the thought but didn't act on it. Not this time.

Instead, hauling in a deep breath, he toed the line he himself had drawn and set his mind, his hands, his lips to the task of easing her back from the brink she wouldn't reach that night.

Tomorrow, yes, but that was another day. Tonight, they had a bare five minutes before they would need to reappear with the other guests.

Luckily, Phoebe was too out of her depth to argue; with enthusiastic applause reaching them through the night, she allowed him to straighten her gown and lead her back through the corridors without protest.

When they joined the throng of guests pouring out of the music room and milling in the hall, no one gave any indication of having noticed their absence. Given the crowd, given the care he'd taken to cover their movements, that wasn't surprising.

As for Phoebe, he kept her arm locked with his and glibly deflected any question directed her way. While she was steady enough on her feet, and he'd ensured her gown was perfectly neat, her color was a touch too warm, and her eyes were still a trifle dazed.

The sight made him wonder how she—oh-so-definite-and-determined Phoebe—would be after . . .

He broke off the thought, smiled at Lady Griswald, then tacked through the crowd to come up by Edith's side.

After delivering Edith and Phoebe to their carriage and seeing them off, he put Audrey in hers, refusing her offer to drop him off at the club. He let her believe that he intended to look in at one of the clubs in St. James; in reality, he simply had to walk, although he doubted even that would help.

He'd probably spend most of his sleepless night imagining inventive ways to murder, slowly, whoever it was who'd harmed Phoebe.

He tried to tell himself that his reasons for seeking out Phoebe at Lady Fleming's alfresco luncheon at Wimbledon the following day were all to do with tactics. He wanted to have his evening free to watch Edith's house and track Phoebe's groom and maid should they venture forth.

In reality, after the previous night he felt driven to complete what he'd started. It was as if his failure to bring his pleasuring of her to a proper and satisfactory conclusion sat like a blot—a big black blot—on his sexual record.

He couldn't let it stand; he had to make it right.

Somewhat to his relief, Phoebe patently agreed. The instant she saw him approaching across the Flemings' lawn, she stopped and stared, her eyes widening first in stunned surprise, then in startled speculation.

He'd forgotten how easy to read she was; he prayed he was the only one viewing the open book of her intentions.

"What are you doing here?" Despite the words, her tone made her underlying hopes abundantly clear.

He took the hand she instinctively offered, bowed, then, straightening, set her fingers on his sleeve. Turning, he surveyed the assembled horde. "I haven't attended a function like this for over eleven years. I assume it's still permissible for couples to stroll the gardens?"

"Well, yes." Phoebe blinked, then let her gaze wander over the guests, the multitude of fashionable young ladies and eligible young gentlemen promenading on the lawn, the matrons and older ladies gathered in chairs and idling groups about its edge, while she imagined . . . "But you can't mean to . . . to slip away and engage in . . . *here?*"

Looking up, she met his green eyes; what she saw there made her heart stutter.

Holding her gaze, he arched a brow. "Why not?"

She blinked again and looked away—from those too-knowing eyes and the too-tempting suggestion lurking in their depths. "I . . . ah . . ."

"Don't you wish to?" His voice had lowered to that seductive tone that invariably sent a delicious shiver down her spine.

She pressed her lips tight against a telling urge to blurt, "Yes, of course," and forced herself to try at least to think.

He shifted nearer. "Last night the soprano's last song wasn't long enough—we could, I thought, continue with the discoveries her brevity forced us to curtail."

Every syllable of the illicit invitation echoed evocatively through her whirling mind, distracting, luring. . . .

She looked across the lawn to where Edith, Audrey, and three of their dearest friends were engrossed in conversation, studiously not glancing their way—as if they hadn't noticed him, a dark and dangerous predator, stalking over the sward to corner her. "I'm positive—" She broke off, cleared her throat, then continued more firmly, "I'm positive that slipping away *privately* will be considered too fast."

He'd followed her gaze to the congregation of matrons and chaperones; now he snorted. "Phoebe, not one of them expects us to stay here and chat and exchange inanities with the rest. They know—or hope they do—why I'm here. They're going to be far more disappointed if we don't disappear for a half hour or so than if we do."

She had a sneaking suspicion he was right. She met his eyes. "Why do they think you're here?"

"To seduce you, of course." The look he bent on her suggested she was being willfully obtuse. "You're twenty-five, well born and well dowered. In their eyes, it's past time someone did."

She held his gaze, knowing that he might well be right—in one sense. Her aunt, her godmother, and the others might indeed hope a gentleman like Deverell would sweep her off her feet—even through seduction—but they would, of course, assume that the end result would be wedding bells.

But she'd said no to marriage and had meant it; she was certain he hadn't forgotten. He'd accepted her stance and offered a liaison instead. What if . . . ? What would they, and the ton, think later?

Did she care?

More to the point, what was the alternative? To endure another night racked with the same restless longing as the last?

Her gaze locked in the green of his, she cleared her throat. Nodded. "All right." She glanced at the assembled guests. "But how?"

Her life was her own to live as she saw fit.

"Simple." His hand trapping hers on his sleeve, he turned her away from the lawn. "This way."

He steered her to where a path led between thick borders backed by dense shrubbery. "Allow me to conduct you on a tour of the delights to be found in such a pleasantly sculpted landscape. Did you know these gardens were originally laid out by Capability Brown?"

"No." She glanced at him. "Were they?"

He nodded. "Luckily for us, less so for Mr. Brown, the Lady Fleming of the time developed an irrational dislike of his open spaces. So she filled them in—with trees and flowerbeds and shrubs, with streams and gardens of this type and that, all interconnecting." He caught her gaze. "The perfect landscape for seduction."

She decided she was going to be bold; with him, there seemed little point in being otherwise. "Why perfect?"

"Because even if there is a crowd present, as there is to-day, it's never difficult to find some place, some enchanted spot in which to engage in . . . whatever one has in mind."

"Hmm. So, speaking as a seducer"—she cast him a glance—"an expert seducer, what spot do you have in mind for us?"

"Speaking as an expert seducer"—he guided her under a hanging garland of wisteria and onto a narrow graveled path—"I'd suggest, naturally, that we choose our spot to best support, if not heighten, the experience."

She frowned. "And what sort of spot will that be?"

"I'll know when I see it."

She looked around while they walked, neither dawdling nor hurrying; she swung along by his side, their steady pace taking them further and further from the house, the lawn, and the other guests. She glanced back at one point and saw nothing but a wall of trees and shrubs. "Do you know where we're going?"

He glanced at her enigmatically. "Yes—and stop worrying. I know precisely where we are."

His tone suggested he wasn't speaking only of the gardens' geography.

They came to a lovely pool where the ornamental stream that wended through the grounds widened, then spilled over a weir. The sound of the gurgling, burbling water was pleasant; she glanced at him, wondering if he would stop there—the spot was reminiscent of his "pretty spot" by the stream at Cranbrook Manor—but he didn't pause.

A little way along, they came upon a sunken rose garden.

Taking her hand, he led her down the steps and along the path between the arching canes laden with heavily perfumed blooms. There was an alcove with a seat thickly cushioned in thyme; she looked at it, wondering—could any spot be more romantic?—but he led her straight on.

Beyond the rose garden lay a truncated vista where the hand of Capability Brown was still detectable. A small white marble temple with columns in the Doric style overlooked a deep pond covered in water lilies. The sight reminded her of the temple by the lake where they'd dallied in the night; she felt sure he would halt there, but he didn't.

He kept walking, neither fast nor slow. His bootheels rang on the paved path edging the pond; she heard the confidence in his stride. He knew where he was taking her, had already chosen which of the many gardens comprising the Flemings' property would best suit them . . . her. His seduction of her.

To heighten the experience . . .

She looked ahead, but a narrow archway through a thick hedge limited her view of the next garden; all she could tell was that it contained trees tall enough to rise above the hedge. Nerves suddenly flickering, her mind raced, cataloguing all the types of gardens they'd passed, and what they'd yet to see. . . .

Without pause, he led her under the arch.

Coolness enveloped them as they emerged on the other side and stepped onto a rougher graveled path that led through an arboretum.

Tall trees closed around them, many old with wide, thick boles. To either side of the path, leaves blanketed the ground, relatively level, spreading to either side. Within a minute, she realized they were no longer on the path; glancing behind, she couldn't see the archway. She was alone with him in the cool glade where shadows lay heavy, dappling as an errant breeze ruffled the high canopies.

His stride slowed.

She recalled very well the last time they'd been in a landscape such as this.

Recalled very well what had happened.

Drawing in a suddenly not quite steady breath, she looked at him.

He halted; letting her hand go, lowering his arm, he slowly turned to face her.

Increasingly breathless, she studied his face. Wondered why it was that when they were alone, he never bothered to disguise his ruthless self behind his charming mask. When he looked at her, she had no difficulty seeing him for what he was—and reading what he wanted, what he intended, in his eyes.

She licked suddenly dry lips and kept her gaze fixed on his, conscious of her body tightening, of her nerves already taut and flickering.

But over what? In anticipation of what?

He'd been studying her face, her features; his gaze came to rest on her eyes. "You aren't frightened of me—and you can't be frightened by this place, not in daylight."

His low, matter-of-fact tone focused her wits. Made her think . . . then she nodded. Found her voice. "I'm not afraid of you." She cast a glance around. "Or of this place." It was a wood, just a wood.

"Good."

The intent in his deep voice had her gaze darting back to him, fixing on him as he stepped slowly, unhurriedly, toward her.

Eyes widening, she instinctively backed, equally slowly, step by step—as she knew he intended her to. He didn't rush or grab, but simply herded her.

Until her back came up against the bole of a tall tree; smooth and ungiving, she let it support her. She licked her lips, watched him close the distance between them, his eyes heating as they followed the tip of her tongue. "Why good?"

The question was little more than a murmur as his hands bracketed her waist and he moved close.

He paused, then replied, "Because I'm going to kiss you, and then I'm going to ravish you, here in the dark wood under the trees." His eyes lifted and met hers; he held her gaze for an instant, then lowered his eyes again to her lips. "And you're going to enjoy every second."

Chapter 11

*H*e kissed her, but this time he hadn't caught her hands; she held them up, palms out, uncertain, then tentatively rested them on his shoulders.

Waiting to see . . .

But he was right; there was nothing in his kiss, nothing in him to frighten her. She knew him, recognized him, felt comfortable and safe with him. His tongue cruised her lips; she parted them, let him enter. His tongue found hers, then stroked, heavy and certain, confident of her response; her senses sighed and yielded.

The kiss went on, grew hotter, more demanding, more commanding of her wits, her mind, her senses. Her body. Held trapped between his hands, braced against the tree, it heated, then smoldered, then burned; he set a steady flame within her, and steadily, ruthlessly stoked it.

His hands slid upward and found her breasts, claimed them, left them heavy and swollen with aching need; his fingers tweaked her nipples to tight, excruciatingly sensitive buds. Even muted by two layers of cloth, his touch—flagrantly possessive—affected her profoundly, sank into her psyche and touched something there.

A darker, stronger passion.

At first she thought it was his, then she recognized it as her own. Realized that with him, not only did she feel it, but she could own it—embrace it.

She liked being held, trapped between unforgiving wood at her back and a passionate man intent on ravishing her. A dangerous like.

An alluring like. One that sparked her senses and made them come alive.

Then one hand left her breast and he reached for her skirts, this time wasting no time in lifting them, in gathering them up, bunching them between them, then sliding his hand beneath.

To find her bare skin, and possess that, too.

He cupped the back of her thigh, bare above her stocking, then ran his hand up, spread his fingers and cupped one globe of her bottom, hand to naked skin. He kneaded, not as gentle as last night—more, she sensed on a spurt of delicious awareness, driven.

That he wanted her she'd never doubted, yet he'd so successfully reined his passions, held his desires under such tight control that she'd got little taste of them . . . until now.

His hand flexed, gripped her bottom; his other hand kneaded her breast. His lips and tongue plundered her senses without quarter, and she sensed . . .

The power in him. His elemental male dominance, the strength, the will, the passion that could so easily overwhelm her, that would allow him to take from her whatever he wished at any time.

Before her thoughts could even coalesce about that realization, he pulled back from the kiss. Just an inch. His hand flexed, caressed her bottom as from under heavy lids his eyes raked her face.

She lifted her lids just enough to see . . . the raw hunger that prowled just beneath his controlled exterior. It was no surprise to discover her breathing was unsteady, too fast, a trifle ragged, but to realize that his was too was a slight shock—albeit one that brought a distinct thrill.

His gaze lowered to her lips. "Those words we agreed to yesterday—they still work."

" 'No,' 'wait,' and 'slow'?"

He nodded, leaned in again. "They'll always work. With me."

That was all he'd wanted to say, to tell her. His lips covered hers and he waltzed her straight back into their fire, the conflagration of heated passion waiting to sear their senses, to consume them.

The hand beneath her skirts shifted, boldly moved to splay over her belly, tensing, claiming, then he wedged one hard thigh between hers, eased her legs wider apart, and his long hard fingers speared down and between, and found her.

Claimed her.

Not just the sensitive spot he'd caressed last night, although he paused to pay homage there and set her senses leaping. This time he reached further, stroking, caressing, parting, then probing, evocatively exploring.

She shuddered. Held against the tree, her mouth all his, her senses careening, she found a fleeting moment to wonder if she would panic, but even before the thought was fully formed it was swept away.

He eased one finger inside her and she gasped.

For one instant, her world teetered, poised on a sensual

brink, then a wave of breathless longing welled and flooded her and washed her helplessly over the edge, drowning out all else.

His hard finger withdrew, then more boldly thrust in; his hand shifted between her thighs, his other fingers touched, caressed—and her senses splintered.

Hunger rose, that darker passion driving it, and she suddenly understood all she'd heard of the act—how addictively tempting it could be.

His tongue found and mated with hers, thrusting to the same steady, relentless plundering rhythm at which his hand worked between her thighs, at which his finger filled her, repetitively intimate. Pleasure uncoiled and spread through her, driven by that unwavering intimate invasion.

At some point, her hands had risen to his head, her fingers tangling in the thick dark locks. Now she gripped and held him to her, boldly kissed him back and made it clear—as clear as she knew how—that she wanted more.

That she wanted *all*.

Deverell sensed her demand and inwardly rejoiced, relieved and vindicated. She wasn't yet truly desperate, but he didn't want her to learn just how desperate he could make her before giving her release—that was for later. Much later.

Right now . . . relief swept him as he set his mind to the task of introducing her to sensual glory. To guiding her senses along the last stretch to release. All the while holding his own clamoring desires ruthlessly in check.

Somewhat to his surprise, his control held firm; it didn't even waver when, his fingers artfully tightening about her nipple in time to the deep stroking of the finger buried in her sheath, she uttered a little scream, smothered by their kiss, then climaxed.

He waited until she slumped, then lifted his head to watch her face. To study the sight as the tightness of passion was washed away, replaced by that most mesmerizing of expressions. He loved seeing that glow on his lovers' faces. On Phoebe's . . . as he looked down on her face, he felt his heart contract.

He kept his hand between her thighs, lightly stroking, soothing more than driving as the last ripples of tension faded. His fingers at her breast idly caressed the tortured bud, drawing out her descent from the peak.

Her flesh was scalding, slick and welcoming, swollen and soft beneath his probing fingers. Every iota of male need within him was focused on that, all but salivating, teased even more by the sweet, musky scent that rose to wreathe his senses.

Yet to his surprise—his great surprise—his passions and desires seemed content to remain harnessed. For now. That was understood, yet . . . when it came to Phoebe, his control seemed, if not limitless, then more definite. Which was curious, given that she stirred that too primitive side of him more than any other ever had.

He studied her face, wondering. Perhaps it was because that more primitive side of him understood and accepted that in order to have Phoebe—to have her as he wished—this was how things had to be.

Step by step, as he'd dictated from the first. At least now he understood why.

It was a matter of trust. First to last, with Phoebe that's what was needed. First, she needed to learn she could trust him, especially intimately. Only once she trusted him would she—could she—willingly lie beneath him, of that he was sure. But once she'd taken that step and given herself to him, then inevitably she would realize she could trust him with all her other secrets, too, with all the rest that made up her life.

When it came down to it, that's what he was after.

Her body, her soul, her secrets—and the rest of her life.

* * *

"Fergus and I wondered," Skinner said, shaking out Phoebe's unusually crushed muslin day gown, "seeing as how you and Mrs. Edith don't have to be at Lady Crackendower's ball until later, if you wanted to slip around to the agency this evening between dinner and leaving for the ball. Seeing as Lady Pelham's going to be seeing Jessica tomorrow."

Sitting in her hip bath, wreathed in steam, Phoebe stopped her vigorous application of the sponge to her skin and frowned. "I would like to, but . . ."

Inwardly muttering, she forced her wits to work. If this lingering lassitude, which seemed to linger even more mentally than physically, was the unavoidable outcome of being pleasured, then it was no wonder half the ladies of the ton so often appeared to be mentally disconnected.

"I'm not sure . . ." She wasn't, but why? It took a minute or more for the reason to materialize through the clouds fogging her brain. "Deverell . . ."

"His man is watching the front, so we can nip out the back and his viscountship'll be none the wiser."

"No, it's not that." Eyes narrowing, she related, as much for herself as Skinner, "He told me he wouldn't see me at Lady Crackendower's tonight because he had other business to attend to."

"Well then—perfect." Skinner frowned at the muslin skirt, then plopped down in a chair. "I don't know what you did today, but this gown has heaps of tiny bits of bark caught in the weave." She started plucking them out. "You need to take better care."

Phoebe lifted the sponge to her flushed cheeks, muting her inarticulate reply. She remarshaled her thoughts. "Be that as it may," she said, lowering the sponge, "I've a strong premonition that his 'other business' will be watching this

house, too—and he's far too clever not to think of the back."
If he wasn't with her . . .

She reminded herself that she was the one who had instigated her seduction in order to distract *him*. And although
while he was with her he seemed totally focused on her, when
he wasn't . . . she had very little confidence that he would be
distracted at all. *She* was the one more thoroughly distracted,
not him.

A state he'd gone out of his way to ensure.

Even now she was amazed at her brazenness, but when he'd
eventually drawn his hand from between her thighs, let her
skirt fall, and then tensed to step away, she'd grabbed his
shoulders and, admittedly in rather elliptical phrases, suggested he take what he wanted. That he stop being so damned
controlled and come inside her.

He'd understood her perfectly, but his jaw and his determination had only firmed. He'd leaned close, one arm braced
on the tree above her head, wound a finger—the same finger
with which he'd earlier pleasured her—in a lock of her hair,
then caught her eyes and told her, bluntly, how it would be
when he did.

In a bed, with her completely naked, not a stitch to hide
behind, with him totally naked, too, and with adequate light
so he could see her as he took her.

The picture he'd painted had been brutally primitive; before she'd even had time to absorb it, he'd swiftly kissed her,
then seized her hand and towed her from the tree—all the
way back to the lawn and the other guests.

After that, of course, her distraction had been complete.

It still was. Thinking of anything else was hard enough,
but keeping her wits focused seemed well nigh impossible.

She continued to ply her sponge while she wrestled with
the possibilities. Tried to. In the end, she sighed and settled

for acting on intuition. "Don't go out tonight—not you or Fergus. I don't want to risk it." Not with Deverell potentially out there prowling. "Send a lad with a message first thing in the morning, as if he were being sent on the usual morning errands. Give Jessica my best wishes for the interview, and tell Emmeline to send word—again by a lad—afterward."

Skinner shot her a sharp look. "You're being very careful with his viscountship."

"If you'd spent much time in his company, you'd understand why."

"Is he really likely to kick up a stink if he realizes what you're up to?"

Phoebe grimaced and gazed into the distance. "I don't know," she eventually replied. "But I don't want to risk finding out."

By the next evening, by the time she and Edith entered Lady Gosforth's ballroom, Phoebe was no longer certain what she might or might not risk.

What she was certain of was that Deverell's step-by-step approach had pushed her to the limit of her endurance. The previous night, even though she'd known she wouldn't see him, her senses had expected to. She'd felt deflated, unutterably bored for the entire ball, unable to find one good moment, take one scintilla of pleasure in the evening.

She hadn't even been able to concentrate on chatting, talking and keeping up with the ton's news as she needed to do. Her mind had simply refused to focus.

A state of affairs that had continued unabated through not just the evening and a restless night but the entire ensuing day. While she had *thought* of Jessica attending her interview with Lady Pelham, thought, too, of numerous other aspects involved in the smooth functioning of the agency, she hadn't been able to convince herself that any action on any such count was urgent—more urgent than fantasizing about when next she and Deverell would meet, and what they would do when they did.

Never before had she been prey to such mindless wool-gathering; it had to stop.

Standing by the side of Lady Gosforth's ballroom near the chaise to which she'd conducted Edith, Phoebe plotted and planned. Luckily, Gosforth House was an excellent venue in which to ensure Deverell came to the point.

Impatience gripped her. When poor Mr. Camberley approached and asked her to dance, it was all she could do to refuse with civility; it was so irritating not to be able to simply state that she was waiting for someone else.

She'd assumed Deverell had been learning where she and Edith would be each evening through Audrey, but just in case, she'd remembered his instructions of where he could be reached and dispatched a note to Montrose Place bidding him join her at Gosforth House. She'd kept the note brief. It was possible, even likely, that he would misinterpret her purpose in summoning him, but that was immaterial.

The important thing was that he should come.

It was after ten-thirty, the middle of the evening, when Deverell strolled through Lady Gosforth's ballroom doors. After exchanging greetings with his host and hostess, who were acquainted with his family, he moved into the room, preparing to search for Phoebe—only to discover her making a beeline for him.

His instincts flickered, but, his glibly charming smile in place, he went to meet her.

"Miss Malleson." Taking her hand, he bowed—instantly felt, through just her fingers, the nervy tension thrumming through her. Straightening, he continued to smile easily as he asked, "What is it?" His tone conveyed his instant alertness, his awareness that something wasn't as it should be.

She acknowledged it with a tight little nod. "I need to speak with you alone. Come with me."

Linking her arm with his, she turned to one corner of the long room. He moved smoothly, covering her hand on his sleeve, looking attentively at her—disguising the fact that she was leading him, not the other way around. "Where are we going?"

"You'll see when we get there."

Before he could pursue that, Maria, Lady Cranbrook, beckoned imperiously; perforce they had to stop and chat before moving on.

He realized that Phoebe was making for a door most of the way down the room. She was giving an excellent imitation of Marshal Blucher, marching in a straight line directly toward her goal. Glancing swiftly around, he noted with some relief that, courtesy of Lady Gosforth's being one of the principal hostesses and her ball therefore being a certifiable crush, the crowd in the room was so dense that their forced march wasn't as noticeable, as revealing as it would otherwise have been.

Relieved on that score—he might whisk Phoebe away from under the matrons' eyes, but he knew what the ton's arbiters would turn a blind eye to, and what they wouldn't, and Phoebe whisking *him* away fell in the latter category—he returned his attention to her, to what had driven her to seek his help. "What do you want to tell me?"

Reaching the door, she opened it, glanced at him. "I'll tell you when we're private."

She was tense, on edge; he followed her through the door without further hesitation. Closing it behind them, he looked around. They were in a corridor; Phoebe led him on.

"It's this way."

"What's this way?" He fell in beside her.

"A suitable place to have our discussion. Now be quiet in case someone hears."

He obligingly kept silent and followed; he'd no doubt learn all soon enough. Somewhat to his mystification, she led him unerringly through a maze of corridors—Gosforth House was centuries old—and then started up a flight of stairs.

"Do you know where you're going?" he whispered.

She glanced back at him, her gaze severe. "Yes." She looked ahead. "I've visited here often."

She volunteered nothing more; he climbed the stairs in her wake, noting the sweet curves of her lush derriere tonight outlined in old gold silk. His hand started to rise before he realized and forced it down again. She seemed troubled; whatever had prompted her to send for him at the club was presumably preying on her mind.

Recalling that something had occurred to trouble her instantly suppressed his libido.

On the upper floor, she skirted a gallery, then led him down another corridor into a distant wing. The sounds of the ball had long faded; the rooms they passed were eerily still.

Unused. He felt sure of it. He glanced around, noting the thin layer of dust on a side table.

Then Phoebe opened a door and went through. He followed; the room beyond lay in darkness.

"Close the door," she instructed from somewhere in the gloom. "Then I'll light a lamp."

He did as she asked, then stood in the darkness before the door and waited.

A spark flared, then moved; a wick caught, flared, lighting Phoebe's face, then settled to burn steadily. Phoebe adjusted the wick, and the circle of light, until then limited to her and the lamp, spread and illuminated the room.

Deverell blinked, then stared.

Phoebe replaced the lamp glass and turned to him.

He couldn't drag his eyes from the room and its furnishings. "Good Lord."

His voice was weak, an accurate indication of the depth of his amazement. It was the most extraordinary room he'd ever seen. Bizarre was the adjective that first leapt to mind, closely followed by astonishing, unexpected, and utterly fantastic.

His jaw had dropped; it took effort to close it. Stunned, he surveyed the chamber. The size of a small parlor, it had been decorated as a cross between a seraglio and some lustful sheik's desert tent, all rendered by an imagination run amok.

The walls were hung with spangled gossamer silk, a divan angled between two walls strewn with brocades and piled with satin cushions. The colors were rich—crimsons, purples, blues, and golds. There were silk tassles everywhere, with brass lamps and candlestands and small exotic inlaid tables scattered here and there. More cushions were piled on jewel-hued rugs. Even the ceiling was ornamented with gilt stars.

"Who . . . what is this place?" Returning his gaze to Phoebe, he discovered she'd walked to him.

"It's Catherine's boudoir—she's Lady Gosforth's middle daughter. She and I were close friends. Although she's married now, she insisted her boudoir be left as it was."

He nearly asked why but decided he didn't need to know; the thought that the room had been created from the fantasies of a young lady boggled his mind enough as it was. The fact that Phoebe patently found that perfectly reasonable boggled it even more. His gaze had wandered to the fantastical décor; he looked back at Phoebe—just as she clasped his face between her hands, stretched up, and kissed him.

Unprepared, his loins ungirded—he hadn't expected matters to take such a turn—and perhaps mentally primed by the suggestive surroundings, he found himself lured into an exchange that too quickly progressed from the sweet to the sultry, and from there in double-time to the flagrantly ardent.

But . . .

It took more effort than he liked to break from the kiss, to wrench his lips from the wanton delights of hers and rasp, "What—"

"We can light more lamps if you like."

He blinked down at her. Why . . . ? "Lamps?"

Drawing back a fraction more, she leveled her gaze—on his cravat. "You insisted on a bed, and light enough to see." She drew in a breath—and set her fingers to his cravat. "So we can light more lamps if one isn't enough—"

"Phoebe." He closed one hand over hers, stopping her from further disarranging his cravat. In retrospect, he'd been slow in picking up the signs, because he'd thought . . . He waited until she looked up at him, until he could see her darkened violet eyes, and the stubborn, indefatigably determined set of her chin. "What did you want to discuss with me?"

He felt obliged to confirm that matters were as he now thought.

"Not so much discuss as address. Us. This—my seduction." Sliding one hand from beneath his, she waved over her shoulder at the red-silk-brocade-draped divan. "There's the bed, we have light, so now it's just—"

"No." Gripping her hand, he lifted it away from his cravat. Retaining his hold, he resurveyed the room, but there really was no question in his mind. He met her gaze. "We are not staging the final act of your seduction here, tonight."

She narrowed her eyes at him, her glance now more ireful than desireful. "Why not?"

He suddenly realized what the real source of the tension

thrumming through her was. It was difficult not to smile with smug satisfaction; preserving an expression of impassivity, he racked his brains for an excuse she would understand, one that wouldn't worry her—one she would accept.

"Because"—he kept his eyes locked with hers—"the final act in your seduction will run for considerably longer than half an hour."

She blinked, then blinked again. "Oh."

"In fact"—the more he thought of it, the more sure he was—"you should think more in terms of several hours."

She started to mouth "several," stopped, swallowed, then nodded. "I see. Very well." She looked past his shoulder for a moment. "In that case—" She tried to step back, out of his encircling arm, but he held her securely.

He looked down at her. "Where are you going?"

She braced her hands against his chest. "If we're not . . . then we should return to the ballroom."

Her tone was determinedly prim. He chuckled, the sound as delightedly devilish as he felt. "You've just handed me yourself for half an hour, in a setting designed for titillation." By a female mind, what was more. He caught her startled, widening gaze as it lifted to his eyes. "You can't possibly imagine I'll refuse."

Phoebe read his intentions in his eyes, clearly writ in the devilish green, and inwardly groaned. This was not a good idea; this wasn't what she'd planned. Then she remembered. "No."

He looked at her; she smiled.

He frowned, clearly considering, then slowly shook his head. "Those words I gave you—they only apply when I'm kissing you, or at the very least have my hands on you. I gave them to you so you won't feel threatened, but you're not in such a position now, so they don't function."

She felt her jaw drop. His gaze had gone past her; keeping

one of her hands locked in one of his, he moved her aside and walked toward the divan, towing her behind him.

He halted and studied the divan. "Especially not after bringing me here. That qualifies as incitement, and with incitement you can't vacillate. Once you've incited, you have to cope with whatever response you get. That's the way incitement works."

She struggled to follow his reasoning, then realized he was talking purely to distract her while he planned. . . . She tugged on his hand. "We really should get back to the ballroom."

"Not yet. We've plenty of time. More than half an hour, really, given the crowd down there."

She was struggling to think of a useful response when he turned and her nerves leapt, but then he sat on the divan. He bounced lightly, testing, then he sighed and reclined back against the cushions, lifting both legs onto the bed so his feet hung off the end, lifting one arm over his head and settling his shoulders into the piled cushions. She stared down at him.

A slow, wolfish, thoroughly untrustworthy smile curved his lips and lit his green eyes. He changed his hold on her hand so his fingers now manacled her wrist. "You're not really going to tell me that you'd rather be weathering the crush down there than attending to my needs?"

Her mouth dried. She considered him for a long moment, then asked, "Your needs?"

"Hmm. Isn't this something like the fantasies you and Catherine dreamed of in creating this room? Having a sheik or sultan capture you and order you to pleasure him? Isn't that how it goes?"

He'd guessed right, and he knew it, but not even in their wildest dreams had either she or, she'd wager, Catherine ever conjured a sheik or sultan who could hold a candle to him.

Aside from all else, he was real—real flesh, hot blood, and very hard muscle. Reclining before her in an unbelievably arrogant pose, one that was doing real violence to her already weakened resistance.

Then something in his eyes changed; she could have sworn his gaze grew hotter, but harder and more ruthless, too.

"Come." He gave a light tug on her wrist. "Kiss me."

It was an outright order in a tone that brooked no argument—one that warned that any resistance, any recalcitrance, would be dealt with in a way she wouldn't want to learn about.

He exerted a steady, inexorable pull. She took a step forward, then another, then found herself sinking onto the divan beside him.

She waited, but he didn't reach for her and pull her down to him; instead, he studied her for a moment, then he lifted his free hand and lightly—oh so lightly—caressed the delicate curls brushing her nape. The touch—so subtle, so unexpectedly evocative—made her shudder and close her eyes.

"Now you're in my harem, you have to learn to be a houri." He waited until she opened her eyes, until she fell into the green depths of his, then stroked her nape lightly again and murmured, "Come—kiss me, and give me your mouth."

Her hands were rising to frame his face before she'd thought, then she tried to think and discovered she couldn't. That somehow the draw, the hypnotic tug he exerted on her, was all consuming, making thinking redundant, at least for now.

She wanted to kiss him. Her lips throbbed as she leaned over him. As she paused with their lips less than an inch apart, letting her breath bathe his, feeling his exhalation brush hers.

Then she closed that last inch and kissed him. Let herself

flow into the kiss, into her memories, into her long-ago fantasies.

He was the sultan, the sheik of her girlhood dreams, a figure larger than life, better than any mortal man could ever be. A better lover, a stronger warrior, a more powerful lord—a masterful seducer.

She opened her mouth over his, sent her tongue between his lips to mate with his, and did as he'd commanded—as she knew he wished—and fed him kisses, kisses more ardent than any she'd imagined gifting any man, more wanton, more abandoned, more urgent and arousing.

He responded, met her and matched her, demanded, but didn't take the reins, refused to absolve her of her duty.

He hadn't released her wrist; his fingers remained shackled about it as she leaned on his chest, her lips fused with his, and felt herself drowning, growing giddy, her wits and senses swirling in the sea of desire she'd evoked.

It was he who broke the kiss, drawing back just enough to meet her eyes. Then his hand rose, sliding across the back of her neck to cup her nape, holding her there, letting her feel the weight and strength of his hand.

Then he released her wrist, reached down, and, with a surprisingly quick few flicks, freed the back of her skirt and tossed it up to her waist.

She sucked in a breath at the cool touch of the air on her exposed skin, caught and held that breath, her lungs seizing as his hand closed possessively over one bared globe.

He caught her eyes, flexed his hand, flagrantly kneading, then, exerting pressure, he drew her lips closer. Just before he kissed her, he murmured, "Now those words apply."

She understood, but as his lips closed over hers and heat arced, sparked, then raced between them, through them, over them, building into a now-familiar conflagration, she knew she wouldn't need to remember his words.

This was her dream, not his, and it was even better than her girlish imagination had painted it. He was her sheik come to life, determined to ravish her, to demand her sexual surrender. . . . She wasn't about to stop him.

This was what she wanted, what she'd brought them here to achieve. The last stage in her seduction . . . she suddenly discovered just how hungry she was, how desperate she could grow to feel his hands on her.

He shifted, then rolled her into the cushions, then rolled again, and she lay beneath him.

She arched and her senses exulted, glorying in the solid hardness of his body over hers, holding her trapped, pinned beneath him. Her naked bottom lay on the red silk brocade, a cool touch at first, but it quickly heated. One hard hand remained beneath her, idly sculpting, for the moment waiting.

His other hand had slid from her nape; palm and fingers now cruised the gold silk of her bodice, taut and straining to contain her already swollen breasts. She arched into his touch, eloquently if wordlessly inviting more. His fingers found the line of buttons closing her bodice, traced, fumbled.

He drew back from the kiss, looked down at the tiny buttons. "Open your bodice."

Another order; there was something in his face, in the hard lines and planes, that sent a delicious thrill skittering through her as she drew her hands from his hair and obeyed.

Any doubt that what she'd glimpsed wasn't real—that his desire for her didn't burn with a raging flame, didn't drive him—disappeared in the instant she slid the last button free. He pushed her hands aside, pressed the halves of her bodice wide, paused for a heartbeat to examine what he'd uncovered—then he bent his head and feasted.

As if he were starving—as if he and his senses could never, would never get enough of her, not enough to satisfy.

She writhed and burned beneath his hands, his lips, his too-knowing caresses. Her gasps and moans, orchestrated by a master, filled the room, each sound another note in a sensual sonata that hypnotized and lured. Each lick, each evocative suckling sent sensation spearing through her; she welcomed every streak of lancing passion, every lapping flame of desire—embraced them, offered herself up to them, and him.

Of course he knew.

Just as he knew that that wouldn't be enough to satisfy either of them. She felt nothing but leaping expectation when he shifted back and between them drew up the front of her skirt. The back had already been trapped high under her back and shoulders when he'd rolled them; with the front lifted, too, she lay all but naked beneath him, her hips and long legs exposed to his gaze, displayed against the red-silk brocade.

She realized, and with difficulty lifted her heavy lids—and saw him, braced above her and a little to the side, looking down. Studying, examining. In that instant he was every inch the sheik intent on claiming her for his own. Then one hand rose, touched, glided over her smooth skin, then the backs of his fingers brushed her curls and she shut her eyes on a sensual shiver.

One of longing, of yearning, of wanting. A hot shiver of desire—one he saw, understood, and set about fanning.

He mapped her terrain, then explored, explicit, suggestive, uninhibitedly bold. He rearranged her limbs as he wished, pressing her thighs wide, opening her to him, then stroking, probing, penetrating.

She arched, restless, wanton, desire all but choking her. Eyes closed, she writhed, threshed, gasped, and knew she was begging. But not just for release. She wanted more—she wanted him inside her.

Where the knowledge, the absolute certainty came from, she didn't know; it was simply there, blazoned in her brain, something her heart, her body, every muscle and sinew and nerve knew as truth.

She wanted him, wanted to give herself to him, sensed that unless and until she did she wouldn't be complete, wouldn't be herself—the self she needed to be.

The first touch of his lips on her mons made her shriek. The first lick and she lost what little breath she still possessed. Then his tongue artfully caressed that tiny nub of sensitive flesh—and she was lost.

Lost in a world of heat and flame and fiery sensation. One he skillfully evoked, then with unwavering expertise guided her through, showing her, letting her feel, teaching her, letting her learn and know. Slowing here, racing ahead there, lingering when she needed it even though she was far past any hope of uttering any words.

At the last, he drew the glory to her, let it infuse her, fill her, shatter her.

Let it sweep her up and carry her beyond the stars for that perfect timeless moment, but then it faded, and as she drifted back to earth, she still felt empty. Incomplete.

At the very last, unfulfilled.

He'd shifted, lifted, and resettled her; she lay cradled in his arms, lying against his chest as the aftershocks of the incredible pleasure he'd wrought coursed through her.

His hands were still on her body, still stroking, but his touch, his intent, was plainly soothing. Yet there was something more that reached her still languid senses; she wondered if she was imagining it—conjuring a worshipfulness, a devotion, a reverence that wasn't truly there.

Dragging in a breath, she forced her lids up and turned her head to catch his eye. "I want you to join with me."

His face was graven, his gaze entirely serious. "I know."

After a moment, he glanced down, at his hand gently, slowly, stroking the side of her breast. "But the time and the place is not yet and not here."

If she'd had more energy—if he hadn't drained her of every last drop—she would have argued, yet she could see . . . she faced forward. Desire and more was etched in the lines of his face, easy to read. Desire and more infused the body against which she sprawled; there was no gainsaying the evidence of the hard rod pressed against her hip, or the sheer needful tension locked in every muscle of his long frame.

As if he could read her mind, he bent his head to hers and brushed his lips above her ear. "Not yet. But soon." His chest swelled, and he continued in the dark, dangerous tone that always sank to her bones, "You are what I desire, what I want. You are what I will have."

His next words reached her on a dark whisper.

"And I'm no fantasy."

Chapter 12

*P*hoebe woke the next morning with golden languor lingering in her veins.

And expectation buoying her heart.

"Soon" he'd said, and he was a man of his word.

With a long sigh, she stretched under the covers, lips curving in remembered, faintly shocked delight, then the rattle of curtain rings reached her. She looked to where Skinner was briskly pulling back the curtains, letting the morning sunshine stream in.

Skinner looked her way. "Good—you're awake. Emmeline sent a message—we've an emergency to take care of."

Phoebe sat up. "An emergency?" She tossed back the covers. "Jessica?"

"No—seems that's going well. Lady Pelham wants her, so Emmeline's sorting it out. It sounds like she's all but settled."

"Then what?" Thrusting her arms into her robe, Phoebe

walked to the chair before which Skinner, anticipating her need, had set her breakfast tray. She sat and looked up at Skinner. "What did Emmeline say?"

Skinner's lips thinned. "The Chifleys' new governess is being hounded by the eldest son. Poor girl's just twenty—it's her first position in the ton. Last night, the bounder tried to force his way into her room. The housekeeper came by just in time. The girl's frantic, but luckily the housekeeper's a friend of one of Emmeline's sisters, and so knew where to send to for help."

Sipping her tea, Phoebe was already making plans. "The Chifleys . . . they're on Dover Street, I think. Edith will know." She thought, then said, "We'll call on Lady Chifley this afternoon and see what we can learn." She looked at Skinner. "Send a message to Emmeline to get word to the Chifleys' housekeeper and the governess that we'll arrange something as soon as we can—possibly as early as tonight if we can manage it."

If the situation warranted it. She'd long ago learned not to rush a "rescue." Much better to take an extra day and be sure, but if after she met the Chifleys' eldest son and got some idea of the household she deemed the young governess at immediate risk, then they would act tonight, no matter the difficulties.

Skinner grunted and went off to send the message.

Phoebe gave her attention to her tea and toast, swiftly reviewing the engagements she and Edith had planned for that day. She and her aunt had an unspoken agreement; as, regardless of Phoebe's age, Edith stood essentially *in loco parentis,* no specific description of the agency and its works, let alone Phoebe's central role in both, had ever fallen on Edith's ears.

She knew, of course, but not having heard the facts stated, she felt no obligation to report to her brother what was, after all, only "female intuition, if not mere speculation"— something Phoebe's father would be the first to discount.

Edith had always, from the first, supported Phoebe's "little crusade." Phoebe hadn't explained what had driven her to take up such a cause, but she'd long suspected Edith had read between the lines and understood. Regardless, if she required assistance of the sort her aunt or her cronies could provide, she only had to ask.

Pouring herself another cup of tea, Phoebe considered how best to engineer a social meeting with the Chifleys' son.

Five minutes later, she realized her mind had wandered. With a guilty start, she hauled it back, faintly appalled at how constantly thoughts of Deverell intruded on her mind. Thoughts of how he made her feel, of the emotions that ran rampant when she was with him—of how much more this liaison of theirs had grown to be, so much more than she'd imagined, so much more addictive.

All day, every day, she looked forward to the night, to being with him, in his arms again, to experiencing the next plateau of sensual delight, not just the sensations but the feelings, too, that welled and cascaded through her. With him, only him. Her lips felt permanently sensitized, her body more alive, every nerve more aware; at her own instigation, she'd become enmeshed in a sensual web, yet the fascination he exerted, the quality in him that held her attention so effortlessly, wasn't that, or not only that.

What it was . . .

She frowned, pondering, then realized.

With a muttered oath, she read herself a stern, mentally strident lecture on where her priorities lay. She had the agency and her purpose in life, and people who depended on her—they had to be her first consideration. Dallying with a too-handsome viscount was all very well, but what lay between them, intense and exciting though it might be, was a liaison, nothing more.

That was all she was prepared to allow, and her first priority ensured that that was all it would ever be.

Deverell wasn't the fulcrum of her life—her work was. She clearly needed to keep that point uppermost in her mind.

Apropos of which . . . after their interlude last night, she'd made it patently, abundantly, insistently clear that she expected to take her last and final step into intimacy tonight. If instead she had to organize and carry out a rescue, then she wouldn't be meeting Deverell in Lady Fortescue's ballroom, and her final plunge into intimacy wouldn't take place. At least not tonight. Courtesy dictated she send him a note to inform him of that fact, *but* . . . if she did, he'd immediately guess she was up to something.

The damned man was already watching the house, making organizing things doubly difficult. Serve him and his arrogance right if he turned up at Lady Fortescue's and discovered she wasn't there. He'd be irritated and annoyed, and doubtless she'd later have to do something to appease him— her traitorous senses came alert at the thought—*but,* she concluded, ruthlessly suppressing them, that would be later, after the rescue; simply discovering her absent from the ball wouldn't tell him anything.

It wouldn't lead him to the agency and her secret.

But that was assuming the rescue would indeed have to be staged tonight. First things first.

Setting down her empty cup, she rose and crossed to her armoire. Opening the doors, she stood back and contemplated the best gown in which to interrogate Lady Chifley.

An hour later, Deverell leisurely descended the stairs at the club, summoned by the succulent aromas of coffee and bacon. Ambling into the dining room, he headed for the table.

Gasthorpe looked up from the sideboard. "Good morning, my lord. There's a message just arrived for you."

Lifting a silver salver, Gasthorpe crossed to the head of the table, where Deverell had elected to sit.

"Thank you." Deverell lifted the folded note from the tray and recognized Montague's neat script. He smiled. "And a very good day it's shaping up to be."

And if he had any say in it, the night would be even better.

Breaking the seal, he spread the sheets, picked up the coffee cup Gasthorpe had filled, sipped, and started to read.

The first three lines had him smiling again. "Well, well."

"Good news, my lord?"

"Indeed." Phoebe's bank drafts—all of them—had been paid to the account of the Athena Agency. Montague had, of course, dug further; the Athena Agency was an employment agency "specializing in the employment of superior young women in genteel establishments."

The further Deverell read, the more he regretted not pressing Montague to take his wager. Neither he nor his man-of-business would ever have imagined the Athena Agency or anything like it as the recipient of Phoebe's considerable largesse.

Following a summation of his financial scrutiny, Montague had listed the agency's address—Kensington Church Street, a stultifyingly proper neighborhood—along with the registered principals of the business, a Mr. and Mrs. Edmund Birtles and a Mr. Loftus Coates.

The Birtles address was the same as the agency's, but Coates lived in Connaught Square, one step away from Mayfair.

Deverell studied the names, then folded the letter, tucked it into a pocket, rose, and crossed to sample the dishes Gasthorpe had left ready on the sideboard. After piling his plate, he returned to the table. While he worked his way through ham, eggs, and kippers, he considered what he knew and what he had yet to learn.

When his plate was clean, he stirred and turned to Gasthorpe. "Has Grainger left yet?"

"No, my lord."

"Good." His smile as he pushed away from the table held a predatory edge. "Tell him to report to the library—I've a new assignment for him."

Rising, he strolled out and up the stairs, wondering what further insights the day's activities might yield. While Grainger watched the Athena Agency, he would see what he could learn about Birtles and Coates—especially Coates. If he had any rival for Phoebe's affections, he wanted to know, but quite aside from that was the obvious question of what a gentleman was doing associated with an agency "specializing in the employment of superior young women in genteel establishments."

Deverell walked into Lady Fortescue's ballroom midway through the evening, intent on finding Phoebe and hearing what she had to say about the Athena Agency.

Unable to help himself, in the afternoon he'd dressed as a laborer and slouched past the agency's twin bow windows, but he'd seen nothing beyond a desk and two chairs—empty— and a counter behind which a woman in her midthirties had been standing perusing some papers. The storefront had looked discreetly prosperous and businesslike, yet not intimidating; the glass in the two bow windows had sparkled, and the paint work had been fresh, with the agency's name picked out in neat, bright script over the door.

The Athena Agency had been outwardly created to

inspire confidence in its well-heeled clients. Even the address, not Mayfair but on the opposite side of Hyde Park and Kensington Gardens, was excellently gauged to strike the right note; very definitely catering to the upper classes, yet not seeking to impose itself on the haut ton.

Such observations had set his thumbs pricking; they were precisely the sort of minor but critical details Phoebe would appreciate.

Other than confirming that Mr. Loftus Coates's abode bore witness to his position—affluent, well-to-do, but not as well connected as one needed to be to move among the haut ton—he'd got little further in his investigations of the man; his servants didn't patronize the local tavern, nor were they well known in the neighborhood shops. A trifle odd, but if Coates was a recluse, as one shopkeeper had termed him, perhaps his household staff was small, and their circle of acquaintance commensurately narrow.

He hadn't yet asked Montague to pursue Loftus Coates; he'd decided to see if Phoebe, once apprised of his knowledge of the agency, might make such an investigation unnecessary. If she capitulated and told him all, he wouldn't need to investigate anyone else.

"I'm exceedingly glad to see you, my lord." Lady Fortescue viewed his bow with a critical eye. "It's past time you joined the throng and made your choice. Audrey's somewhere here—I'm sure she'll introduce you to any young ladies you've yet to meet."

Deverell clung to his charming smile and omitted to inform her ladyship that his choice was made, his interest fixed on only one lady, and she was no longer so young. Or so innocent, except in the biblical sense.

Leaving Lady Fortescue to the business of managing her guests, he headed for the corner where he'd glimpsed the tip of a red ostrich feather swaying above a crimson turban.

It was indeed Audrey; she was seated beside Edith, heads together, Lady Cranbrook alongside. He greeted Lady Cranbrook, then Audrey, so that it appeared perfectly natural that he should chat a trifle longer with Edith.

"Miss Malleson?" he asked. Somewhat to his surprise, Phoebe wasn't hovering nearby. After last night, after her stringent comments regarding her expectations for tonight, he'd fully expected her to waylay him the instant he crossed the threshold.

On the other hand, after last night, perhaps she'd decided to play least in sight, just to force him to exert himself.

Edith's washed-out blue eyes smiled rather sadly up at him. "I'm afraid Phoebe's indisposed, my lord. Such a shame. She's at home tucked up in bed—she must have eaten something that disagreed with her."

From the word "indisposed," his instincts had gone on high alert, yet for the life of him, he couldn't tell if Edith was lying or not. Couldn't tell if Phoebe truly was lying moaning in bed or . . .

He smiled commiseratingly and made some remark. Instead of moving away, he remained beside the three older ladies, chatting easily, yet the conversation engaged only the surface of his brain.

The rest was racing, assessing, evaluating. The bottom line was he wasn't inclined to believe Edith's tale.

Unfortunately, he couldn't cite pricking thumbs as evidence of any duplicity.

Lady Cranbrook claimed their collective attention with some tale—and he recalled that at Cranbrook Manor it had been Phoebe herself who had whisked the maid away.

The pricking in his thumbs was joined by an icy sensation at the back of his neck—an infallible sign that danger threatened. In this case, he was clearly not its target. Phoebe was.

His mind tenaciously followed the logical paths: Phoebe

had most definitely and unarguably expected to meet him here tonight at Lady Fortescue's ball. She'd made a very large point of that. If instead she was whisking some maid away tonight, then the necessity had to have been sprung on her—she'd certainly known nothing of it last night—but how had she learned of the need?

How did she learn of any such situations, those necessitating the whisking away of maids? Even more to the point, if she and her agency were behind the maids' "abductions," for want of a better word, then with respect to any action she had planned tonight, how had she gathered the necessary intelligence on the house, the surrounding streets, the household's habits?

A glimmer of an answer took shape in his mind. In Grainger's absence, he'd set one of the footmen from the club to watch Edith's town house and follow Phoebe and Edith on their outings. While Deverell had been dressing, the lad had looked in to report no unusual activity and had tendered a list of the houses Edith and Phoebe had visited that day.

Deverell had forgotten to read the list; he'd left it on the dresser at the club.

Inwardly wincing, he turned to Edith. It took him no more than a minute to subvert the conversation, then to separate his and Edith's discussion from Audrey's and Lady Cranbrook's.

"So unfortunate that Phoebe fell ill. Did you and she visit many households today?"

Edith smiled sweetly, encouragingly, up at him. "Only three. Two this morning—old Lady Crenshaw and then later Mrs. Fortinbras, but then this afternoon, Phoebe insisted on calling on Lady Chifley." Edith heaved a put-upon sigh. "I really don't know *what* Phoebe was thinking—Lady Chifley is always so tiresome, endlessly reciting all her equally tiresome sons' exploits, as if they were in any way distinguished."

A touch of color appeared in Edith's lined cheeks; she lowered her voice. "Spoiled, you know—every last one."

"Oh." Deverell raised his brows, feigning polite interest. In reality, his interest was rabid. "How old are her ladyship's sons? I don't believe I've ever met them."

"Oh, you wouldn't have," Edith assured him. "They're much younger. Only the eldest is down from university yet, and although it pains me to be so blunt, Frederick can hardly be termed a welcome addition to the ton."

Deverell fought to keep a frown from his face. "Why's that?"

Lips firming, Edith lightly rapped her cane on the floor. "He's objectionable. *Quite* objectionable." She met Deverell's eyes, her normally limpid gaze razor sharp. "Phoebe thought so, too. We met him briefly before we left Lady Chifley this afternoon."

Deverell looked down into Edith's old eyes and couldn't decide if she knew what she was telling him. The terrifying thought bloomed that she did and was doing so deliberately. . . .

He straightened, then swept her a bow. "Pray excuse me."

Edith smiled, sweet and soft and unterrifying again. "Of course, dear."

With a nod for Audrey and Lady Cranbrook, he turned on his heel and rapidly quit the ballroom; seconds later, he left the house.

The instant he set foot inside the club, Gasthorpe came hurrying from the back of the hall.

"My lord, Grainger sent a message just five minutes past. About half an hour ago, Miss Malleson drove up in a carriage to the back of the agency. She went in. Shortly after, she and two men—one her groom—came out and they left all together, once more in her carriage. As per your orders, Grainger remained on watch at the agency."

Deverell shut the front door behind him and comprehensively swore.

Whisking maids away, objectionable sons. It wasn't difficult to guess what Phoebe and her agency—he was perfectly sure it was hers—were up to. Or why.

But this . . . unless managed carefully, "abducting" maids from the center of London was an action guaranteed to be fraught with dangers—plural, not singular.

Mentally kicking himself for not asking Edith the obvious pertinent question, he refocused on Gasthorpe, standing before him, waiting to assist. "Where's Chifley House?"

A narrow alleyway ran along the backs of the large houses on Dover Street; Deverell found Phoebe, cloaked and hooded, a slighter shadow picking her way down it alongside a bulky, heavier shadow moving with a ponderous, lumbering gait.

A few yards wide, the alley was bounded by the high stone walls along the rear of each property. Sliding into the dense shadows about its mouth, Deverell followed Phoebe and her guard, a good fifty yards behind. He wanted to see what happened, how their "abduction" was orchestrated, before he made his presence known. He'd already identified one major strategic error on their parts and capitalized on it; their carriage was pulled up to the curb on Hay Hill, just past the alley mouth. Their driver sat alert on the box, reins in his hands, ready to drive off, meanwhile keeping watch on the carriages and passersby traveling up and down Berkeley Street across the end of short Hay Hill.

The carriage should have been positioned before the alley mouth, not beyond it. To the inexperienced, beyond seemed safer—easier to leap in and drive off, escaping any pursuers racing up the alley. If the carriage were before the alley mouth, the pursuers might intercept it—that was how that reasoning went. However, with the driver facing away from the alley mouth, he hadn't seen Deverell approach from the rear and slide into the shadows, hadn't noticed him gliding in the wake of Phoebe and her guard.

The lumbering giant, too, although clearly alert and watchful, was searching every shadow except those behind him.

Phoebe slowed, looking up at the backs of the houses. Deverell guessed she was counting; Chifley House was in the middle of the block, halfway down the alley. As she swung to walk on, he noticed she was carrying a small shielded lantern, presently fully shielded. The night was dark, overcast, with no real moonlight; with the tall town houses rising on either side, the alley was one small step from pitch black, yet she made no attempt to use the lantern to light her way.

The damned woman knew what she was doing was dangerous. That she should do everything possible not to draw attention to her presence in the alley.

Lips grimly set, Deverell hugged the darkest, densest shadows along the opposite wall and steadily closed the distance between them.

The giant reached out and touched Phoebe's shoulder. When she halted and looked his way, he gestured to a door set in the grimy alley wall.

Again, Phoebe looked back along the alley, scanning the houses; her gaze didn't swing far enough to detect Deverell, now twenty yards away.

Phoebe nodded. Deverell strained his ears, but neither she nor her guard spoke. The giant reached for the door latch and lifted it, but it was locked. Phoebe stepped closer; partially unshielding her lantern, she shone a narrow beam on the old, heavy lock as the giant crouched down and went to work on it.

Deverell could have had it open in seconds; the giant took

two minutes, but eventually he rose and nodded to Phoebe. He lifted the latch and eased the door open just enough to confirm that it was no longer barred. Then he glanced at Phoebe.

She looked down, fiddling with the lantern, then looked up and nodded to the giant.

He swung the door open, held it wide with one huge paw, stepping across Phoebe, shielding her with his bulk. Phoebe ducked and angled the lantern beneath his brawny arm, then unshielded it.

The light beamed out, then was shuttered. Once, twice. Then came a pause, a count of seven, followed by one last flash of light, then Phoebe stepped back, reshielding the lantern. The giant pulled back, swinging the door almost closed—then they waited.

Seconds ticked by, then the quiet was broken by a distant shout, muffled within walls. Before the sound faded, pattering footsteps, faint, then growing louder, reached Deverell's ears.

He saw the startled glance Phoebe shot the giant, then another muted bellow reached them, this time more definitely from within Chifley House.

The footsteps reached a frantic crescendo. The garden door was wrenched open; the giant stepped back as another female figure, hooded and wrapped in a cloak with a small traveling bag clutched to her chest, shot out into the alley.

It was instantly apparent that something was wrong. Babbling hysterically, the maid pointed frantically back at the house.

Phoebe and the giant looked.

From the house, a furious male voice rang out, then pounding footsteps rattled like gunfire in the night, racing closer.

Phobe swooped, putting her arm around the maid, urging her to flee.

The giant swore, hauled the door shut and turned, sweeping his arms, protectively herding Phoebe and the maid on.

The door at his back flew open.

A young man appeared, lips drawn back in a vicious snarl. He took in the figures before him in a blink; before the giant could turn, he raised his arm high. Deverell heard the blow rather than saw it—deduced the cosh the young man had used on the giant before he saw it dangling from the man's hand.

The giant crumpled and went down.

Poised in the shadows, every muscle tensed to act, Deverell waited, willing Phoebe to travel the few yards more to take her past him, so neither she nor the maid would be between him and their attacker.

But Phoebe had heard the giant's grunt; she glanced back and saw him hit the ground. With a stifled cry, she pushed the maid on. Completely disregarding the vicious gentleman clambering over the giant's fallen bulk, she rushed back, her attention fixed solely on the giant.

Deverell bit back an oath and glided forward, still concealed by the dense shadows.

To his surprise, the gentleman didn't spare Phoebe so much as a glance but, swearing like a trooper, started after the fleeing maid. He still carried the cosh in one hand and hefted a suspiciously thin walking stick in the other.

The maid glanced back, saw; with a smothered sob, she came stumbling along. Deverell stepped out of the deeper shadows into the middle of the lane—into her path. She shrieked as he materialized in front of her. His gaze beyond her, fixed on the gentleman—presumably the eldest Chifley scion—he caught the woman by her shoulders, in a few efficient moves divested her of her cloak, then pushed her on. "Go! There's a carriage waiting at the end."

He'd kept his voice low, but his tone wasn't one any sane

person questioned. Terrified, the maid gulped and fled.

As he'd expected, Chifley took him—a tall, large male shielding his fleeing quarry—for another lumbering guard. Spewing profanity, Chifley tossed aside the cosh and ripped the scabbard from his swordstick.

Brandishing the lethal blade, he came at Deverell.

Balanced on the balls of his feet, Deverell waited, still helpfully cloaked in shadows . . . until just the right moment to whip the cloak up, entangling the slim blade. Then he twisted and wrenched.

Chifley made a gurgling sound of surprise as the rapier was hauled from his grasp.

Deverell flung both blade and cloak aside, unbalancing Chifley. It was so easy after that. One powerful punch driven from the shoulder connected perfectly with Chifley's out-thrust jaw and the bastard's eyes rolled up, then silently, like a limp rag, he sank to the ground.

A panicked sound from behind him had Deverell glancing back. Contrary to all wisdom, the maid had stopped, perhaps paralyzed by fear. Her back to the stone wall, one fist pressed to her mouth, she was battling to hold back hysterical sobs. She was quivering uncontrollably.

He held up a hand, palm out. "Stay there."

Eyes huge, she managed a shaky nod.

Turning, he swiftly scanned the backs of the nearby houses. People had to have heard; they had no more than minutes if they were to get away unseen.

A few quick strides brought him to Phoebe and the giant. She'd managed to wrestle the huge man into a sitting position against the wall. Ignoring her and her utterly shocked gaze, he bent and spoke to the giant. "How bad is it?"

One hand to his head, the man glanced up at him, then winced. "Near to cracked m'skull." He sucked in a breath, then added weakly, "Luckily, it's thick."

Deverell managed to make out the words through the giant's heavy Scots accent. He nodded, then reached for Phoebe; closing his hands about her shoulders, he physically lifted her and set her on her feet. "Get the maid, and get into the carriage."

His tone brooked no argument, no dissension; when she hesitated, looking down at the giant, Deverell gritted his teeth and tersely added, *"Now!"*

Even she heard the warning. With a wary glance at him, she went.

Deverell shifted to the giant's side; as the man struggled to his feet, Deverell grasped one huge arm, ducked, and, pulling the arm over his shoulder, hauled the man upright.

He was unsteady on his feet; clamping one arm across the man's back, Deverell guided him up the alley. Glancing ahead, he saw Phoebe shaking out the cloak she'd disentangled from the rapier, then she swung it about the maid's shoulders and solicitously urged her on.

"Thank ye." The giant staggered forward as fast as he could; he'd accepted Deverell and his help without hesitation. "Someone musta heard that rooster. I'm thinking we need out of here right quick, afore they gather their courage and come looking."

"I'm glad to hear one of your little band has some sense." Ahead, Phoebe and the maid reached the mouth of the alley and turned toward the carriage.

"Aye, well. It's the first time anything's gone wrong." As they lurched toward the alley mouth, the giant added, "I keep telling her it ain't safe, specially fer the likes of her, but will she listen?"

Deeming the question rhetorical, Deverell made no answer. He was, however, determined that when he spoke to her, Phoebe would definitely listen—and learn.

* * *

Fifteen minutes later, he looked out of the carriage window as the huge trees of Hyde Park slipped past.

They'd escaped the alley and Hay Hill without anyone seeing them. Reaching the alley mouth, he'd seen Phoebe hovering before the open carriage door, watching. She'd caught his eye, and even over the distance she'd sensed his displeasure. Turning, she'd quickly clambered into the carriage.

He'd bundled the giant in, then followed, creating a crisis. With both him and the giant inside, space was tight; he'd ended sitting alongside Phoebe, with the still shivering maid opposite and the giant, whom he'd recognized as Phoebe's groom, wedged into the corner opposite Phoebe.

She was worried about the giant. In light of that, he'd held his tongue, biding his time. He would much rather have been across from Phoebe, able to see her face; as it was, in between quick, concerned glances at the giant, she kept it studiously averted.

Regardless of what she thought, what he could imagine she might fondly wish, she wasn't going to be able to fob him off, not after this evening's work.

And once he'd learned the whole of her secret, again no matter what she might fondly wish, she would not—not ever again—embark on any similarly dangerous enterprise such as he'd stumbled on—and rescued her from—tonight.

Just the thought of what might have happened had he not followed her . . .

Jaw setting, he kept his gaze on the park and continued to keep his thoughts to himself. For the moment.

The maid's hysteria had abated somewhat by the time the carriage turned off the cobbled street, maneuvering to enter, then rolling down a narrow lane running along the back of a long row of shops. Eventually, the horses slowed and the carriage was brought to a rocking halt.

Deverell glanced out at the rear of the narrow building behind which they'd stopped. "The Athena Agency, I presume?"

He looked at Phoebe, met her startled gaze.

When she said nothing, he reached for the carriage door, swung it open, and stepped down into the lane.

The driver was scambling down, concern on his round face. He, too, was a large man; Deverell had seen him before—in the lane by Cranbrook Manor wood.

Dropping to the ground, the driver eyed Deverell as he straightened. "Here, Fergus? You all right?"

"Aye," came from within the carriage. "We'd best get this lot inside—just make sure you tie m'horses up good and tight."

Deverell said nothing. Reaching into the carriage, he took Phoebe's hand and assisted her down, then did the same for the maid, who looked uncertain and faintly shocked by his courtesy.

Phoebe looked on, a frown in her eyes. She'd halted a few feet away, making no move to go inside. He knew without thinking that she was debating whether or not it lay within her power to dismiss him, to somehow send him away.

The driver went to the carriage door, leaning in to assist the giant. Leaving him to it, Deverell moved to Phoebe's side; gripping her arm above the elbow, he quietly murmured, "Don't bother even thinking it."

He didn't meet the sharp look she threw him. Lifting his head, he called, "Grainger?"

There was a rustle behind some barrels nearby, then Grainger stepped into view. "Yes, guv?"

"Keep an eye on the horses. We won't be long."

"Aye, guv."

Rather more than a trifle shaken, Phoebe watched Fergus,

now out of the carriage but leaning heavily on Birtles, pause to have a word with the lanky lad, who had clearly been keeping watch on their premises.

How had Deverell found out? How long had he known? How much had he learned?

Most importantly, what would he do with his newfound knowledge?

His fingers tightened about her arm. Head rising, she allowed him to steer her toward the back door. Miss Constance Spry, the Chifley's ex-governess, a quiet, rather timid but sensible young woman with excellent references and unimpeachable background, meekly followed; regardless of what had transpired, Phoebe felt entirely justified in having embarked on their precipitous rescue, inadequately planned though it had been.

Miss Spry's situation had been desperate. That had been apparent when, that afternoon at Chifley House, leaving Edith with Lady Chifley and the two other matrons who'd called, Phoebe had stepped out onto the terrace and seen, on a path to the side of the small garden, the petite governess struggling in the arms of Chifley, valiantly fighting to avoid being kissed. Phoebe had deliberately scuffed her shoe, causing both to look up; Miss Spry had grasped the moment, wrenched free, and run.

Chifley had looked at Phoebe, then looked after Miss Spry and laughed. Cruelly. It had been clear he would be after her, with even greater determination, at the first opportunity. Nothing was going to stop him until he'd ruined her; the fact that she was a vicar's daughter probably only incited him more.

Letting Miss Spry escape, with a sneer on his face, Chifley had started, deliberately, toward Phoebe. She'd turned and stepped back into the drawing room, feeling physically ill.

To her relief, within minutes of Chifley joining his doting

mama and her cronies, Edith, clearly struggling not to curl her lip, had declared that they had to leave.

Across the room, Chifley had bent an openly lascivious look on Phoebe; he'd certainly seen her well enough to recognize her. In the alley, however, in the dark, his attention had been fixed on poor Miss Spry. If he had recognized Phoebe, shock would have brought him up short; she felt reasonably confident he hadn't, that at least in that respect her secret was still safe.

Nearing the agency's door, she glanced back. Fergus was coming on slowly. She briefly scanned his face and inwardly winced at the pain she saw there. That was the only real regret she had over the night's events.

Despite the obvious drawbacks, even having Deverell find them had had its benefits; he'd rescued them, but more importantly he'd meted out some degree of punishment to Chifley, which was more than she would have been able to do.

For that, and his help with Fergus, she was willing to at least treat him civilly, even though he'd clearly been spying on her.

Reaching past her, he opened the back door; turning, head high, she led him inside.

The door gave onto a small dark hall; a few paces brought them into the large spacious kitchen at the rear of the shop.

Emmeline had been sitting knitting by the fire, with Jessica at the table nearby, quietly chatting. Both looked up eagerly as the sounds of the group's arrival filtered into the large room . . . then both women's faces blanked as Phoebe came forward and they saw Deverell, prowling larger than life, behind her.

Emmeline and Jessica quickly came to their feet. An awkward silence fell as the others shuffled in. Phoebe walked to the hearth, bent to warm her hands at the cheery blaze; the instant everyone was in the room, she turned and waved at

Deverell, who had come to stand alongside her. "This is Lord Paignton."

She said nothing more. The difficult silence lengthened, then Fergus groaned. Shuffling to the table, he slumped into a chair. "Begging y'r pardon, Miss Phoebe, m'lord, but m'head's fit to split."

Emmeline gasped, blanched; dropping her knitting on her chair, she hurried around the table. "Good Lord—what happened?"

She didn't wait for any explanation; she fretted and fussed, dispatching Birtles for clean rags and Jessica to fetch a bowl of warm water.

Phoebe stood by the fire and let the mild pandemonium reign; she knew it was Emmeline's way of coping, not just with the shock of Fergus's injury but with the even bigger shock of having a man like Deverell in her kitchen.

He was the epitome, outwardly at least, of the type of gentleman Emmeline had had good cause to flee years before. Phoebe glanced sideways at him, wondering if perhaps he might feel, or be made to feel, awkward enough to leave. He was frowning—at first she thought at Emmeline, but then she realized he was looking at Fergus. More specifically, at Fergus's cracked head.

Phoebe noticed Miss Spry, white-faced, her worldly goods clutched to her chest, trying to look inconspicuous against one wall. When Jessica returned with the bowl of water and placed it on the table by Emmeline, Phoebe beckoned to her. "Jessica—this is Miss Spry. Perhaps you would be good enough to take her upstairs and show her where she can rest."

Ignoring the looming, attentive presence by her side, Phoebe smiled reassuringly at the governess. "You'll be perfectly safe here. Once Emmeline has tended to Fergus, she'll come up and see you settled. Go with Jessica." Switching her gaze to Jessica, she added, "We won't need either of you again tonight."

Jessica nodded, a trifle overwhelmed, and turned away.

Although Miss Spry's eyes remained unnaturally wide, she bobbed a curtsy. "Thank you, miss." Then she swallowed, cast a fleeting glance at Deverell—one Phoebe noted wasn't so much frightened as awed—and said, "I owe you and your friends here more than I can ever repay. I won't forget."

Inclining her head with a certain quiet dignity, Miss Spry joined Jessica. Together, they slipped from the room.

Deverell heard stairs creak as the two young women climbed to the rooms above the shop. He returned his gaze to Fergus; after several more minutes of Fergus's grunted protests and Emmeline's exclamations and largely ineffectual fussing, he stirred. "Here—let me see."

He went forward, rounding the table to where Fergus sat slumped, his head propped in his hands. He noticed the stark fear that flashed in Emmeline's eyes but gave no sign that he realized it was due to his approach; she fluttered, but then, fists clenching, stood her ground on Fergus's other side.

"It's a . . . a *monstrous* crack." Emmeline wrung her hands as he leaned over Fergus, gently parting the man's thinning, curly hair to examine the severe contusion left by the viciously wielded cosh. Emmeline set her chin. "He should have a doctor see to it."

That had been her central plaint, one Fergus had thus far refused to countenance. However, the wound on the back of his skull was larger than Deverell had expected to see. It was mostly laceration, but . . .

Holding up three fingers a yard in front of Fergus, Deverell asked, "How many fingers?"

Fergus glanced up. A moment passed before he said, "Three."

Phoebe drew nearer; Deverell didn't need to look to sense

her increasing concern. He straightened. "I think Emmeline"—he nodded to the older woman—"is right."

Emmeline blinked, shocked.

When Fergus shot him a frowning glance, he added, "I tended enough battlefield injuries to know what needs a surgeon and what doesn't, and while I doubt it'll prove incapacitating, that wound needs to be looked at."

"A surgeon?" Phoebe glanced at Emmeline. "I can't think of whom—"

"If I could suggest," Deverell said dryly, "my colleagues and I at my private club have a surgeon on call, one who's accustomed to dealing with injuries such as this, and similarly accustomed to being discreet." He met Phoebe's eyes. "We can take Fergus there—it's not far—and I'll summon Pringle, our surgeon."

Looking down, he met Fergus's eyes, narrowed in pain. "Pringle knows more about such injuries than any man alive. He can check you over, then we'll all feel much happier. At the very least, he'll clean the wound properly."

Emmeline looked as if she couldn't believe her ears, as if she couldn't quite believe he'd offered to help.

Phoebe was regarding him, also with suspicion in her eyes, but not for the same reason.

He met her gaze and faintly raised his brows. He did indeed want her at the club, away from her people so he could question her—something he was reluctant to do before those here, all of whom clearly saw her as their mistress-cum-leader. That wasn't a position he wished to undermine; he simply wanted answers to his highly pertinent questions.

Her people also seemed uncertain over whether or not he posed a threat to her, and them, too; he didn't think he did—wasn't entirely sure why they were viewing him as they were—but that was another reason for shifting her interrogation to more conducive surrounds.

And if her concern for Fergus gave him the leverage to accomplish that, he wasn't too noble not to use it.

He continued to look at her, awaiting her decision—as did everyone else. She hesitated, but her concern for Fergus was stronger than her wariness of him and his plans. She nodded. "That's a very"—her lips thinned—"kind offer."

He suppressed a grin; she'd guessed his plans.

The next few minutes were filled with yet more fuss, during which he learned that Emmeline's husband, Birtles, was the man who had driven the carriage. He suggested that Birtles remain at the agency, his home, while Grainger drove Edith's carriage.

Fergus fretted about entrusting his cattle to the youthful Grainger; Deverell countered with the unarguable—that Grainger cared for and drove his matched grays.

Three minutes later, he led Phoebe out to the carriage, following Birtles and Emmeline, who were guiding the still unsteady Fergus between them. In short order, they were in the carriage and Grainger was driving them through the streets. Phoebe glanced at Deverell but said nothing; the lack of privacy was a major impediment—Fergus was sitting on the seat opposite.

For his part, Deverell was content to wait; they were, after all, heading into his domain.

Chapter 13

*P*hoebe stared out of the carriage window at the houses slipping past. Those hosting entertainments were well lit; guests were departing from some, the clop of horses' hooves and the revelers' gay voices ringing in the air. The evening was well advanced; a few blocks away in Mayfair, the haut ton would be gathering shawls and reticules and preparing to leave their balls.

She owned to a fleeting wish that she'd been among them and not facing a situation that could at best be termed difficult—but then Miss Spry would have been ruined. Jaw setting, Phoebe dragooned her wits into battle order and turned them on Deverell.

On how she was going to cope with him.

He was clearly going to be a very real problem. Indeed, after witnessing all he had that night, he'd become a real threat to her enterprise.

Tucked in the corner of the leather seat, her face turned

from him, she was nevertheless aware of him beside her—of his hard body, warm and alive, of steely muscles coupled with an incisive mind. Of his strength, not just physical but on numerous other planes as well.

He would be a formidable adversary. Could he be converted into an ally?

Or if not that, could she at least persuade him to keep silent?

She couldn't say; she would have to feel her way. The carriage turned down a quiet street. She inwardly grimaced. After he'd so blatantly used Fergus's injury to jockey her into coming to his club—into meekly walking into the lion's den—of one thing she felt sure: He would use whatever advantage fate handed him, wield whatever power he held and call in her mounting debts of gratitude to pressure her into telling him all—everything he wanted to know.

How to avoid that was what *she* needed to know.

The carriage slowed, then halted. Deverell leaned past her, opened the door, then stepped out. Turning, he offered his hand; clasping her fingers firmly, he helped her down to the pavement.

She looked about while he sent his lad—Grainger—hurrying up to the house. He returned in less than a minute with a footman; a precisely dressed, rotund, butlerlike individual followed.

While Grainger and the footman assisted Fergus from the carriage, overseen by the butler, Deverell led her up the paved path, past neat bushes and shrubs toward steps leading up to the house's—club's—front door. She glanced left and right; the building was similar to other houses on the street, in no way extraordinary. Number 12 Montrose Place flew no flag to indentify it as a club for wealthy gentlemen.

"This is your club?" She felt compelled to confirm that.

"Yes." Deverell glanced back at the others. "The Bastion Club."

He guided her up the steps and through the open front door. In the hallway—tiled and recently painted, fresh but rather austere, quite definitely masculine with its lack of ornamentation or anything as softening as a vase of flowers—he lingered, waiting for the others.

When all four were inside and the butler had shut the door, Deverell nodded toward Fergus, who seemed exhausted. "Put Mr. McKenna in the small parlor. Grainger—stay with him." To the butler he said, "Send for Pringle. Ask him to examine Mr. McKenna thoroughly—he took a nasty knock in the line of duty."

The butler bowed. "At once, my lord."

Deverell glanced at Grainger and the footman easing Fergus into the room to one side of the front door, then he looked again at the butler. "Are any of the others in this evening?"

"No, my lord. Just yourself."

"In that case, we'll break with tradition. Miss Malleson and I will be in the library." Releasing her, he lifted her cloak from her shoulders and handed it to the butler.

As if visiting a gentleman's club was an unremarkable event, she shook straight the skirts of her midnight blue walking gown—long-sleeved and buttoned to the throat, it helped her blend with the night—then straightened.

Deverell's fingers closed about her elbow; he turned her toward the stairs. "Summon us if we're needed. And send Pringle up when he's finished with McKenna."

"Yes, my lord." The butler hovered at the bottom of the stairs. "Shall I bring tea?"

Deverell glanced questioningly at her. She considered, then looked at the butler. "Thank you—that would be welcome."

Having something between them other than just words might be helpful.

Deverell steered Phoebe up the stairs, his fingers wrapped about her elbow more in case she required support than in any sense of restraint. As they gained the first-floor landing, he glanced at her face. Head high, she showed no sign of nerves, of being unsettled.

Most young ladies, even twenty-five-year-olds, could be excused for feeling decidedly shaky after the events of the evening. Releasing her, he opened the library door and stood back for her to precede him; she swept in, spine stiff—she was clearly made of stern stuff.

Following her inside, he closed the door and reflected that that was just as well; he had very little patience for feminine fluster.

He watched as she walked slowly across the room, taking in the quietly luxurious, distinctly masculine furnishings, the deep leather armchairs, the small polished tables scattered between, the well-stocked bookshelves and the sporting magazines lying discarded here and there.

Reaching the fireplace on the other side of the room, she glanced up at the wide mirror above the mantel, briefly studied his reflection in it, then looked down and bent to warm her hands before the sprightly fire dancing in the hearth.

He remembered she'd done the same in the agency's kitchen, yet the night wasn't that chilly, and her hands, when he'd taken them to help her out of the carriage, hadn't been cold.

She was nervous—or at least on edge—after all.

He headed toward her. She looked up and turned to face him. He waved her to an armchair angled beside the fire. While she moved to it and sat, he drew another around, positioning it across the hearth but further back from the flames. He sat and studied her.

He'd intended from the first to use the library; having Pringle see McKenna in the small parlor had simply been a useful excuse. They'd set aside the small parlor for meeting with females, but it was simply too small for his present need. If he paced, or if Phoebe paced, in the small parlor they would have been too close. Far too close given the subjects their discussion was slated to encompass and the instincts it was sure to abrade.

Let alone the feelings—the reactions, the emotions— already roiling through him.

Settling in the chair, sinking into the cushioning leather, Phoebe flicked a glance at the door, concern for McKenna patently riding her. Distracting her.

"He'll be all right." His subtle emphasis suggested that his reassurance didn't extend to her well-being.

Her eyes fastened on his face, her blue-violet gaze sharpening . . . then she shivered delicately. Crossing her arms, she rubbed her palms up and down her upper arms, as if she truly were cold . . . but the library was pleasantly warm.

He inwardly frowned but kept the expression from his face. She wasn't just unsettled; she was in shock but doing her damnedest to hide it.

A sound at the door had him turning; seeing Gasthorpe carrying a tray, he waved him in. Waiting while Gasthorpe solicitously laid the tray on a table close by Phoebe's chair, he grasped the moments while she and the club's majordomo consulted on who would pour and the need for sugar lumps to deal with the unsettling tilt and swing of his emotions, a sudden upsurge of concern for her swamping his violent feelings of just a few seconds before.

"My lord?"

Gasthorpe's voice drew him back; seeing the majordomo holding the teapot aloft, he shook his head. "No—I'll take a brandy."

He had a strong suspicion he was going to need fortification to get through the coming discussion without either misstepping and failing to learn all he now knew he absolutely had to know, or worse, queering his pitch irretrievably with Phoebe.

Watching her sip her tea, he let his concern for her wash through him, not fighting or trying to suppress it but letting it spread, sink in, and so gradually subside. Leaving his earlier, underlying feelings still standing, still turbulent, powerful and remarkably strong, a roiling, surging clashing sea swirling beneath his tightly reined temper.

Not just coloring his temper but giving it an edge quite unlike any he'd experienced before.

A clink of crystal reached him, then Gasthorpe appeared by his elbow, proffering a glass half-filled with amber liquid. He took it and nodded a dismissal. Gasthorpe bowed and withdrew.

He sipped, watched Phoebe cradle her cup between her hands and gaze at the fire. What he felt—for her, about her—wasn't familiar. He wasn't even sure why he felt as he did. But given that she now meant this much to him, given their ever-deepening, soon-to-be-consummated sexual connection, given that he wanted her as his wife not just because it was a logical decision but one defined and driven by something far more powerful than reason—given, therefore, that he would have to learn to deal with her, a being he definitely didn't completely comprehend—given all that, then exercising all due caution was assuredly the path of the wise.

She swallowed, then drew a deep, fractionally shaky breath, and held it—and he felt, once again, the ground shift beneath his emotional feet.

As if he were standing on quicksand, from both his point of view and hers.

"What, exactly, is the business of the Athena Agency?" He kept the words uninflected, let nothing more than even-tempered curiosity color them.

She studied him for an instant, then coolly replied, "That's none of your concern."

He held her gaze, let a moment tick by, then calmly stated, "Think again."

When she merely arched a brow, unimpressed, and said nothing, he took another sip of brandy, then evenly said, "Correct me if I'm wrong. You—through the agency—have been assisting female servants to escape from their employment, presumably when they become the target of unwanted advances from their male employers, or males associated with their employers. You've been using the income from the fortune you inherited from your great-aunt first to establish and subsequently to support the agency. You own the building the agency is housed in, but Mr. and Mrs. Birtles and a Mr. Loftus Coates are the named principals of the business."

Her face registered not just shock but another emotion that quickly resolved into outrage. "*How* did you learn all that?"

"I checked." Even now he was amazed, prey to a combination of surprise, fascination, and frank admiration that she had not only conceived the notion but had engineered it, given it life, and, as far as he could tell, successfully run the business for years.

Spine rigid, she'd narrowed her eyes at him. "Checked how?" Then understanding dawned. Her jaw dropped; for an instant she was speechless. "You . . . you used your . . . your contacts to investigate my finances?"

Her rising tone was a warning, one he ignored. He nodded.

Fury sparked, lighting her eyes, her whole countenance. "How *dare* you!"

Spots of color rose to her cheeks; she all but vibrated with righteous indignation. The reckless sea of emotions he was holding down surged in response to the accusation in her eyes; it would be easy, so satisfying, to let them erupt, but . . .

"Phoebe . . ." Outwardly unperturbed, he held her gaze, then quietly stated the bald truth, "When it comes to you, to matters involving you, matters that in any way might prove dangerous to you, there's little I wouldn't dare."

Phoebe heard the ring of abject honesty in his words. Inwardly aghast, battling to conceal it, she read the unsettling, disconcerting, ineradicable truth in his eyes.

Not only did he know, incontrovertibly beyond any hope of her disguising the truth, far too much—far more than was safe—but being him, the type of man he was, he would never let such "matters" rest.

And, *damn!*—she'd brought this down on her own head! She'd encouraged him to engage in a liaison with her—without having thought it through. Without having recalled, not until now when she was faced with the inevitable out come, that gentlemen like him had a tendency to assume responsibility for the women in their lives.

In a blink, she jettisoned any idea of him turning a blind eye, of her convincing him—no matter what she said or how long she argued, no matter any distraction or inducement she might offer—to simply walk away and let things be. Let her and the agency carry on as before.

But . . . there had to be a way. If he was a wall blocking her, there had to be some way around him—over or under or past.

She tried desperately to think, but her brain felt literally torn, wrenched and shaken, racked with worry for Fergus, laced with guilty regret that her rush to save Miss Spry had led to his injury, and simultaneously rocked by the realization that Deverell now had it in his power to completely overset all her careful work.

If he told *anyone*—Edith, even though she supported her without knowing the details, even Audrey, who was so eccentric yet would surely draw the line over a lady of the haut ton owning and actively operating an employment agency, let alone consorting with servants and members of the lower orders as she necessarily did—the entire enterprise she'd worked so hard and so long to establish would come tumbling down about her ears.

The man who sat in the armchair opposite quietly watching her was beyond doubt the most potent threat to her—on all levels—that she'd ever even imagined, let alone faced.

Eyes locked on his, green and unwavering, she assimilated that. Along with the fact that he'd made no threats, no decrees, no statements of intent. That he was waiting.

She thought back, reviewing their exchange . . . realized. Drawing in a slow breath, she shifted, easing her tense back. "What do you wish to know?"

He heard the question for the capitulation it was but gave no sign of gloating. "How do you know which females need rescuing?"

She drained her teacup, set it down, then told him of the network that operated throughout Mayfair and the major country houses, the housekeepers and butlers who knew each other, the interconnecting mesh of family and relatives who worked here or there, in this lord's employ or that lady's. "It's not hard to hear of the problem households if you're listening in the right quarters. Emmeline worked in a number of establishments, and she has seven sisters and two brothers, similiarly employed. Through them and her, word gets passed back to the agency."

"And then?"

"And then . . ." She drew breath and went on, "If we need to rescue someone from an actual residence, as is usually the case with a governess, I visit with Edith or one of my other aunts. It's not that difficult to arrange. I don't make direct contact with the young woman involved—that's always done through the housekeeper or whoever in the household alerted us in the first place."

"You go there to reconnoiter, to study the house and the approaches to work out how to mount your rescue?"

She could read nothing—neither was there disgust nor condemnation—in his tone. "Yes." She rose and started pacing before the hearth, rubbing the fingers of one hand, remembering various rescues they'd staged. "If, on the other hand, the girl's a lady's maid, dresser, or companion, and therefore likely to travel, it's often easier to rescue them from other houses."

"Such as the maid you rescued from Cranbrook Manor— Lady Moffat's lady's maid. I take it that was Jessica?"

She cast him a glance, then nodded. "Lord Moffat has a roving eye, and roving appetites as well."

She sensed a reaction then, a clear response, a tightening of muscles, a swift, involuntary flexing of steel instantly suppressed—but she had no notion what it meant. She didn't feel it was directed at her, but he remained so calm, so outwardly contained, that even though she could sense he was reining his reactions back, holding them in, even though she could see in his darkened eyes that he wasn't as unengaged as he was taking care to appear, she still couldn't tell what he was thinking.

What he might be considering doing with the secrets she was revealing.

She paced back and forth, casting quick glances his way; he'd fallen silent, thinking, eyes narrowed, face set, the angles unforgivingly harsh.

There was no sense in beating about the bush. Halting before the chair she'd vacated, she drew herself up, clasped her hands before her, trying not to clench her fingers in too obvious trepidation, and faced him. "What are you going to do?"

He blinked, looked up, and focused on her face. Frowned. "Do?"

The incomprehension in his face—as if he had no idea that he held the fate of something she'd worked for years to achieve in his hand, that it was his to smash at his whim— ignited her temper. It flared, infusing her with an almost frenzied fury, lighting her eyes. "Yes," she hissed. *"Do!"*

Flinging her hands in the air, she abandoned her suppli- cant's stance and fell to pacing again—a great deal more vigorously. "I'm perfectly well aware that the ton would be horrified to learn of my 'enterprise.' That one word from you to almost anyone, but especially to my father, would bring the whole to a crashing halt!"

Agitated, she wrapped her arms about her, swung to face him, and again demanded, "So what are you going to *do?*"

"Ah." Deverell nodded to indicate he understood her ques- tion. What he didn't understand was how he should answer.

Being able to rapidly assess any situation was an ability he'd taken for granted for years—until now. Now he couldn't decide—didn't know what he felt, didn't even have clear in- stincts to guide him. A species of horror over what he could imagine she'd been doing warred with admiration, even pride, at her novel tack and the courage and commitment she'd displayed in getting such an "enterprise" underway, let alone keeping it active.

He kept his eyes locked with hers and drew a long, deep breath—more than anything else to give his head a moment to clear. She was keyed up, tense, on edge; the last thing he wanted to do at this point was to take a wrong and poten- tially seriously damaging step with her. One rather less civi- lized part of him was seriously irritated that she'd think he would harm her in any way whatever. Against that, the same primitive side wanted to roar at her over the danger she'd been courting, as exemplified by the evening's events . . . but roaring at her wouldn't help—him or her—especially as he had no intention of disrupting her enterprise.

"Who's Loftus?" That was one thing he hadn't yet learned. It was a point that might prove decisive.

She narrowed her eyes until the blue-violet seemed purple; her jaw had set long ago. "Tell me what you're going to do first. I don't want him damaged by anything that happens—he doesn't deserve that."

He frowned at her, but his heart wasn't in it. Her tone painted Coates as another of her people, someone she felt obligated to protect. There was none of the heightened trepidation that would signal Coates meant more to her than, for instance, McKenna.

"What I'm going to do. . . ." His mind grasped a situation it recognized—negotiation—and finally got to work, seeking the right words, the phrases, the best approach to achieve his objective. An objective that hadn't, of itself, at any stage been in doubt. The instant he'd learned of her "enterprise," he'd known without thinking what he wanted.

But she had to agree.

He had to persuade her.

To cede him what he now had to have.

"Very well." Holding her gaze, he evenly said, "Consider my position. I now know you regularly put yourself into situations that are utterly and unquestionably beyond acceptable for a tonnish lady—both in terms of your reputation and even more in terms of your personal safety."

She frowned, irritated. "It's not usually dangerous."

He arched a brow. "Tell me . . . what would you have done if I hadn't been there tonight? You and little Miss Spry would have been left facing an enraged man, one who'd come chasing a small and helpless female with a cosh in one hand and a swordstick in the other. Allow me to inform you rational argument wouldn't have worked."

She had the grace to blush; he suspected she also quelled a shiver. "That was the first time any such trouble has occurred."

"Indeed. It did however occur, and it occurs to me that you owe me a debt in that regard."

Lips compressed, she studied him, then asked, "Where are you headed with this?"

His lips eased, but his smile was intent. He kept his eyes fixed on hers. "Knowing what I now know, the ton at large would consider me unquestionably obliged to inform your father." Her eyes flared; he held up a staying hand. "However, there is an alternative—one that would be acceptable to me and to the ton should they ever learn of the matter. That alternative requires me to make myself responsible for your protection, both in terms of your reputation and your physical safety."

Her eyes narrowed, darkened. She held herself very still, then quietly stated, "That's the definition of a husband."

He shrugged lightly, still holding her gaze. "Husband, protector . . . lover. Call the position what you will, it's one I and the ton recognize. Either one of the three could apply in this situation."

He intended to claim all three positions, simultaneously, eventually, but saw no reason to push the point. Not yet; now was not the time.

Phoebe studied him for a long moment, then swung and slowly paced. A minute ticked by, then she halted and looked at him. "What would this—being my protector in this case—entail?"

"You would have to include me in any action to do with your enterprise that could in any way harm your reputation or even remotely put you in danger." He tilted his head, considering, his eyes on her. "Or, indeed, brought your enterprise into danger. Protecting it would be a necessary part of protecting you."

She frowned. "And if I agree, you'll allow me to continue—the agency to continue—as it has to this point, unchanged? Without interference?"

That last was the part she couldn't bring herself to believe.

But he nodded without hesitation, his green gaze unwavering. "Provided you abide by my stipulations, then you and your people will be free to proceed as you always have, with the one proviso that if there's any danger, I will step in and do whatever is necessary to ensure your safety—and that of your people and your enterprise as well."

She was confused—not by his offer but by the fact that he'd made it. She couldn't make him out; she didn't understand him or his motives.

Watching her, Deverell felt that for the first time that night, some control over events was returning to him. He gave her a moment more, then arched his brows. "Well?"

He knew very well that she had no real choice. She knew it, too.

She continued frowning at him, but then, in clear capitulation, she drew a long breath and nodded. "Very well. On the basis of what you just said, I accept your proposition."

"Good. Now who's Loftus?" It was a point that bothered him, this unknown male.

To his relief, his concern was misplaced. Loftus proved to be a reclusive middle-aged philanthropist who'd learned of the agency's work through his housekeeper, when she'd hired a girl from the agency and he'd questioned the forged references the agency had provided. Since learning of them and their enterprise some three years before, Loftus had supported them in myriad ways, both financial and practical.

"He's one of our best sources for new positions for the girls we help. Despite his restricted lifestyle, he hears of things in his circles—wealthy merchants who are looking for a well-trained governess, or who need a lady's maid for their daughter. That sort of thing."

Loftus was clearly not an enemy; indeed, be might well prove to be an ally.

A knock on the door had them both looking that way. When he called, "Come," Pringle walked in.

Deverell rose and greeted him. He introduced Phoebe as McKenna's employer.

Pringle bowed; straightening, he stepped back as Gasthorpe slipped past to remove the tea tray. "I've checked the wound, cleaned and treated it. McKenna's lucky he has a thick head— beyond a headache that might last a few days, I doubt he'll suffer any lasting injury. The wound itself should heal well enough, and give him no further trouble."

Deverell thanked the dapper surgeon; Phoebe smiled, added her thanks, and gave him her hand. After bowing over it, Pringle withdrew; Gasthorpe had already left with the tray.

One glance was all it took to tell Deverell that Phoebe's mind had refocused on McKenna. He'd got the vital agreement he'd wanted from her; it seemed an opportune moment to move on and let that point rest.

"Come." He waved her to the door. "Let's see how McKenna feels, and if he's up to it, I'll see you both home."

She nodded and headed for the door; opening it for her, he followed a step behind her as she went down the stairs. "McKenna—he's your groom as well as your coachman?"

"My father hired him to be my groom when I was eight. Whenever I stayed with my aunts, which was most of the time, he took on the role of coachman as well. He doesn't like to be idle."

Deverell said nothing, but the suspicion that Lord Martindale had hired McKenna to be rather more than a groom—that Fergus had become her coachman to ensure he would be able to watch over her when she was out of the house—solidified. McKenna considered himself her guard; that was why he'd accepted Deverell's assistance so readily.

Why, when Deverell followed Phoebe into the small parlor and Fergus looked up, he studied Deverell for only an instant before giving his attention to Phoebe. Fergus knew Deverell posed no threat to her.

Deverell stood back and let Phoebe fuss, then stepped in and rescued Fergus. McKenna assured Phoebe he was perfectly well able to withstand the journey to Park Street.

"Grainger will drive us," Deverell said. "You can travel in the carriage, then Grainger can stable the horses—all you need do is watch and tell him where."

Fergus grunted, but assented.

Grainger had been waiting by the door, still eager over being a part of what he viewed as an adventure. In short order, Deverell had them all organized; he guided Phoebe, once again cloaked and hooded, down the path behind Fergus, Grainger, and a now largely redundant footman to the waiting carriage.

Minutes later, they were rolling, slowly and ponderously, through deserted streets. The ton's entertainments were long over; while gentlemen might while away the rest of the night at their clubs in St. James, in Mayfair all was quiet and largely still. Lights had been doused, doors locked and bolted. There were few people of any sort out upon the streets.

Fergus had insisted he was recovered enough to ride up top, alongside Grainger, leaving Deverell alone with Phoebe in the dark confines of the carriage.

Through the heavy shadows, he felt her gaze on his face, not exactly suspicious but wary. He didn't react, made no move to reengage her in discussion of her enterprise or anything else.

There was, as he'd told her, a correct time, a correct place, for everything. Their right time and place was nigh; he didn't need to do anything but wait.

Under Fergus's direction, Grainger guided the carriage into the narrow lane that ran alongside Edith's Park Street town house, leading to the mews backing onto the end of the long garden.

Grainger halted the carriage in the mews. They all climbed down quietly. His hand beneath Phoebe's elbow, Deverell arranged with Fergus that after helping him unharness and stable the horses, Grainger would help him up the stairs to his room above the carriage house.

"I'll see Miss Malleson inside." Deverell glanced at Grainger. "When you're finished here, head back to Montrose Place."

"Aye, sir." Grainger snapped off a salute, then crooned to the horses, urging them to pull the carriage to the stable.

Fergus nodded his thanks and followed.

Grasping Phoebe's arm, Deverell turned her; the garden gate, a thick wooden door set in the high wall along the side of the garden, faced the lane.

After one last glance back, she let him lead her around the corner to the gate. "Thank you for helping with Fergus. He's not as young as he used to be."

"None of us are." The gate was unlocked; swinging it wide, he steered her through.

Other than a sharp glance, she said nothing more regarding Fergus, but pointed to a key hanging on the wall by the gate. "You should lock the gate after you when you leave—toss the key back over the wall and I'll pick it up tomorrow."

He'd simply lock the gate without the key but saw no

reason to mention that. She led him along the path toward the kitchen door, then diverged onto a connecting path that skirted the back of the house.

He'd wondered how she came and went; the answer was the French door to what he guessed was the morning room. It, too, was unlocked; opening it, she led the way inside.

Phoebe wasn't surprised when he followed her into the darkened room. She never left lights burning; she knew the house more than well enough to find her way to her chamber in the dark.

What did surprise her—what brought her up short before she'd reached the spot where she'd planned to turn, give him her hand, thank him, and bid him good night—was the sharp click of the lock on the French door.

Halting, she started to turn—and discovered he'd followed much closer, much more swiftly and silently than she'd supposed.

He was behind her, close.

She stilled, and he moved closer yet, one large hand sliding about her waist, gently but definitely trapping her against him.

He bent near; she felt his chest at her back, his thighs bracketing hers as he drew her against him. Felt his fingers brush aside the curls at her nape, then his lips touched, brushed. Closing her eyes, she fought to quell a too-revealing shudder and failed.

Then his voice, deep and dark and sinfully dangerous, brushed over her ear, slid across her senses. "This night is not yet ended . . . for us."

He hadn't forgotten; she'd thought he had.

Every nerve in her body came alive, awoke on a rush of anticipation at the promise of long-desired gratification.

She hesitated, not quite believing the moment had come. "Here?"

Even to her ears the question was purely curious.

His lips cruised her nape. "I'm staying at the club—I can't take you to my bed there. So . . ."

He paused, and she waited, breath bated, wondering why she felt as if she'd been captured. Why she felt so deeply thrilled.

His hand shifted across her waist, pressing more firmly; his strength flowed around her, indescribably male, primitively real in the dark.

Then he pressed a hot, wet, open-mouthed kiss to her nape, on her spine, then ordered, his voice gravelly and harsh, "Take me upstairs to yours."

Chapter 14

*H*e followed close behind her as she led him up the stairs. Not touching her, yet close enough that her nerves constantly leapt, unstintingly aware of him.

As they stepped into the gallery and she turned to the front of the house, he leaned close and murmured, "Where's Edith's room?"

"At the back." A restless sleeper, her aunt had always preferred the quieter room, but these days Edith invariably drank a tisane on retiring, after which she could be counted on not to stir until morning. By then . . .

They neared the door to her room.

"Your maid?"

"Asleep." Skinner didn't wait up for her on the nights she performed a rescue; her maid needed to be awake and about early the next morning in case there were any unexpected details requiring attention.

As she reached her bedchamber door, an acute awareness

that she was alone with a man in the dead of night, that there was no one near, no one who would hear any scream or moan, swept over her. No one to interfere; no one who would save her. She was even more aware, to her tingling fingertips aware as she reached for the door latch, that the man in question was immensely powerful—strong, masterful, used to his own way—used to seizing what he wanted, and that if he so wished, he could do whatever he wished with her. To her.

And he would.

That was his intent as he followed her through the door.

Why she wasn't frightened was a mystery; instead she felt a lancing thrill of excitement, of eager anticipation.

Yes, she'd wanted this, wanted him to want her, and get to the point of taking her, but in the back of her mind a question had lingered: Would she balk at the last moment?

Would her old fears, those fears he'd inadvertently prodded to panicky life but which subsequently he'd been canny enough to circumvent, rise up and prevent her from learning what she so desperately wanted to know, from experiencing all she had thought she never would, even now, even with him?

To her immense relief, the answer seemed to be no.

She halted in the middle of the floor and turned to face him.

He'd closed the door; he walked unhurriedly toward her, looking about, taking in the large four-poster bed with its emerald silk draperies tied back with tasseled cords. The ornate headboard sat against the outer wall; the two windows flanking it looked over the street.

The curtains over both windows were tightly drawn, blocking out even the moonlight; the room was lit only by the flickering glow of a small oil lamp on her dressing table. He glanced around; to her surprise, he seemed to be examining the furniture. Reaching her side, he pointed to the three three-armed candelabras set about the room, adorning the chest of drawers, one of the bedside tables, and the small Pembroke table she had her breakfast on.

"Light those."

A frisson of expectation slithered down her spine. A bed, he'd wanted, and light . . . light so he could see her as he took her. She remembered his tone as he'd said that; the promise in his voice echoed in her mind as she gathered the three candelabras, lit one candle from the lamp, then used it to light all the others.

From behind her came shuffling sounds; grasping two of the candelabras, she turned—to discover he'd moved both bedside tables out so one stood midway down each side of the bed, about three feet away from it.

He gestured to the tables. "Place those there."

She did. While she returned to fetch the last candelabra, he strode to the Pembroke table.

Her heart was galloping when she raised the candles. Turning, she saw that he'd placed the small rectangular drop-leaf table parallel to the end of the bed.

She approached, the table between them.

He nodded to its polished surface. "Put that there."

She did, careful not to spill any wax.

As she straightened, he reached over the table and caught her hand. Drew her around the table to him as he turned and surveyed the bed, awash in the golden glow cast by the nine candles. "Perfect."

Releasing her hand, he slid his arm about her waist, gathered her to him as he looked down and caught her eyes.

Caught her chin on the edge of his other hand and tipped her face up. Let his gaze linger on her features, then again met her eyes. "Now . . . to my next requirement."

Her, naked, with not a stitch to hide behind.

The words slid through her mind as he bent his head. Her lids fell.

His lips covered hers, supped, sipped, then his thumb pressed on her chin; he opened her mouth and swept in.

And simply took—as he wished, as she wanted.

He demanded and she gave, he commanded and she yielded—gladly, willingly, eagerly. It was a game, one she'd learned, one he'd taught her—one she was desperately keen to play. One that gave her all she needed, and promised even more.

Then he drew back and looked down. "Take off your bodice."

Without a blink she set her fingers to the tiny buttons closing the long-sleeved bodice, separate from the skirt, very ready to shed the already-too-tight garment; her breasts had firmed even though he'd yet to caress them, already hot and aching for his touch. While she worked her way down the long row of buttons, he filled his hands with her bottom and molded her against him, shifting against her in a flagrantly suggestive way, cradling the hard length of his erection against her soft belly.

Then her bodice was open; she swiftly shrugged it off—but with a gasp stopped halfway, her arms still entangled, her head arching back as he lifted her against him, boldly licked one furled nipple through her chemise, then having dampened the material, swirled his tongue around the aching peak, closed his mouth around it, and suckled. Hard.

She shrieked—managed to swallow the worst of the sound, but then he transferred his attention to her other breast, and she moaned.

He stripped the bodice from her arms, let it fall. Immeasurably grateful, she raised her arms, sank her hands into his hair, and clutched him to her as with lips and tongue he feasted—and gave her her fill.

Until she burned.

His hands had continued to knead her bottom, sending waves of sensation surging deep within her. Building, growing, a burgeoning need.

Then his grip eased and he let her slide down until her feet touched the floor.

He raised his head, and she realized his breathing was ragged—nearly as ragged as hers. "Your skirt and petticoats—take them off."

As much a growled plea as an order; her fingers were at her waist, flicking the ties undone, before she'd thought.

Instinctively she understood. *Her, naked,* was something he wanted her to give him—to gift to him. In return for the pleasure she knew awaited her in his arms, it was a gift she was more than willing to bestow.

Her skirts and petticoats hit the floor, and his hands were on her. His lips claimed hers again, and this time it was different—this time he wasn't anywhere near as in control; this time he tasted dangerous.

Wonderfully, powerfully alive—wholly male, wholly driven. By desire, for her, for her body, to take it, claim it, possess it. To make her, and it, his.

All his. Every inch, every nerve. Every leaping pulse.

Every gasp, every moan he wrung from her.

She clasped his face between her hands and kissed him back. As wanton as he was flagrant, as abandoned as he was masterful.

As giving as he was demanding.

As yielding as he wished.

As she wanted.

For oh, she wanted this—the fire, the passion, the heady desire, the uninhibited whirling of her senses.

The heat, the flames that licked, then roared, the molten fire in her veins.

And he was with her this time, not an observer of her pleasure but a wholly engaged participant—and she rejoiced. Exulted in the hard grip of his hands as he held her, the unslaked lust that edged every caress, the desire that burned and turned his body to hot iron, unforgiving and searing, the hunger—urgent and needful—that drove every ravenous kiss, every greedy, grasping touch.

It was she who abruptly caught her breath, broke the kiss and pushed back from him—so she could grasp the hem of her chemise and strip it off over her head.

His hands closed about her and he hauled her against him before the silk left her fingers. She gasped at the contact of bare skin to clothes, then his lips came down on hers and he drank her cry as his fingers squeezed tight about one furled nipple.

She arched in his arms, the movement shifting her sensitized skin against his clothing, abrading thousands of nerve endings alive and flickering beneath her flushed skin. His hand left her breast and possessively roamed, over her waist, her belly, to her curls. He speared his fingers through them, then pressed one hard leg between her thighs, forcing them apart; his fingers slid between, found the flesh he sought already slick and swollen. He cupped her, and thrust first one, then two fingers deep.

Nails digging into his biceps, she hung on as he worked his fingers within her, then withdrew and returned, again and again, pushing her on, harder, faster, more ruthlessly than before.

She couldn't catch her breath, physical or sensual, couldn't stand against the fiery tide he called up and sent raging through her.

He pressed deep and she shattered, came apart in his arms, her cry muffled by his lips.

For long giddy moments all she knew was sensation, and

the reassuring strength that held her, surrounded her, lifted her. . . .

He laid her on her sheets, the covers discarded, trailing over the end of the bed, her head on her pillows, her hair tumbling down to spread like dark red flames around her head. Her limbs he arranged in a feminine sprawl, one more revealing than she would have chosen, her arms out from her sides, leaving her breasts exposed, legs flat to the sheets but with one knee bent to the side . . . she blushed when she realized that he was looking at her, examining her as he stood at the end of the bed, toeing off his shoes, stripping off his clothes.

The candles bathed her in golden light, but it was his gaze that kept her warm.

That heated her through, and gave her the courage to lie there, wantonly asprawl, and let him look his fill.

The urgency investing his every movement filled her with a sense of awe—that she, her body, his desire for her, his need to possess it—could affect him, the highly controlled, usually so contained, ruthless and powerful gentleman to such an extent.

To the point that his hands shook as he lowered them to the buttons at his waist.

Lifting her gaze over his ridged abdomen, over the sculpted planes of his chest, lightly laced with crinkly black hair, over the breadth of his heavily muscled shoulders and upper arms, the strong tendons in his throat, she reached his face—and saw . . . a ruthless intensity that should have sent her fleeing.

That should have shaken her to the core, frightened her, pricked her old fears to new heights . . . yet didn't.

His gaze was on her body, wholly absorbed, wholly focused and intent.

The sight of his face, of the stark, unforgiving intent to

possess that was etched so clearly in the patrician planes, struck her like a blow to the chest—to her heart.

His trousers hit the floor; he stood naked before her.

She didn't let her gaze drift down. Instead, when his gaze rose and collided with hers, all fire and passion and need, she raised her arms, opened them to him—offered her body and herself to him.

His eyes narrowed for a second, drinking in her surrender yet knowing it wasn't. That it was more, something other, something else.

Something he was powerless to resist.

He knelt on the bed, crawled, a large prowling beast, the short distance to her. With one hand, he rearranged her legs, spreading them apart; he came up between, one arm bracing alongside her shoulder taking his weight as he fitted his hips between her widespread thighs.

As he reached between them and set the broad head of his erection to her entrance. He nudged a fraction in, then removed his hand, planting that palm on the other side of her. Caging her. Holding himself above her as he slowly thrust into her.

Watching her.

As he eased inside her and her body stretched, adjusted— as her lungs tightened, her eyes widened . . .

He swooped, bent his head and captured her lips—and heat exploded within her all over again.

He knew exactly how to call forth her fire, how to make her writhe and burn beneath him. How to make her yearn, and gasp, and want. To make her arch and demand—

He thrust deep—one powerful flex of his spine and he impaled her.

Pain struck like lightning, searing her. Her muscles clenched; she remained arched, head back, eyes closed, gasping, her fingers locked on his upper arms. Her body all his, offered and now taken, claimed irrefutably. . . .

The pain faded.

He drew back from the kiss, just far enough to be able to focus on her eyes. His breath harsh and sawing bathed her lips as she forced her lids up and met his gaze.

Greener, darker, burning.

"Are you all right?"

His tone was steady, even, but the words were so gravelly she took a moment to make them out.

Took another moment to consider her answer. To register the feel of him, hot and hard buried so deeply within her, so foreign, so indisputably male, so strangely welcome. To register the weight of him holding her down, his hips pinning hers to the bed.

To realize she was safe and . . . that pleasure beckoned.

She met his gaze, licked her lips, then looked at his. "Yes."

It was the last word she uttered for some considerable time.

He'd said he would teach her and he did; he taught her more than she'd imagined there was to learn about the pleasure she could find in a man's arms.

In his arms.

Her mind made the correction instinctively; she didn't question its rightness. Instead she devoted herself, her mind, her senses, her body to his lessons.

To the heat and the slick dampness of their joining, to the play of their bodies one against the other, to the tantalizing brush of skin against skin—hers silken soft, his harder and hair-dusted, more abrasive over flesh that was also harder, heavier—his body impressed itself on hers in myriad sensual ways.

His lips and fingers explored her face, her lips, her throat, her breasts, treated her to caresses that traced the long line from her waist over her hips to her knees; every touch was more intense, heightened, colored by the fact that this time he was joined with her.

Clever fingers and palms lingered on her flexing thighs, sculpting, tracing, making her even more aware of the steady rocking rhythm as his body rode hers, primitive and triumphant, then with a gentle nudge he lifted one thigh, curling it about his hip, tilting hers beneath him, opening her to a deeper, more intimate penetration, to a deeper, wholly glorious binding.

The golden candlelight washed over them as he guided her ever onward through a landscape that was familiar yet different, where the colors were stronger, the feelings more intense, sharper, where her senses were more alive, more hungry, more needy, more vulnerable. More open. He whispered guttural words of encouragement as, helpless, she writhed beneath him. As he introduced her to the mindless craving, to the blinding need to touch, to feel, to climb, to spin the sensual pleasure out and out and out, to find and reach that elusive peak of glory.

She gasped, eyes closed, fingers sinking into hard muscle as pleasure surged higher, as her nerves tightened and coiled. And still he pushed her on, steady, unwavering, relentless.

Deverell braced his arms and rose above her, looked down on her as the reins of passion slithered and slipped from his grasp, as, breath ragged, he thrust more deeply, then deeper still into her welcoming body, flushed and writhing beneath him, wantonly seeking both her pleasure and his.

Her hands clutched in desperation, then eased, released, drifted—only to clutch again as the next wave of passion caught her and lifted her higher.

And higher.

He was nearly blind with need, with sheer lust and wanting. Every long stroke into her scalding sheath, every instinctive clamping clasp of her slick flesh about him—the most evocative embrace a woman could bestow on a man—pushed him further, drove him harder, made it that much more difficult to cling to control.

Yet he fought and kept his pace slow, steady, unrelenting—the only way possible to spin the road out long enough to let her go at her own pace. To let her find her way up the mountain to the peak—rather than having him whip her up, use his expertise to harry and hurry her. In some detached corner of his mind he knew that was important, that in this she should never know—never would need to know—just how much power he wielded over her, how completely subject to his will she was. That she was so much less strong, not just weaker in body but in knowledge and expertise, that if he so chose, in this she could be his victim.

He wouldn't so choose, and she wouldn't be, but she didn't need to know she could be.

So he fought to guide and not to drive, to let her find her own way. . . .

To heaven. She came to it in a rush, in a glorious, mind-numbing crescendo of desperation; he watched her crest, watched her body rise beneath his, clinging, holding, then helplessly surrendering, letting go and releasing.

At the last moment, he bent his head and drank her cry, in a sudden surge of primal possessiveness ravaged her mouth—

And his reins snapped. Broke. Flew apart.

His body plundered hers, desperately seeking—and then he was there, joining with her, senses reaching and twining with hers, his body hers as hers was his and the glory fused them.

He was lost, in that instant blind, deaf and dumb, beyond

thought or words or reason. Held above her, his body shuddered, racked by pleasure one last time as he emptied himself into her yielded flesh, into the hot, indescribably soft haven her body had become.

His, all his.

With a groan, he surrendered, let himself down upon her, wrapped her in his arms and held her close.

Two hours later, Deverell lay back on Phoebe's pillows and ruthlessly channeled his thoughts away from the soft, warm, too-tempting female body curled with her back against his side.

She fitted perfectly, heaven-made for him.

And his rapacious needs, but that was one of the realizations he was battling to block from his mind. Later would be soon enough to dwell on such matters. Now . . . now he needed distraction.

The candles had guttered, plunging the room into a comfortable dark. His eyes had adjusted; it was almost pitch black, but he could make out the furniture, enough to be able to rise, dress, and leave without noise.

Not that he had any intention of doing so just yet.

Once again he steered his mind away from the prospect of what might transpire between now and him leaving. Jaw setting, he refocused on other things—any other thing that might fill his mind; he had to at least give her a little more time to recover from what had, even to his jaded senses, been an engagement of significant and quite startling sensual dimensions.

Dwelling on elements of that engagement wasn't going to help.

The only other thing engaging enough to distract him was his wider plans for her, and how they were progressing. All in all, he was pleased, indeed, smugly satisfied. The unexpected chance to learn the secret of the agency wasn't an opportunity he could have passed up; he'd had to grasp the moment to pressure her into telling him all . . . not that she had. She had carefully avoided any mention of what had moved her—a well-bred, wealthy young lady of the haut ton—to embark on such an esoteric career.

His eyes narrowed in the darkness; the reason wasn't hard to guess. Some bastard—some marauding wolf in gentleman's clothing—had tried to force her. . . . He cut off the thought, blocked the mental vision; his reacton to it was too violent and might disturb her, still slumped and slumbering by his side. Regardless, said ravening wolf had clearly not succeeded in raping her; his actions, however, had left scars.

He would never forget the fear he'd inadvertently triggered, more than once. He'd overcome it, worked his way around it, but that fear had been deeply etched. She was—as he'd known from the first moment of setting eyes on her—a sensual woman. Highly and richly so, the sort of woman made for men like him who could match and fully appreciate them. Yet that fear had blocked her path, had prevented her from enjoying her own nature, from developing and taking pleasure in it as she could and should, from being all she could be . . . but he was there now.

Tonight had been fated in more ways than one, a scheduled step in his plan to use her sensual nature to persuade her into matrimony, yct after learning the true nature of her agency and how she ran it, after guessing the connection to her fear—regardless of any plan, he would have made love to Phoebe tonight, compelled to demonstrate that her fear was only a hurdle, not a barrier, that all the pleasures a woman could enjoy could still be hers.

And on some other level entirely, after the dangcrs of the night he'd felt driven to capture and possess her, to make her finally, ineradicably, and indisputably his.

He shifted, seeking a more comfortable position, more in his mind than in the bed. The emotions she evoked in him were not entirely familiar; even the familiar urge to conquer and possess was edged with something deeper, more fundamental and powerful.

Those new and altered feelings made him uneasy, a trifle wary, but he had his goal before him, and that hadn't changed. Not in the slightest.

He wanted Phoebe as his wife, was now beyond determined on that. Beyond committed. And on that path, he was progressing well.

This evening she had, albeit under duress, accepted him as her protector. An hour ago, entirely willingly, she'd accepted him as her lover. Of the three positions he'd so sapiently named, he had only one more to claim, but wisdom dictated he consolidate his hold on the two he'd claimed tonight before he made a bid for the last.

He glanced at her. Hair deliciously tousled—as it never otherwise was—she looked like the houri he'd told her she should train to become.

A niggle intruded, his imperative need to ask her about the man who had harmed her. He would one day, but instinct suggested now was not the time to raise that issue—their intimacy was too new, too fragile.

So . . . as there was nothing he could sensibly do to strengthen his position as her protector, wisdom dictated . . .

Turning toward her, he raised a hand, set his palm to the curve of her naked shoulder, then slid it slowly down.

Phoebe came awake to find her body had woken before her, that it was already heated, responding in wanton abandon to caresses so explicit she might have blushed if she hadn't already been so flushed. So filled with sultry passion.

Lying on her side, sunk in her bed, with Deverell a hard,

hot male wall behind her, she closed her eyes and followed the intimate play of his fingers. Let her senses submerge beneath the tide of sensual longing.

Felt the tide catch her, felt desire swell and rise.

She murmured his name. Before she could turn to him, he leaned over her, raising her upper thigh, bending her knee, pressing it to the bed . . . he slid into her. Slowly, smoothly. Deep.

Until the hard hot length of him filled her.

Then he withdrew and pressed in again, stretching her sheath, filling her to the hilt, to the point where she felt he was nudging her heart when he thrust the last inch.

She heard a gasp as he repeated the slow, deliberate movement, realized that it was hers, that her fingers had tangled in the sheet, clutching spasmodically as he continued to ride her in this different way. Continued to pleasure her deeply, unhurriedly, languidly.

Over and over. The conflagration within her built, and built, the end approaching much more quickly this time— but then he slowed, eased back, penetrated her less deep ly . . . and the firestorm, denied, retreated, shrank back.

Hovered. Then he returned to thrust hard and deep; the flames roared and greedily rushed in—only to be denied yet again . . . and the pleasure grew.

Burgeoned, filled her, sank to her bones.

Filled her mind, captured her senses.

She wanted to give the pleasure back to him, wanted, in an instant of startling clarity, to lavish on him the same sensual delights he was so assiduously giving her. But how?

His weight held her pinned, his chest to her back, one heavy arm snug over her waist, his hand cradling her breast, long fingers stroking, gently kneading in time with the rhythm of his loving.

She tried to twist to catch his eye but couldn't, tried to

shift her hips against him, then realized and tightened about him as he pressed deep.

And was rewarded when he halted, buried deep within her, and hissed in a breath. He held it for an instant, then exhaled and picked up his rhythm again.

He leaned close; his lips traced the curve of her ear, then his breath brushed over it. "All you have to do is lie there and be ravished."

Coming out of the dark behind her, his tone, deep and gravelly, was perfectly gauged to send a shiver down her spine.

His lips returned to her ear, lightly brushing, then he pressed a kiss to the sensitive skin beneath it, then trailed light kisses down the taut line of her throat. Then he spoke again. "Naked, in the dark of the night, in this bed . . . you're mine, remember? My houri, my pleasure slave, to do with as I wish."

He eased his shoulders back, released her breast, and sent his hand skating down, over her waist and around to evocatively stroke her bottom. "To possess as I wish. Like this, with your lovely arse to my groin, your body supple, soft and pliant, prone beneath me, helpless to prevent me taking all I want, as I want."

Against the pillow, her lips curved. She didn't think she was entirely helpless. . . .

Lasciviously, seductively, she squirmed, flagrantly encouraging him to do his worst. To take her more aggressively, more definitely. To ride her more deeply.

Blatantly challenging him to forget about her pleasure and take his, to slake his lust in her very willing body.

He hissed in another breath. She tightened her inner muscles, simultaneously wriggling . . .

He swore. And the dam broke.

His hand clamped about her hip, ruthlessly held her down

as he shifted, adjusted, then did as she wished. Set aside his control and took her without restraint.

The fire howled through them both, harsh and hot, ravenous and greedy. It burned and consumed, cindered all constraint, left them both gasping, senses reeling, struggling to see, to know, to grasp.

The pinnacle of pleasure.

And the consequent bliss.

The first shattered them, ripped and shredded them, hurling their senses beyond the world.

The latter fell on them, doused the last flames, enfolded them in the cocooning arms of satiation, and healed them.

Wracked, exhausted, they lay slumped in the bed, wrapped together, unable to move, the thundering of their hearts one beat in their veins.

She couldn't breathe, but she didn't care. At the last he'd roared her name, and at the last she'd been there, with him, together, in no way apart.

Hours later, he rose. Phoebe sensed more than felt him leave the bed; she turned and watched as he gathered his clothes in the dark, then started to dress.

He glanced up, saw she was awake. "It's nearly dawn—I have to go."

She heard the reluctance—real, sincere—in his voice and was inwardly delighted. From him, she felt sure reluctance at this point qualified as a compliment of the highest order.

Recent events had, she decided, made decorum redundant; she let her gaze roam the planes and bulging muscles of his body, the long lines, the dips and hollows she'd gained a much better sense of, indeed, appreciation of, through the last hours. There was absolutely nothing there she didn't like.

Settling back on the pillows, she let her gaze rest on him and let her mind explore the changes the hours had wrought.

In her, courtesy of him and his particular brand of loving.

She wasn't such an innocent that she didn't know that the way he approached her, the words he said, the fantasies he created in her mind and fed were deliberate, knowingly gauged to seduce and sensually ensnare her. And she wasn't such a prude not to acknowledge that he was right, that all those things were not only necessary, needed to ease her past her old fear and into intimacy, but they also heightened and deepened her enjoyment of the act.

From the first, he had read her very well, and while she wasn't at all sure she approved of that ability, she couldn't pretend she didn't appreciate the outcome.

Gone was her fear, vanquished—made as redundant as modesty and decorum, at least between them.

So yes, she felt . . . blissfully sated all the way to her toes, her body glorious and more alive, more whole, more real, more engaged with the world, and she owed it all to him. Gratitude was what she should have felt, but as her gaze rested on him, she was very aware that it wasn't simply gratitude that filled her.

Inwardly, she frowned. She wasn't sure what she truly felt, only that it went deep and stirred her in ways she hadn't before encountered.

He sat on the bed to pull on his boots. She stared at his broad back and wondered.

She didn't want him to leave, although she accepted he must. But it was her certainty that she wanted to see him again, to invite him to her bed and her body the next night, and the next, that troubled her.

Such a fascination—wanton and real, unfettered now they'd indulged to the point of intimacy—wasn't going to make her life, the decisions she would need to make, any easier. Her simple plan to embark on a liaison, short-lived and soon over, had headed down a track she hadn't intended . . . and now he'd learned about the agency and her secret, her "little crusade."

The events of the past night had created an upheaval in the landscape of her life. How should she respond?

As he rose, glanced at her, then came around the bed, she rephrased her question: How was she going to manage him?

He halted beside the bed and looked down at her. After a moment, he reached out, with the fingers of one hand lightly stroked her cheek. Then he caught her chin, tipped it up, leaned down, and kissed her—gentle and sweet.

"Take care." He breathed the words against her lips, then released her and straightened. He hesitated, then said, "I'll call on you later in the day."

With a nod, he turned and silently crossed the room. Even though she was watching, she barely saw the shadow that was him open the door and slip through, then the door closed, and he was gone.

With a sigh, she sank back and stared up at the dark canopy. There was simply no sense in imagining she might draw back and bring their liaison to a quick end, not before she'd fully explored all the pleasures to which he could introduce her and, even more, learned of all the ways in which she could pleasure him.

Learning one without the other seemed immensely unwise; if he was going to be able to hold her senses hostage, she wanted to be able to reciprocate. That, to her mind, seemed eminently sensible; she shouldn't give him—or any man—any unnecessary advantage.

As matters now stood, every time Deverell came near her, she felt an illicit thrill—an expectation of forbidden, deeply sensual delight. Every time his eyes met hers, every time he touched her, however innocently, she thought of being with him, alone, in his arms.

Now she would think of having him between her thighs,

or behind her, of the indescribable pleasure of him joining with her.

Of course, he was the only man with whom she could imagine engaging in such activities, so obviously the time for her education in this sphere was here and now.

With him she had a chance to explore all that fate had left her ignorant of, and there was no way she would turn aside from that. No matter the risk . . . if she was honest, to her heart. It was that that had stirred when minutes ago she'd stared at him through the dark.

She pushed the thought away; in attempting anything worthwhile, there was always some risk. Witness the agency.

Tugging the covers up, she snuggled down. As matters now stood, there was nothing to prevent her from accepting Deverell's standing offer to fully experience her sensual self, to explore her own nature and come to know and understand the full gamut of all as a woman she could be.

That was important, as important as all else.

"And he already knows about the agency."

Closing her eyes, she willed herself to sleep; to her surprise, she succeeded.

Chapter 15

L ate that morning in a town house in fashionable Arlington Street, just around the corner from St. James, Malcolm Sinclair paused outside his guardian's study. After an
instant's hesitation, he raised a hand and knocked.

"Come in!" Henry barked from within.

Opening the door, Malcolm did as he was bid.

Henry sat behind his massive desk, papers spread before
him. An imposing figure with steel gray hair, he was engaged in transcribing a judgment; a downward twitch of one
corner of his thin lips was his only acknowledgment of
Malcolm's presence.

Unperturbed, Malcolm quietly shut the door and crossed
the room on silent feet.

Henry glanced up from beneath beetling brows as Malcolm gracefully sat in the chair facing the desk. He scruti-
nized Malcolm's impassive countenance, and as usual could

read nothing in it. "Well?" he demanded, his brusque tone giving warning of his ire over having been disturbed.

Malcolm dutifully reported, "It appears we have a problem."

Settling himself elegantly, he observed his guardian's harsh-featured face and waited with his customary patience. Others sitting in that particular chair would have felt apprehension, certainly a degree of nervousness, but Malcolm had been Henry's ward from the age of six; he'd grown accustomed to his guardian's arrogant and contemptuous severity, inured to the effect of his unmitigatingly hard and ruthless presence.

While Henry believed his was the superior intellect, Malcolm knew better; he, however, saw no reason to correct Henry's mistake.

Henry humphed and returned to his writing.

The *scritch-scratch* of his pen continued, the dominant sound in the room. Malcolm let his gaze roam, taking in the gleam of wooden stocks, of finely wrought iron and steel, the glint of brass inlays, the sleek, destructive lengths of the numerous pistols mounted on the walls. Henry's obsession with pistols—for obsession it truly was—never failed to amaze him, a curious insight into the incalculable folly of an otherwise careful man.

To Malcolm the assembled pistols, valuable antiques and rarities though they were, were merely guns, tools to be used if necessary but otherwise relatively uninteresting objects.

To Henry they were passion. And desire—definitely desire.

Indeed, his desire to acquire one of Napoleon's personal pistols had reduced Henry's funds to the almost embarrassing. And now with the final end of the war, there were pistols from defeated French marshals coming onto the market. Henry was eager and ever-greedy for funds.

He finally came to the end of his paragraph. He looked up to dip his nib in the inkpot. "What problem?" He didn't bother looking at Malcolm.

"That sweet little governess we were to pick up from Chifley. She's gone."

Henry paused, then lowered his pen, and finally looked at Malcolm. *"Gone?"*

Malcolm toyed with the idea of making Henry repeat himself but decided against it. "Indeed. She ran away—or should that be escaped?—last night. According to Chifley it was organized—there were others, including guards, waiting in the alley to help her get away."

Henry's lip curled. "And you believed him? That posturing bantam can't keep his pants buttoned. Are you sure he didn't give her a poke and she fled into the night?"

Malcolm smiled thinly. "In the normal way of things, a likely possibility, I'll allow. However, in this case, I'm inclined to believe him. Aside from his disgruntled manner— I'd swear the girl had eluded his manly embrace—he's sporting a bruise on his jaw that certainly didn't come from the door he told his mother he'd walked into."

Frowning, Henry set down his pen. His expression darkened as he considered the possibilities, as Malcolm had already done. Pale eyes narrowing, Henry tapped a yellowed fingernail on the parchment before him, the final judgment on a man's life, now forgotten. "That sounds like we have some other gang pursuing the same game as we—*in our territory.*"

Malcolm inclined his head. "There's more. I'd heard rumors that female staff had gone missing while attending house parties with their mistresses. As that action wasn't here, in Mayfair, it didn't seem relevant, and indeed, the first two instances could have been mere coincidence. Now, however, another lady's maid—Lady Moffat's—has vanished from

Cranbrook Manor. Together with this latest incident . . ." He gestured deferentially. "I think your deduction may well be correct." He paused, then diffidently asked, "What are your orders?"

Henry's eyes narrowed to shards of flint. "Find out more." He paused, then his fist clenched and his voice took on a darker note. "If there's a gang of interlopers operating around here, they're poaching on our turf. Clearly we need to teach them a lesson. *And* exact retribution."

Trust—it was all about trust. In wooing Phoebe, it was the most vital element he had to establish. And in that respect, Deverell felt he was progressing exceptionally well. All he had to do was capitalize on his success to date and further deepen her implicit trust in him.

His way forward was clear. Of necessity, women trusted the men they slept with; now Phoebe had allowed him into her bed, into her body, he'd cleared that hurdle and had gained that most fundamental of trusts, but it was unquestionably in his best interests to consolidate his position and allow that trust to deepen, as it naturally would over time, over more interludes.

Until eventually she was sufficiently enamored of him to happily entertain the notion of marriage.

He hadn't lost sight of his ultimate goal, and now that she'd entrusted him with her secret life—her involvement with her agency—he had another facet of her trust to pursue.

Apropos of that, he presented himself at Edith's town house at noon. The butler showed him into the morning room—the French door of which he'd locked on his way out seven hours before.

Phoebe was there, along with Edith. After exchanging greetings with her aunt, he turned to her. "I wondered if you'd care to take a drive in the park, Miss Malleson?" When she looked at him blankly, he added, "Or perhaps, as the day is so fine, we might venture a trifle further."

To Kensington Church Street, for instance.

She blinked. "Oh. Yes. That is . . ." She drew breath and found a smile. "Thank you. A drive in the park would be pleasant. That is"—she turned to Edith—"if you're sure you can manage without me, Aunt?"

"Oh, indeed, indeed." Edith beamed at Deverell. "It's only Lady Hardcastle's this morning. I'll do perfectly well on my own."

"In that case, if you'll wait, my lord, I'll fetch my bonnet and cloak." Phoebe rose and headed for the door, then paused and glanced back at Edith. "You will remember if you meet Lady Purcell . . . ?"

Edith smiled and waved her on. "Of course, dear. If I see her I'll drop a word in her ear."

With a nod, Phoebe turned and left.

Once upstairs, she summoned Skinner; while she set her bonnet over her hair and tied the wide ribbons under her chin, she explained she was going to the agency to check on Miss Spry and Jessica, too. "She'll be leaving with Lady Pelham tomorrow—I must check that she has everything she needs. How's Fergus?"

"Still laid down upon his bed." Skinner gave Phoebe's cloak a sharp shake. "Luckily that lad of his viscountship's has called around and offered his services—said as his viscountship said as he ought. Fergus said he helped him last night. Seems the old Scot's willing to trust his horses to the lad, so he'll drive Mrs. Edith to her engagements today. Fergus swears he'll be better come evening."

Phoebe glanced at Skinner's tight expression; she was worried about Fergus, and about Phoebe, too. Phoebe had told her about the trouble at the Chifleys' and how Deverell had helped them. Skinner's opinion of "his viscountship" had noticeably mellowed.

Standing, she let Skinner swing the cloak about her shoulders, then, tugging on her gloves, she went downstairs.

Deverell stood waiting in the front hall. "Edith's gone to get ready for her visit." Taking Phoebe's hand, he turned to the front door.

Phoebe shot him a sharp look as she walked beside him. She'd jumped at the chance to visit the agency; she hadn't until that moment wondered why *he* was so keen. He appeared his usual, arrogantly confident self; going down the steps beside him, she told herself it was merely understandable curiosity on his part—a wish to know how the agency worked, given that he'd elected himself its protector as well as hers.

A niggling little voice murmured that men like him were wont to take charge, to insist on running any enterprise. Jaw setting, she let him hand her into his curricle; they would see about that—just let him try.

"How much does Edith know of your little enterprise?"

The question pulled her back to the present; picking up the reins, he set his grays trotting.

She took a moment to find the right words to answer. "She knows, yet she doesn't." She caught his eye as he glanced at her. "Edith's one of those people you don't have to explain things to—she's terribly *knowing*. She sees and understands, and somehow just *knows*. And in this case, she and I have left matters like that—if she hasn't been told, then if Papa asks, she can with a clear conscience say she's heard nothing."

Somewhat to her surprise, Deverell nodded, accepting her odd description. "But if you were to disappear, or she needed to contact you urgently, would she know where the agency is?"

"No, but everyone else in the household knows. And she knows they do. She'd simply ask Henderson to send a message to me."

He nodded again. "So why is Edith having a word with Lady Purcell?"

She inwardly grimaced; she'd hoped he hadn't picked that up. "Because although Edith knows no details, she does understand the thrust of the agency's work. Lady Purcell is Lady Chifley's sister, and a much more sensible sort of lady."

His eyes narrowed. "Edith was with you when you met young Chifley yesterday afternoon."

"Yes, so she's guessed enough to see the value in mentioning to Lady Purcell how troubling she found her nephew's behavior when we called . . . and then Lady Purcell will no doubt hear of the governess who ran away, put two and two together, and being the sort of female she is, she'll take her sister aside and have a stern word in her ear, and with any luck Lady Chifley will be much more careful over what sort of female staff she brings into her household."

A moment passed, then he murmured, "Very neat."

He tooled them through the busy thoroughfares around the park, then turned into Kensington Church Street, drove past the agency and around to the rear. Drawing rein in the lane, he deftly backed the curricle into the narrow space immediately before the agency's back door, moving the horses out of the laneway before halting them and applying the brake.

As he stepped down—a distinctly strange sight in that locale, with his drab, many-caped greatcoat and glossy Hessian boots—two urchins, wide-eyed and wondering, came sidling down the lane to stare.

Deverell saw them; he beckoned. They edged closer, unsure, but then he spoke, asking them if they could keep an eye on his horses.

Phoebe couldn't see what he passed them, but their faces lit, they nodded and pocketed his largesse, then took station at the horses' heads. Deverell went with them, showing them how much rein to leave loose, then giving them the ribbons. Then he rounded the carriage and handed her down.

Phoebe eyed the large, powerful grays. "Are they safe?"

She glanced back at Deverell in time to see his lips twitch.

"I assume you mean the boys, but yes, my cattle are excellently well behaved."

She read the message in his amused green eyes: Excellently well behaved, just like their owner. She humphed and led the way inside.

Emmeline was in the kitchen, standing over the table kneading dough. Miss Spry stood beside her, grinding nuts. Birtles sat in the chair by the fire, keeping out of the way. He grinned and rose as Phoebe entered; he nodded to her, then rather more warily at Deverell as he appeared behind her. "M'lord." His gaze returned to Phoebe. "How's Fergus?"

"Improving but still under the weather. He swears he'll be well by this evening." With a smile for Birtles, Phoebe went to Emmeline. "Biscuits?"

Emmeline had frozen, her gaze on Deverell; she shook herself, looked down at her hands, then nodded and resumed working her dough. "I thought to send some with Jessica tomorrow—for the trip." Emmeline glanced at Miss Spry beside her. "Constance kindly offered to help."

Phoebe pulled a straightbacked chair to the table and sat. "I hope you've recovered from your ordeal? It was certainly a shock, having him chase you like that."

Constance Spry glanced up and met her eyes; a small smile curved her lips, then she looked back at the mortar in which she was grinding almonds and walnuts. "It helped seeing his lordship hit him. Now whenever I think of him, I see his eyes rolling back and him going down like a sack of onions."

Phoebe grinned at the image; busy with Fergus, she hadn't seen what Deverell had actually done, only the results. "Before I leave today, we must talk—you, Emmeline, and I—so that we have some idea of what sort of position will best suit you. But first, I must speak with Jessica."

Emmeline nodded, her gaze fixed on her dough. "She's upstairs packing."

Behind her, Phoebe could hear Birtles and Deverell talking, something about horses. He seemed inoccuous— well-behaved—enough, and Birtles well knew his wife's difficulty over large and powerful gentlemen; Birtles wouldn't let anything upset Emmeline.

Reassured, Phoebe rose and headed for the stairs.

She found Jessica in the small room at the rear of the first floor, carefully folding her few belongings and setting them in her battered satchel. She looked up and beamed when she saw Phoebe, and quickly bobbed a curtsy. Phoebe smiled back, well-pleased; the panicked look had gone from Jessica's eyes. Just a few days with Emmeline and Birtles, free of any hint of threat, and Jessica was once again the bright, cheerful lass she should have been.

"You'll manage very well with Lady Pelham. Just remember . . ." Perching on the edge of the narrow cot, Phoebe described her ladyship's eccentricities, and also gave Jessica a potted history of the family, so she would know what gentlemen she might expect to encounter, without making a point of it informing her that they were all rather old and staid, and therefore unlikely to pose any problem.

Downstairs, Phoebe heard a deep voice saying something, then the bell on the front door of the agency tinkled, and the door shut. She inwardly frowned. Had Deverell gone out?

Rising, she wagged a finger at Jessica. "One thing—if ever you do run into any difficulties of that nature again, do remember that you can always return to the agency. But in

Lady Pelham's household, you won't need to worry—her housekeeper and butler are excellent people."

Jessica blew out a breath. "It'll be such a relief, miss, not having to guard against . . . well, you know, every minute of every day." Jessica rushed on to thank her; Phoebe held up a hand, stemming the flow, and told her to enjoy her work with Lady Pelham, and that would be thanks enough.

Leaving Jessica reassured and firmly focused on taking up her new position, Phoebe returned downstairs. She turned right along the narrow corridor that linked the shop at the front with the kitchen. As she reached the kitchen's threshold, she realized the voices she was hearing—Emmeline's and an indistinguishable male rumble—were coming from the shop; when she glanced into the kichen, Constance was alone, neatly forming the dough into shapes on a baking tray.

"Just tell me where. Up here?"

Startled, Phoebe swung around. The cultured accents were Deverell's. She walked quickly to the archway giving onto the shop, trepidation rising. Was Emmeline alone with him? Was she panicking . . . ?

The sight that met her eyes brought her up short. Far from panicking, Emmeline was directing a viscount—a large, powerful, overwhelmingly male lord—as to precisely where she wished several big boxes containing various files to be placed on the high shelf running along one side wall.

Setting one box on the shelf, Deverell stepped back, dusted his hands, then turned to pick up the next. He saw Phoebe, met her eyes. He hesitated for a second, then hefted the box. "Seeing I was here to keep an eye on you all, Birtles stepped out to order some coal."

He said it as if it were the most normal thing in the world for a viscount to be left at the beck and call of females running an employment agency.

"A little to the right, my lord, if you would." Apparently

subject to the same delusion, Emmeline stood back and pointed. "With a little bit of space between—that way Birtles will be able to grab each easily when we need it down again."

Deverell followed her directions without a murmur, then turned to heft the next box.

Mentally shaking her head, Phoebe stood in the archway and struggled not to stare.

That was the start of a very odd week. If she'd paid more attention to the incident with the boxes, perhaps she would have been rather less surprised by, or at least better prepared for, the subsequent developments.

Over the following days, having gained an inch, Deverell steadily invaded her world. And not just her daytime world but that of her nights, too; having once found his way to her bedchamber, he had no difficulty retracing his steps on the following and subsequent nights, much to Phoebe's confusion.

She wanted him there, in her bed, yet every night she felt she was falling deeper under his spell, deeper in thrall to the magic they wove, not independently but together. That was the most enthralling aspect—the give and take, the reciprocity of pleasure, of desire, of need.

There was so much she'd yet to learn, yet every night's lessons only made her more eager, more curious, more involved.

A dangerous situation.

An unsettling portent.

The days proved even more confounding. Deverell had an amazing knack of reading people, and therefore knowing just how to smooth feathers, as he'd proved with Emmeline. And therefore Birtles. Within forty-eight hours, he'd become an accepted member of her little band, viewed by all the others as one of them. Even Skinner, who hadn't actually met him but had only heard of his exploits from Fergus, jetti-soned her heretofore prickly view of "his viscountship"; she still irreverently called him that, but her tone made it clear the title was no longer one of contemptuous dismissiveness.

Unlike her easily-won-over staff, Phoebe was signifi-cantly more suspicious, not of his good intentions or his trustworthiness but of the wisdom of allowing a gentleman like him too great an involvement in her domain.

She kept expecting him to take charge. Indeed, she was firmly convinced he wouldn't be able to help himself, that he would at some point find the temptation simply too great and, with the best of intentions, usurp her position. Through those first days she remained constantly on guard, keyed up, ready to repel any encroachment on his part—and time after time he met her eyes, smiled, and waited for her decision.

It was thoroughly disconcerting, and not a little discom-posing, to find herself constantly wrong-footed over him, al-beit only in her mind, in her expectations. It was equally lowering to realize that he read her as well as, if not better than, he read all the others; he seemed to know just how far he could go without triggering her defenses, unerringly to know when stepping one inch further would bruise her toes.

And he'd stop. And defer to her.

After six days of constantly watching him, of constantly having him around, both at the agency and in the evenings at her elbow in the ton, helping here, assisting there, pro-tecting always, even she mentally threw up her hands and consented to be impressed. Consented to admit, if only to herself, that he was one of that exceedingly rare breed of gentleman who did not constitutionally require to be for-ever in charge.

Not that she told him; he needed no encouragement.

And *then* she discovered that, courtesy of his particular talent for business, he was perfectly happy to sit down with the agency's ledgers and accounts and add, check, balance, and record—all with an ease that bespoke considerable experience—and her resistance crumbled.

As she'd remarked to Skinner that evening while primping to meet him at Lady Parkinson's ball, any man willing to step in and spare her that ordeal was worth tolerating.

Skinner had humphed and cast a glance at her new gown. "Tolerating . . . is that what this is?"

She'd blushed and said nothing more.

A week after Jessica had happily left for her new life with Lady Pelham in the country, Phoebe sat in the agency's kitchen with Emmeline by her side, going over their lists of female staff looking for positions, discussing possible matches with their list of households looking to hire.

Their "rescue work" comprised only a small part of the agency's activities, a necessary condition to allow them to successfully and unobtrusively place their special clients. After four years of operation, the agency boasted a considerable list of female staff placed, had an enviable if select reputation among those seeking work in the capital, and a significant clientele among the households of the ton whose housekeepers returned again and again when looking for maids, dressers, governesses, or companions.

Deverell listened to Phoebe's and Emmeline's comments with half his mind; the other half was engaged in matching recent receipts with a list of projected costs. The agency didn't have a budget; he'd decided it needed one, and as finance was one area in which Phoebe seemed happy to give him free rein, he was engaged in formulating one.

An activity that kept his mind sufficiently busy and his boots under the agency's table—alongside Phoebe's.

The bell over the agency's front door tinkled; they all looked up and heard Birtles, minding the counter in the shop, greet whoever had walked in. "How was Harrogate, sir?"

Phoebe and Emmeline exchanged surprised and delighted glances, then Birtles continued, "Come you in then, sir. Miss Phoebe's here and will be right pleased to see you."

Deverell rose as both Phoebe and Emmeline pushed back their chairs and stood to greet a large, older gentleman, white-haired and well-dressed, neat yet rather somber.

"Loftus." Smiling, Phoebe advanced, hands outstretched.

"Mr. Coates." Emmeline beamed.

Loftus Coates took Phoebe's hands in his, a shy, avuncular smile wreathing his face. "I fear the waters didn't agree with me, so I returned somewhat earlier than I'd anticipated."

Coates's gaze had found Deverell; his voice died away.

An easy smile curving his lips, Deverell rounded the table and offered his hand. "Deverell—Paignton, for my sins." He still hadn't got used to his title.

Coates released Phoebe's hand and gripped his.

Deverell continued, answering the question in Coates's mind, "I'm assisting Miss Malleson in her endeavors."

"Oh?" To Coates's credit, he showed no inclination to retreat. He looked at Phoebe.

Deverell looked at Phoebe. And waited.

She met his eyes briefly, then looked at Coates. "Indeed." She glanced again at Deverell. "Strange though it may seem, Paignton has indeed been very helpful." She gestured to the chairs about the table; as they all moved to sit, she went on, "We had a spot of bother while rescuing our latest special client."

Coates frowned; he waited for Phoebe and Emmeline to sit, then took the chair opposite Deverell. "Spot of bother?" He considered Phoebe for an instant, then turned his gaze on Deverell. "I take it there was some threat that Fergus and Birtles couldn't handle?"

Meeting Coates's dark eyes and seeing the real concern therein, Deverell recalled thinking that Loftus Coates might well prove an ally. Inwardly congratulating himself on his farsightedness, he nodded. "A cosh and a swordstick."

Coates's lips thinned; he turned a reproachful gaze on Phoebe. "My dear—"

She stopped him with an upraised hand. "Before you begin any lecture, I've accepted Deverell's offer of . . ." She caught herself before saying "protection," caught his eyes for a brief moment then smoothly continued—"an additional escort, additional help whenever we perform a rescue."

Coates studied her for a moment, then transferred his gaze to Deverell. After a moment, he nodded. "Very well. I'll say no more on that head. Instead, I'll ask what I came here to learn—is there any special client you need help with placing? If you performed a recent rescue, I imagine there is."

Phoebe nodded and proceeded to tell him of Miss Spry. It quickly became apparent that Coates had a large network of acquaintances and business associates, wealthier merchants, bankers, and the like.

"A governess of impeccable character with some experience with very young children. I really don't think she'll be difficult to place, my dear." Coates smiled at Phoebe. "Leave it with me. I should have an answer in a day or two."

Phoebe exhaled. "If you can manage it, we'd all be very grateful. She's a lovely young woman, but we've nothing in our books that would be suitable, and with the news about the Chifleys' loss still doing the rounds in the ton, I fear it wouldn't be wise to look in those circles."

"No, indeed. Not for Miss Spry, and not for the agency, either." Coates glanced at Deverell, then looked back at Phoebe. "You really do need to exercise great care, my dear. No placement is worth the risk of jeopardizing all the good work the agency still has before it."

It was a gentle rebuke, yet Deverell was grateful to Coates for making it; it absolved him of the need. At present he was doing his best not to tell Phoebe things she didn't want to hear, but he could only go so far down that road.

Phoebe grimaced but merely rose as Coates did.

Deverell rose, too.

After shaking hands with Phoebe, Coates turned to him. "Perhaps, Lord Paignton, you could spare me a few minutes?"

Deverell smiled. "Of course." Avoiding Phoebe's immediately suspicious gaze, he waved to the front door. "I'll walk you out."

With a gracious nod, Coates accepted; he turned back to Phoebe. "I'll be in touch in a few days, my dear." With a nod to Emmeline, Coates turned and followed Deverell up the corridor.

They both nodded to Birtles at his post behind the counter, then Deverell held the door for Coates and followed him onto the pavement. By unspoken agreement, they strolled a few yards until they were beyond the agency's windows.

Coates halted; he stared across the street and awkwardly cleared his throat. "I assume I don't need to inquire as to your intentions, my lord."

Deverell waited until Coates turned his head and met his eyes. "No."

Coates studied his eyes, then nodded; Deverell glimpsed fleeting relief in his. "In that case, might I ask your . . . ah, stance as to Miss Malleson's activities with the agency. I should tell you that I've assisted in my small way for over three years, and in that time I've come to admire and, figuratively speaking, greatly applaud the work Miss Malleson has accomplished in saving so many poor girls from . . . from . . ."

"An unenviable and undeserved fate?"

"Indeed." Chin firming, Coates nodded. "Just so."

Deverell looked down, frowned slightly as he considered

his position—considered the right words to describe it. "I see no reason—none whatever—to disapprove of Miss Malleson's intent with regard to the females she rescues. Indeed, like you, I find her actions admirable. However, I cannot, and will not, permit her to place herself—or indeed, as I've informed her, any of her people or the agency itself—in any danger. Of any kind."

Looking up, he met Loftus Coates's eyes. His voice firmed. "My stance, therefore, is that as I have no wish to curtail her activities, I must of necessity join in them—but as her protector, her shield. That's my purpose in joining her little band—keeping Phoebe, and all her works, safe."

Coates held his gaze for a moment, then briefly smiled. He held out his hand. "Thank you. I believe we understand each other. It's a relief to know Phoebe has such a shield. If you ever need assistance of the sort I'm able to give, I'll be honored to provide it."

Deverell smiled and gripped Coates's hand. They parted, and he returned to the agency, still smiling, just a little smug.

He knew what he was doing, or at least he'd *thought* he did. But as the days went by and he learned more about the agency's operation and scope, Deverell found himself increasingly drawn in. Not just because of Phoebe, because it was her enterprise, the daytime activity about which her life revolved, but for the purpose itself.

Two nights later, lying pleasantly sated beside Phoebe in her bed, he stared at the canopy above and pondered the depth of his developing interest in the agency's work. Perhaps it wasn't such a fanciful notion that a man like him, one who had spent so many years in pursuit of his country's greater good, should be attracted to the battle Phoebe was waging. The scale might be a great deal smaller, the field more circumscribed, yet it was still a battle between good and evil, between right and wrong—and it was waged largely undercover, yet another aspect that made the whole seem comfortable and familiar to him.

He felt like he belonged. As if working alongside Phoebe, keeping her and the agency safe, was a position that had been crafted especially for him—the answer to the restless, unsettled feeling that had gripped him over the past months. His lack of purpose . . . but was it fair or right to make Phoebe's purpose his?

Beside him, she snuffled, wriggled closer, her bottom to his side, then sank back into slumber.

Inwardly smiling, he turned his mind to the day just passed, and those before that. He was starting to find a certain rhythm, a pattern to his days; he was actively searching for it, constructing it. During the mornings he generally left Phoebe to her visits with Edith; it was essential for her to maintain her position as Edith's "shadow," always there, always listening, learning, quietly questioning. She often returned from those visits with information on households and possible positions for the agency's clients. Over those morning hours, he took care of any estate business, looked in on Montague, and dealt with any business matters requiring his attention.

In the afternoons, he usually dropped by the agency; by the time he'd chatted with Birtles and learned from Emmeline about the day's developments, Phoebe would have finished her afternoon visits and would join them. The next hour or so would be spent on agency business. His background enabled him to offer novel solutions to some of the problems; every such instance sent a glow of satisfaction through him, somewhat to his surprise.

But it felt good. His association with Phoebe's agency was bringing him a return he hadn't expected. He was increasingly grateful to them—especially Phoebe—for accepting his services, for allowing him into their circle.

His wandering thoughts drifted over the past day, one not so routine. Lady Castlereagh had hosted a picnic at the family's estate in Surrey; Edith had declared she would be too tired by the drive, so he'd driven Phoebe down in his curricle and spent the day at her side. His appearance in that position had further fueled speculation, but of that Phoebe thankfully continued to be oblivious. She'd remained focused on her goals—keeping her ears open for possible positions—and in that, he'd seen a chance to assist.

Leonora, Countess Trentham, had been present, along with Trentham's redoubtable great-aunts. Recalling that his fellow Bastion Club member and his wife accommodated a startlingly large number of older ladies in their various households, he introduced Phoebe and stood back.

Until her marriage, Leonora hadn't spent much time in the ton; she and Phoebe hadn't previously met. He wasn't, however, the least bit surprised when they seemed to recognize each other as kindred spirits. By the time he and Phoebe parted from Leonora, the women were well on their way to becoming firm friends. Leonora, by no means blind, had invited Phoebe to call, and there had already been mention of the Athena Agency.

While the ladies had chatted, he'd considered the network of households, of wives and their friends, that courtesy of their marriages the Bastion Club members were creating. And those members and their wives he would trust with his life—and also, therefore, the secret of the Athena Agency.

There was a possibility there for expanding the agency's work, but that was a prospect for the future, for after he'd made the speculation in Leonora's and so many other ladies' eyes a reality.

He dwelled on the vision—Phoebe as his wife. Soon; the

time for broaching that issue was not yet, but approaching. Just as well.

Aside from all else, there was the not-so-minor detail that he couldn't—wouldn't—willingly sleep anywhere but beside her. Some nights ago when Phoebe had sent a note that Edith had been too tired by their day's outing to Richmond to attend any evening entertainments, he'd grasped the opportunity to drop by the gentlemen's clubs, simply to show his face and hear any story doing the rounds; afterward, he'd decided it was too late to disturb Phoebe.

Instead, he'd spent a hellish night in his previously perfectly comfortable bed at the club. Time and again, on the brink of sleep or just beyond, he'd reached for Phoebe and she hadn't been there.

He'd barely slept a wink. At some deeper level, his nerves— or was it his emotions?—had felt abraded.

He wasn't interested in repeating the experience. It had been unsettling to realize how important she'd become to him; that was an aspect, something he knew was a growing and burgeoning aspect, of his wooing of her that he hadn't foreseen but saw little benefit in dwelling too much upon.

Once she was his wife, that unexpected and unsettling craving would be satisfied, so all he needed to concentrate on was marrying her and the rest would take care of itself.

Fixing his mind on that goal, he turned and slid his arms around her, curled about her, and let his dreams claim him.

The next evening he joined Phoebe at Lady Walker's ball. Audrey was present, too; she sat beside Edith, her sharp eyes narrowed, studying him as he bowed, chatted to Edith, then moved on to take Phoebe's hand.

Sincerely hoping his aunt would keep her questions—on his imminent nuptials, he had not a doubt—to herself, he raised Phoebe's hand to his lips, kissed, then looked over the sea of heads as the musicians struck up.

"How useful—a waltz." He caught Phoebe's eyes. "Shall we?"

She smiled and assented, allowing him to lead her to the floor. Buoyed by the clear expectation in her eyes, he swung her into his arms and swept her into the swirling throng.

He waited until they'd completed their first circuit, until she'd all but sighed and relaxed in his arms, before asking, "How's our latest special client?"

"She's recovering well." Phoebe met his green eyes; she still found it astonishing to be discussing such matters with him. "From what she's told us, we got her away just in time."

They'd run another rescue three nights before; Deverell had watched over the proceedings more or less over her shoulder the whole time, but all had gone well, exactly as planned.

A slight frown darkened his green eyes. "Emmeline mentioned there might be two other outings in the offing. Are there always that many?"

That many female staff needing rescue from their masters.

"Yes, and no. This is the busiest time of year for it."

His frown grew more puzzled. "Why? Just because it's the Season?"

"No—it's because of what happens at the end of the Season. It's almost May. By June the ton starts to remove to the country, so for female staff feeling under threat, the choice is to escape now or risk being trapped on some country estate where the man involved will have even more time on his hands and the houses are bigger."

She paused while he whirled her around the end of the room; once they were heading back up it, she added, "And in terms of finding another position, now is the time. The ton in particular does little to no hiring during summer—ladies tend to wait until they're back in town."

He raised his brows. "I hadn't thought of it like that." After a moment, he refocused on her eyes. "So how many are you expecting?"

She lightly shrugged. "All I can be sure of is that there will be more."

He inclined his head; he drew her closer as again they whirled through the tight turn at the end of the room, but this time he didn't ease his hold. This time he kept her close; she wasn't even sure he was conscious of it. That it wasn't an instinctive part of his reaction to a subject she increasingly realized he found disturbing.

In the sense that he felt he should do more.

"You know," she said, acting on a whim, her voice low, just for him, "I realized some time ago that we couldn't save every girl, every woman. That it's simply not possible, that not being able to help some is a fact of life, one we have to accept."

His eyes had fixed on hers; holding his gaze, she continued, "Edith calls my hobby a 'little crusade'—as usual she sees to the heart of things. But I've accepted, as we all must, that we can't change our world—that we can't eradicate this particular evil. That we *can* only do what we do, but what we *mustn't* do is imagine that because we can't fix the whole problem, that what we do accomplish isn't worthwhile."

A long moment passed; the waltz was ending when he replied, "Edith's indeed very wise—it seems you've inherited the trait." He whirled her to a halt, then lifted her hand to his lips and kissed. Met her eyes and smiled. "Successfully helping the girls and women we do is, indeed, sufficient justification."

She returned his smile, let him set her hand on his sleeve,

then together they moved into the crowd, stopping to chat here, to exchange greetings and news there, to learn what was happening in the wider ton.

As they left Lady Fergurson and moved on, Phoebe smiled to herself; he'd grown almost as glib as she in eliciting useful information from ladies young and old. "Don't forget to tell Emmeline about Mrs. Caldecott looking for a new companion."

His lips curved but he made no reply, simply steered her to the next likely source.

When he'd first made it clear he wasn't going to stand stoically by and simply watch what she did, she'd had serious reservations over how "helpful" he would be. Instead, quite aside from his glib tongue and charming smile—potent weapons within the ton—and his unusual background both as a military spy and also in business, which was proving so useful in other areas, there was the surprising yet undeniable fact that his simple presence at the agency had had an unexpected but powerfully positive consequence.

Emmeline's rapid acceptance of him she'd put down to his charm and his undoubted ability to soothe women's fears.

What she hadn't immediately realized was that while every "special client" reacted at first sight of him with instinctive suspicion if not outright fear, just by being himself he allayed those fears and transformed even the most hardened suspicion to something close to fascination.

Not with him personally, but with what he represented.

It had taken her a little while to realize what a potent message his being at the agency, assisting as he was, was sending to their most vulnerable clients.

They'd seen the dark side of powerful gentlemen; he was the light to that dark, the living proof, one they could see with their own eyes, weigh with their own wits, and so realize that not all men like him were evil. That while some men outwardly like him were dastardly predators, others were protectors and defenders.

As all their "special clients" needed to work for their living and could not therefore avoid gentlemen like him, it was vital that they realize not all such men were dangerous. More, it was something they needed to learn and accept before they could with confidence go back into the arena in which they had to work.

A subtle but powerful boon. No woman who had ever been a victim would forget the look of a true predator, but they did need to learn to look first, before they ran screaming into the night.

She glanced at him, tall, large, and subtly protective by her side, and let her lips curve. Looking ahead, she had to admit he'd surprised her; indeed, he'd trumped her expectations on virtually every count.

It was the Misses Berry who first set her inner alarm bells ringing. Rated among the biggest gossips in the ton, they were unsurprisingly interested in Deverell's presence by her side.

Too interested.

Phoebe had known the sisters for years, but she'd never seen Mary quite so fixed on interrogating a gentleman of Deverell's ilk. As for Agnes, she quite openly believed . . . that there was something rather more than a liaison in the wind.

Inwardly blinking, Phoebe took a mental step back. As if from a distance, she heard Deverell, unperturbed by the old ladies' interest, deal with their arch queries without revealing anything at all. Unfailingly charming, he made their excuses; she bobbed a curtsy and let him lead her away.

She refocused and suppressed a violent urge to look around. To search other faces, to see what others thought. Were thinking, imagining.

The Misses Berry were intelligent, as astute as they could hold together. If they thought . . . then presumably they were receiving the wrong message.

One quick glance at Deverell's face confirmed he was truly unperturbed, that the old ladies' suppositions hadn't bothered him in the least. She couldn't believe that he, of all men, hadn't read their comments as she had.

Which meant . . .

Eyes fixed forward, Phoebe drew in a deep breath.

It was clearly time to set certain matters straight.

Chapter 16

*T*heir relationship was a liaison, nothing more.

While waiting in the darkened morning room for Deverell to appear, Phoebe considered all that had changed in the past weeks—and all that hadn't.

He'd changed her mind about a host of subjects; he'd surprised her at almost every turn. He'd taught her of things she hadn't known—about the interaction between men and women, and not just on the physical plane. He'd opened her eyes in many ways, educated her senses, and left her with a much deeper appreciation of men like him.

What hadn't changed was their future—for each of them their ideas of what their future would be.

He'd intended to marry her at the outset, but when she'd made it clear she wasn't interested, he'd readily rescripted his desires and accepted a liaison instead. Since then, he'd given no indication he'd reversed that acceptance, that he'd changed his mind and was again contemplating marrying her.

For her part, while she could now see the attraction, or certainly more attraction than previously, her reservations remained. . . .

She frowned. Didn't they?

A sound outside the uncurtained windows had her looking up. Across the moonlit garden, she saw the gate swing open. Deverell appeared, shut the gate, took the key off the nail and locked it, then replaced the key and came striding across the lawn, directly to the French doors.

She watched, intrigued, but he paused before the doors for no more than a second before the lock clicked open and he stepped inside.

Concealed in the shadows, she stood. The movement immediately locked his gaze on her, but he recognized her in the same instant; the sudden tension that had flared abruptly dissipated.

Equally instantly, he sensed something was wrong. Head tilting, he approached. "Phoebe? What is it?"

"I . . ." Eyes wide, she stared at him; she'd forgotten that in the dark he always seemed much larger, much more . . . ruthless, determined, forceful, intimidating. Much more male.

His gaze, narrowed and searching, traveled her face. He raised a hand; in desperation she caught it in both of hers, held it between them as she drew in a quick breath and said, "I wanted to talk to you. About . . . about what people are thinking. Expecting. I think we need to consider—"

"The only thing we need to consider is what we want." Shifting closer, Deverell turned his hand and captured one of hers. "What's between us comes from us, and concerns only us—it's not a matter the ton has any say in, not in any way." Raising her hand, he turned it and pressed his lips to her wrist. Felt the telltale flutter of her pulse, her immediate response as his lips caressed.

Through the shadows, he held her gaze. "You want me,

Phoebe, and I want you. For tonight, that's all we need to consider."

That's all he was prepared to allow her to consider, because what else she wanted to consider . . . the way she'd spoken, her tone, her tension, told him without words that he couldn't yet risk that, that despite his recent successes the dominoes had yet to fall decisively his way. The time to speak of matrimony was definitely not yet.

He was too experienced in strategy to risk such a vital thing, not until he was certain of victory.

She was still gowned in the green silk creation she'd worn to the evening's balls. Still holding her hand, holding her captive, he reached out and brushed his thumb over the peak of her breast—and watched it pebble under the silk.

Heard her breath hitch, let his fingers lightly caress the swelling mound . . . deliberately spun a web he knew would hold her, at least in this setting, at least for tonight.

"I want you to imagine something." He let his voice deepen to a more hypnotic note. "You've been sitting in the dark, just as you were, and a dark stranger appears. You rise to escape, but he catches your hand."

His eyes on hers, he shifted his fingers about the hand he held, sliding them down to manacle her wrist. "You want to flee, but he holds you—and touches your breast."

He continued to lightly caress the taut silk. Continued to hold her gaze. "You're quivering." She was, a fine tremor of desire. "You want to flee but you can't—you know what he wants, what he intends to do with you. To you."

She did. Phoebe's mouth was dry. She couldn't drag her eyes from his, couldn't pull her mind from his spell. Couldn't free her senses from his hold.

"Your biggest problem," his voice went on, pure suggestion sliding into her brain, "your biggest *secret* is that you want what he wants, too."

He was right, and he knew it. His confidence was blazoned in his steady gaze, in the seductively arrogant curve of his lips.

"So you're going to do exactly what he tells you." He let a moment elapse, then continued, his tone hardening, "What I tell you."

Again he paused; when next he spoke his words were clearly an order. "You're not to make a sound. You're not required to speak." His tone remained even, uninflected; he had every expectation of being obeyed. "The first thing you're going to do is turn around and lead me—your dark stranger—to your bedchamber."

She hesitated; she knew she could say no, simply refuse and insist they talk, and he would sigh and allow it . . . but he transparently didn't want to discuss that point, and if he didn't, did she really need to? Now, at this moment?

The truth was she'd much rather learn what he planned to do to her—all the details. Would much rather experience that than engage in a discussion she had a sudden premonition she wasn't as prepared for as she'd thought.

She drew in a tight breath, opened her mouth to agree—he silenced her with a finger across her lips.

"No words. Once we're inside your chamber with the door closed on the world, moans, sighs, screams, and breathless cries are permitted—but no words." He held her gaze, and she felt the strands of his web tighten about her. "Now lead me upstairs."

They moved through the dark house in silence. He retained his hold on her wrist. When they reached the door to her room, he halted her. Reaching past her, he closed his hand about the doorknob, then, leaning close, his voice low and dark—that of the dark stranger—said, "Once we go through the door, I'm going to direct you in a fantasy. You'll do exactly as I say, without hesitation. Although I'll be with you—and you'll know that—the fantasy starts here. You've come upstairs late, the rest of the household are long asleep. You go into your room—and as far as you know, you're alone."

On the last word, he set the door swinging wide. "Go in."

She stepped across the threshold into his fantasy, and his fingers slid from her wrist.

She took one step and felt him like a shadow moving into the room behind her. Turning, she saw the door standing open; stepping back, she shut it.

"You believe you're alone in your room. You start to undress, thinking of your lover."

He was just another shadow at the periphery of her vision, moving outside the circle of light cast by the candelabra she'd left burning on her dressing table. She moved to the table, sat, and unpinned her hair. Picking up her brush, she ran it through the heavy tresses.

"You think of your lover—what he would see if he were here. What he would be thinking."

She heard the armchair shift but didn't look that way. Something else moved on the floor. She finished brushing her hair, then stood, rounded her dressing stool, and saw that he'd shifted the armchair back so it stood to one side and a little behind the cheval mirror he'd moved out into the room.

He was sitting in the armchair, booted foot on one knee, elbow on the chair arm. Watching her.

She reached for her laces, saw her reflection in the mirror. Her bodice was tight; she breathed a sigh of relief when the laces unraveled and freed her aching flesh.

"You imagine your lover is here, with you. Watching you undress."

That wasn't difficult; she could feel his gaze, already burning, on her. And knew the sensation would only grow hotter.

"You disrobe as you imagine you would to tantalize him."

Lids at half-mast, she held up her bodice with both hands beneath her breasts and drifted across the floor until she stood directly before the mirror, far enough back so that she could see her reflection from her head to her toes. She studied what she saw—the rather tall, slender woman with the mahogany-red hair, skin pale where the candlelight reached it, dappled in mystery down her other side. Slowly smoothing her hands down over her body, she inched the gown to her waist, then steadily lower until her palms brushed her thighs, then she let the gown go and watched in the mirror as it slid, susurrating to the floor.

She drew a deep breath, filled her lungs, watched her breasts rise above the scooped neckline of her chemise. It was fastened with tiny buttons down the front; she set her fingers to them and slowly, steadily, slid them free—until the chemise gaped open to her waist, exposing the inner swells of her breasts and the shadowy valley between.

Head tilting, she considered her reflection, studied her face, the expression of sensuality that seemed to be slowly investing her features. She let her gaze roam slowly down. Her garters flirted with the hem of her chemise.

She glanced to where the dressing stool stood, then reached out and hooked it closer so one corner was before her. Lifting her right leg, she placed her foot, still in her low-heeled dancing pump, on the stool, then with both hands slid her garter—slowly—down her leg, taking her silk stocking with it, until at the last she removed shoe, garter, and stocking in one smooth movement.

The chair creaked as he shifted. Hiding a smile, she dealt with her other garter, stocking, and shoe in the same way, then pushed the stool away and straightened.

Her expression had subtly altered, grown more sultry, her

lids heavier, her lips fuller. One knee slightly bent, she toyed with the open edges of the chemise, then boldy reached down, grasped the hem, and, still slowly, drew the garment off over her head. . . .

Her gaze locked on the mirror. Hand extended, she froze—not from fear of any kind but from fascination. He'd seen her naked any number of times, but she hadn't—she'd never had any real idea of what he saw, how she looked to his eyes.

What she saw in the mirror . . .

Was that truly her? She could feel his gaze, scorching and intense, wholly fixed. Wholly caught. Did she, her body, truly have that much power?

Then he spoke and she had her answer; his voice had deepened further, taking on the gravelly, rasping tone she now recognized as betokening desire. "Cup your breasts— caress them as he would."

Faintly shocked at the suggestion, she did as he said, and shuddered.

"Close your eyes."

She did, her fingers still shifting, stroking satin skin.

"Imagine how it would feel if he were with you." A silent pause, then she sensed him behind her. "Imagine his hands on your skin."

Imagination was heightened by sensation, merged with it seamlessly. His hands roved her body freely, but he knew her now, so well that his hands followed her script without direction. He touched her as she wished to be touched, as she dreamed of him touching her, yet not a word was spoken, not a glance exchanged.

She stood before him, before the mirror, naked, eyes closed, and he gave expression to her dreams, converted them to reality.

His hands slid over her skin, each caress more evocative

than the last, building the fire inside her, sending it spreading beneath her skin, heating her.

Seducing her all over again.

Then his fingers splayed over her stomach, evocatively flexed, then slid lower. To artfully, tantalizingly caress her curls, then lightly, oh-so-lightly probe the soft flesh behind.

She sucked in a breath against the constriction banding her lungs. Cracking open her lids, she looked into the mirror, and saw him, a dark, dangerous shadow behind her, his shoulders wider than hers, his head bent as he studied her body, watched as his fingers played . . .

Then he lifted his head and saw her watching. Watched her watching his hands move evocatively, provocatively over her body until she shuddered and let her lids fall.

His hands eased, then left her.

"You wish your lover were here—you want to feel him inside you. But he isn't."

He'd moved back from her; she wasn't sure where he was.

"So you let your hands fall, open your eyes, put on your nightgown, then blow out the candles and get into bed."

She obeyed but didn't see him. She picked up her lawn nightgown from the chair in which he'd previously been sitting, drew it on over her head, did up the buttons, then returned to the dressing table and doused the candles.

And caught a glimpse of him, a denser shadow near the bed. She headed for it; as she reached it he spoke from the darkness along the other side.

"You get under the covers, lie on your back, draw the covers to your chin, close your eyes, and compose yourself for sleep."

Wondering, she did as he said, settling and closing her eyes, then relaxing.

"That's when you realize you're not alone—that there is, indeed, a man in the room with you. A man who's been watching you undress lasciviously. Your lover? Or another? You don't know, you can't tell. The room's too dark for you to see, so you keep your eyes closed, feign sleep, and wait to see what he, whoever he is, will do."

Straining her ears, she heard him moving unhurriedly about the room, undressing. Then came silence.

Suddenly the covers were lifted, and the bed bowed beside her, then he shifted closer and she could feel the hard hot naked length of him stretching alongside her.

He settled on one elbow, looking down at her; she could feel his gaze on her face, sense his looming nearness.

Then he reached across her and caught her hand, caught the other and locked both in one of his; raising her arms, he pressed her hands into the pillows above her head.

And leaned nearer. "Open your eyes."

She did; all she could see was a large dense shadow looming over her in the dark, all she could sense was the hard male strength of his body poised half over hers.

"Who am I?" The words drifted through her mind. "Your lover? Or the dark stranger?"

His attention had drifted to her lips. They throbbed.

"Both," she murmured, instinctively arching, testing his hold on her hands, aching to feel his lips on hers, to feel his body along the length of hers.

She heard a deep chuckle, then he obliged and kissed her. Ravenously.

Cocooned in the dark, he was as she'd said, both her lover and a dark stranger—a forcefully seductive male intent on taking from her all he wished, on wringing from her every last gasp, every last iota of surrender.

She had her own agenda. She wriggled and squirmed until he shifted over her, pinning her to the bed—and her senses sighed in delight, in satisfaction and building expectation. Why she so craved his weight was a mystery, but she had no time to pursue it, caught, held effortlessly in a wild mating of mouths, of lips melding, tongues tangling—while he opened the front of her nightgown and laid her breasts bare, set his free hand to the swollen mounds and made them ache.

Then he pulled back from the kiss, looked down, then lowered his head and devoured.

Her hands still anchored above her head, she could do nothing but gasp, arching helplessly, beyond thought offering her flesh for his delectation.

For his appeasement and her satisfaction.

For his pleasure and her delight.

She twisted sinuously beneath him, caressing the hard rod of his erection, flagrantly inviting, suggesting, luring.

And succeeded in stoking his fire as he was stoking hers, succeeded in adding an edge of driven passion to his already tense muscles, succeeded in invoking a dangerous shadow of deeper, darker desire.

She shifted again and he swore.

Between them, he reached down, wrenched the front of her nightgown to her waist, with his thighs spread hers wide, then settled heavily between.

She writhed and suceeded in brushing the blunt head of his erection with the slick pouting lips of her entrance.

He hissed and went still, a tremor of unruly passion barely leashed rippling, a threat and a promise, over and through him.

She arched again, blatantly inviting; she was scorched and open and so empty—she ached to feel him inside her, filling her, thrusting deep.

"Tell me what you want." The order rasped across her senses.

Trapped in mindless need, she sobbed and squirmed, but he held her down.

"Tell me. Say the words. Do you want to be ravished? Do you want me to ravish you?"

"*Yes!*" The plea escaped her on a gasping sob as she fought to free her hands.

But he held them down, held her trapped beneath him in the dark as he covered her lips with his and ravished her mouth, covered her, and thrust deep into her body.

She cried out—in pleasure, not pain—tried to arch and meet his next thrust but with his body hard and hot, unyielding and powerful, he allowed her not even that much sway.

In the dark, freed by her plea, her wanton invitation, he rode her hard and deep, filling her body, overwhelming her senses.

Ravishing her in truth.

And all she could do—all he let her do—was rejoice in the primitive taking, in the powerful, unfettered act. And glory in the raw passion that drove him, the greedy, needful hunger, the stark, undeniable evidence of his desire for her.

As her senses tightened, coalesced and started the now familiar climb, she shuddered, gasped, and embraced all he gave her. She might be the one ravished, but he was giving more than taking . . . or perhaps his taking was a form of giving.

That was the last semicoherent thought she had as with one shatteringly deep thrust he brought glory crashing down on her. Sent her spinning into the golden void, then with a guttural shout, he joined her.

They clung, lips touching, brushing, fingers tangling and clutching as they struggled to gasp, to breathe as the storm winds of passion buffeted them, wracked them, as desire raked one last time, then receded.

And left them exhausted, wrung out, flung like flotsam and jetsam on some distant shore, together, still whole, yet irrefutably changed.

*   *   *

Phoebe still felt faintly skittish, uncertain of just what had changed and how, when she arrived at the agency that afternoon to discuss placements with Emmeline.

Deverell was there, long legs stretched out under the table, the agency's account books scattered before him; he looked up as she walked in, met her eyes—rapidly read them, then smiled. At her, for her. A private, knowing, yet reassuring smile.

Without conscious thought, her lips curved in response. Inclining her head, she swung off her cloak and dropped it on a chair. "Well, then." She slipped into the chair beside Emmeline, next to Deverell. "Let's get started. Has Loftus found anything that might be suitable for Miss Spry?"

Deverell returned to his books, and she gave her attention to Emmeline.

Ten minutes later, Loftus arrived and joined them. With a nod to Deverell, he took the chair on Emmeline's other side and tossed a note on the table.

Phoebe pounced on it, eagerly opening it and scanning the information inscribed within.

"I think those people might do for Miss Spry." Loftus had returned yesterday and demanded a full accounting of Miss Spry's background and credentials. Clasping his hands on the table, he nodded at the note in Phoebe's hands. "They're gentry, wealthy enough, well-connected enough, a trifle scatterbrained, the pair of them, but as kindhearted as any you'll find. They've found themselves with a rapidly increasing family, and when I visited them a few hours ago, it was abundantly clear they're in desperate need of help."

She and Emmeline peppered him with questions about the Follingworth household, located in Bloomsbury.

"Three under five years old, and another on the way?" Emmeline nodded direfully. "She'll certainly need more help than just a nurse, or even two."

"The position certainly sounds perfect for Miss Spry." Phoebe glanced at Loftus. "Are they actively searching for a governess?"

Loftus smiled, a trifle smug. "They hadn't thought of it, but they're thinking of it now. I mentioned the Athena Agency—I fancy you'll hear from Mrs. Follingworth within the week."

Phoebe tilted her head, fingertips tapping, eyes bright. "Bloomsbury, and a family with no connections to the Chifleys, indeed moving in quite different circles. That should be safe enough, provided we hide any mention of Constance's recent employment."

Emmeline rifled through a stack of papers, consulted one, then shook her head. "We'll have to get her a reference to cover it. The date's on her one before that, wishing her well for her new position, what's more, so we can't hide the gap."

"So we need a forged reference." Phoebe grimaced. "You can't—you've done too many recently."

"And you can't," Emmeline returned, "for the same reason." She looked at Phoebe. "So now what? We can't get Constance to write one herself."

A silence fell. Loftus broke it, clearing his throat. "I daresay I could write one—pretend it was from a Mrs. Loftus."

Phoebe and Emmeline just looked at him.

"No—you can't." Deverell met Loftus's eyes. "Nor can I." He smiled. "Wrong sort of hand."

Phoebe nodded. "Thank you, Loftus, but Deverell's right—it has to be a lady's hand." She frowned. "I can't ask Edith—"

The bell over the front door tinkled. They heard Birtles, minding the counter, say, "Good afternoon, ladies. Can I assist you?"

A soft shushing of skirts brushing the floor was followed

by the sound of the door closing. Emmeline pushed back her chair and rose.

"Actually, I was wondering if my niece was here—Miss Malleson?"

Widening, Phoebe's eyes flew to Deverell's.

"And I believe my nephew might be here, too—Deverell. You might know him as Paignton."

There was no doubting Audrey's extremely well bred accents any more than Edith's softer tones.

"Sounds like an invasion." Deverell pushed back his chair and rose.

Phoebe muttered something unintelligible and followed him as he headed down the corridor to the front room.

"Ah—there you are!" Audrey saw them first. She was wielding an ornate lorgnette, an appropriate final touch to her costume. Draped in silks of various gold and green hues, a brassy satin turban fixed with an oval of pearls swathing her head, she was currently affecting the Egyptian style.

Deverell nodded. "Aunt." He bowed to Edith, expression mild. "To what do we owe this unexpected pleasure?"

Phoebe jabbed him in the back—as much, he suspected, for his languid drawl as his words—as she pushed past him. "Is something wrong?"

"No, no, dear." Edith was looking about her curiously, taking in the desk and chairs, the boxes on the shelf, the counter. "We just, well, we wanted to see . . ."

Audrey snorted. "We decided if Deverell could visit you here, then we could, too. We've been assisting you much longer than he has."

Deverell managed to swallow his laugh, but knew it showed in his eyes as he met Phoebe's, still mystified.

Edith patted her hand. "I decided it really was time I *knew*, dear—especially after whoever it was knocked poor Fergus on the head. I was really quite bothered, and it never does for a lady not to know what's going on in her own household. Or even pretend not to know."

Emmeline had hung back at the mouth of the corridor. Seeing her, Edith smiled. "And who's this?"

A trifle stunned, Emmeline hurriedly bobbed a curtsy. "Mrs. Emmeline Birtles, ma'am."

"Hmm—you're familiar." Wielding her lorgnette, Audrey studied Emmeline. "Now where . . ." Suddenly Audrey's magnified eyes widened; she let the lorgnette fall. "Great heavens! You're that missing companion—what was the name?—Miss Ponsonby, that's it. You went missing from Lady McAllister's summer house party. . . ." Audrey frowned. "But that was years and years ago."

"Five years," Phoebe supplied. She cast a pleading glance at Deverell.

"Perhaps"—moving around them, spreading his arms he herded Audrey and Edith toward the corridor—"we should retreat to the kitchen and you can meet all those here out of sight of any passersby. To begin with"—with his head he indicated Birtles as they passed—"this is Birtles, Emmeline's husband. He and Emmeline manage the agency."

Both Edith and Audrey smiled at Birtles, who blushed and bobbed bows.

Audrey looked ahead. "So how, exactly, does the agency work?"

"Come and sit down," Deverell coaxed, "and Phoebe will explain."

Phoebe cast him a speaking glance but followed Audrey down the corridor. Edith followed, with Emmeline behind her; Deverell brought up the rear. He stepped into the kitchen to find that Loftus hadn't seized his chance and escaped via the rear door and the laneway but, despite what Deverell had realized was extreme shyness, had stayed to help them face this latest development.

Of course, he hadn't known what he would be facing, but at least Audrey hadn't raised her lorgnette in her usual, high-bred, intimidating way. Instead, she stood at one end of the table, looking rather blankly at Loftus, standing, holding his hat before him, blinking rather dazedly at the other end.

Phoebe helped Edith to a chair. "This is Mr. Loftus Coates. He's been a benefactor of the agency for some years." She glanced at Loftus and smiled encouragingly. "This is my aunt, Mrs. Edith Balmain, whom you've heard me mention so often."

Clearly uncomfortable, Loftus bowed stiffly. "Ma'am. It's a pleasure to make your acquaintance."

Deverell moved around Audrey to set a chair for her; one of her hands snaked out, caught his arm, pinched through his sleeve. "Introduce me," she hissed under cover of Edith's delighted returning of Loftus's greeting.

She hadn't taken her eye from Loftus. Detaching her hand from his sleeve, Deverell drew out a chair. "It seems to be our afternoon for aunts—allow me to present mine, Miss Audrey Deverell. She's also Phoebe's godmother."

Loftus gathered his courage, faced Audrey, and bowed. "Miss Deverell."

He didn't meet Audrey's eyes, for which Deverell didn't blame him; Audrey always had a rather daunting effect on men of her generation. Holding the chair, he glanced at her.

To his surprise, her gaze fixed on Loftus, she moved past the chair, extending her hand. "Mr. Coates."

Loftus eyed the slender fingers presented to him, swallowed, then reached for them and shook them.

Audrey beamed at him. "It's intriguing, and rather reassuring, too, to learn that these children have had wiser counsel to call on in their endeavors."

Retrieving her hand from Loftus's slack grasp, smiling, she turned and took her seat.

As he moved to take the chair beside her, Deverell shot a glance at Phoebe; she arched a quick brow in return, and moved to the chair beside Edith, motioning Loftus to resume his.

Instead he cleared his throat and remained standing. "I really should be getting along." He turned his hat between his hands. "I just called by—"

"Nonsense!" Audrey turned the full glamor of her smile on him. "Both Edith and I would be devastated to think that our advent had disrupted your meeting. Indeed, I would be grateful if you would stay—your perspective on the agency's work would greatly assist us." Audrey looked around, her intrigued glance including Emmeline. "I find myself quite fascinated by the agency's enterprise."

Turning back to Loftus, Audrey waved him to sit. "Please, do stay, Mr. Coates."

Refusing such an entreaty was patently beyond Loftus; he hesitated, then drew out his chair and sat. Audrey turned her bright gaze on Phoebe. "Now then, dear—do tell us how things work."

Phoebe glanced at Deverell, drew in a deep breath, and proceeded to outline the various activities of the agency. Both Edith and Audrey put questions, insightful and at times rather startling in their candor; Audrey turned a query Loftus's way and drew him into the discussion.

Seated beside Edith, opposite Deverell and Audrey, Phoebe couldn't help but remark how very much at ease with those of lower station Audrey was. For all her wisdom, Edith was more reserved in engaging with Loftus, and even more so with Emmeline, but Audrey was transparently specifically interested in the roles both played, and equally patently recognized no social boundaries, encouraging both to freely engage with her, and succeeding.

Edith was also interested and intrigued, but raised as a

Malleson within the haut ton, hemmed in by numerous dreadfully stuffy relatives, she found it more difficult to relax among ordinary people. Although Audrey had an equally august background, and arguably an even more stuffy and high-in-the-instep family, she'd made a career of being unconventional.

And Deverell was the same. Seeing the understanding glance he exchanged with Loftus, remembering the ease with which he'd won over Fergus and Birtles, and even Emmeline, his easy way with Grainger—from whom Phoebe had now learned enough to appreciate Deverell's appointing the boy as his groom as a "rescue" of sorts—she realized that Deverell's interest in and facility in engaging so easily with people of lesser degree weren't, as she'd supposed, an outcome of his military service but the result of something deeper, more like an inherited ability.

It was one she valued. She'd lost her own "distance" from others long ago, courtesy of recognizing, first with Emmeline and then all the others, that women of any station were subject to the same threats, the same fears. The same emotions as they progressed through life. That regardless of the quality of their gowns, their cultured speech or their knowledge of ladylike accomplishments, they were the same and equally worthy of help.

Of respect.

That wasn't something Deverell had had to learn; it was a tenet he'd absorbed long ago. So long ago it was a part of his character; he was as open-minded and unconventional as Audrey, and equally likely to protect a maid as he was a lady.

And that, Phoebe realized, as she watched him lean forward and deflect Audrey's attention from Loftus—so that Loftus could catch his breath—was quite an amazing find in a gentleman like Deverell, in a man of his class.

* * *

Five nights later, Phoebe lay warm and sated in the billows of her bed, sleepy but not yet ready for sleep; eyes closed, she drifted in the dark and marveled at the turn her life had taken.

Turns. It wasn't simply the presence of the heavy male body sprawled beside her, one muscled arm slung over her waist, holding her protectively even in sleep, that was different. He'd made a place for himself there, in her private world, but he'd been equally assiduous in carving out a place in the agency and claiming it.

What she found so amazing was that, even there, be it in Kensington Church Street or in the lanes and alleys where they waited to whisk away the frightened women they rescued, that place he'd claimed was by her side—not in front of her, not instead of her, but with her. Alongside her.

He'd cast himself as her partner.

Through the darkness she glanced at him, at the slice of his face she could see—he was sleeping slumped on his side, his face burrowed into the pillow—and she was still astonished, irredeemably fascinated that a man such as he, a man such as she knew him to be, could be so . . . amenable. So willing to adjust, to mute what none knew better than she was his natural inclination to command, to instead defer to a woman—worse, *a lady!*

The only times he'd shown any tendency to take the reins had been during their rescues; he hovered, not liking the locations, the surroundings—the danger to her. She knew without words that he didn't like her being part of the group who went out at night to rescue the women, but he'd accepted, reluctantly, that no woman hoping for rescue was likely to willingly go with him or Birtles—or indeed any man. It had to be Phoebe; she could reassure the girls as no one else could. So he chafed, but when all went according to plan, he drew back and let matters proceed as she directed.

He'd managed to not just allay her fears on that score but open her eyes to a raft of possibilities that, prior to his advent into her life, she would have sworn were *im*possibilities.

Indeed, that day had brought a fresh round of observations and revelations. For some time she'd wanted to visit two of their resettled "special clients" to see how both girls were faring. Hearing of her wish, he'd offered to drive her into Surrey, to the two villages serving the country estates at which the girls now worked. Emmeline had written and made arrangements for the girls to meet Phoebe at the local inns.

That morning Deverell had driven her into the country, to the meetings. He'd sat a little apart, keeping watch over her and the girls while she and they had chatted, but when it had come time to leave, in both cases he'd risen and approached, and with his easy smile and a few charming words had eased each girl's instinctive fear. He'd spoken with her in the girls' presence, openly acknowledging his commitment to the agency, and more subtly to Phoebe herself. Each girl had blinked, startled that he—a gentleman of the very sort they had such bad memories of—would think and behave as he did.

Each had readily accepted his offer of a lift back to the gates of their place of employment; both had departed reassured and, Phoebe had no doubt, a trifle less inclined to paint all powerful gentlemen as blackguards.

The journey back had been another revelation; he'd questioned her as to the girls' attitudes after rescue, their needs—emotional as well as physical—to best enable them to recover from their ordeal. To best eradicate the resultant fears.

Remembering, she let her lids fall; he'd been totally focused, completely absorbed, not just interested but . . . again, the word that fell into her mind was committed. He had some plan evolving in his head, on that she would wager, but he hadn't yet mentioned it, hadn't yet proposed it.

She'd intended to interrogate him that evening at Lady Hubert's rout; instead, she'd spent much of the evening acting as *his* protector. Most of the balls and parties they'd previously attended—that she and Edith habitually graced— hadn't been those at which the matchmaking mamas predominated, but her ladyship's rout was one of the premier events of the Season, which was now in full swing. Despite Deverell's clear preference for her company, they'd been approached by a steady stream of ladies keen to try their hands, as well as those of their charges at detaching him from her skirts.

He'd clung tight, and more than once she'd felt the need to employ her wits and her tongue to shield him. Really, some of the more brazen suggestions had made her blush for her sex.

She shifted in the bed, letting her leg brush his. If she were truthful, she'd startled herself by recognizing in herself a reaction she'd seen in him when other eligible gentlemen had tried to capture her interest.

In him, she'd labeled it possessiveness; in her . . . was it any different?

And if she had the right to feel so, didn't he?

Numerous incidents during the rout had brought one point home: He needed a bride, a wife of the right caliber to help him, to assist him with the social round he'd inherited along with his title. She'd learned more of his circumstances from comments let fall by various ladies during the evening—and also from Audrey, now she'd taken to frequently looking in at the agency—enough to understand that his need was real.

Partnership.

The word revolved in her mind, as if she were mentally tasting it.

He'd become her partner in her enterprise, but what of his? He had a calling he needed to follow, just as she had. But was that any of her business?

The answer depended on what lay between them.

If what they now shared was in truth the liaison she'd assumed it would be, then it should be on the wane, attraction and desire fading, both of them starting to turn aside, their attention drifting. Yet if anything, the opposite was happening; they were growing more connected, their lives, hopes, and aspirations more intertwined by the day—and on his part that was unquestionably deliberate.

So if this wasn't a liaison, what was it? A partnership, yes, but where did that end?

When she'd insisted on a liaison, she hadn't known, hadn't imagined a relationship like what was developing between them could exist—could possibly be.

But if it could . . . ?

He'd changed his mind once and accepted a liaison. What if she now changed hers?

Would he, could she persuade him to, change his back?

Did she want him to?

The concept and the question wreathed through her mind, and followed her into her dreams.

Chapter 17

"There you are, dear." Audrey dropped a neatly written reference on the agency's kitchen table before Phoebe. "Do you need any more?"

Phoebe picked up the letter, read it, then looked up and smiled. "Not at present. But thank you—this will be perfect."

"Of course. Do let me know when you require another." With a wave, Audrey drifted back up the corridor; they heard her taking her leave of Emmeline, behind the front counter, then the front door opened and shut.

Deverell glanced at Phoebe; they shared a smile, then he returned his attention to the account books. When appealed to over a forged reference for Miss Spry, Audrey had been delighted to oblige. She and Edith had seized on the provision of such references as one way they could contribute to the agency's work; he suspected Audrey took great delight in inventing households, and with her artistic bent she had no difficulty disguising her hand so she could create references from multiple imaginary ladies.

"With this," Phoebe murmured, setting aside the reference, "Dulcie should be able to secure that post with Lady Huntwell."

And yet another of their "special clients" would be settled. But Phoebe had been speaking the unvarnished truth when she'd warned this was their busy time; they had three more rescues pending.

The front door opened and shut once more; Deverell lifted his head. With Phoebe, he listened to the voices in the front room; it was a woman who'd come in—her voice and Emmeline's were too soft for him to make out their words.

The woman didn't remain long; as soon as the front door shut again, Emmeline came down the corridor.

Halting in the archway, from where she could retreat to the front if anyone entered, she showed them a puzzled, frowning face. "Well—that's a strange thing, to be sure."

"What is?" Birtles came in from the lane, a sack of potatoes in his arms. "Where'd you want these?"

Emmeline pointed to the pantry, then answered his first question. "That was my sister, Rose. She popped in to tell me that that girl she'd mentioned, from her friend Mrs. Camber's household that she and Camber thought needed our services—well, it seems the girl's up and gone of her own accord."

Deverell frowned.

"Run away?" Phoebe asked.

Emmeline nodded. "That's what Camber said. She'd spoken to the girl—she was being pursued by her master's nephew—and she, the girl, had seemed keen to have us help her, but this morning the girl was gone. Camber thought as perhaps she grew so desperate she didn't want to wait and simply fled."

They all thought of a young maid fleeing into the streets of London.

"Well," Phoebe said, her expression grim but resigned, "we can only help those who come our way."

Emmeline nodded and headed back to the front counter. Birtles humphed and went out to fetch the rest of his purchases.

Phoebe returned to sorting her lists; Deverell eyed her bent head and wondered. Had the maid run away or . . . ?

Try as he might, he couldn't guess what it was he sensed hovering just beyond perception's reach.

On the opposite side of London, Malcolm Sinclair climbed the three steps to the recessed door of a tall, narrow building located off Threadneedle Street in the bustling heart of the city. Pushing open the outer door, he entered; without looking to right or left, he ascended to the first floor. The rooms at the end of the corridor overlooking the street housed the offices of Drayton and Company, Mr. Thomas Glendower's business agent.

Malcolm tapped peremptorily on the office door and entered.

Less than a minute later, he was shown into Drayton's sanctum. Drayton, average in every physical way, mild-mannered but yet a skilled and exceedingly thorough man-of-business, was already on his feet behind the desk, a smile wreathing his countenance. "Mr. Glendower—a pleasure as always, sir."

Smiling faintly, aloof and distant, Malcolm shook Drayton's hand. "I trust all goes well?"

"Indeed, sir." Drayton waved Malcolm to the chair before the desk; he waited until Malcolm elegantly sat before sinking back into his own chair. "You'll be pleased to know that the position we took in Bonnington and Company has already paid a substantial dividend."

Drayton continued, giving Malcolm—Thomas Glendower—a detailed report on his considerable portfolio.

Malcolm listened intently, but while one part of his mind registered facts and figures, another part circled, as always, as ever, checking, considering, assessing and evaluating his options and his decisions, his moves in the game, on the chessboard of life, of which Drayton and Thomas Glendower were one.

Potentially a vital one.

Henry knew nothing of Thomas Glendower, and even less of Malcolm's facility with finance, with business and the raising and profitable management of capital.

On coming up to town, moved by a distantly perceived, possible, but vague need, Malcolm had amused himself by setting up his alias and his accounts with Drayton, initially as a means of concealing, and at the same time doing some thing useful with, the sizeable sum he'd amassed through his years at Oxford.

Young gentlemen liked to wager, to play cards for exorbitant sums, sums those who gambled with Malcolm usually lost. Honorably, legitimately—he never resorted to cheating. That was the thrill, the test, the challenge. Over the years, he'd come to view his role in the light of teaching his colleagues a valuable lesson—one sadly few took to heart. Unless one was a whiz with figures, it was unwise to play with one who was.

But what had started as an amusement had grown to an absorbing interest. Malcolm now knew that finance and making money was the area in which he excelled, and which gave him the greatest satisfaction.

Well and good. As a consequence, however, Thomas Glendower and his portfolio now meant a great deal to Malcolm; they were creations of his he would fight to protect.

His more superficial mind reported that Drayton had been his usual hardworking, indeed inspired, self. That was what had drawn him to the man—like Malcolm, he was motivated as much by the thrill of successful investment as the money. As he invariably did while sitting in Drayton's chair listening to his enthusiastic report, Malcolm congratulated himself for his foresight in choosing Drayton—and in setting up such an excellent way of quietly salting away large sums of cash.

Drayton came to an end. "Excellent!" Malcolm smiled, still aloof but showing his approval. Reaching into his pocket, he withdrew a wad of notes—the cut he'd skimmed from the payment for the last two women passed to the white slaver traders.

Despite his perennial desire for cash, Henry was exceedingly lax about keeping a close eye on what should have been his; he'd made no attempt to check the amount Malcolm had stated they received in return for handing over the prettiest maids in London, snatched from the households of lords and dukes. As always arrogantly certain—forever arrogantly blind—Henry blithely believed Malcolm handed over the full sum.

Such naïveté had Malcolm inwardly shaking his head every time he thought of it. In reality, fifty percent of the cash handed over had from the first made its way into Mr. Thomas Glendower's accounts.

Nonchalantly dropping the notes on Drayton's desk, Malcolm stated, "Add that to my account. Invest it as seems fit. That opportunity with the Northern Canal, for example, might suit."

Drayton's eyes had lit. He reached for the money. "Indeed, sir—an excellent choice."

While Drayton counted the notes and directed his clerks to enter the sum into various ledgers, Malcolm let his mind return to the aspect of his current enterprise that, increasingly, was preying on his mind.

Henry, arrogant and blind, was a potential liability. When, with becoming meekness, Malcolm had speculated on the dangers of depositing sums of cash received from crime into one's own bank account, Henry had laughed contemptuously; his reputation and position, he claimed, would forever protect him from any investigation.

Perhaps in the past that had been so, but Malcolm had heard enough whispers to suggest that the authorities were becoming more vigilant, certainly less *laissez-faire*. But while Malcolm could and would quite happily turn his back on the white slavers and walk away—he didn't need their money; he preferred to make his by safer means—Henry was another matter. He was now addicted to the funds their association with the trade brought in—or more specifically, addicted to the pistols that money allowed him to buy.

Unfortunately, he was also being a pig-headed fool and refusing to take the obvious precautions.

Malcolm abhorred fools, and pig-headed ones were the worst. But what he really didn't like—what preyed on his mind—was the potential weakness in his own defenses that Henry now represented.

So . . .

Drayton spoke; Malcolm looked at him, smiled, and rose. Their business concluded, he allowed Drayton to show him out. The instant the office door shut behind him, he let his mind refocus on the problem he could see looming.

Henry would run his own race, and there was nothing Malcolm could do, nor felt compelled to do, in that regard. He and Henry had managed to rub along for nearly fifteen years; it was time to move on. As soon as he turned twenty-one, in just a few short weeks, and assumed control of the fortune his father had left in Henry's charge, he would act, and step out from Henry's shadow—sever the umbilical cord that had until now kept him tied.

Meanwhile, however . . . descending the stairs to the ground floor, Malcolm narrowed his eyes. It would be wise to give some thought to shoring up his own position in the event that Henry was caught.

Tricky, but there were ways and means, and in the circumstances he wasn't at all averse to using them to ensure he didn't get caught, too. Considering his options, he pushed open the front door and strolled out into the street.

"Three rescues in one week—that's a record!"

Phoebe clinked her glass with Deverell's; smiling delightedly, she beamed at their small band gathered around the agency's kitchen. "Thanks to our excellent team—Birtles, Fergus, Scatcher, Grainger, and Deverell"—she inclined her head to each in turn—"all three went off smoothly. And thanks to Emmeline, Loftus, Audrey, Edith, and myself, we already have one of our special clients placed, and potential positions to pursue for the other two."

Birtles raised his tankard high. "To the Athena Agency!"

Everyone cheered and drank.

Lowering his mug, Deverell looked around at their unlikely crew. Goodwill and high spirits overflowed on all sides; three rescues in such a short period was indeed an achievement.

Scatcher, the owner of the shop to the left, a clearing house for antiques and antiquities of dubious provenance, was an unprepossessing rogue whose rather grubby exterior hid a heart of considerable warmth. He'd been highly wary of Deverell but had accepted him on Phoebe's word; for his part, Deverell was willing to admit that despite Scatcher's questionable business practices, his sharp eyes, quick wits, and well-honed instinct for self-preservation were of excellent value in a lookout.

On their last rescue, Scatcher had spotted the watch in good time to prevent them being discovered.

The notion of Scatcher and Audrey, let alone Edith, rubbing shoulders was a flight of fancy Deverell had never imagined he'd see, but there they were, all three earnestly debating the positions they were lining up for the girls they'd rescued.

Loftus stood beside Audrey—or rather she stood beside him. His aunt invariably gravitated to Loftus's side, but no matter how carefully he watched, Deverell couldn't tell whether her interest was driven purely by curiosity or . . . something else. Regardless, he'd never seen Audrey's usually peripatetic attention so consistently focused on one object.

Turning from Emmeline and Birtles, Phoebe tucked her hand in Deverell's arm and nudged him toward Loftus at the end of the room. "You know, the only thought dimming my enjoyment in our week's work is that there existed three situations from which we had to rescue those girls."

He closed his hand over hers on his sleeve and gently squeezed. "True." He'd thought of that himself. "But as you once so sapiently remarked, we can only do what we can, and trust in God to take care of the rest."

"Hmm . . . I don't recall saying all that—not the last bit, anyway—but you're right." Phoebe met his eyes. "I wanted to thank you not only for not being difficult over the agency, but for joining us. We couldn't have managed all three in one week, not before, not without you and Grainger to help."

"Grainger and I are enjoying ourselves," Deverell dryly returned. "Never doubt it."

"Nevertheless." Phoebe looked ahead to the small group before them. "You know," she murmured, lowering her voice, "I've rarely seen Edith so animated—so involved. Actively helping us has been good for her."

Deverell grinned. "It's the slightly scandalous nature of the enterprise that so thrills her. Audrey's been corrupting her."

Phoebe laughed and they joined the others, and the celebration continued for some time.

Later that night, as he let himself in through the French doors of Edith's morning room and silently went upstairs, Deverell came to a decision, one he'd been hoping not to have to make.

That evening they'd attended Lady Carnaby's ball, not so much a crush as a highly select gathering. There'd been a number of eligible gentlemen present, dropping by more to be seen among that circle than to cast their eyes over any young lady.

At one stage, he'd been dispatched to fetch Audrey and Edith refreshments. He'd been waylaid, caught by Lord Grimsby and then Lady Hendricks; by the time he'd reached the small salon where the refreshment table was located, Phoebe had been standing alone beside Edith for some time. On his way back, a glass of orgeat in each hand, he'd paused just inside the ballroom to check—to verify that no gentleman had taken advantage of his absence to approach Phoebe.

None had, or if they had, they'd already left; she'd still been standing beside Edith, chatting to Audrey.

The sight had brought home an anomaly he'd noted but hadn't fully analyzed; Phoebe was unquestionably attractive, yet although gentlemen looked, and certainly noticed, few ever approached her.

He'd originally thought that had been due to his attentive and openly possessive presence; now . . .

A gentleman had ranged alongside him, his gaze fixed in

the same direction. Handsome, a blood of the ton a few years Deverell's junior, the man had clearly been studying—assessing—Phoebe. Turning his head, Deverell had studied the newcomer, until the man had noticed, met his eyes, and smiled—somewhat sheepishly.

"I was just thinking . . ." With his head, the man had indicated Phoebe on the other side of the room, considering her once more. "Dashed attractive, don't you think? Pity, really."

He'd blinked. "Pity?"

"Well, yes." The man had glanced at Deverell. "You must have been in the wars if you don't know."

He'd nodded, acknowledging the supposition. "What don't I know?"

"That Miss Malleson over there—the lady we've been studying—is one to avoid. At least if you prefer your hide whole. The edge of her tongue can slice like a saber. She ought to come with a warning: Deadly, approach at your peril."

"Is that so?" He'd struggled to hide a grin, but then he'd looked again at Phoebe . . . and sobered. "Why? Do you know?"

The gentleman had shaken his head. "No clue. As far as I know, she's been that way ever since she came up to town. Any number have tried, but all have ended up slinking away to lick their wounds." After a moment, he'd added, "Mind you, I did hear that some brave soul has tamed the dragon, but as he doesn't seem to be anywhere in sight, no doubt she's put him to rout, too."

It had been tempting to claim the title of St. George, but he'd resisted. With a nod, he'd parted from the gentleman and tacked through the crowd, eventually returning to Phoebe.

Along the way, he'd recalled her initial response to his interest; she'd tried her level best to drive him away. While with him she hadn't succeeded, other gentlemen wouldn't have found her methods of repelling them as entertaining and amusing as he had.

All of which led to his one remaining question, the question he'd hoped she would answer without him having to ask it. What had happened to raise her defenses? The same incident almost certainly had driven her to begin the agency.

Reaching her door, he paused, then gripped the handle and turned. The time had come; he had to know.

Somewhat to his surprise, she was standing before one of the windows, still dressed in her ballgown. The curtains were open, looking down on the quiet street below. Arms folded beneath her breasts, she glanced over her shoulder and saw him, smiled, then turned back to the view.

He came up behind her, placed his hands on her shoulders. "What are you doing?"

"Just . . . thinking." She leaned back against him, resting her shoulders against his chest. "After our celebration today it just seemed the right moment to reflect . . . on how we started, what we've gone through, and where we are now."

He didn't say anything, just slid his hands down her upper arms, then slipped them around her waist, wrapping his arms around her, holding her against him.

Glancing at her face, he saw her smile, sensed its quality; she was looking back with satisfaction.

"The first year—the year after I rescued Emmeline—we set up the agency, me, Emmeline, Skinner, Fergus and Birtles, who'd followed her. He was the gardener at the estate she'd been at; he left and followed her and worked for two years to persuade her to marry him."

Deverell devoutly hoped it wouldn't take him that long to persuade Phoebe.

"That first year, we rescued two maids. The second year we rescued four. That was when Loftus joined us—we tried to place one of the maids in his household, but he realized her reference was a fake and came around to the agency. Once he learned the whole truth, he left, and we feared the worst—but then he returned and said he wanted to help. He's gradually helped more and more with the years."

"And you've rescued more and more women every year."

"Yes." Her expression the epitome of content, she nodded. "Last year, we managed nine. This year, we've already done eight special clients, and there's more to come."

"One tomorrow night." Deverell laid his cheek against her hair, tightened his arms a fraction, held her closer. "And you shouldn't forget the more public successes—thanks to the agency's operations any number of female staff have been placed in good, and safe, positions."

"True." Happiness ringing in her voice, Phoebe tried to turn.

Deverell tightened his grip and prevented it.

Surprised, still smiling, she leaned to the side, trying to peer into his face, but he kept his cheek pressed to the silky fall of her hair. "What is it?"

He sighed. "Phoebe, I have to ask—I have to know." He didn't have the words to explain why, no reasons, just emotions, and he was discovering he was no master of those.

"What?" she prompted, her hands closing over his at her waist.

"I want to . . . *need* to know what happened to you that made you start the agency."

She said nothing for a full minute, but he didn't press, didn't speak; the continuing suppleness of the body beneath his hands, the relaxed curve of her back against his chest, reassured him that she wasn't reacting defensively. She was thinking.

Eventually, she murmured, "That was a long time ago."

"Regardless. Please tell me."

She sighed and leaned fully back against him, her head

resting against his shoulder, her fingers gripping his. "I was at a house party with my aunt Marion. I was seventeen, not yet presented. The party was one of the first of that ilk I'd attended—a highly select group of guests gathered at the country residence of a senior peer. It was an honor to be invited, and for me, green as I was, a thrill to be there."

Her voice grew distant; he sensed she was looking down the years at a scene well remembered, but in some respects fading. "We'd been there for three days. It was the night of the Grand Ball our hostess had decided to hold. It was a magnificent event—people came from all around. A lot of attention was paid to me. I confess I felt somewhat overwhelmed, almost giddy, drunk on enjoyment. The ballroom was filled to overflowing. Other salons nearby were full, too. It was a warm night, and I started to feel almost suffocated. I was looking for Marion, but I was surrounded by young gentlemen, all asking me to dance, all chatting—I didn't know how to break away.

"But then . . ." Her voice changed. After a moment she went on, her tone flatter, more distant. "A gentleman, one of the guests and a close friend of the host, came to my rescue. Or so I thought. He kindly . . ." She paused, then went on, "He dismissed the younger men, telling them I needed a moment of peace to find my whirling feet, then he suggested we go for a stroll in the gallery. Everywhere else was crowded—he said the gallery would be cool and quiet, the windows open to the fresh air. I wanted to speak to Marion, to let her know where I'd be, but he assured me there was no need. It was a house party, not a London ball."

Phoebe paused; after a long moment, she went on. "I let him lead me away, but the gallery he led me to wasn't the main gallery about the head of the main staircase, but another in a separate wing, one containing nothing but bed-chambers, and therefore at that hour quite deserted. The gallery was as quiet and cool as he'd said. It was also unlit and full of shadows, alcoves, and embrasures.

"I wasn't comfortable but . . . I told myself I was imagining things. That my imagination was running amok. I didn't see the danger—didn't *believe* in the danger, until it was too late."

"What happened?"

She tightened her hands over his, instinctively reassuring, yet . . . some part of her still quivered. "He started to say things—to make lascivious suggestions. I was shocked, and showed it, but that only inflamed him all the more. I remember the look in his eyes." She shivered; she had to swallow before she said, "He backed me against the paneling."

He didn't know what moved him to it; if he lived to be a hundred, he still wouldn't know. He stepped sideways, beyond the edge of the window, drawing her with him, smoothly turning her, then backing her against the wall. "Like this?" He moved closer, trapping her between the wall and him.

The light coming through the window was weak, yet enough for her to see his face. Her eyes had widened; they searched his, then, her voice a touch firmer, more in control, she nodded and said, "Yes."

"What did he do then?"

"He tried to kiss me."

"Tried?"

"I fought him, wouldn't let him."

He bent his head and covered her lips with his, forced hers wide and kissed her without restraint. As forcefully as he wished, plundering, taking—until they were both reeling.

Lifting his head, he looked into her hazed eyes. "You don't have to fight me—you like being kissed by me."

She blinked, struggled to find enough breath to say, "Yes."

"And then?"

"And then . . ." Her gaze grew distant; after a moment,

she licked her swollen lips. "We were struggling. I was trying to break free, but he was much stronger than me—he
kept me pinned against the wall and started to pull up my
skirts."

"Like this?" With one hand, he grasped her skirts and
drew them up, bunching them in his fist.

Eyes locked with his, she drew in an unsteady breath.
"Yes." The word shook, but it wasn't fear but desire that made
her voice quaver.

He lowered his head so that his breath washed over her
lips. "And then?"

This time, when she tried to lick her lips, he swooped and
captured her tongue, drew it into his mouth, then released it.
"What happened next?"

Her breasts swelled as she drew in a breath. "He pushed
one of his legs between mine—forced my legs apart."

"Like this?"

He lifted her slightly, pressing one rock-hard thigh between hers, forcing her to ride the tensed muscle, ruthlessly
stimulating her even through her rucked skirts.

She gasped, let her head fall back against the wall. "Yes—
like that." But then she shook her head, frowning. "No—not
like that. With him it didn't feel good." He pressed and she
gasped. "Nothing like—"

"Nothing like this, nothing like with me."

"No . . . that was awful. This is . . . nice."

That was what he'd wanted and hoped to hear, a reassurance that her past wouldn't—couldn't—come between them,
not now, not later. He waited until she refocused on his eyes.
"What then?"

She dragged in a huge breath. "Three maids came into
the gallery, carrying warming pans for the guests' beds.
They were chattering—they were almost on us before they

realized. They gasped and fell back. Then they froze. They didn't know what to do. He'd twisted to look at them—I shoved, he staggered back and I broke free and fled."

He paused, then said, "There's no maids here."

She focused on his eyes, saw him clearly. "No." Her lips softened. "Nothing to stop you . . . from taking me."

He looked into her eyes. "Only you."

She studied his eyes, his face, then reached up with one hand, slid her palm over his nape, speared her fingers into his hair, and drew his lips to hers. "I don't want you to stop."

She breathed the words, then sealed his lips, and kissed him. Deeply.

He drew her skirts higher, trapped them at her waist, reached between her spread thighs and found her. Ready and swollen, wet and wanting.

It was the work of a minute to open the placket of his trousers, to free his aching staff and slowly, steadily, bury it deep in the hot haven she so ardently offered.

She sighed into his mouth, then arched as he lifted her higher against the wall, wordlessly urging him deeper.

He thrust in and she moaned; when he lifted her legs she wrapped them about his hips and clung. Gasping as he held her there, impaled, fully open, fully his.

It was a strange and wonderful loving, full of sighs and strangled moans, of intimate penetration accomplished beneath their clothes, and an even more evocative acceptance. Her body clasped his, again and again, holding him deep within her. There was no rush, no uncontrolled, out-of-control driving passion—just a simple wish for pleasure, a search to find it, give it, receive it in full measure. To wring every last scintilla of sensation from the moment, from their joining.

And at the last, when their senses were gorged and their nerves shredded and the frantic moment was upon them, when heat seared through their veins and for that glorious instant ripped them from the world, they still clung, wrapped together, savoring every last instant together.

The wave caught them, lifted them high, then flung them into ecstasy.

Once it faded, they fell back and collapsed across her bed, too exhausted to move, too sated to care.

Their labored breaths filled the air; he thought he could hear their hearts still thundering.

The tumult gradually faded. Relaxed beneath the arm he'd flung across her waist, Phoebe suddenly giggled. Eyes bright, she turned her head and looked at him. "That was . . ." She raised a hand, or tried to, then let it fall back to the bed. "*Wonderful*! Remarkable. Just don't ask me to move any time soon."

He snorted. "We'll just lie here for an hour or two, until I figure out which way is up."

She laughed, apparently delighted by the weakness she'd caused. The sound washed over him, a wonderful note that sank to his bones, evocative and intensely satisfying—just as satisfying, he decided, as the breathy little cry she always uttered when she climaxed.

After a moment, he struggled up on one elbow. He looked at her face, drank in her blissful expression. Debated, but he had to know. "What happened then?"

Lifting the lids she'd allowed to fall, she regarded him through the shadows, then sighed; her expression changed as she looked into the past.

"I ran all the way back to my room. I summoned Skinner and she came. She stayed with me. Later, when Marion looked in to ask where I'd got to, I told her I'd had a headache. Skinner and I discussed it—at the time, there was nothing I could do. If I'd made any protest . . . in those circles, in the circumstances, some wouldn't have believed me—they'd have whispered that I was making such claims to make myself interesting—while others would have known I spoke the truth but wouldn't have wanted to know. And above all else, there was the embarrassment, not just for myself but for Marion, too, and our hostess, who'd been nothing but kind."

"Other than inviting a gentleman to her house who she must have known preyed on young ladies."

Phoebe considered the naïve innocent she'd once been. "Indeed. Other than that."

A moment passed, then Deverell asked, "Who was he?"

She looked at him, met his eyes, and decided against telling him he didn't need to know. He didn't, but not because he didn't have the right to ask, especially not after what had just passed between them. "He . . . I took my revenge on him a few years later, once I'd learned how it could be done."

He frowned. "How?"

"I learned he'd married for money and was dependent on his wife's family, and therefore her support. I'd spent more time with Edith by then, and I'd learned how gossip works in the ton." She held his gaze. "His wife didn't know—she had no idea, but from all I could see she was the only one who didn't have some inkling. I started a rumor—very easy when people credit Edith with knowing everything there is to know and assume I'm in her confidence. It was a simple matter to say I'd heard from someone else . . . his wife heard it from any number of sources and started watching her husband. Within days, she had proof the rumors were true. Ever since, she's kept him a virtual prisoner in the country. She holds his purse strings, and given what she learned, she keeps a very tight grip on them."

She paused, then added, "In the end, I hit him where it hurt him the most—in his pride. He's something of a laughingstock now, for everyone knows why he's confined to his estate. And of course his wife never holds house parties."

Deverell studied her eyes, then nodded. "Remind me never to get on your wrong side." The gentleman he'd met at the ball hadn't been all that far wrong. Deadly—approach at your peril.

She chuckled and closed her eyes. "But now I've told you all my secrets, I want to know one of yours."

He blinked, considered. "I don't think I have any secrets— none that you might want to know."

"Ah, but you do." She opened her eyes and found his. "Tell me—why is it that with you, no matter what you do, no matter how . . . how forceful you are, how dominant, how frightening, how revulsed and panicked I would feel were it any other man but you doing the things you do to me—" She paused, then holding his gaze simply said, "Why is it that with you, the same things are so enjoyable?"

He looked into her eyes, shadowed in the dark, for a long moment, then bent his head and brushed her lips with his. "Because all the others are wrong—and I'm not. Because"— he touched his lips to hers, breathed over the delicate curves— "I'm the right man for you."

She asked no more questions. After a long, lingering, gentle kiss, they undressed in the dark, let their clothes fall where they would, then climbed under the covers and found sleep in each other's arms.

"What do you mean, she's *gone?*" Sitting at the agency's kitchen table beside Deverell, the accounts spread before them, Phoebe stared at Emmeline.

"Disappeared." Emmeline nodded grimly from the mouth of the corridor. "Just like that other one, only this time the girl *knew* we were coming for her tonight—so why would she run last night?"

Deverell glanced toward the front of the shop. "Is that the housekeeper?"

"Yes. Mrs. Stanley. She's the one helped organize our rescue. She's embarassed, but"—Emmeline shrugged—"it's hardly her fault."

Deverell glanced at Phoebe, then looked at Emmeline. "Ask Mrs. Stanley to step in here. Let's see if we can't shed some light on what happened."

Ushered to the kitchen by Emmeline, Mrs. Stanley nervously clutched her tapestry bag. Seeing Deverell and Phoebe, her eyes grew round; she quickly bobbed, regarding them with unbounded amazement. When Deverell politely invited her to sit, she looked uncertain.

"Oh, go on—they won't bite." Emmeline nudged her into a chair. "Just answer their questions and let's see what we can work out."

Mrs. Stanley perched on the edge of the chair and swallowed. "She—Lizette—was looking forward to getting away tomorrow with the agency. I swear I can't make head nor tail of why she vanished last night—she's not a silly girl, not Lizette."

"Vanished?" Deverell kept his expression encouraging, as unthreatening as possible.

"Yes—one minute she was heading upstairs, and this morning she was nowhere to be found."

"Her clothes, her belongings—are they still in her room?"

Mrs. Stanley nodded. "Must have been some powerful urge to have her leave them, but"—she shrugged—"who's to say?"

Deverell didn't like the notion that was forming in his head. "I believe, Mrs. Stanley, that you or the butler should inform the watch of Lizette's disappearance. Granted it's unlikely that they'll find her, but in the interests of justice, that should be done."

Mrs. Stanley nodded glumly. "Aye—I thought perhaps we should, but sure as eggs are eggs, they'll never find hide nor hair of poor Lizette—no more'n they did with Higgins's Bertha."

Deverell leaned forward. "Who?"

"Mrs. Higgins as is housekeeper for Major and Mrs. Wrigley on South Audley Street. Her parlor maid Bertha, handsome girl who'd been with her six years, suddenly up and vanished two weeks ago, just like Lizette." Mrs. Stanley shook her head. "Higgins reported it to the watchhouse, like you said, but nothing came of it. And she hasn't seen Bertha again."

Deverell debated but decided he had to know. "This Bertha—you said she was a handsome girl. And I assume Lizette was, too?"

"Oh, aye. Right lookers, the pair of them. Well, have to be, don't you, to be a parlor maid these days."

Deverell made no reply; he stood as Mrs. Stanley got to her feet. Other than repeating his advice that she report Lizette's disappearance, he said nothing more; a minute later, the bell tinkled and the front door shut behind the housekeeper.

Birtles, who had sat through the interview in the chair before the fire, looked at Deverell as he resumed his seat. "You think there's something behind this—these maids who up and disappear after arranging to leave with us?"

Deverell glanced at Phoebe, saw the same question in her eyes, and in Emmeline's as she came back from seeing Mrs. Stanley out.

"I think," he said, choosing his words, "that these disappearances are becoming too frequent to overlook. Three, all in the space of two weeks, all attractive girls—the sort who work in the mansions of Mayfair." He definitely didn't like what he was thinking.

"The same area we mostly work in," Birtles observed.

"Indeed." Deverell kept his reaction from his face. "Be

that as it may, I can't see any way we can pursue this—other than via the watch."

Not unless they had something more to work with. He turned that conclusion over and around in his mind, examining it from every angle, and couldn't fault it. He knew too little to alert anyone—even those who would back his instinct that something nefarious was going on.

He glanced at Birtles, who was as sober as he. "Until we clear up this mystery of the missing maids, we'll take every precaution."

Phoebe grimaced. "Well, we won't have to worry tonight—we no longer have anyone to rescue."

Chapter 18

"Here she comes." Phoebe pointed to a slight, cloaked figure creeping up the area steps at the rear of one of the town houses fronting Curzon Street.

Deverell spared the hesitant figure no more than a glance before returning his gaze to the dense shadows shrouding the narrow alley in which he and Phoebe stood waiting, partially concealed in the lee of their carriage.

This was the sixth rescue he'd helped organize, and the one he liked the least. Although only yards from the wide thoroughfares of Mayfair, they stood in a maze of alleys, lanes, and interconnecting mews; there were too many entrances onto the scene, all draped in darkness—too many approaches from which others could come at them largely unseen.

He kept telling himself that this wasn't a battle, that Phoebe and her people weren't troops he was positioning to repel an attack, yet that's how his mind kept seeing the moment—how his instincts kept prodding him to react.

Phoebe shifted beside him, her attention on the maid creeping out into the alley, her gaze locked on the dark carriage. One hand on Phoebe's arm, restraining her, Deverell gripped, then released his hold. "Go to her."

He didn't need to whisper twice; Phoebe swept forward, walking quickly, decisively. Cloaked and hooded, she was nevertheless clearly female; the frightened maid, also cloaked, drew herself up, clutching her bag to her chest defensively, but she didn't bolt.

Deverell scanned the area again; his thumbs were pricking. Fergus was on the box; Grainger was further down the alley watching their escape route, while Birtles was keeping watch at the head of one of the alleys to their rear. Scatcher was about, too, hugging the shadows a little ahead of the carriage.

Every instinct Deverell possessed urged him to walk with Phoebe, to stick by her side, yet if the maid saw him there, large and menacing, she might panic and flee. Phoebe had a knack of reassuring with a few words, so that while they still eyed him, and to a lesser extent Birtles and Fergus, with wariness and suspicion, the girls would nevertheless trust Phoebe enough to leave with them.

Phoebe reached the girl and spoke with her. Deverell saw some of the brittle tension in the maid's figure ease. She peered toward the carriage. Phoebe turned and beckoned.

He started forward—and a chill touched his nape.

In that same instant he saw a shadow between him and Scatcher move, sliding out of a narrow gap between two houses. Blinking, he shifted into a run—there were more of them pouring out of the narrow gap. Behind him came the sound of an oath and scuffles.

Followed by the unmistakable cacophony of a fight.

He waved at Phoebe. "Get to the carriage!" She'd turned and was staring past the carriage at the altercation behind it.

Two men erupted out of the area behind the maid—shoving her aside, they flung themselves on Deverell.

He had to stop and deal with them. A flurry of quick, punishing blows, a kick to one knee and they were down, rolling and groaning on the rough paving.

Deverell swung around, rapidly assessing. Scatcher had fallen on the rear of the group between him and Phoebe; despite his stature, he was giving a good account and Grainger was pounding to his relief.

But one man had won through; he'd reached Phoebe. He was standing before her and the maid, looking from one to the other—it was ludicrously obvious he'd been told to "grab the woman" and didn't know which one to seize.

He seized Phoebe.

Deverell saw red.

The man started to drag her down the alley; she resisted, slapping at him with her free hand.

The man cursed, stopped, lifted his arm to backhand her across her face—

Deverell's fist connected with the man's face instead.

He wrenched Phoebe free. "The carriage!" He pushed her toward the maid, then squared up to the bruiser, who'd staggered back, bellowing in rage. Regaining his balance, he lowered his head and charged Deverell.

But the man hadn't been taught to fight in the same arena Deverell had; with a few quick jabs followed by a satisfying roundhouse, Deverell felled him.

He spared only a moment to confirm that Scatcher and Grainger were holding their own, then turned and raced back to the carriage. Dragging the nearly hysterical maid, Phoebe had just reached it and opened the door.

"Get in!" She pushed the maid to the door.

Deverell reached them, grasped the maid about the waist and hoisted her into the carriage, then grabbed Phoebe and bundled her in after her. He slammed the door shut. "Stay there!"

There was no one on the box. The horses were shifting, restive, but not yet panicking.

He ran to the rear of the carriage. Birtles had been overwhelmed by three men, but Fergus had jumped down and gone to his aid. Laying about with his whip, he'd dragged the bruised Birtles free, but the hyenas were still circling.

The three attackers froze when Deverell appeared out of the night and ranged alongside Fergus and Birtles, now upright, albeit unsteadily.

Eyeing him, swiftly calculating the odds and deciding they were no longer in their favor, the three exchanged glances, then turned and fled.

Fergus swore and started after them. Deverell caught his arm and hauled him back. "No—let's get out of here."

Recalled to their purpose, Fergus nodded and lumbered back to the carriage. Deverell supported Birtles as far as the carriage door. "Get inside."

Leaving the big man to clamber in, Deverell went to the horses' heads and peered down the alley. The three who had tangled with him had staggered away; he glimpsed one of them disappearing down the narrow gap.

Further down the alley, wreathed in shadows, Grainger and Scatcher were still standing—but so were two of their assailants.

Deverell turned; in two strides, he reached the coachman's steps and swung up. "Go—we'll pick them up on the way."

Fergus released the brake and eased the reins; eager to get away, the horses jerked and clattered forward.

The two attackers facing Scatcher and Grainger heard; glancing around they saw the carriage lumbering down upon them.

They turned and fled down another of the narrow alleys.

"Get on!" Deverell waved Scatcher and Grainger to the carriage.

Scatcher came running; Grainger hesitated, wanting to give chase, but then obeyed. Fergus slowed the carriage; both men scrambled up to the footmen's positions over the boot.

The instant they were aboard, Fergus whipped up his horses. He drove out of the dark alleys into the nearly deserted streets and headed toward the agency.

Beside him, Deverell settled on the seat. "Take a roundabout route."

It wasn't until she sat down at the table in the agency's kitchen that Phoebe had a chance to analyze what had happened. Sinking onto a chair, she looked around—at her people, as Deverell referred to them.

He was there, sitting alongside her, his hands wrapped about a steaming mug. He and Fergus had tended to Birtles's bruises while she and Emmeline had soothed and reassured the panicked maid. The girl, Molly Doyle, was now huddled under the covers on one of the narrow cots upstairs, thanking her stars for salvation.

A cup of tea appeared in front of Phoebe. She looked up and smiled her thanks as Emmeline took the chair beside her. Birtles sat slumped in the next chair, sipping what Phoebe suspected was an extra-strong hot toddy.

Fergus rose from the fire he'd been stoking and took the chair at the end. The back door opened and Scatcher and Grainger, who'd been taking care of the horses, came in. Emmeline rose, helped them to tea, then resumed her seat.

Deverell glanced around as Scatcher and lastly Grainger sat. "Good—we're all here, more or less intact. We came out of that well, but . . ." His gaze traveled around the table, taking in the faces, finally coming to rest on Phoebe's.

"Who were they? Why did they attack us? And will they attack us again?"

"Wasn't any doing of the household—the nobs the girl was fleeing from," Birtles said. "Wrong sort of bruisers. And they weren't young bloods out for a lark, neither."

Scatcher nodded. "Lowlifes, they were—right rum customers."

"Did you recognize any of them?" Deverell asked.

Scatcher shook his head. "Not from this side of town, nor yet, if you ask me, from the East End, neither." He sipped, then said, "Southwark, most like."

"What's most worrying me," Fergus said, his Scots accent slow and lugubrious, "is the why of it."

That was worrying Phoebe, too.

Fergus glanced at her, then looked at Deverell. "Could it be that last time, and perhaps one time before that, they got to the girls first, but this time, we did?"

Deverell hesitated, then admitted, "It looks suspiciously like that. But what—" He broke off, looking down at the mug cradled between his hands, a frown drawing down his dark brows. "Bear with me—let's talk this through. This other gang . . . if we assume they're behind the other disappearances we've heard of, then it seems they're targeting a specific sort of female." He glanced around the table. "You all saw Molly Doyle?"

Puzzled, Fergus, Scatcher, and Grainger shook their heads.

"She's Irish, another parlor maid, and strikingly pretty, if not beautiful. Mrs. Higgins described the other two girls—Lizette and Bertha—as 'right lookers.' It appears this gang is kidnapping beautiful parlor maids, and of course Mayfair has the best selection of those."

"But . . . why?" Emmeline gave voice to the obvious question.

Deverell's expression was grim. "I can think of only one reason. This other gang are procurers for white slave traders."

Emmeline sucked in a shocked breath; horrified, Phoebe held hers.

Birtles blinked. "I didn't think that happened anymore."

"It does," Deverell said, "but it operates in cycles. They'll plague London for a few months, maybe a year, then fade away—but then it's Bristol's turn, or Liverpool, or Southampton. Over the years, they've likely become more selective—beautiful, preferably untouched young women will give the best return in their dastardly trade."

He paused, then concluded, "It appears the blackguards have returned to London."

"So," Phoebe said, "while we're *rescuing* the same sort of girls—for of course it's the most attractive female staff who are subjected to unwanted attentions—this other gang is trying to kidnap them."

"Exactly." Deverell met her eyes when she looked at him. "And that's why we're going to have to do something about this, because short of halting the agency's efforts with 'special clients,' it's inevitable we'll run across this gang again." He paused, then added, "Or more specifically, they'll come looking for us."

"In the night, in the narrow alleys." Fergus nodded direfully. "While we're rescuing the girls—they'll know where to find us."

"Bad enough," Deverell grimly returned, "but it'll be even worse if they follow us back here. That we can't have—it's something we must never risk."

They all murmured agreement to that.

Deverell waited a moment, allowing everyone time to assimilate the situation, then quietly said, "That leaves us facing a choice—a choice we have to make, more or less now, tonight."

Phoebe turned to him. "What choice?"

He met her gaze. "We have two options, two paths we can take. One, we do nothing to stop the slaving gang— nothing to draw attention to the agency. We pull back and hide until the wolves finish prowling London's streets and move on to their next field. That may be weeks, or it may be months. We'll have to cease all rescues and leave threatened girls to fend for themselves until it's safe for us to act again. We can't even be a safe house, taking in girls if they can find their way here by themselves. Even that could lead the wolves to our door."

A deep murmur of resistance rippled around the table.

He held up a staying hand. "Before you say no to that option, consider this. This agency has rescued a number of women over the years—and will rescue many more in the years to come *if* it remains in existence. If we refuse to temporarily call a halt, we'll put the future of the agency—and the rescue of all those women in the years to come—at risk."

Everyone was grimly sober; all frowned, weighing his words.

"How much risk?" Phoebe eventually asked, a clear bite to her tone. "What's the other option—you said there were two?"

"The second option is to stop the slavers."

Fergus looked worried. "How? We came out all right tonight, but next time there'll be more of them, and there aren't more of us."

Deverell felt his lips curve. "Yes, and no. I hadn't imagined taking them on in the back streets at night. That would be foolhardy. However, I have contacts who'll know exactly how to deal with them—indeed, I imagine they'll be only too *happy* to deal with them once I inform them that such a gang is active. However, in doing that, and while they're being dealt with, which may take a week or so, we'll have to be more vigilant than ever—we must *not* draw attention to the agency's 'special clients.' Not official attention—while the agency's actions in helping 'special clients' is not of itself illegal, some of the methods employed would not meet with general approval. And we'll still need to avoid the attention of the slavers."

He glanced around, meeting all the gazes, ending with Phoebe's. "We can act against them—with luck the authorities will catch them, but at the very least they'll be driven from London and the agency will be able to continue its work in safety. But in alerting the authorities there's a risk that they'll discover what the agency's secret role is—it's the reason we've stumbled on the gang. We can take care to keep our heads down in any upcoming rescue over the next weeks while the authorities are dealing with the gang, but we can't completely foresee—and therefore can't completely manage—what might happen once we inform the authorities."

Frowning, Phoebe held his gaze, wondering why he was watching her so intently—why he was speaking more to her than anyone else.

"So," he concluded, "there are two options, two paths. Both will work. One is completely safe but lets the slavers be. The second is risky but, with luck, will mean the end of this gang at least."

His gaze remained steady on her face. Phoebe sensed he was waiting . . . then she realized. She cleared her throat and looked around the table. Everyone was waiting on her— on her decision.

Her people, her agency . . . her decision.

She looked back and found Deverell's eyes, looked into

the steady, unwavering green. Drew strength and certainty from his gaze. "I don't think there's any real choice—we can't allow slavers to operate without trying to stop them. The agency's reason for existence runs directly counter to theirs." Drawing in a decisive breath, she glanced around the table. "I believe we should take the second path. We need to alert the authorities."

No one had argued. Deverell had accepted Phoebe's commission to do whatever needed to be done to alert the authorities and set them on the trail of the slavers. In turn he'd impressed on everyone else the need to conceal the agency's special operations from all those not already aware of them.

Climbing the club's stairs the next morning after breakfast, he recalled his and Phoebe's later discussion, once they'd been alone in her bedchamber.

Although he'd couched the risk as being to the agency, there was an equal risk to her—to her reputation. Should it ever become known she was the owner of an employment agency, let alone that that agency specialized in rescuing female servants from sexual exploitation, she would be ostracized. Such was the hypocrisy of the society in which they lived.

When he'd made that point, Phoebe had looked at him then waved the matter aside. Not lightly—she'd seen the danger—but without hesitation.

Quite apart from all else, all he now felt for her, for that alone he would stand by her forever.

She had a well-honed grasp of right and wrong, of which rules could be broken, which bent, and which were inviolable. And a feel for those risks one sometimes had to take. For one of his background, his past history, he couldn't wish for better in a wife—for an understanding and a pragmatism that augered better for their future.

Walking into the library, he headed for the writing desk set in one corner.

Half an hour later, he summoned Gasthorpe. "Have these delivered as soon as possible." He handed the majordomo letters addressed to Viscount Trentham and to the Marquess of Dearne at their London residences. "And give this"—he added a folded note to the pile—"to Crowhurst when he wakes."

Gasthorpe had informed him over breakfast that Gervase Tregarth, Earl of Crowhurst, had arrived late last night, having driven up from his estates in deepest Cornwall. From Deverell's point of view—and, he suspected, Gervase's as well—that was perfect timing.

Gasthorpe eyed the missives with interest. "Is something afoot, my lord?"

Gasthorpe had been a sergeant major throughout the wars; he could scent imminent action.

"Indeed." Deverell rose. "I'm convening a meeting here this afternoon." He hesitated, then added, "Miss Malleson will be attending, which will shock the others but can't be helped. Given our numbers, we'll need to use the library."

"Indeed, my lord. Rules are all very well, but we need to be flexible. What time, my lord?"

"I've nominated four o'clock, but it might be later. I'm sure Trentham, Dearne, and Crowhurst, as well as Miss Malleson and I, will be here at that time, but I'm not sure at what hour the last of those I'm summoning will be able to join us."

Gasthorpe looked his question.

Lips twisting, Deverell clapped him on the shoulder and headed for the door. "Wish me luck—I'm off to Whitehall to beard a lion."

A hungry, frustrated, disaffected lion who seemed perfectly ready to savage *something* that deserved it.

Sitting in front of Dalziel's desk, watching the elegant gentleman who for ten and more years had been his commander mentally sift the information Deverell had just finished laying before him—the evidence of missing maids, the "rescue" that had been disrupted, the nature of the men involved—Deverell wondered how much longer Dalziel—Royce whoever-he-was—would continue to search for his last traitor.

They'd been close to success last month when Jack Warnefleet had been in town, but at the last moment Dalziel's "last traitor"—the one he'd hypothesized must exist and who they now knew was flesh and blood—had slipped from their net. He'd killed his henchman to do it, but that only bore witness to the man's ruthlessness.

Dalziel's ruthlessness had never been in question. Although his expression remained as enigmatic as ever, his dark brown eyes held enough frustration for Deverell to read.

Just what that augered Deverell wasn't sure; he'd come hoping for Dalziel's support in an administrative sense—he could open doors with just a message, get attention from any branch of the authorities, insist on things no one else could. Regardless of his failure over his last traitor, he still wielded significant power. But . . . there was a restless tension in Dalziel Deverell recognized—the need to act, to do, to accomplish something even if the most desired goal remained out of reach.

Battle nerves, they'd called it. The impulse to act that one often had to fight against in the hour prior to the first charge. That those who'd served in the same secret arena as Deverell had had to learn to suppress, to not act precipitously and bring disaster down on their heads. Yet in Dalziel's case it wasn't so much a matter of timing as of release—of having no outlet for the frustrations his pursuit of the last traitor had generated.

Failure was something Dalziel's temperament was not well suited to absorb.

Abruptly Dalziel's gaze refocused on his face. "Slavers."

Just the word, uttered in that deep, ineffably cultured voice, with an inflection dripping so much more than disgust told Deverell that administrative assistance was the most minor of the support he was going to get.

"This agency—how safe are they?"

"For the moment, safe enough. There's no information the slavers are likely to find that will lead them to it."

Dalziel nodded. Decisively. "Very well—you can count me in. Slaving in any form is bad enough, but to have a gang operating on London streets, seizing women—women they pick and choose assisted by someone in the ton—is anathema, beyond condemnation. That they made a mistake and nearly grabbed Miss Malleson only illustrates that the danger is not confined to the lower classes.

"And you're perfectly right—we can't leave this to the overworked watch. Besides"—Dalziel's dark eyes glinted with the predatory inclinations of a born marauder—"as some of the culprits are likely to be members of the ton, the watch will be hampered where we will not."

We, Deverell noted.

"So—how are you proposing we go about this?" Dalziel's gaze was now deceptively mild.

Deverell wasn't fooled; his ex-commander was spoiling for a fight—he was just glad they were on the same side. "I've called a meeting at the club for four o'clock this afternoon. Crowhurst will be there, and most likely Trentham and Dearne. St. Austell, Torrington, and Warnefleet are all on their estates—by the time a message reaches them and they return to town, it'll all be over."

"Indeed. And I daresay, recently married as they are, they might have other calls on their time." Dalziel had looked down, consulting a diary; Deverell couldn't tell if that last comment was uttered tongue-in-cheek or as a statement of fact.

"Four o'clock at the Bastion Club." Dalziel looked up and met Deverell's eyes. "I'll be there."

Early that afternoon Malcolm again braved his guardian's study to sit elegantly at ease in the chair before Henry's desk. And possess his soul with saintly patience.

Eventually Henry looked up, narrow-eyed, from the dispatch box through which he'd been leafing. Stony-faced, he regarded Malcolm. "Well?"

With diffidence perfected to an art, Malcolm flicked a speck of lint from his sleeve. "We caused them some grief, but . . ."

Henry scowled. "But *what?*" He dumped the red dispatch box down on the desk. "They were supposed to be *taught a lesson.*"

"Oh, I'm quite sure they got the point." Malcolm frowned slightly, the gesture for once entirely genuine; he was puzzled, his instincts for self-preservation stirring uneasily. "I was watching the action from a doorway nearby. They didn't see me—but I have to admit I didn't like what I saw."

Henry's scowl grew blacker. "What the devil do you mean?"

Malcolm hesitated, replaying the scene again in his mind. "One of the other crew . . . he could fight. And no, I don't mean he was a brawler or a pugilist or anything of that nature. Not even a devotee of Gentleman Jackson—he was far more effective than that."

In his mind he saw again the tall, lean, menacing figure— saw again how he moved, the controlled strength, the incisive, decisive application of same. "He was . . . something quite different, and definitely dangerous. I didn't get a good look at him, but if I had to describe him, I'd say he had the build of a guardsman."

"Hmm." Henry shut the red box and pushed it aside. "It

sounds like they—whoever they are—have recruited some talent."

"There was something else." Malcolm met Henry's eyes. "There was a woman there—one of them, helping to get the girl away."

"A *woman?*" Henry raised his brows, then snorted. "I don't know why I'm surprised. Probably your 'guardsman's' doxy."

Malcolm inclined his head noncommittally. "Chifley also babbled about some woman being in the lane when he rushed out—he, too, assumed she was some doxy assisting the other gang. *However*"—he waited until his tone brought Henry's cold gaze back to his face—"if it was the same woman I saw last night, she's no doxy. She's of the ton. I can't put a name to her, but I've definitely seen her about this Season."

Henry's eyes narrowed; Malcolm could almost hear the thoughts chasing themselves through his brain.

Then Henry's jaw set. "Go out into the ton—it's the height of the Season, balls and parties aplenty, and you have the entrée everywhere. Find out who this lady is." Henry's eyes grew colder; they gleamed like ice. "Don't approach her—not in any ballroom. Learn her name, and then we can arrange a private meeting to ask her who she's working with. I'm sure we'll be able to convince her to tell us all."

Henry was clearly relishing the prospect. Malcolm was rather less sure of tangling in any way with the man he'd glimpsed in the alley.

He waited. When Henry said no more, absorbed in considering some scene Malcolm had no real wish to see, he dutifully inclined his head. "I'll start quartering the ton tonight."

Henry came to himself, glowered, then nodded curtly and reopened the dispatch box. "Tell me the instant you learn who she is."

* * *

"He's coming here?" Tristan raised his brows high. "Well, well—he *is* keen."

Phoebe considered the look on Tristan's face, then Christian's; guessing what she was thinking, Deverell explained, "Our ex-commander is very much a law unto himself."

"Whoever his self may be." Gervase caught Phoebe's eye. "He goes by the name of Dalziel, but that isn't his true name. What his real name is and why he's kept it a secret is a mystery we're collectively determined to solve."

Christian and Tristan had arrived early; Gervase hadn't bothered going out. The three had been waiting in the library, relaxed in armchairs with glasses of brandy in hand, when Deverell had ushered Phoebe into the room.

The others had come to their feet with alacrity; they'd beamed and lined up to be introduced. No hint of censure regarding Deverell's cavalier dismissal of their no-female-except-in-the-front-parlor rule had surfaced, not even via a look. Once they'd all settled again, Phoebe in the armchair at the focal point of the room with a glass of the finest amontillado in her hand, the others flanking her in a rough circle, Deverell had found himself glad that there were still ten minutes to the hour, leaving him time to reassure Phoebe over Dalziel.

"Some weeks ago, we learned his real first name was Royce," Christian said, "but unfortunately that doesn't get us far. We're not sure if it's his first first name, or his third or even fourth—or even a formal given name at all, come to that."

"We did learn that Lady Osbaldestone and at least two of the other grande dames know him in his real guise." Deverell picked up the tale. "But although we tried our best to interrogate—and when that didn't work, wheedle, trap, or in any other way coerce the information from—said ladies, we learned nothing beyond that they also know the reason he keeps his identity a secret."

"So," Tristan said, "beyond the name he actually goes by, he remains as big a mystery as ever."

Phoebe smiled. "I imagine that's one mystery none of you can let be."

They all paused, considered, then shook their heads.

"He knows all our secrets," Gervase said. "Only fair we should know his. Apropos of that"—he looked at Deverell—"is there any specific connection between your game and his obsession? Is that why he's so eager?"

"Highly unlikely," Deverell said. He'd already given Phoebe a potted history of Dalziel's last traitor. "I think the reason for his interest is more that he's frustrated and restless with no enemy to sink his teeth into, so he's perfectly happy to turn his attention to my game, and sink his teeth into my enemy instead."

The others chuckled.

Christian nodded. "Yes, I can imagine that."

"One thing that did occur to me," Deverell said, "was that if we needed further proof that whatever he did during the war he didn't spend the entire time behind his desk, his present reaction provides it. If he'd been nothing more than a pen-pusher, he wouldn't be feeling inactivity pinching now."

The other three nodded sagely.

In the distance, they heard a peremptory knock fall on the front door.

At the same instant, the clock on the mantelpiece chimed the hour.

Phoebe waited, eyes on the door. When it opened, and the club's majordomo bowed the visitor in, she fully expected to be somewhat disappointed; after all the talk of mystery and menace, she didn't truly believe their ex-commander could live up to the picture they'd painted.

One glance told her she'd been wrong.

He was more—much more—than they'd led her to believe.

She watched the other four rise and go forward to meet him, to shake his hand and exchange greetings. She didn't bother listening to their words beyond registering that although his voice was like theirs, deep and well-modulated, his tone always held an edge—a warning that words and tone could slice; more than the others, he used his voice as a weapon.

Outwardly, he was superficially one with the others—immaculately turned out in coat, waistcoat, breeches and boots, with a perfectly tied cravat; his hair was dark—sable brown—while his features bore the unmistakable stamp of their shared Norman ancestors.

She took all that in in one comprehensive glance, then concentrated on what they hadn't told her—all else that she could see as he moved among them.

Deverell was graceful, elegant, and strong, as were the other three club members. Their ex-commander, however, took all three qualities to the extreme. Phoebe had lived all her life in the ton, but she'd never, ever, set eyes on a man like this one.

There was something that lived just beneath his surface, something that prowled. Something infinitely more dangerous—something that frankly shouldn't be permitted in any well-bred drawing room.

And then he was moving toward her, his dark gaze fixed on her, Deverell bringing him to her to introduce.

She rose, feeling trapped in that predatory gaze. Deverell and the others were dominant men, but they weren't like this.

This man was too much—definitely too much. Too dangerous, too powerful—too male.

All her reservations over large and powerful men returned

in a rush. She glanced at Deverell. He caught her wide-eyed look, arched a quizzical brow, then he was by her side, his hand under her elbow.

Just as well; it stopped her from curtsying.

His touch reassured and anchored her. She heard him introduce her and remembered just in time to offer her hand.

Dalziel took it in his; his fingers were cool, their pressure undisturbing as he bowed over hers.

She drew breath and managed a passable smile.

Releasing her hand, he smiled in return—effortlessly charming, just like Deverell. "It's a pleasure to meet you, Miss Malleson."

She uttered the prescribed reply and they parted; he moved away to accept a glass of brandy from Tristan. She sank back into her chair, able to breathe again. As the others all sat, she realized why she'd instinctively started to curtsy. Deeply.

She'd seen Dalziel before—not met him, only seen him. At some party one of her aunts had given long ago. The memory was hazy. Deverell started to speak, and she put it aside to tease out later.

Deverell had told the others little beyond the fact that he'd stumbled on a slaving gang operating in Mayfair. Early this morning, he'd spoken to her of the need to reveal to his ex-colleagues, as well as Dalziel, the full scope of the agency's operations. If they wanted their help, they needed to trust them with the whole truth. She'd agreed, and now she'd met them she had no doubt that had been the right decision.

But as she listened to Deverell explain the agency, how they learned of their "special clients'" needs and then arranged to whisk the girls away and resettle them, she wondered how such behavior sounded to them—whether they would be shocked that a lady of her station, unmarried, should be not just involved in but the instigator of such an enterprise, correcting a wrong ladies such as she weren't supposed to know of, or at least were supposed to hide any awareness of. Would they view her as vulgar?

While Deverell was speaking, she kept her gaze on the glass of sherry in her hand. When he came to the end of his description of the agency and paused, she drew breath and looked up, swiftly scanning the circle of faces.

Tristan was the easiest to read; his eyes were wide in patent amazement heavily tinged with approval. "What an extremely *laudable* goal."

"Indeed." Gervase raised his glass to her. "A commendable endeavor."

"Felicitations on your courage, Miss Malleson." Dalziel inclined his head to her, his dark eyes trapping hers. "The only element I find disturbing about your enterprise is that it has reason to exist." His face hardened and he lowered his eyes. "Would that it didn't."

"True," Christian said. "However, as we're dealing with reality—indeed, must deal with it—your endeavor is worthy of the highest respect. Would that more ladies looked to such activities rather than their usual often ineffective charities."

"Speaking of which, would you mind, Miss Malleson, if I told my wife of your agency?" Tristan asked. "It's the sort of enterprise in which I know she'd love to be involved."

Blushing under their fulsome praise, Phoebe admitted that she'd already met Leonora and they were meeting again. She gave Tristan permission to explain about the agency; rather surprised, she found herself promising to allow Leonora to assist.

"So that's the agency as is," Deverell resumed. "What happened . . ."

While he described the recent events—the girls who'd disappeared before they'd been rescued and the latest fracas—Phoebe surreptitiously studied the others, considering not just their words but all she could see of their reactions.

They were like Deverell in multiple ways—strong, large, inherently sensually charismatic, powerful, arrogant, dominant and wealthy gentlemen who, although warriors at heart, were driven not by the urge to dominate and own, to capture and exploit, but by a need to protect and defend.

Although the least easy to outwardly read, Dalziel was in that respect the clearest example; although all of them felt it, his anger at those who gave the agency reason to exist was more hard-edged, more potent, more clearly sensed.

Raising her head, she gazed around the circle; all were focused on Deverell and his words. She no longer had the slightest doubt that enlisting the aid of these gentlemen was the right thing to do. She felt perfectly safe trusting them with the agency's secrets, and hers. In entrusting the agency's defense to them.

As had happened with Deverell, as she looked around the circle she felt not a little amazement, a small voice in her head noting that it wasn't only Deverell who was like this— large, powerful, sensual—and *safe*.

Reaching the end of their evidence, Deverell paused, then stated the inescapable conclusion. "These kidnappings are specific. They're targeted. Not just any maid who happens to walk by, good-looking or not, but specific girls of a certain age, a certain high standard of beauty."

"Which means"—Christian narrowed his eyes; normally a gentle gray, they'd turned as hard as stone—"*someone*, almost certainly someone of the ton, is, for want of a better term, identifying the targets."

Deverell nodded. "Indeed. It can't be any butler or other member of anyone's staff."

Gervase humphed. "They don't see enough other staff to be useful in that regard, not given the fussiness of white slavers."

"So," Tristan said, his tone full of disgust, "it's one of us." He glanced at the others. "So to speak."

"Indeed." Dalziel's drawl promised the darkest retribution. "Which is why it's so fitting *we* should hunt him down and ensure appropriate justice is dispensed."

Phoebe blinked and glanced around. Far from looking startled, the others were all nodding, perfectly serious, grimly so.

"Which brings us to our first question," Deverell said. "How?"

Phoebe sat back and listened as they threw suggestions and observations back and forth. It was rather unsettling to sense—to have demonstrated so clearly—this other side of them, the ruthless, implacable side. In their pursuit of whoever was aiding the slavers, and the slavers themselves, they acknowledged no such things as limitations, only hurdles to be overcome.

In this guise, they were as frightening, as scarifying as any other man she'd ever met, yet Deverell was one of them . . . and listening, she could see what drove them, what fueled their driving passion in this—what ultimately would drive them to victory in this. They saw it as their right and proper place to defend the weak and the helpless against those who would harm and exploit.

That was their role, what they'd been born to do—their birthright, one they'd each long since claimed. They knew that, lived that, understood that—and now she did, too. She would never be wary of men like them again.

Gervase sat forward, his glass cradled between his hands. "If one of the ton is involved, and we know that's so, then it's money that's behind it."

Dalziel nodded. "Agreed. I can think of some rather less savory motives, but regardless, money will be the major attraction."

"So," Christian said, "what can we surmise about this someone? I can't imagine they're female."

Tristan grimaced. "It's possible, but is it likely? There would have to be some connection with the slavers—some agreement—and I can't see any female regardless of her need of funds being able to pull that off. Too dangerous, too likely she'll end up as part of the goods."

"So our quarry is a man," Deverell said. "One who lives in London, very possibly for most of the year, most likely in Mayfair, and given the households from which maids have disappeared, he moves in the best circles."

Christian added, "He may not be *known* to be in need of funds."

Dalziel inclined his head. "That would be too easy."

"However," Deverell said, "there are ways to inquire, people who would know."

Christian grinned. "I assume you haven't retired from the business world. How far can your contacts reach?"

Deverell narrowed his eyes. "Quite possibly far enough. I'll have them put the word out tomorrow and see what we can learn."

Dalziel was turning his glass between his long fingers. "I'll see what I can ferret out by less direct means. We're looking for someone with a hidden need of cash—there are always whispers."

Deverell met Christian's eyes; all of them wanted to know what "less direct means" their ex-commander had at his disposal, but none were game to ask.

"Meanwhile," Dalziel went on, "the rest of you can see what you can learn from the watchhouses. Concentrate on those surrounding Mayfair. See what you can learn about missing maids—from there and any other sources you have to hand. We should try to get dates for all the disappearances we can find." He met Deverell's eyes. "With luck, if either you or I can identify a likely villain, we can check to see if he was the recipient of unexplained largesse on or around those dates."

Deverell nodded. "Even more, it might be possible to track him through such payments. Difficult, but the more dates we can identify, the more one account will stand out— regardless of whether he's using another name to conceal the payments."

"True," Christian said. "And then there's the slavers themselves." He grinned, but it wasn't a humorous gesture. "I'll ask around my underworld contacts and see what they've heard, but white slavers by their nature tend to be criminal nomads without strong connections to the local scene. I'll check nevertheless—no telling where we might have some luck."

"And then there's the docks." Gervase nodded to Tristan. "Between you and me, we should have that covered. And Jack Hendon's in town, too. Whoever our villains are, there have to be ships involved, and of that someone's bound to know."

"On top of that," Dalziel put in, "I'll officially alert the water police. My understanding is that white slavers generally gather their goods on shore, then call a ship in—too suspicious to have a ship with no specified cargo simply standing out from shore. The dock and port authorities have been much more vigilant in recent years."

Dalziel glanced around; all the others were nodding, thinking, but there were no further suggestions. He met Phoebe's eyes. "It's enough to start with," he said, "but I would also suggest that keeping a covert watch on the Athena Agency premises would be wise, at least until we know who our tonnish villain is. We have no idea what insights he might be privy to, so making sure the slavers don't call around to put the agency permanently out of business seems a sensible precaution."

The other four readily agreed. Dalziel smiled faintly at Phoebe; she smiled, rather tightly, back. The unnerving man no doubt thought he'd done her a favor—and quite possibly he had. But all she could think of as the meeting broke up was how she was to explain to Emmeline and the still frightened Molly, let alone the other women who dropped by at the agency, that there would be an assortment of large, dangerous, powerful—but *safe*—gentlemen hovering, flitting back and forth, keeping a protective watch on them all.

Chapter 19

*L*ater that night, Phoebe sat at her dressing table brushing out her hair and thinking over the events of the day.

Meeting Deverell's colleagues, learning what they planned to do, how they planned to catch the white slavers, had been intriguing, but looking back on the episode, what truly amazed her was that she had been invited to attend. And accepted as a necessary presence. She'd said little but hadn't felt excluded. Time and again they'd glanced at her for confirmation; if there'd been anything with which she'd disagreed, she'd been given ample opportunity to say so. And any comment she might have made would have been listened to and addressed, of that she felt sure.

It had felt strange to be treated so . . . much like an equal. As Deverell treated her, true. Perhaps men like him, like the others, saw partnerships with ladies as the norm, or at least mundane enough to be accepted without a blink.

That, she well knew, was certainly not the common thinking among fashionable gentlemen.

Uttering a soft snort, she laid aside her brush and reached around her neck to unhook her pearl necklace. She'd told Skinner she wouldn't need her tonight; she hadn't yet undressed, because she wanted to talk to Deverell.

First. For that, clothes would help.

After leaving his club, they'd gone to the agency to tell the others their news. Emmeline had blinked, expression blanking on hearing that there would be four other gentlemen—all large ex-guardsmen like Deverell—haunting her kitchen over the next few weeks; she'd gone very quiet.

She'd taken Emmeline aside and they'd gone up to see Molly; there, she'd explained that the other four were *just* like Deverell, that there was absolutely nothing to fear from them—that indeed, both Emmeline and Molly could rely on them if they had any need.

Somewhat to her surprise, Emmeline had blinked again, thought a moment, then smiled and assured her all would be well. If they were *just* like Deverell, then, or so it seemed, both Emmeline and Molly were quite looking forward to meeting them.

She didn't hear so much as a footstep before her door opened; she glanced around and saw Deverell already inside, shutting it behind him.

Noting her state of dress, he arched a brow as he approached.

Rising, she gave him her hands.

"Excellent!" He took her hands in his. "I was going to warn you not to undress."

"Oh?" She was surprised; he tended to want her out of her clothes as soon as possible. "Why?"

His lips twisted. "Because, as I seriously doubt I can persuade you to spend the next few weeks—until we catch the slavers and their supporting cast—locked up safe and secure in this room, I want to teach you a few tricks to defend yourself in the event a man grabs you like that blackguard did last night."

"Oh." Intrigued, she asked, "Should I punch him?"

He gave her a long-suffering look and lifted one of her hands. "Make a fist. Tight."

She did. Then he did the same, holding his fist alongside hers.

"See the difference?"

She grimaced. "Yours is nearly three times the size of mine."

"True. My wrist is also at least double the size of yours. If you try to punch a man you're liable to hurt yourself more than him. But we'll come to what you can do in a moment. First"—he recaptured her hands by locking his fingers around her wrists—"you need to break free."

She studied their hands, held between them. The man who had grabbed her last night had had hold of just one of her wrists and she hadn't been able to pull free; Deverell had shackled both and he was larger and stronger. "Can I?" She glanced at his face. "Is it possible?"

He smiled. "Oh, yes. Rotate your arms upward and outward."

She blinked, then looked at their hands and did—and his hands were forced from hers. "Oh!"

"You have to do it much faster than that, or he'll realize and resist, but if you do, it's almost impossible for anyone to hold onto you like that." He recaptured her wrists. "Try it again—quickly this time."

She did. They repeated the exercise a number of times; each time she sensed him using more of his strength, yet she always managed to break his hold. "Well!" she said when they stopped. "I had no idea it was that simple."

He grinned. "It's not—that just stops him from holding you by the wrists. Wrists are the easiest way to hold a woman, but once you've broken his hold, any determined attacker is going to grab you—your body—next."

He demonstrated, seizing her about the waist before she could leap back. He held her before him. "Now what do you do?"

She looked at where her hands had come to rest against his upper sleeves. They looked ridiculously tiny. "Not a fist."

He laughed. "No. Unless you have no alternative, don't resort to your hands. If a man's holding you like this, face-to-face, you have a much better weapon."

She frowned. "What?"

Lifting a hand, he tapped her forehead. "That's the thickest bone in your body. Use it—butt him with it. If his nose is in reach, aim for that. If not, even the chin can hurt—"

She tried it.

He broke off and staggered back a step, blinking. "Yes." He blinked again, lifting a hand to his chin. "Just like that. Very good . . ."

"Oh, heavens! Did I hurt you?" Hands outstretched, she closed the distance between them.

He frowned at her. "I'll recover. But it occurs to me that the first rule you in particular need to learn is: Don't let the villain catch you in the first place. When that ruffian grabbed you last night, he spent a good few seconds deciding which of the two of you to grab, and both of you just stood there and waited for him to make up his mind." He put her away from him—a good yard away. Lowering his head, catching her eye, he forcefully stated, "If a man comes for you intending to catch you—*run!*"

He took one step toward her. She swallowed a shriek and bolted behind the armchair.

"Good." He pushed the armchair, sending it careening away. He came for her again.

She turned and fled toward the bed, but he was on her. Wrapping one steely arm around her waist, he locked her to him, bent his head and said, "Don't rely on being able to break his hold, or on butting him"—he moved his head aside as she tried it in reverse, but the difference in their heights meant her head hit his shoulder—"just run like the devil, because if he catches you he's going to lift you." He demonstrated, swinging her off her feet, half tucked under his arm. "And then you're quite helpless."

She gasped, struggling to right herself and discovering he was correct; she was indeed helpless.

"Actually, there's two things you can do if he grabs you like that—*before* he lifts you." Deverell swung her back up and set her on her feet again. He nudged the heel of her pump with the toe of his boot. "Don't try this on me because it hurts like the devil, but if you're wearing heels like these, you can smash one down on his instep. With luck, he'll let go of you, and then you can—"

"Run." She glanced back over her shoulder at him. "What else?"

"The other thing you can do—not a good option but a last resort—is to collapse in his arms. Just let yourself fall. It's very hard to hold onto anyone who's gone boneless."

She tried it and saw what he meant.

"But," he said, deftly readjusting his hold, "if you do that, you have to be ready to break away immediately his hold on you loosens, because as soon as he realizes, he'll grab you more securely, as I've just done."

He hauled her up. "So, you see, running and not getting caught is the first and best option, because once he has hold of you, he's going to lift you, and throw you—"

He tossed her on the bed.

She bounced, then swallowed a shriek as he followed her, trapping her beneath him. She caught her breath and looked into his eyes, then smiled like a cat and lifted her arms, winding them about his neck. "I take it that's the end of my lesson?"

She knew perfectly well where his attention had veered. "Yes." He looked down at her, at her lips. "For tonight."

Artfully she shifted beneath him. "So what now?"

"Now"—he reached for her laces—"we concentrate on getting you undressed."

So he could soothe the other set of clamoring impulses that had beset him. He'd done everything he could to protect her, put in place every guard, every sentry he could, but he couldn't forever be by her side. The knowledge irked; the fact that in this day and age he couldn't lock her in some tower until all danger was past abraded nerves and feelings he hadn't known he possessed.

The only relief, the only succor, the only balm that seemed to soothe his primitive self was to possess her. To remind himself he could, that she was his, willingly and completely.

As he spread her thighs and eased his aching erection into her slick, scalding heat, some part of him sighed, let go, and embraced paradise, and her.

"If you'll excuse us, Lady Harting, my aunt is beckoning." Phoebe smiled sweetly at her ladyship, a harridan if ever there was one, less sweetly at her niece, who was staring most unbecomingly at Deverell, and smoothly steered him away.

He leaned closer as they maneuvered through the crowd. "Is Edith waving? I thought she was at the other end of the room."

"She is, but another of my aunts might be here somewhere—who knows?" They were at Lady Gifford's ball, a major event. Five days had passed since Deverell had called in his friends to search for the slavers; for the past five nights they'd circulated through the ton, alert to any whispers, although as yet they'd heard none. But at every ball, every party, she'd had to exercise herself on his behalf—in his defense. She glanced at him critically. "I cannot believe how many matchmaking mamas seem to think you're fair game. Are you carrying a sign I can't see that declares Open Season?"

Deverell grinned; looking ahead, he patted her hand where it lay, possessively gripping his sleeve. "It's just one of those crosses men such as I have to bear. Within these halls we're the hunted, not the hunter. It's a sad, sad reflection on our times."

Phoebe looked at him, then snorted and faced forward. After a moment, she said, "You might try to be a little more dismissive."

He could, but he was deriving far too much satisfaction from having her wield her tongue and her wits in his defense. She was surprisingly good at it. "You need to polish your skills. This is clearly not a type of action you've engaged in much before—protecting gentlemen from the importunings of gorgons and their charges—and who knows? You might find you need such talents in the years to come."

For instance, when she was his wife.

Phoebe merely humphed and turned him toward the refreshment room. "After dealing with Lady Harting—was she the *fourth?*—I'm parched."

He dutifully steered them through the milling throng. The ton was galloping toward the Season's zenith with its customary hedonistic fervor, and to cap it all, last week Princess Charlotte, the Princess Royal, had married, casting those females with matrimonial intentions into a heightened frenzy. Every ball was packed, every entertainment an unmitigated crush, with matchmaking mamas lurking at every turn. He would much prefer to retreat and avoid such events, but Phoebe still needed to circulate, to keep her ear to the ground over households, potential problems, and most importantly suitable placements for the women on the agency's books, both those from its conventional activities as well as their special clients.

Reaching the refreshment room, a side salon thankfully less crowded, he procured two glasses of champagne.

Phoebe lifted one from his fingers. "There's an alcove of sorts where that window's screened by those palms. Let's go over there."

He nodded and trailed her across the salon to where the positioning of the palms and the window created a nook—in public view, indeed giving a view of the ballroom, yet affording a degree of privacy.

Phoebe stepped into the alcove and with a small sigh of relief turned to face him. Her gaze went beyond him, idly scanning the guests swanning about the ballroom. He sipped and looked at her face, studied it—saw and savored the subtle dropping of her veils now she was alone with him.

It was moments like this when they were alone, two together yet in some indefinable way as one, that he felt the urge to mention marriage most strongly, when he felt their complementarity—their ability to work together for the agency and more widely in society itself—showed so strongly that it couldn't be denied, and he couldn't believe she wasn't aware of it, that she didn't see it as clearly as he.

Ever since she'd admitted him to the select circle who knew about the agency, they'd steadily grown closer. Although he'd intended that to happen, and done all he could to promote it, he was nevertheless amazed at how readily and how deeply their lives had intertwined. She had to see, to know by now that their marriage was meant to be.

To him there was no question, none at all. The only question remaining was when to broach the subject, and for his money the answer was as soon as possible, which realistically meant as soon as they'd successfully dealt with the white slavers and the associated threat to the agency.

He took a sip of champagne and inwardly vowed that the instant all danger was past, he'd ask Phoebe to officially be his.

As if following his thoughts, she stirred and glanced at him. "I'm dying to hear what came of your meeting today. There's no one near enough to hear, so tell me—what have the others found?"

Phoebe knew he and his colleagues had met that morning to pool all they'd thus far learned and decide which avenues to further pursue. Deverell had, without her prompting, kept her apprised of all he heard, but they usually had to wait until they were alone in her bedchamber. But her impatience was building; with the threat of the white slavers hanging over the agency, she found it difficult to concentrate on the mundane.

He shifted, glancing around, confirming no one was within earshot. "Regarding the females who've gone missing over recent weeks, through the watchhouses we've now got information on eight. Six were from Mayfair, or near to it, all working in households of the ton, not just wealthy but of a certain social standing. The other two were merchants' daughters, both very beautiful, and in both cases they personally interacted with gentlemen of the haut ton coming to buy their fathers' wares."

"So assuming we're correct and the villain is some member of the ton, he would have met them in their fathers' businesses."

Deverell nodded; those two girls had been snatched from the gardens of their homes. He had to work to keep all grimness from his face, to keep his expression charming and light, as if he and Phoebe were swapping inanities. "So we've now got dates for eight kidnappings. I'm hoping that somewhere, employing his usual thorough and stunningly far-reaching methods into which I don't care to inquire too closely, Montague, my man-of-business, will be able to trace payments matching those dates to some account."

Phoebe raised her brows. "Can that be done?"

"Yes, but not easily. And unfortunately, not quickly. But if money's his object, then some trace will be there." Unless the man was wise enough to keep his dastardly windfall under his mattress, but if he was eager for the funds . . . "The other possibility is that he's spending the money, or had some pressing need—Dalziel's set his contacts to trawl through the clubs and report any unusual or urgent debts or unexpected profligacy."

Phoebe frowned. "How do you think this man, the tonnish villain, works—how does he interact with the smugglers?"

"The more we learn from the underworld contacts Gervase, Tristan, Christian, and I have been speaking with, the more it seems likely our man is acting as the procurer we labeled him. According to those who might be expected to know, white slavers don't like to show their faces—they don't like to grab their wares themselves. Traditionally they've relied on locals they entice into working for them—it's the locals who identify the best targets, arrange the kidnappings using local men, and then deliver the girls to the slavers. In this case, however, the usual locals aren't being used. Although the underworld suspected white slavers were back, no one knows who their new procurer is, a situation that's making everyone uneasy, not least because this new procurer is making the old ones look bad. He's been handing over excellent goods and he's been operating for some time without any alarm being raised—without alerting the authorities, or leaving any clue as to who he is."

Phoebe was silent for a moment, then asked, "Where do they keep the girls?"

"From what we've gathered, their base is generally a warehouse—it'll be one of myriad legitimate warehouses somewhere along the river behind the docks. Locating it would literally be like searching for a needle in a haystack."

Phoebe drew in a sharp breath. "So the girls who've been seized are beyond our reach?"

"Not necessarily. They gather their cargo in the warehouse, but once they have their quota, they have to move them to their ship. We're much more likely to be able to identify the ship—we decided today to forgo any attempt to locate the warehouse and concentrate instead on locating the ship. If we can identify it, we can rescue the girls." He paused, then added, voice low, "It's unlikely they'll be harmed—the slavers will get more for them if they're untouched and beautiful. They'll be well fed and well housed."

"But prisoners," Phoebe said, abiding anger in her voice.

Deverell nodded. "Tristan's spoken with Jack, Lord Hendon, another ex-operative and friend of Tony Blake, one of our members. Jack owns Hendon Shipping, one of our largest shipping lines—he has all the contacts we need to keep a tight watch on the river, and now Dalziel has alerted the water police, Jack's working with them. They know what they're doing. They're quite sure no slaving ship has slipped in and out in recent weeks, so the ship for this cargo is yet to arrive."

"So we'll have a chance to rescue the girls?"

"With luck, yes." Some other guests were drifting their way. Deverell took Phoebe's elbow and guided her out of the alcove, back toward the crowded ballroom; there was nowhere else to go. "Once they have a full load"—he lowered his voice—"they'll call in their ship. They'll have it sail up openly—it'll be carrying some legitimate cargo to explain its appearance in the Pool and most importantly its need for a dock. When it docks, the cargo will be openly put off, and the girls secretly loaded in its place, then the ship will put out again, most likely claiming it's headed for Southampton or to some other port for its next cargo. Once out at sea, they instead set sail for wherever their secret cargo is bound."

"So . . ." Eyes narrowing, Phoebe imagined how it would be. "We'll have to wait until the last moment, just before they put the girls on board."

Straightening, Deverell nodded. "We'll have to wait for them to bring the girls to us."

The surging crowd neared; they were forced to put aside their discussion and pretend to enjoy the ball.

We, she'd said—and he'd said *us.*

As dawn approached the next morning, Phoebe lay snug and warm beside Deverell in her bed and, eyes closed, let her thoughts roam, let herself poke, prod, and assess the subject that increasingly impinged on her mind.

She'd changed. She'd come a long way from her blanket distrust of strong and powerful men; quite aside from the one slumbering naked beside her, she was now in league with a crew of them, and far from recoiling, she appreciated them and their attributes more every day. As for Deverell . . .

He'd become much more than just another of "her people," those who worked with her in the agency and elsewhere, lending their support to her "little crusade." Indeed, he wasn't even just the best and closest; he was her lover and protector in truth—and over the last weeks of working together she'd come to realize he'd coalesced those positions into something more.

He'd become her personal champion.

Others, she'd realized, viewed him so—not just his colleagues but also Emmeline and Birtles, Fergus, and, even more telling, Skinner. They all viewed his position—their relationship—as right and proper, something to be not just accepted but encouraged. Which was interesting, considering their previous views of men such as he, every bit as negative as hers had been.

Her lips quirked. In a quite amazing turnaround, *she'd* become an advocate of strong and powerful gentlemen. A certain type of strong and powerful man. To her surprise, she'd discovered she could accept him as her champion without turning a hair.

All that was strange enough, but what was steadily herding her mind in a truly startling direction was the sense of sharing growing between them now they'd joined forces in defense of the agency. Initially she hadn't imagined he would have any real concern for it beyond the fact that it took up much of her time and posed a certain danger, but as the weeks had progressed she'd realized she'd underestimated him—that his increasing involvement with the agency, its works and its defense was driven by sincere interest.

Sincere appreciation of the value of the work and a wish to contribute. He was like Loftus in that regard, an unexpected godsend.

It was that sense of sharing, the increasing sense of partnership engendered and consolidated as over the last weeks they'd worked together that drove her thoughts. Of shared goals, shared commitments . . . shared lives.

That was where her thoughts invariably led her.

There was no denying that their support of each other in spheres beyond the agency had also grown instinctive and constant. She suspected he was as aware of it as she—which left her wondering what his thoughts on their relationship were, whether they'd headed down the same path as hers.

They were lovers, yes, but he needed a wife. He'd said so from the first, but the last weeks in the ballrooms had brought home to her just how real his need truly was.

And how easily she could fulfill it.

And how willing she now was to do so.

She, Phoebe Mary Malleson, was actively considering marriage. For years she'd imagined she never would; now she couldn't imagine not pursuing the path her thoughts were urging her down.

And she was fairly certain that if she suggested it, he would agree. It had been she who had declared against it when he'd first raised the subject, so it would need to be she who reopened it and resurrected the prospect he'd initially proposed.

She thought of that—how to reintroduce the subject, how he might respond.

Beside her, he stirred, reaching for her beneath the covers; finding her, he hugged her close and sank back into slumber. It wasn't yet dawn; she didn't need to wake him yet.

So she let him sleep while she grappled with the amazing fact that regardless of what his initial reaction might be to her suggestion that they wed, she—her heart, her mind, her entire being—was determined to persuade him that putting his ring on her finger would be the best thing he could possibly do—for them both.

Malcolm Sinclair stood at the side of Lady Rathdowne's drawing room and wished there were more shadows in the room. He didn't appreciate the attention of the young ladies, and even less that of their hard-eyed mamas who looked him over measuringly, wondering if he were suitable prey.

His appearance was no help, but at least his age afforded him some protection; many knew he'd yet to attain his majority, that he was rather too young to be thinking of matrimony just yet. Still, too many noted him for his comfort.

Her ladyship's soiree was the third event on his evening's calendar; he had two more balls to call in at if he drew a blank there. He'd spent the past week trawling the ton's entertainments, something of a penance, yet even if Henry hadn't ordered him to find the lady in the alley, he would have done so anyway; to his mind, self-preservation was a worthy goal.

It had finally dawned on him that the major balls at which young ladies made their come-outs were not the right venues in which to seek his quarry. Rational conjecture suggested she would be older—a widow or a daring matron perhaps. So he'd shifted his field to the more select entertainments such ladies frequented.

The more reasonable numbers were an added benefit. The relative lack of crush enabled him to stand quietly by the side of the room and systematically quarter it.

His gaze passed over her at first, but then she straightened from speaking with an old lady seated on a sofa and turned to a large gentleman. . . .

Malcolm recognized them both, or at least he thought he did. The lady moved and he was sure of her, but the man? He hadn't seen him as clearly; no matter how he racked his memory, he couldn't be certain of him.

But of her he assuredly was.

Doing his best to merge with the wall, he studied the couple; they were directly across the room, but the intervening guests provided a sufficient screen—he could observe without fear of being noticed.

Then the musicians in the adjoining salon struck up a waltz. The gentleman turned to the lady and spoke; with a smile—she really was remarkably attractive if a trifle long in the tooth—she gave him her hand. Excusing themselves to the old biddy on the sofa, they headed for the dance floor.

Malcolm didn't follow; fixing his gaze on the old lady, he was surprised to find he knew her. Edith Balmain. She'd been a friend of his parents and had spoken kindly to him some months before when she'd encountered him in Bond Street.

There'd been an easy familiarity in the way the other lady had interacted with Edith; a relative or connection was Malcolm's educated guess.

Smiling faintly, he moved away from the wall and crossed the room. He paused to glance in at the dancers on the way and saw his pair revolving as if there were no others on the floor. They made a handsome couple, but to Malcolm's sharp eyes there was more to it than that; he'd take an oath they were lovers—that the unknown gentleman was her paramour.

Filing the observation away, he continued his progress, deftly avoiding two young ladies to approach the sofa, and Edith Balmain.

"Good evening, Mrs. Balmain." He bowed easily before her, an eager, innocent light in his eyes. "Malcolm Sinclair, ma'am."

She had sharp blue eyes; they regarded him with interest. "Malcolm—how nice to see you again, my boy. Are you well?"

"Indeed." He let his gaze sweep the room. "I've just started going about a trifle—finding my legs in this arena, so to speak."

"I'm sure the hostesses will be delighted to welcome you. Your mother was a favorite of many, you know."

He knew very little about his mother; the comment made him pause, but the waltz wouldn't last forever.

Edith's blue gaze was searching his face. "As I recall you're finished with your studies, is that correct?"

"Yes—I came down last year, but I've been traveling with friends until a few months ago." He drew a quick verbal sketch of his travels; time was running short. He ended with a restless glance around, followed by an ingenuous, "Are you here alone, ma'am?"

She smiled, understanding perfectly—or so she thought. "No, no—I'm here with my niece, Miss Malleson. She's dancing at present but will no doubt return shortly."

"Oh!" Malcolm turned his head to look toward the dance floor. "Was she the lady who was with you a few minutes ago? With some gentleman?"

Edith smiled. "Yes, that was she. Deverell—Viscount Paignton—was with her."

"Deverell?" Malcolm frowned as if trying to place the name. "I don't believe I recognize him."

Edith waved, dismissing his effort. "You won't. Deverell spent the last ten years of the war in France, behind enemy lines. He was last on the town, or indeed anywhere in the ton, when he was your age and you were in the schoolroom." Tilting her head, Edith studied him. "If you wish, I'll introduce you."

There was a twinkle in her eyes that made it easy for Malcolm to, with suitably labored tact, disclaim all need to be introduced to either Miss Malleson or her escort. Edith accepted his reluctance readily, assuming he was nervous or shy or both.

Employing the most boyish version of his ready charm, Malcolm took his leave of her as the last chords of the waltz sounded. Quitting her vicinity, he retreated in good order and immediately left the house—before she could think to point him out to Miss Malleson and Paignton.

For the moment, he'd learned all he needed to know about them; they didn't need to know about him.

* * *

It wasn't Phoebe Malleson who bothered Malcolm but the gentleman in whose arms she'd been whirling, the gentleman who'd looked at her as if she were his all. The gentleman who had spent the last ten years of the war behind enemy lines. Malcolm was exceedingly glad he'd learned that little tidbit; he'd gnawed at it through the night and brought it like a well-picked bone, along with his other observations, to deposit before "his master" at the earliest opportunity.

"Phoebe Malleson, you say?" Eyes narrowing, Henry set down the book he'd been reading. "She's Martindale's daughter—his heiress. He became a recluse after his wife died. The girl goes around with her aunts—she has a round dozen of them—but as I heard it not one of them could get her wed, heiress or no."

Malcolm, in his customary seat before the desk, murmured, "I found her with one of her aunts, Mrs. Edith Balmain. I don't know about Miss Malleson not being weddable—she had a gentleman dancing attendance on her." He went on to describe Paignton, watching for Henry's reaction—which was dismissive.

"Never mind him—have Miss Malleson seized and brought here." Henry's eyes gleamed coldly. "It shouldn't take much persuasion to get her to tell me who the leader of this other gang is. No doubt he'll prove to be some disreputable lover." He snorted contemptuously. "Women, ladies or not, they're all the same. Serves Martindale right, allowing her to roam with only females to watch over her."

Malcolm had to bite back an acid comment. Had to work to pitch his voice to its usual diffident note. "You don't think Paignton might be the man?"

"*Paignton?* Deverell, as he's known?" Henry's tone made it clear how ludicrous he found the suggestion. "You need to learn to read men better, boy. Deverell's not the type—he's not just ex-guards, he's one of Dalziel's crew. All King and

country to the death and no holds barred along the way."
Henry snorted. "There's not a chance in Hades that one of
them would be involved in slaving." Harsh amusement lit
his eyes. "Even if they thought of it, their next thought—of
finding their ex-commander on the doorstep asking them to
please explain—would be guaranteed to make them pass
the chance by. No—whoever Phoebe Malleson is helping
whisk these girls away, it won't be Deverell."

Oh, *wonderful!* Deverell was *that* sort of man. Malcolm
fixed his gaze on the handsome pair of pistols mounted on
the wall behind Henry until he was sure his voice wouldn't
betray his scorn. Then he tried again. "There's definitely
something between them—Deverell and Phoebe Malleson."

Henry's brows rose, faintly supercilious. "She wouldn't
be the first lady to have dallied along the way with some
less-than-suitable customer. Perhaps she's got Deverell on
her string now, but the other one is blackmailing her. That
might well be it—if she's looking to land Deverell, then the
last thing she'd want is a past lover showing his face."

He paused, then nodded as if convinced by his arguments. He fixed Malcolm with an ice-cold stare. "Get her
here."

Malcolm hesitated, then, his expession utterly blank, inclined his head and rose.

Chapter 20

*T*he work of the agency had to go on. Deverell repeated that dictum several times each hour, reminding himself why Phoebe needed to swan through ballrooms and drawing rooms filled with frenetic hordes.

Tonight, they'd already graced the Dalrymples' ball and the Cavendish event; they now stood in Lady Melvin's ballroom, surrounded by a garrulous throng. Despite his experience, he was having to work to keep a charming expression plastered on his face, rather than give vent to a snarling growl. The apogee of the Season was nigh, and those of the matchmaking sorority who had yet to succeed were growing desperate—desperate enough to disregard all warnings and take a concerted tilt at him.

Luckily, Phoebe stood firm in his defense—only fair, given his sole purpose in being by her side, there to be tilted at, was to protect her.

"This is madness," she murmured as a surge of people

toward the dance floor sent a rippling jostle through the crowd.

"Quite." He drew her nearer, protectively, into the lee of his body. "But for some incomprehensible reason, the ton's hostesses engage in exactly the same behavior year after year. Are female memories really that short?"

She shot him a reproving look, but her lips had curved. "I want to find Lady Canterbury. I heard she's looking for a new parlor maid. I know Lord Canterbury is safe enough, but I'm not sure who else is in their household."

Meaning whether there were any untrustworthy males lurking. "I'm fairly certain Canterbury has no sons." Lifting his head, he scanned the gathering. "I last saw her ladyship over by that corner." He caught Phoebe's eye, arched a brow. "Do we assay forth and hunt her down?"

She grinned. "You make it sound like a military exercise."

"If you want my opinion," he returned, head bent so his words fell by her ear as they moved forward into the press of guests, "there are more than a few ladies among the ton who could give any general lessons."

Looking ahead, she laughed, yet as he steered her through the throng, his senses, his instincts, were alert and alive, very much as if this were indeed a battlefield. Until the slavers were caught and all threat to Phoebe and her enterprise removed, he would remain on guard; Phoebe wouldn't set foot outside at night without him by her side. During the day, if he wasn't with her, then she was either at the agency or with Edith, Audrey, or Loftus, and always under Fergus's watchful eye.

He and Fergus had an agreement—Phoebe would never be without one or the other hovering. Whether she'd noticed that yet or not he didn't know, but he saw no reason to draw their close guarding of her to her attention. No need to precipitate futile argument on that score.

Later that evening in the carriage rattling back to Park Street after the last of their selected entertainments, it was Edith who inquired as to the progress of their investigations. He brought her up to date; they'd long jettisoned any notion of keeping the seriousness of the situation from Audrey and Edith. Audrey was spending quite a bit of time with Loftus, and he was no match for her interrogatory wiles. So what Loftus heard, Audrey knew, and therefore Edith knew, too.

"Tristan and I managed to track down two of the men who accosted us in the alley while we were rescuing Molly Doyle." He glanced across the carriage at Phoebe; she was hanging on his words. "Both had been hired specifically for that event. Neither knew by whom—they both described the person they dealt with as a young man, *not* a gentleman, not well-educated but well-spoken enough, not well-dressed so much as neat. The implication was that this hirer is of a type who can appear in their seedier world without inviting notice, but he's not widely known—not someone anyone seems to know well enough to identify in any way."

Phoebe raised her brows. "But they worked for him? He clearly hadn't any difficulty gathering quite a band."

Deverell's lip curled cynically. "He pays well—that's really all men like that care about, and he kept his word and paid them the rest of what he'd promised even though they singularly failed to seize Molly Doyle or inflict much damage on us. In that, he was clever—word will have gone out among the bruisers and thugs-for-hire that he's trustworthy in that regard. I doubt he'll have trouble hiring men as and when he needs them.

"However"—Deverell grimaced—"among the teeming multitudes of London, as this hirer is not known to the established underworld and he comes and goes and never uses the same taverns twice, then our chances of tracing him are minuscule."

Phoebe frowned. "He seems rather clever for someone of that ilk."

Deverell hesitated, then said, "The men we spoke with, and apparently their colleagues, assumed the young man was working under the direction of someone else. When he told them what to do, it was as if he were reciting orders from some master. They all had the impression that he was acting as a servant, although he never mentioned any other."

"So," Edith said, her nomally soft voice sharp, "the procurer—who we suspect is of the ton—has a hirer, a man of lower class to handle the less savory aspects of his trade."

Deverell nodded. "But if we can't locate the hirer, then we can't follow him back to his master. So in terms of identifying the procurer, our best and indeed only remaining way forward is through tracing the money that's presumably behind it all."

"Has your man Montague learned anything there?" Phoebe struggled to read Deverell's face through the shadows.

A wolfish grin flashed. "We live in hope. Montague sent word late today that he's nearing the end of his researches and believes he may have turned up something. However, he's insisted on reviewing all the evidence himself. We've arranged a meeting for the afternoon of the day after tomorrow so the rest of us can share any news we've gleaned—I'm hoping Montague will have a name to give us by then."

He went on to briefly outline for Edith the steps taken to keep watch for the slaving ship and their plan to rescue the girls already in the slavers' clutches. Having heard all that the previous night, Phoebe leaned back against the squabs and mentally reviewed all that had recently been going on around the agency and its work.

They'd rescued two more girls since Molly Doyle; in both cases, the instant the need was identified Deverell had stepped in and organized a swift and heavily guarded operation utilizing his friends and their undoubted expertise. Both rescues had gone off without a hitch.

If they could drive off the slavers she would on one level be satisfied enough; the agency could continue its work untrameled—and indeed, with the additional support the recent weeks had brought, would be stronger and more effective than ever.

But the existence of their "procurer" sent an icy chill through her; that someone like that could exist, circulating in their privileged world yet preying on the most vulnerable, indeed using their position to do so, filled her with a repugnance impossible to swallow. Impossible not to act upon.

She glanced at Deverell; even veiled by the shadows, not only his impatience but also his steady confidence were easy to read. She caught his eye, let something of her own anticipation show. "So by the end of the day after tomorrow, with luck you might know the procurer's identity."

He met her eyes and nodded. "It's what we're all waiting for—and then we'll act."

Late the next afternoon, every sense alert, Malcolm moved unhurriedly through the sulphurous murk hanging low in the crowded passage known as Swan Lane, not far from London Bridge.

Buildings pressed close on either side; regardless of their appearance, all were occupied—any could be hiding interested eyes, yet the late-afternoon fog was a dense veil, obscuring vision beyond a few feet. Sounds echoed eerily in the enclosed space; the immediate smells of woodsmoke, rotting refuse, sewage, and the metallic whiff of the fog were all overlaid by the unmistakable stench of the nearby docks.

Malcolm's destination loomed on his left; soundlessly he turned up a flight of narrow, rickety steps and climbed to the tiny room tucked above the rough tavern after which the lane was named. He paused on the landing and looked down the steps, listening to the cadence of the scuffling foot traffic below. No disturbance, no change; he didn't think anyone had seen him, let alone followed him.

Satisfied that the stairs would give warning of anyone tempted to creep close enough to listen outside the door—always a risk in this neighborhood—he lifted the latch and went in.

The room was dusty and cramped; squeezed beneath the rafters, it held a bare wooden table supporting a single candle, already lit, three stools, and nothing else—other than Jennings, propped on one stool, patiently waiting, a dutiful and thankfully intelligent lackey.

Jennings rose.

Closing the door, Malcolm smiled easily, removing the dark, wide-brimmed hat he'd worn to disguise his shining head and fair features, neither of which belonged hereabouts. For a second, he studied Jennings—round face, stocky build, neat and clean, looking oh-so-like a tradesman's son. He was the same age as Malcolm but in experience a world apart; considering the ready smile Jennings returned, Malcolm cynically wondered which way Jennings would jump if his loyalty were ever tested.

Not that it mattered; Jennings was not, when it came down to it, his principal line of defense. Should he be caught and persuaded to speak, anything Jennings might say would only support Malcolm's own assertions—that Malcolm was merely his guardian's pawn, nothing more than a higher-level lackey, the next rank up from Jennings in a heirarchy controlled with an iron fist from the top.

Jennings thought the careful plans Malcolm related came from Malcolm's unknown governor, to wit Henry, while

Henry thought that all the plans of how to accomplish the abductions and deal with the white slavers had originated with the likewise unknown contact, Jennings.

Only if Jennings described in Henry's hearing the instructions Malcolm had regularly communicated, which supposedly came from his governor, would there be any reason even in Henry's mind to question the construct Malcolm had created. And how likely was that?

Drawing out one of the stools, Malcolm sat. "We have another job. Not *quite* the sort of thing we've done before." He met Jennings's eyes, read the eagerness therein, grimaced and let a hint of uncertainty—the first he'd ever displayed before Jennings—slide through his voice. "If it were me . . . frankly, I'd leave this lady be. This is too rich for my blood—too risky."

He paused, frowning, letting Jennings see how troubled he was. "But the governor's set on it, so . . ." With a shrug and another grimace, he outlined what men would be needed, where and when the snatch was to take place, and exactly how it was to be done.

Jennings's eyes widened at the details, but Malcolm had chosen him not just for his so-average appearance but also for his nimble wits. Despite taking no notes, Jennings could be relied on to remember every detail, no matter how minor, how seemingly inconsequential, and given the implications of the where, when and how, he needed no further explanation of the risks.

After a moment of thought, Jennings nodded. "I know where I can get two reliable men smart enough to do exactly as I tell them, and a suitable carriage." He met Malcolm's eyes. "But given the danger, are you sure we shouldn't have more men?"

Malcolm shook his head. "According to my governor, in such an area more than two men would invite attention, and that we wish to avoid at all costs. The danger will come not from seizing the lady but from being noticeable and thus traceable on the way to the second house."

Jennings frowned. "You're right—this is certainly different to the others—but," he shrugged, "I'm sure we'll pull it off."

"Indeed." Reaching beneath his cloak, Malcolm drew out a purse and tossed it on the table. It clanked; Jennings eyed it, mentally weighing it, then nodded and reached for it.

"Offer more than the usual rates if the men haggle." Malcolm rose and met his lieutenant's eyes. "Just make sure we have two good men to carry out the deed and that they stick to the plan exactly."

Jennings nodded and pocketed the purse.

Placing his hat back on his head, settling it so the wide brim shaded his face, Malcolm turned to the door. His hand on the latch, he halted, hesitated. His motto was: Caution was always wise. He turned back.

Jennings looked at him inquiringly.

Malcolm's features remained set; inwardly, he smiled. "One thing—if on the day after tomorrow I fail to show at our next meeting, then you'd best assume that regardless of our carefulness my governor's been found out. If that happens, I'd strongly advise you to disappear. Not just from the area, but from London."

Jennings held his gaze unblinkingly, then said, "I've an aunt in Exeter—I might take myself down there to get some sea air."

Malcolm let his lips quirk, a touch rueful. "An excellent idea."

With a nod he turned to the door.

Jennings rushed to ask, "But what about you?"

Facing the door, Malcolm smiled, letting his true emotions show where Jennings couldn't see them. "Don't worry about me. Even if the minions of justice bring my governor down, I doubt they'll be concerned with a mere message-bearer."

One, moreover, who'd taken care to appear an innocent-led-astray.

Raising his hand in farewell, Malcolm opened the door; without looking back, he left the tiny room.

As he threaded his way back through the dingy alleys, he swiftly reviewed his defenses. All were in place. All were rock solid. Jennings had been the only possible chink, and Malcolm now had the sealing of that in his control.

If Henry were caught, through either this latest folly or some other foolishness Malcolm knew nothing about and therefore couldn't guard against, it would be impossible to hide his involvement. He'd realized from the first that his best defense was to remain in plain sight, but disguised.

In this case, the disguise he'd used for years with Henry, and which his guardian fondly, firmly, and irrevocably believed encompassed the true reality of Malcolm Sinclair, was essentially unassailable. It would protect him from anything beyond the mildest of repercussions; indeed, he'd own to surprise if he was even considered worth a formal warning.

As his boots struck the cobbles of a major street, he smiled cynically. If he played his cards well, he might even be viewed as a victim.

He was an excellent cardplayer. If Henry bought down their house of cards, his next challenge would be to see what hand he could get himself dealt out of the wreckage.

Pleased with the analogy, he whistled beneath his breath as he headed back to Mayfair.

Aside from all else, he had only a few days before fate would lift him into a new world, one in which he would be entirely his own master.

In just four days, he would turn twenty-one—and assume

control of the inheritance he'd worked so diligently to protect from Henry's depredations.

The following afternoon, Phoebe stepped out of the morning room onto the narrow terrace that gave onto the lawn of the walled garden of Edith's house. Inside, lying down on the chaises in the drawing room after their afternoon's exertions, Audrey and Edith were idly swapping anecdotes, eyes shut, recovering.

Smiling, Phoebe stepped onto the lawn and ambled, equally idle, down the path that followed the wide flowerbed along the laneway wall. It was after five o'clock and the sun was dipping below the rooftops, but the stones of the wall still held the full day's heat; it was the perfect time for a lady to stroll without need of a parasol.

She often strolled at this time, the hiatus between the afternoon's entertainments and the ritual of dressing for the evening. The lingering warmth of the day released the perfume from the blooms nodding in the border; she stooped to sniff a red rose, marveling as she always did at the richness of the scent.

Normally, she used these quiet moments to organize her thoughts, to review the day from the perspective of the agency and consider what the evening might bring, how she could best use its entertainments to further the agency's aims. Today, however, she was fully engaged in suppressing her thoughts—from holding them back when they wanted to rush ahead. Soon Deverell would learn the identity of the dastardly procurer. Would he know today? Had Montague sent word to their meeting? Or had they already learned the answer via some other route?

Regardless, who was the man? Was he someone she knew?

More importantly, how would Deverell and his colleagues

choose to act? Would they move today? Would he tell her first? Or . . . ? "If I don't stop thinking," she muttered to herself, "I'll drive myself insane."

She glanced across the lawn to where Fergus sat on a bench by the house, mending a bridle. Continuing on, she passed the gate in the wall; reaching the back corner of the garden, she paused to admire a rosebush covered with fat pink blooms.

The sound of the back door opening had her glancing around. Milligan, the housekeeper, looked out. Seeing Phoebe, she beckoned and called, as she did most afternoons, "Mrs. Balmain's called for tea in the drawing room, miss. I'm just about to take it in."

Phoebe waved to show she'd heard and turned back to the house. "Thank you, Milligan. I'll come in."

Milligan noticed Fergus on the bench nearby. "You'd better hie yourself in, too, before my scones go cold."

"Scones, heh?" Fergus laid aside the bridle. He looked across at Phoebe, returning up the path, then turned and followed Milligan through the kitchen door.

Phoebe didn't hurry; it was so pleasant outside. She'd passed the garden gate and was halfway back to the morning room when a soft thud sounded behind her, followed immediately by a child's wail.

"*Noooo!* M'ball! How'm I gonna get it back?"

Turning, Phoebe located the ball that had bounced on the lawn, then rolled a little way. From beyond the wall came sounds of an agitated conference debating the wisdom of climbing the high wall to retrieve the ball.

Quickly walking back, she picked up the ball; hefting it in one hand, she walked toward the gate. "Don't climb the wall! It's got glass shards along the top. Wait a minute and I'll bring your ball out to you."

She thought of tossing the ball back over the wall, but she

couldn't be sure they wouldn't miss it, and then it might bounce into the garden across the lane, inhabited by a very large bullmastiff. Lifting the key from the nail, she slid it into the lock, then turned; the bolt fell. Grasping the heavy latch, she pulled the gate wide—and blinked at the empty lane.

The sound of rushing, retreating footsteps reached her. Puzzled, she stepped through the gate, looking toward the street—and caught a fleeting glimpse of three urchins fleeing around the corner as if the hounds of hell were snapping at their heels.

"Well." Astonished, she halted.

In the same instant she realized she wasn't alone.

She sucked in a breath and whirled—

A black bag dropped over her head. Letting the ball go, hands rising to grasp the cloth, she dragged in a breath to scream.

A hard calloused hand caught each of hers.

She parted her lips—a band of material was cinched over her mouth. It was pulled tight and tied about her head; she only just managed to keep the band from pressing between her lips and pushing the cloth into her mouth.

For a moment, she was fully engrossed with that battle, then, as her senses snapped back to the outer world, she felt her arms being bound to her sides, then her hands were yanked forward and her wrists secured tightly before her. Before her head steadied she was lifted, carried between two men a short distance back along the lane, then loaded into a carriage, laid on the floor like a rolled-up rug.

The carriage door was shut on her; the carriage tipped as one of the men climbed up. "Shut the gate."

The words were a deep, grumbling growl. A second later, she heard a muted thump as the gate closed.

Almost immediately the carriage tipped as the second

man joined the first. The carriage jerked, rocked forward, then rumbled down the lane and out into the street.

From the opposite side of Park Street, along which he'd just happened to be strolling, yet another elegant gentleman out enjoying the pleasant afternoon, Malcolm watched the carriage bearing Miss Phoebe Malleson rattle down the street, then turn the corner and head deeper into Mayfair with an air of grim resignation.

He shook his head and strolled on. It was a stupid move, unnecessary—there were plenty of maids in Mayfair; it would have been easy to avoid whatever group Miss Malleson was a part of—and unacceptably dangerous.

The more he learned, the more he felt certain Henry's reading of the situation was wildly fanciful. The other "gang" wasn't in league with the white slavers, nor yet any other arm of the flesh trade—they were the wrong sort of people and there were no obvious connections. If left to his own much more cautious devices, Malcolm would have investigated the true nature of the other gang's activities; given they, too, were operating if not outside the law then certainly on its fringes, and given that people of the caliber of Deverell and Miss Malleson were involved, there might well have been some nugget of information he could have exploited to nullify any threat the other gang might have posed.

But the ways of wisdom, of caution, had deserted Henry. Malcolm would have had to advance his case in highly forceful fashion to convince his guardian of the folly of his approach.

And that he hadn't been prepared to do.

Arguing successfully with Henry—while he could certainly have done it—would have shattered his disguise. The veils he'd spent years artfully weaving would have fallen from Henry's eyes, and then he would have known the truth—and if he then later fell, he would take Malcolm with him.

Malcolm had witnessed Henry's vindictiveness too often to doubt it would—if given cause—be turned on him.

One of the hallmarks of the wise was that they avoided the pitfalls that ensnared lesser mortals. Malcolm had absolutely no intention of becoming ensnared in the web he had to this point managed for Henry.

Especially as it was Henry's overweening arrogance that was set to bring the whole crashing down. "His territory" indeed!

Reaching Piccadilly, Malcolm crossed the street and strolled along the edge of Green Park. He paced along the pavement, swinging his cane, to all appearances a gentleman contemplating the beauties of the day.

Looking back on the last months, revisiting decisions in light of the looming debacle, there wasn't, despite all, much else he could have done. Last December, with less than six months to go before Malcolm gained his majority and control of the fortune his father had bequeathed him, Henry—who as Malcolm's guardian had complete control of that fortune until he came of age—had started toying with the funds, withdrawing small amounts here and there to feed his craving for acquiring pistols.

Malcolm had had to find an alternative source of cash sufficient to satisfy Henry's spiraling need, and quickly—that had been the only reason he'd mentioned the white slave traders and the possibility he'd seen there.

Henry, predictably, had leapt on the idea.

A product of Malcolm's creative mind, the possibility, when he'd pursued it at Henry's direction, had transformed into a lucrative reality. And so it had started, and so it continued, and Henry, now addicted, would never allow it to cease.

Until he was caught.

Whether in the absence of Henry's need Malcolm would have developed his notion of assisting white slavers to the point of actually doing it, he honestly couldn't say. He often thought of such schemes, but purely in a theoretical way; never before had he converted theory into practice.

Even now, even though it had been his concept and it had worked, although he was grateful for the experience he'd gained, he felt not the smallest ripple of regret at the notion that Henry would soon be caught and the white slaving scheme would end.

In three days, he would be free of Henry; a whole world of ways in which to make money was out there, and he intended to explore. Yet until then . . .

Increasingly certain Henry's capture was in the wind—kidnapping the all-but-affianced bride of a man like Deverell seemed a certain way of bringing the full weight of the authorities down on one's head—Malcolm paused at the corner of Arlington Street and considered the façade of Henry's house.

Miss Malleson would by now be in the mews behind the house, if not already within it.

Cold-bloodedly considering that, he concluded that perhaps it was time that Henry was caught. Of course, as a member of an august arm of "the authorities," Henry considered himself beyond reach, indeed quite literally above the law.

In his mind, Malcolm weighed all he knew against Henry's conviction of his own invincibility.

Then he stirred and walked on, past Arlington Street and on toward White's in St. James. There would be plenty of acquaintances there to see him, many well-connected friends with whom he could dine.

Regardless of who had weighed the odds correctly, him

or Henry—and he knew who he would wager on if he were a wagering man—given what would most likely transpire once Miss Malleson was in Henry's clutches, there was no need whatever for Malcolm to be anywhere in the vicinity.

Chapter 21

On the carriage floor, Phoebe suffered through every jolt, every rattle, until she felt like her teeth would come loose. When the carriage finally came to a blessed halt, she exhaled with relief—as well as she could past the gag.

She hadn't been able to move an inch. Her hands were too well tied; she hadn't been able to loosen the bonds. The fabric of the hood was fine woven and black; she couldn't even distinguish daylight through it.

But she knew she was still in London; the carriage hadn't gone that far—the ordeal over the cobbles hadn't gone on that long. The familiar sounds of the capital reached her ears, muted by the hood but otherwise undimmed. If she had to guess, she would say they were still in Mayfair, or close to it.

By the clatter outside, the echoes of the horses' hooves as they shuffled and of men's voices and boots, the carriage was in some narrow space between houses—probably a mews.

Before she could think further, the carriage door was

wrenched open. Hands—large male hands—grabbed her, hauling her out; there were two of them as before, but this time one hefted her over his shoulder.

"I'll take her in. You wait with the horses."

"Aye, but hurry up." The second man sounded nervous. "This ain't the sort of place I like to hang about. Yer never know when a constable might stroll by. The watchhouse ain't far."

The man carrying her grunted, then turned. For some moments Phoebe had all she could do to fight back waves of dizziness; the man was carrying her like a sack of potatoes with her head dangling down his back, her legs locked to his chest under one beefy arm. With her arms bound and her tied hands trapped beneath her, she couldn't brace or in any other way steady herself against the rocking of his gait.

Then, thankfully, he slowed and stopped. Her senses returned to her; she could hear and feel again. From the coolness reaching her, he'd carried her into a house, presumably by some back door to a lower floor. No kitchen smells, no warmth. A cellar?

"This way."

Beneath the hood, she blinked. A well-modulated voice, accents unmistakable—a tonnish butler.

Then they were moving again, but slowly; she concentrated on the surroundings, on what she could learn, instead of letting her senses focus on the nauseating effect of being held upside down with the man's burly shoulder pressing into her middle.

She could hear the man's footsteps and the butler's as he preceded them. Stone flags at first, then they climbed a short flight of steps and came out onto tiles. That lasted for a little way; she sensed they were in an enclosed space—a corridor?

Then they went through a doorway and the walls fell back. A hall?

A tiled floor still, but then the footsteps became muffled; a rug. The man slowly swiveled, balancing her weight, reached for something—and started to climb.

Wooden stairs.

She continued to track their progess through what seemed to be a fashionable house. On reaching the first floor, the butler led the way down a carpeted corridor. Phoebe counted the paces, one of Deverell's rules echoing in her head.

If you're caught and can't do anything else, concentrate on learning as much as you can about where you are, and your captors.

He'd continued giving her lessons and advice on defending herself, on how to react in various adverse circumstances; somewhat to her surprise, his words hovered high in her mind, almost as if he were there, watching over her.

But this was no test, no game. This was all too real.

She counted, remained focused. Twelve paces from the stairhead, the butler paused; she sensed him moving—opening some door?—then the man carrying her grunted and changed direction.

He passed through a narrow portal; Phoebe felt one side brush her shoulder. Then he climbed.

Steep, narrow stairs—servants' stairs?

Under the hood, Phoebe frowned. That seemed an odd place for servants' or attic stairs. Equally, it seemed odd that attic stairs were starting from the first floor. Almost all houses in Mayfair and surrounds had attics above the second floor, not the first.

Could they have somehow come in on the first floor rather than the ground floor? No—what she'd thought was the front hall had been tiled. Tiles were rarely found in first-floor galleries—they had timber floors and runners.

So what were these stairs—where were they taking her?

The stairs, eleven of them, ended; the man angled himself

and her through what was clearly a low, narrow doorway. With a grunt the man straightened; she felt him look around.

"Put her on the bed."

The man moved to obey the butler's command. Phoebe tensed, then she was hoisted off the man's shoulder and dumped—exactly like a sack of potatoes—on a raised mattress.

The panic she'd managed until then to hold at bay welled. She wriggled, then rolling to one side desperately searched with her halfboots for the edge of the bed. The butler muttered an oath and started forward.

" 'Ere—none o' that." The rough man grabbed her feet; anchoring each ankle in a beefy fist, he held them together and pressed them down on the bed.

She threshed, trying to break free, but with her hands so well tied she could barely move.

"Here," the butler said, then she felt her feet being lashed together.

Bad enough; they then secured her lashed ankles to one side, then the other—presumably to bedposts—fixing her feet midway between.

When they stepped back, Phoebe tried to move her ankles and found the most she could manage was an inch either way. Worse, she could no longer shift around because she couldn't put her soles to the bed to gain leverage.

She sensed both men watching her, assessing their handiwork.

"That'll hold her." The butler's voice was superiorly smug.

She heard him move. "Come," he said. "I'll inform the master she's here and give you a note so you can claim the rest of your fee."

They left. Phoebe listened. A key turned in the lock of the

narrow door, then she heard a creak as they went down the stairs. Straining her ears, she caught a distant muffled thud . . . and then she heard nothing more.

She was hooded, gagged, and bound, helpless on a bed in some strange room in some gentleman's house. Only two rough men and the man's butler knew where she was. And now "the master" was about to be informed.

Who was he?

The procurer? Was this his way of striking back at the agency and her? He'd learned who she was; what was he planning to do?

Her mind tried to run in a dozen directions at once; she couldn't focus, couldn't think. . . .

Deverell would come for her. He *would* find her. He wouldn't rest until he did.

How? She hadn't a clue, but just as smothering panic rose once more, she remembered that he'd hoped to learn who the procurer was, possibly by that evening. Possibly very soon.

Once he knew he would go to Park Street to tell her, find her gone, and guess . . . then he would come.

She'd just reached that reassuring conclusion when the stairs beyond the door creaked.

Instantly alert, she listened—and heard a key inserted in the lock, then the bolt clicked and the narrow door opened. She felt the slight draft, then the faint eddy as someone large moved into the room.

The door closed.

Blind, gagged, helpless, she lay on the bed, fear sliding through her; ruthlessly she trained her senses on the man who had entered and was standing at the foot of the bed studying her. She forced herself to remain perfectly still.

He eventually stirred. "Good. I'm glad to see that you're being sensible, my dear."

A hand tapped her booted foot, and she jumped.

"Hysterics are so tiresome. And in this case, I assure you they would be entirely unrewarding."

The voice was harsh, hard, but very definitely cultured. Well-bred, well-educated—a man of the ton. Of her class, of her station.

He was also not young. Hearing Deverell's strong, calm voice in her mind, Phoebe forced her panicky senses to her will and set them to glean every snippet of information she could about this man—her enemy. According to Deverell, you could never tell which little snippet might save you.

Over the increasingly loud thudding of her heart, she listened as he continued, pacing slowly back and forth between the door and the foot of the bed. "I want to assure you, my dear, that I fully comprehend your position. I realize you've discovered yourself in a bind, shall we say, and have accepted the only viable way out. Situated as you are, I can see that satisfying your lover—ex-lover, I assume—by assisting him in snatching maids for the slavers is a price many ladies in straits such as yours would willingly pay given that Deverell is now hovering so encouragingly."

Under the hood, Phoebe frowned. What on earth . . . ?

He halted; she sensed him studying her. "Handing over a few pretty maids is hardly to be counted in the scales against becoming Viscountess Paignton. And, of course, Deverell is exceedingly wealthy to boot."

Phoebe blinked. He thought she was being blackmailed by an ex-lover into helping him snatch maids?

For one moment, indignation and affront rose and swept through her, swamping all fear. How *dare* he imagine . . . ?!

But he did. Perhaps there was some chance of salvation there.

He spoke again, pacing once more; she listened avidly, noting every word, every nuance.

"All I wish from you, my dear, is the name of this man—your disreputable ex-lover. You need have no fear that in telling me his name, you will invite repercussions—I promise you I will take care of him. You will, quite literally, never see him again."

There was a cadence to his speech, a heaviness, a weight carried in the harsh yet clearly enunciated, ponderously delivered periods that was both unusual and striking.

"Should you comply, I give you my word that you will suffer no injury from me or my associates." She sensed him pause and glance at her. "You will note that I have no reason to fear you, or any knowledge you might glean from this encounter, as you will hardly be so foolish as to call anyone's attention to your involvement—active involvement, I might add—in the white slave trade."

Silence fell. He was standing at the foot of the bed, watching her.

Another moment ticked by, then he said, "Well?"

A wealth of arrogant demand infused the word; he was waiting for her response and wasn't used to being kept waiting.

Idiot! Phoebe's temper sparked. She mumbled from behind the strip of material still gagging her.

"Ah! Your pardon, my dear. How remiss of me."

He moved to round the bed; Phoebe prayed he'd remove the hood from her head.

Then he was by the side of the bed and leaning over her—panic again bloomed. She fought to subdue it, to not cringe and press away from his hands as he reached about her head. She had to hold her breath and grit her teeth as he searched, all but physically holding back her reaction as he felt about her head—then he found the knot, jerked and untied the strip of material. She forced herself to raise her head so he could unwind the strip. Then he pulled it away.

The hood, the hood!

But no—he stepped back from the bed and left the hood in place. Her heart thudding uncomfortably, Phoebe huffed out a disgusted breath—the hood moved, lifting briefly off her face, then settling down again . . . but now she could see.

If she squinted straight down on either side of her nose, she could see a sliver of room beyond her tied feet, beyond the end of the bed.

"Right then, my dear. Now what is your answer? Speak up—what is this man's name?"

Beneath the hood, she moistened her lips and dragooned her wits into order. "Umm . . ." Not for one minute did she trust his assurance that he wouldn't harm her; if she told him a name—any name, given she had no disreputable blackmailing ex-lover—there was nothing to stop him killing her . . . or worse.

He was of the ton; he would consider her ruined goods at best—a female with no status and no rights. If he was, as seemed all but certain, the procurer they'd been searching for, then he had no honor, nothing she could place the slightest faith in.

"I . . . ah." She dragged in a huge breath, felt her whirling thoughts steady. "I need to consider . . ."—on an afterthought she tacked on—"my lord. I need to think *carefully* of my situation. It's not as . . . as simple and clear-cut as you suppose."

There was a second's hesitation, then came, "Indeed?"

His voice had grown horridly cold. She battled to quell a shiver and not shrink from where he stood by the bed.

After a moment's fraught silence, he moved; he started to pace again. He rounded the corner of the bed and fell to pacing back and forth across its end—and she could see him!

Phoebe swallowed a gasp. She knew him! Or at least she had seen him before. His name escaped her, but he wasn't a total stranger. Just one glance at his heavy frame, at his fastidious attire, confirmed he was of the haut ton. Her "my lord" hadn't been amiss. Who the devil was he?

She peered at his face, what she could glimpse of it as, head bowed, hands locked behind his back, he slowly paced. He was older, in his fifties, she imagined; his hair was gray-white, a pewterish shade. He was of average height, heavily built, pigeon-chested; every movement shrieked of the reserved, stiff-rumped arrogance too often found in men of his age and class. She couldn't see his eyes, but his features were unremittingly harsh; he was scowling ferociously.

What she saw gave her some clue to his character. She cleared her throat. "Please . . . I realize it's an . . . an imposition, but if I could have a little time to gather my wits and recover—the jolting in the carriage was dreadful—they left me on the floor, you know. And then being carried upstairs I nearly swooned." It wasn't too hard to make her voice quaver, to instill a suggestion of tears in her tone. She sounded like the sort of sniveling female she abhorred, but . . .

He flung a scowl her way; she got an excellent view of his face, of the shaggy brows overhanging flintlike eyes. Memory stirred, but it was still too elusive for her to pin down.

He studied her; a touch of derision crept into his expression. "Two hours," he snapped. "I have business to attend to." He turned to the door. "I'll return once that's complete." Halting with his hand on the latch, he glanced back at her. "But I'll expect to have that name from you when I do—no more prevarication. You will not find me inclined to indulgence then."

His gaze grew colder, his voice harder. "And if you think to deny me, my dear, I'm afraid your circumstances will become most unpleasant. As you no doubt know, white slavers are not in the least fussy over the station of their goods, only that they are handsome—and in that respect, my dear, do remember that you qualify."

He watched her for a moment, as if waiting for some sign she appreciated the full portent of his words. When she remained perfectly still, he swung on his heel, pulled open the door, and went out.

Phoebe didn't breathe until she heard the lock click, followed by the telltale creak of the stairs as he went down.

Then she exhaled, dragged in another breath, and gave mute thanks she'd managed thus far.

But what now? She had two hours; she had no illusion that he wouldn't return, that he wouldn't insist on having a name.

She wasn't going to lie there and wait for him to come back.

Getting free of her bonds was her first task. The cords lashing her arms to her sides passed just above her elbows; wriggling, she bent her arms up, raising her hands to where she could examine the cords securing them. Unfortunately, with her elbows trapped at her sides, she couldn't raise her hands to her face, couldn't use her teeth to attack the cords about her wrists.

Temporarily defeated, she decided to see if she could get the hood off; after much wriggling and shifting of shoulders and head, she managed to work the hood back and back, until the front edge lay over her brow.

She huffed out a free breath; at least she could see. She took a moment to study her surroundings. It was a strange room—not large but reasonably comfortable with a perfectly adequate bed. While not luxurious, it was certainly no dungeon. In addition to the bed—a four-poster as she'd imagined, but with no canopy above—a small chest of drawers sat beside the door, with a taller chest against one side wall with a porcelain basin and pitcher atop it.

Phoebe wondered whether there would be any water in the pitcher but doubted it. She looked up and around, studying the strangest aspect of the room—it had no windows. There was a large skylight in the ceiling, but it was far too high for anyone to reach, even standing on the bed or the taller chest.

With a sigh, she returned her gaze to her hands and the cords binding them. No matter how she contorted hands and wrists, she couldn't reach the knots with her straining fingers. Squinting down, desperation rising, she saw the heavy pearl brooch pinned between her breasts.

She had it free in an instant; holding it up, she examined the pin. The brooch was heavy, the pin long and sturdy. Carefully maneuvering it between her fingers, she got to work—painstakingly unpicking and unraveling the cords lashing her wrists.

It was a long, slow, laborious process, but she could see she was making headway. She was determined not to be lying on the bed helpless when that dreadful man returned; while working on the cords, she went over in her mind all Deverell had taught her. The knowledge that there were things she could do to protect herself calmed her, gave her determination a focus.

An hour might have passed, but finally the cords fell and her hands were free! Resisting an urge to cheer—she had no idea if anyone was beyond the door—she lay back, smiling up at the ceiling as she massaged her wrists, then she pushed herself upright and set to work on her other bonds.

Within minutes, she was sitting on the edge of the bed, rubbing her arms, swinging her legs. Carefully, she stood. She crept to the door and put her ear to it. It was a thinnish panel, yet she could hear nothing, sense no one close on the stairs. Recalling how cramped and narrow they were, and that there was another door at their foot, she assumed that if there were any guard, they'd be beyond the second door in the corridor below.

She felt safe enough to walk to free up her limbs.

Eventually, however, she returned to sit once again on the side of the bed. Clasping her hands in her lap, she forced herself to face what had to be faced.

What if Deverell didn't learn the identity of the procurer that day?

"There's a ship standing out in the Thames—the *Maire Jeune*, out of The Hague."

The clock on the mantelpiece of the Bastion Club library chimed six times; the five men gathered in the armchairs paid it no heed as Tristan continued, "They put off their cargo of fleeces yesterday and say they're waiting to take on a new cargo. But there's no cargo registered by any merchant or shipping line for that ship. The captain claimed his agent is negotiating for one, but no one's sighted any agent. The water police are keeping a close watch on the ship from afar—they were careful not to raise any suspicions with their 'customary inquiries.'"

"So we have the ship," Deverell said. "Now we need to be sure of catching them before they slip the girls on board and hoist anchor late one night."

In the depths of one armchair, Dalziel stirred. He drew out a small notebook from his inside coat pocket. "What's the ship's description? I'll send an alert to the naval captain in Falmouth, just in case she slips our net. No sense not being thorough."

There were very few people who could be that thorough. Deverell held his tongue and waited while Tristan gave Dalziel the information and he jotted it down.

"Send your alert via Charles." Gervase caught Dalziel's eye when he looked up. "That's the sort of message he would love to deliver. It'll make him feel included."

Dalziel's lips twitched, but he inclined his head. "Indeed.

St. Austell will be the perfect messenger." He looked around the group. "So what else have we gathered?"

They each reported, but other than the news of the ship, there was little real advance beyond what they'd known days before.

"So," Deverell concluded, "tracing the money is still our surest route to the procurer."

"Is there anything more we can do on that front?" Christian asked.

"I doubt it." It was Dalziel who answered. "I can vouch that Montague is thorough and uncommonly tenacious over such matters. He has contacts I'd give my right arm to learn of." His long lips twisted. "But he's the soul of discretion—which is presumably why he has such astonishing connections."

Which, Deverell surmised, was a subtle hint that although Montague might know of Dalziel, there was no point pursing his identity through that most upright man of business. Deverell had to admit the idea had crossed his mind; Montague managed the affairs of some of the most wealthy and influential families in the land.

He recalled he hadn't mentioned Montague's last message. "Montague might have turned up something by now. He was spending today checking. I told him about this meeting—I was hoping he'd have learned something definite by the end of the day."

They all looked at the clock; it was nearly six-thirty.

Christian rose and fetched the decanter; Dalziel asked after Christian's underworld contacts, whether they might be inclined to assist in bringing down the slavers.

They were discussing that possibility when the knocker on the club's front door was plied with uncommon force. Repeatedly.

From downstairs came the clatter of Gasthorpe's and the footman's footsteps as they ran to open it.

In the library, eyes met. They all sat up, sat forward, set glasses down.

Voices reached them, all male, agitated. Then numerous feet came pounding up the stairs.

As one, the five rose and turned to the door as it burst open.

Fergus stumbled in, Grainger on his heels, Gasthorpe a step behind.

Fergus fixed his gaze on Deverell, literally wringing the cap he held between his huge hands. "They've got her, m'lord—the blackguards have kidnapped Miss Phoebe."

Deverell's world tilted. A cold wave washed through him, leaching out all warmth; ice crept behind it, desolate and bleak. His heart stopped, his body felt like stone—locking him in place despite the overwhelming impulse to race to Park Street, to look for clues, tear London apart if need be. . . .

He managed a step forward.

Beside him, Dalziel put out a hand and halted him. "No." There was a quality in that steely voice that even now commanded.

That dragged Deverell, all but quivering under the restraint, back to the real world. He hauled in a breath, held it.

"Find out all you can first," Dalziel quietly continued, "then we'll all be able to help."

The sense in that was undeniable. Deverell expelled the breath locked in his lungs and nodded. Motioning Fergus to a chair, he sank slowly back into his, breathing deeply, desperately searching for a calm that had been destroyed.

He fought to curb the black panic roiling through him. He'd never felt its like before—it was so difficult to breathe— but Dalziel was right; Deverell forced his mind to focus.

Fergus slumped onto the straight-backed chair Gervase set for him. Deverell met the Scotsman's anguished gaze and realized Fergus was flaying himself; she'd been in his care.

He kept his tone even. "What happened? Start from when you last saw her, but quickly."

Fergus nodded and dragged in a breath. "She was walking in the rear garden like she always does late afternoon. They—Miss Audrey, Mrs. Edith, and Miss Phoebe—had come back from their afternoon rounds. The two ladies laid down in the drawing room and Miss Phoebe went for her constitutional."

Christian leaned forward. "She walks every day at that time?"

"Aye."

"It's a walled garden," Deverell put in. He nodded to Fergus. "Go on."

"Milligan—the housekeeper—called to Miss Phoebe that Miss Edith had rung for the tea tray. Miss Phoebe was down the back corner of the garden. She said she was coming and started back, and then Milligan called me in. I went." Fergus looked shattered. "But she was halfway back to the morning room—no more than twenty yards—and the back gate was locked, I'd checked it, and there's shards along the top of that wall. How did they get in and grab her?"

"Was the gate still locked?"

"No." Grainger had come to stand beside Fergus. "I'd gone past earlier—the key was on the nail and the gate was locked, but when we checked after she'd gone, the key was in the lock and the gate was shut but unlocked."

"No one heard anything?" Tristan asked.

Fergus shook his head. "Nor saw anything, either. We asked everyone."

"She opened the gate." Deverell frowned. "Why? She's not witless, and she knew she was in danger." After a moment, he answered, "Someone must have lured her out with something she assumed was safe."

No one commented.

"Time." Dalziel fixed Fergus with his dark gaze. "How long was it before you realized she was gone?"

Fergus grimaced. "Half an hour or so. We thought she was with Mrs. Edith and Miss Audrey, but then Mrs. Edith sent the maid down to ask where Miss Phoebe was as her tea was getting cold."

"So." Dalziel steepled his fingers. "Half an hour, then time to ask about, then your journey here." He glanced at the clock. "An hour, at least, but not much more."

Fergus nodded.

Deverell opened his mouth—before he could speak another knock fell on the front door. A polite knock.

Gasthorpe had gone downstairs a few minutes before, presumably to summon all the footmen and boys who ran messages for the club members. A murmur of voices rose from the front hall, then footsteps, steady and sure, climbed the stairs.

"My lords." Gasthorpe stood back and waved the visitor in.

Montague appeared in the doorway. He glanced around at the tense assembly. His gaze touched each face; most he didn't know, but his lids flickered in surprise when he saw Dalziel. He hesitated for a fraction of a second, then his gaze traveled on to Deverell's face. "I do hope I haven't called at an inopportune time, my lord."

"Not at all." Deverell felt hope bloom; setting his jaw, he waved Montague to a chair. "You've found a name?"

Looking unusually grim, Montague sat. "I have." He glanced again at the others, all except Dalziel. "My news, however, is of a highly sensitive nature. . . ."

"In the circumstances, I'll ask you to speak freely before all here—Miss Malleson was kidnapped an hour ago and

we've no time to lose. We all need to know the identity of
the gentleman who's been assisting the white slavers."

Montague's round countenance registered his shock, but
he quickly set it aside. He glanced at Dalziel, then looked
back at Deverell. "In that case . . ." He drew a deep breath
and stated, "There are only two accounts in all the city's
banks that show sizeable deposits consistently made at or
about the time each missing girl vanished."

Deverell opened his mouth to demand just the name—
Montague stayed him with an upraised hand. "You need to
hear this. I'll keep it brief, but you will need to judge the
validity of what I've learned."

Puzzled, Deverell frowned, but reluctantly nodded.

"One account is an investment account belonging to a Mr.
Thomas Glendower, a young man of good family with a
knack for investing. However, the payments made into that
account are not as consistent in amount and timing as the
deposits to one other account."

"Whose?" It was Dalziel who demanded.

Montague looked at him. "Henry Hubert Lowther, Lord
Lowther. He's one of the law lords."

A stunned silence followed, then Christian said, "I can
see why you were so hesitant to name him."

"And why," Dalziel said, "you wanted us to hear the
proof."

"Indeed." Montague's lips tightened. "But there's more."

It was Dalziel's turn to hold up a hand. "Does anyone
know where Lowther lives?"

No one did. Deverell looked at Grainger. "Go and ask
Gasthorpe."

Wide-eyed, Grainger rushed off.

All those remaining returned their gazes to Montague.

Who looked more than grim. "Be Lowther who he may,
the facts are inescapable—indeed, they are otherwise

impossible to explain. I didn't trust to anyone else's interpretation—I went and looked at the records myself. All highly irregular, of course, but I trust you'll overlook that. What I found . . . every time one of those girls went missing, Lowther deposited two hundred and fifty pounds into his account. *Every* time. I traced his estate income, which is pitifully little but is his only other income. Against that, he's withdrawn large sums. Those sums pertain to purchases of notable pistols—he's an avid collector apparently well known as having all but bottomless pockets."

Gervase blinked. "But you just told us he doesn't. That he has very little income."

"Indeed." Montague's eyes glinted. "Given his lordship's status, I dug deeper—to make sure I hadn't missed any other explanation, any other possible source of funds. Instead, I discovered that his lordship has teetered on the brink of a financial abyss for the last year and more. It's the guns—he's bought far too many. With neglible income coming in, he had an imperative financial motive for seeking additional funds. Indeed, he's been tampering with his ward's accounts as well, although as yet they have suffered only minor depredations."

"Only because he found a better source," Tristan said. "Selling maids into slavery."

Deverell had been juggling Montague's information. "What you're saying is that without the money from the slavers, Lowther would be bankrupt."

Montague nodded. "That's *precisely* the case."

All of them knew what bankruptcy would mean to a man of Lowther's standing. Dalziel put it into words. "The end. *Point nonplus.*" He rose, as did the others.

Grainger and Gasthorpe appeared at the open door.

"Where's Lowther's house?" Deverell asked. Even he heard the violence in his tone.

"Wait," Dalziel countermanded. "We should let Mr. Montague depart, with our sincere thanks. He doesn't need to hear what we intend to do."

Briefly, Montague met Dalziel's eyes; for one instant, Deverell thought he might argue, but then he inclined his head. "Indeed." He glanced at Deverell. "I'll leave you gentlemen to do what needs to be done."

The words had a ring of finality.

Montague left.

At a nod from Deverell, Grainger blurted, "Arlington Street. Number 21."

With a word of thanks, Deverell dismissed Grainger and Fergus, signaling Grainger to close the door. The instant it was shut, Deverell turned to Dalziel.

None of them had sat down again. Dalziel had picked up his glass of brandy and drained it; he was setting it down when Deverell cocked a brow at him. "Still in command?"

Dalziel met his gaze, then straightened and smiled—beyond dangerous, beyond ruthless, beyond merciless. "With such a quarry?" He left the question hanging for a heartbeat, then answered, "Definitely."

Deverell hesitated, weighing up what he could see in Dalziel's eyes, read in his expression—that if anyone was going to bring Lowther down, it had better be Dalziel, who had authority enough to withstand any resultant furor. He nodded. "You're right. So—how are we going to play this hand?"

She felt almost calm.

Phoebe leaned against the wall beside the door, the heavy chamber pot she'd discovered under the bed cradled in her hands. From where she stood, she would hear the creak of the stairs, would be warned when her captor returned for her answer.

Her answer, she'd decided, would be best delivered in

white porcelain. She'd ransacked the room; the chamber pot was the best weapon—it was heavier than the pitcher.

It would, she hoped, at least slow the man down, enough for her to rush down the stairs and, with any luck, lock the lower door behind her. She knew houses like this; if she could break free for a few minutes, she could reach the front door and safety. That was her plan; the rest would be easy.

She looked up, noting that the light was fading from the sky. Evening was drawing in; her two hours had to be almost up.

Resistance was risky, but she didn't believe she had any real choice. Despite what he'd said, this man—their procurer—was one no woman should ever trust. Were she to give him a name, she might find herself dispatched to the white slavers without delay—and then how would Deverell find her? He'd admitted they couldn't locate the warehouse, so rescue would come only when the slavers tried to take her aboard their ship—and how many weeks might pass before that happened?

Quite aside from any other danger, her reputation would be ruined—making it impossible for her to act on Audrey's excellent advice and seize the life she'd absolutely decided should be hers.

Regardless of any other consideration, she was not about to let their beastly procurer stop her from becoming Deverell's wife.

She was unquestionably the best wife for him; she was almost certain he would agree.

Her lips lifted wryly; she was honestly amazed at herself—at how completely determination, conviction, and sheer brazen stubbornness ruled her, at how little real purchase fear possessed.

Her present situation was far worse, far more scarifying than the incident in her past; she knew it, yet she was no longer the naïve seventeen-year-old she'd been. It wasn't just the years that had passed that had changed her but how she'd spent them; most especially it was the last month and all Deverell had taught her, on so many levels, that left her not just determined never to be any man's victim but confident she didn't need to be. That there was every reason to fight and no reason to expect to lose.

Men like their procurer didn't always win, because there were other men, better men, who would annihilate him. All she had to do was escape and leave them, the right sort of large and dangerous gentlemen, to take care of the rest.

That, to her mind, was as things should be.

Escape was her goal—and as soon as possible thereafter, she would speak to Deverell about marriage. If, in extremis, everyone made a vow to God about what they would do if they were saved, then that was her vow. It was senseless to carry on as they were; theirs was no true liaison. They were living in each other's pockets, sharing each other's lives— they might as well marry and have done with the charade.

So she would tell him—

Creak.

Phoebe sucked in a breath. A key slid into the lock.

Silently she took up her position behind the door. As it swung open, she hoisted the chamber pot high.

Pewter-gray hair—she didn't wait to see more but brought the pot whistling down.

He glimpsed movement at the last second and ducked. Instead of cracking the pot over his crown, she dealt him a glancing blow. He staggered.

Phoebe gasped as the pot slipped from her hands and crashed on the floor, shattering into dozens of pieces.

His face contorted in a furious snarl, the man turned on her.

He grabbed her wrists.

She remembered, rotated her arms, and broke his grasp.

He was stunned for an instant; she stepped in and brought her knee up hard and fast, but she wobbled on a pot shard—her blow landed, but not precisely in the right spot.

But the snarl evaporated; his face turned purple. He sucked in a furious hissing breath and grabbed her shoulders. He tried to shake her, but they were both off-balance . . . for a moment they wrestled, pot shards crunching beneath their feet, then Phoebe remembered and butted him in the face.

He was shorter than Deverell and had his head lowered—she hit the side of his forehead with hers. Hard.

He howled—music to her ears!—but his fingers only bit more deeply into her shoulders.

Phoebe cursed and looked down, trying to locate his feet to smash her heel down on his instep—

"My lord—my lord! You must come quickly!"

Breathless and agitated, the butler's voice came from the bottom of the stairs.

Phoebe lifted her head, glanced at the open door.

"There's a gentleman arrived. He's asking for you on some urgent matter. He won't be denied."

Phoebe dragged in a breath to scream—

With a massive effort, the man heaved her from her feet, swung her, and slung her across the room.

She hit the floor and slid into the wall, winded, but with her hands she managed to keep her head from cracking against the paneling.

Looking up, breathless, she saw the man—their procurer—standing before the door, dragging in a huge breath.

His color was high, choleric; his cold gray eyes, filled with fury and vindictive hate, pinned her. His hands shook as he tugged down his sleeves. "I'll deal with you later." His voice was a low, raspy growl, nothing like his previously deliberate diction. "And then the slavers can have you!"

He spat the last words at her, then went out of the door, slammed it shut, and locked it.

Phoebe struggled to her feet; she raced to the door and pounded on the panels. *"Deverell! I'm here!"*

She paused to drag in a breath, listened . . . and realized that she couldn't hear the man's or the butler's footsteps receding. They'd closed the door at the bottom of the stairs; as she'd suspected, it cut off all sound.

No point screaming.

Lips twisting, then setting, she went back to the bed, circling the pot shards to sit on the side.

She'd assumed the visitor was Deverell, but what if it wasn't?

If it wasn't . . . the beast was going to come back once he'd dealt with the interruption, and now he knew she was loose in the room. What would he do?

Looking down, she kicked at a pot shard. More to the point, what was she going to do?

Chapter 22

Concealed in the shadows of Lord Lowther's drawing room, through the partially open door Deverell watched Dalziel, Christian, and Tristan as they waited just inside Lowther's front hall for his lordship to appear.

The butler had opened the front door to them; given no real choice, he'd reluctantly admitted the three gentlemen he'd seen waiting on the stoop and, rattled by Dalziel's subtly menacing demand, had rushed off to summon his master. Tristan had silently reopened the front door; like wraiths, Deverell and Gervase had slipped in and taken up their station in the darkened drawing room. Deverell glanced at Gervase, beside him in the shadows; it was their task to search the house, if Phoebe were there to locate and release her while Dalziel and the others kept Lowther engaged.

Over two hours had passed since Phoebe had been strolling in Edith's garden; their best guess was that she would be held somewhere in this house. Lowther would want to question her, to learn about her involvement with whisking maids away; given her station, it seemed unlikely—unnecessary—for him to have had her taken elsewhere. Not yet.

That Lowther was at home seemed to confirm their assessment.

They waited; silent in the dark, Deverell thanked heaven the discipline of patience was still his. Cold dread had swamped him at the first word of Phoebe's kidnapping; everything he'd learned since had only intensified the sensation. Given her past, this was surely the worst terror that could have befallen her. He might have eased her trepidation, blunted her ingrained, now instinctive fear and the panic that arose from that, but he had no way of knowing how she would react to the present situation and its implicit threats, how deeply fear might grip her, how badly it might affect her.

How terrified she might be.

The thought of her terrified shook him to the core, unleashed a torrent of emotions and a compulsion to act unlike any he'd felt before, to rescue her, defend her, protect her. Above all, to keep her safe.

While he waited, focused and alert, all attention locked on doing just that, the detached, usually totally cynical part of his brain pointed out the obvious with breathtaking clarity—he felt like this about Phoebe because she was his life. The center of it, the lynchpin; without her, all the rest would fall apart.

He'd imagined he would be the center of her life; instead, she was the fulcrum about which his life revolved. Without her, he'd be lost.

As soon as this was over, as soon as he had her safe, he vowed he would ask and insist that she marry him. No more delays, no more waiting for her to see the obvious on her own; if she hadn't noticed by now, he'd just have to make the matter plain—and show her why, every single reason why, she simply had to marry him.

Heavy footsteps came quickly down the stairs—more than one man. Lips set, Deverell resisted the urge to peek out; he and Gervase faded back into deeper shadow as the footsteps halted before Dalziel.

"Dalziel?" Lowther already sounded rattled. "What's this?"

A fractional hesitation—fleeting but there, enough to alert both Deverell and Gervase—then Dalziel murmured, "My apologies for disturbing your nap, my lord." Another brief but meaningful pause. "It seems you've taken a knock on the head."

"What? Oh, that. It's nothing—bumped my head on a drawer. Clumsy thing to do, but nothing to worry about." Lowther paused to draw breath. "Now, what brings you to my door?"

"I fear I need to consult with you on a legal matter. I believe you're acquainted with Dearne and Trentham?"

"Yes, of course." Lowther hesitated, then coughed and stepped back. "If you'll come into my study . . . ?"

Deverell glanced at Gervase as they listened to the four men move down the hall.

"Nap?" Gervase mouthed.

Face set like stone, Deverell pointed upward. From Dalziel's comments, Lowther was disheveled and injured; his lordship had been involved in some fight moments before— and he'd come from upstairs.

Lowther's voice, pitched between petulance and belligerence, faded; a door toward the back of the hall shut.

Deverell waited a heartbeat, then cautiously looked out. The butler, a tall, severe man, stood listening outside what was presumably the study door. As Deverell watched, the man grimaced, then walked off through the swinging doors leading to the rear of the house.

A touch on Gervase's arm and Deverell was moving through the hall. Swift and silent, he reached the stairs; keeping to the edge of the treads, he climbed without a sound. Gervase followed at his heels.

At the top of the stairs, they paused, glancing around, listening, confirming that as expected at this time of day there were no staff abovestairs. Exchanging a nod, they separated; quickly, thoroughly, methodically, all in complete silence, they searched the first floor. Finding nothing, they went up to the second; from there, they progressed to the attics, treading more warily in case any staff were in their rooms.

They found nothing. And no one.

Halting in the narrow attic corridor, Deverell faced Gervase—and saw his frustration mirrored in his friend's face. "We've missed it."

Gervase nodded. "No sign of a struggle, not even a rumpled bed to account for Lowther's disarranged state. Dalziel wouldn't have mentioned it if he didn't think it pertinent, and Lowther wouldn't have excused the injury if it wasn't bad enough to be obvious."

The cold dread intensified, invading Deverell's gut; like a fist, it gripped, turning his innards to desolate ice. Hauling in a breath past the constriction banding his chest, he turned, resurveying the doors to the rooms on either side. "So we search again. It's here, but hidden."

It had to be. *She* had to be.

This time they worked together, one tapping on a wall, the other in the next room confirming that the wall was indeed shared, that there was no extra space between. They worked as fast as they could; how long Dalziel could spin out his fabrication of a legal consulation they didn't know.

They cleared the attics, then the second floor; the only spaces they found were taken up by cupboards. Descending to the first floor, they continued; it didn't take them long to establish that the larger rooms were all as they should be. Frustrated, in Deverell's case with a species of icy panic sliding through his veins, they halted in the corridor a little way from the main stairs.

"This is crazy." Hauling in a tight breath, Deverell raked his hand through his hair. "There has to be something here."

Gervase grimaced. After a moment he said, "Are we wrong?"

Deverell didn't want to think it, but in his present state, he wasn't even sure his earlier deductions were rational. The panic welling inside him was unlike any he'd known. He'd faced death, several times, without such turmoil. Without such desperate, driving, gut-wrenching compulsion to act to fend off the soul-destroying desolation looming.

He *had to* find Phoebe. He was barely aware of clenching his fists with the effort to smother an urge to roar her name. Lips thin, pressed tight, he looked down, then growled, "Somewhere here there's something to be found."

Lifting his head, he looked along the corridor to the stairs. "Let's talk to the butler."

He took a step and something crunched underfoot. He looked down, then crouched. Lifting a pottery shard, he held it up so Gervase could see.

"Odd." Gervase looked right and left. "This place has been swept recently."

Deverell narrowed his eyes. "What if Lowther didn't hit his head, but someone hit it for him?"

Gervase met his eyes, then looked around. "Where is the question." Then he pointed to the side of the corridor past

Deverell. "Is that another sliver? There—at the bottom of those doors."

Deverell swiveled, looked, reached out, and fingered the thin white fragment, then rose, examining the narrow doors in the corridor wall. "Looks like a closet." He pulled the handle. "It's locked."

Gervase ranged beside him. "Why lock a closet?"

"Indeed." Deverell felt in his pocket. In a few seconds, the doors were unlocked. He tugged them open.

Shelves packed with towels and linens faced them. As one, he and Gervase took a step back, scanning the top, the sides, the floor of the cupboard.

"It's a hidden door," Gervase said.

Deverell nodded. "There must be stairs behind it, concealed in the cupboards in the rooms on either side. We need to find the catch."

Towels and linens flew, then reaching to the back corner of one shelf, Gervase grunted. "Got it."

Deverell stepped back. A click sounded. Gervase joined him as the two halves of the cupboard swung out from the center, pivoting at the sides to reveal a dark set of very steep, narrow stairs leading upward. They could just make out another door at the top of the stairs, beyond a wide last step.

"Well, well," Deverell breathed.

Gervase tapped his arm. They communicated by signal; they didn't know if Phoebe was alone or with a guard.

Seconds later, Deverell crept silently up the stairs, leaving Gervase at their base, guarding his back.

In the room at the top of the stairs, Phoebe had returned to stand against the wall beside the door, but this time on the other side. The beast would expect her to be behind the door; he might well swing it back hard to hit her.

Head back against the wall, she tried not to think about

what she intended to do. The beast had left her no choice; she was not going to be his victim.

Her gaze drifted to the mound of white porcelain fragments on the floor by the chest of drawers. She'd broken both the pitcher and the bowl in her quest for a decent weapon. In her right hand, she clutched the long, thin, daggerlike piece she'd fashioned; she'd lagged half its length with the cord with which she'd been tied so she could grip it tightly. The exposed tip was definitely sharp enough to slice through skin; how much more damage it would do she would soon find out.

The stairs creaked.

She sucked in a breath. Waited.

But he waited, too. More cautious, this time.

She would only get one chance at him—in the instant he came through the door. She couldn't hesitate, couldn't fail. Her future and Deverell's depended on it.

The lock scraped.

She breathed out, sucked in another breath and held it. Clutched the dagger shard and tensed . . .

The door flung open, shoved forcefully as she'd foreseen. It banged against the wall.

A man stepped in.

Eyes closing, she swung with all her might, driving the daggerpoint hard for his chest.

Deverell saw, grabbed her wrist lightning quick, crushingly in that first instant, but he immediately gentled his hold as he held the point of the wicked-looking makeshift dagger away from his waistcoat. She gasped and fought his strength. "Phoebe."

Her eyes flew wide, lifted to his face.

For an instant she simply stared at him, then the dagger fell from her fingers, all the fight drained out of her and she flung herself at him. "Oh, thank God—it's *you!*"

She clutched him, hugged him—then pulled back and

framed his face. "How did you find me? That man, whoever he is—"

She broke off as Gervase poked his head through the doorway. He looked her up and down, grinned, then looked at Deverell. "I'll tell them."

Deverell nodded. He couldn't speak. He could barely stand as relief and so much more poured through him.

Turning, Gervase went quickly down the stairs.

Dragging in a still-too-tight breath, Deverell returned his attention to Phoebe, looked at her for an instant—at her face, her eyes, glowing and alive, undimmed . . . then he hauled her into his arms and hugged her until she squealed. Even then, eyes closed, battling emotions that were simply too strong, he had to breathe deeply again before he could force himself to ease his hold and set her back enough to examine her properly.

Her afternoon gown of green cambric was rumpled and crumpled, but not torn; numerous heavy dark red locks had come loose from her chignon, but otherwise he could see no damage. No sign she'd been molested.

Most reassuring was the clear, open expression on her face and the martial light gleaming in her violet eyes.

His reaction was so profound it all but rocked his world.

Hands cupping her shoulders, he looked into her face, met those bright eyes, and struggled to behave normally. "Are you all right?"

"Yes." She nodded. Far from swooning or even wilting, she seemed energized. "I hit him with the chamber pot, but he ducked and it broke. Then he tried to grab my wrists but your maneuver worked—much to his amazement. I tried to knee him but he shifted—I almost got him, though. And then . . ." She frowned lightly. "I can't remember what more, but then his butler called him away. He flung me aside but I wasn't hurt."

She was babbling but seemed quite chuffed at her resourcefulness.

Then her eyes found his. After a moment, she tilted her head, then said, "I might not have defeated him, but thanks to what you taught me—to *all* you've taught me—he didn't harm me. And now you've rescued me, so . . ."

He expected her to say "all is well"; he would have sworn from her tone that that was what she intended. Instead, her pause lengthened. He waited; buffeted by relief, joy, triumph, pride in her, appreciation of her courage and so much more, he was still battling to find his emotional feet.

Then her expression sobered; her chin set, determination in every line. "As soon as this is over, the first chance we have to speak alone, we must talk."

He blinked. Talk? While one part of his mind had him nodding in complete agreement, another part was scrambling to fathom her direction. Most especially the source of her sudden serious determination.

She glanced at the door, a frown forming. "Who was Gervase going to tell?"

Mentally shaking his head, somewhat desperately realigning his wits, he refocused on what lay before them. "The others—Dalziel, Christian, and Tristan. They're speaking with Lowther, distracting him. They weren't going to come to the point until we had you safe."

Casting a last glance around the room—it was concealed between other rooms *and* in between two floors, which was why they hadn't discovered it earlier—he steered her to the door. "Come—we should go downstairs."

Gervase knocked on the study door, then opened it and walked in.

Seated in the chair before the wide desk, Dalziel turned to look at him. Tristan stood to one side, close to the wall, arms folded; Christian stood in a similar position on the other side of the desk, at ease yet focused.

Lowther sat rigidly upright behind the desk, trying to hide incipient panic behind a belligerent scowl.

Closing the door, Gervase walked forward and answered the others' unvoiced question. "We found her. She's with Deverell." Halting behind the chair Dalziel occupied, Gervase held Lowther's gaze. "The room she was in was concealed."

"Is that so?" Dalziel's brows rose as he turned his dark gaze back on Lowther. "How very unwise."

Lowther had paled. He tried for blustering anger. "I don't know what you're talking about. If you're insinuating—"

"The time for insinuations is past." Dalziel's voice, although not raised, left no doubt that he, and not Lowther, was in charge of the interview. "Perhaps I should tell you what we already know."

Calmly, succinctly, he outlined their case against Lowther, citing the evidence tying him to the kidnappings of eight separate women. Christian, Tristan, and Gervase stood not exactly unobtrusively around the room, their gazes resting on Lowther, their condemnation explicit in their cold silence. Lowther glanced at them, read judgment in their eyes; his gaze drifted back to Dalziel.

He swallowed.

There was no hope; he saw that. His face—he—seemed to age before their eyes.

Reaching the end of his recitation, Dalziel asked, "Who was your contact among the white slavers?"

Lowther blinked, twice, then with peevish arrogance stated, "I don't know—I don't consort with such people."

"A nice distinction—you simply take their money. So how was the information relayed from you to the gang who organized the abductions, and how were the resultant payments delivered to you?"

Lowther hesitated. After a moment, he said, "My ward—Malcolm Sinclair."

A curious stillness descended on Dalziel. When he spoke again, his voice was softer, lighter—and wholly frightening. "Your ward. Correct me if I'm wrong—Sinclair's been your ward from the time he was a child."

Curtly, Lowther nodded.

"And you've involved him in this business? Or did he involve himself?"

Lowther snorted. "Malcolm's nothing but a pawn. He does what I tell him. Under my direction, he made the contacts and acted as courier, ferrying information and money back and forth."

"And that's the full extent of his involvement?"

Lowther compressed his lips, then conceded, "He has friends from his Eton and Oxford days—I encouraged him to cultivate them. They proved excellent sources of information about pretty maids and the like—the usual young men's gossip. Malcolm would bring the information to me and I would decide what was useful, what not."

"So Sinclair's role was entirely of your making?"

Lowther's lip curled. "Malcolm's weak—he lacks backbone. He's bright enough but totally indecisive, inclined to be overcautious to the point of doing nothing. He might think of schemes, but he would never actually *do* anything about them."

After a moment's silence, Dalziel murmured, "A pity, perhaps, that you didn't follow his lead."

A deep coldness threaded through his voice, one that chilled to the marrow. Already pasty-faced, Lowther blanched even more.

The silence stretched; none of them moved.

Lowther, increasingly ashen, sat frozen, immobilized as the full weight of all that had been said—and not said—sank into his brain. Eventually he blinked, and the belligerent but brittle defiance that had held him upright until that moment started to fade.

Dalziel glanced at the others. "Perhaps you would give me a few minutes with his lordship. I'll join you in the drawing room."

All three recognized an order when they heard one, especially one delivered in that quiet, deadly, almost disembodied voice. They exchanged glances as they went to the door. Each cast one last glance at Lowther—sitting behind his desk, his pallor ghastly, his eyes fixed straight ahead, the wall behind him sporting six fabulous examples of his obsession, the obsession he'd sold women into slavery to satisfy—then they quietly quit the room and closed the door, and left Lowther staring at his fate.

For long moments, a clock ticking was the only sound to break the silence.

Then Dalziel spoke, his tone colder, icier than the grave. "Well, my lord?"

Slowly, Lowther refocused and met Dalziel's dark gaze.

There was only one answer he could make.

Deverell cocked his head as he heard the study door open.

He and Phoebe were waiting in the now fully lit drawing room, she occupying an armchair while he paced.

On one level, he wanted to face Lowther and exact vengeance in blood, but aside from him having no intention of leaving Phoebe's side, given the depth of his cold fury it was perhaps as well that he left Lowther's punishment to others. Luckily, if there were any man alive he trusted to see justice served, it was Dalziel; he had to be content with leaving the matter in his ex-commander's experienced hands.

"Lowther!" Phoebe shook her head and sipped the tea the

butler had hurried to bring her—after she'd leveled a strait glance his way.

Deverell had noticed and questioned her; she'd confirmed the butler's involvement and complicity in her imprisonment. Quelling his initial impulse to rend the man limb from limb after he'd delivered the tea, by the time the butler reappeared with the tray, he'd decided on a more fitting course.

Courtesy of the time he'd spent at the agency, he now had a much finer understanding of life belowstairs; he'd suggested and Phoebe had agreed that they should simply mention the man's behavior to Scatcher and Birtles, and leave them to arrange his fate.

"I still find it mindboggling." Phoebe set her cup on her saucer. "A *law lord,* and if your recollection is correct, one specifically involved in drafting the laws on slavery."

The study door shut; Deverell heard the others' footsteps nearing.

Halting, he grasped their last moment alone to look at Phoebe—to drink in the sight of her, calm and in large measure composed, safe and unharmed, to let the knowledge wash through him. . . . He turned as the others filed in.

"No doubt about his guilt," Christian growled. "It was written all over his face." He saw Phoebe, smiled charmingly, and sat on the chaise opposite her. "Where was this room he'd locked you in?"

Between them, Deverell, Gervase, and Phoebe explained what had happened regarding Phoebe's capture and subsequent rescue, then Tristan and Christian described what had transpired in the study.

"Lowther knew what was coming before he'd even sat down," Christian said, "what with me and Tristan standing there, two peers whose word would be beyond question as witnesses."

"I've never sat through an interview like that." Tristan shook his head. "When Lowther began, he was convinced he could bluster his way out of any net Dalziel might construct, but even before Gervase joined us he'd tripped himself up twice by reacting to information he shouldn't have known. Dalziel's frighteningly acute—he seizes on tiny reactions, and from that seems to know just where to slip in the knife and pry. . . ."

Tristan paused, then went on, "Then Gervase came in, the kid gloves came off, and it was all over."

Deverell asked about the contact with the slavers; the others had just finished explaining about Lowther's ward when they all heard the door of the study open, then almost immediately shut.

All fell silent and listened.

Strolling, prowling footsteps sounded on the tiles, then Dalziel appeared in the open doorway.

He scanned the room; his gaze found Phoebe, and he inclined his head.

She nodded back, not quite smiling. Unsure.

Everyone watched Dalziel. There was a tension in him, one all the other men recognized, one that pricked their instincts and brought them alert in expectation of some greater danger, as if seeing in him a fleeting glimpse of a lethal edge finely honed.

A shot rang out, echoing and crashing in the confines of the house. In the study; there was no doubt in anyone's mind where the sound came from or what it meant.

No one moved, then shouts and running footsteps rolled up from the rear of the house, spilling into the hall. Dalziel turned his head, looked, then he turned back and met Phoebe's wide eyes. "My apologies." The deep voice was even, undisturbed. "But it had to be done."

Shocked, but puzzled, too, Phoebe held his dark gaze.

"You suggested he take his life." Her tone held no condemnation, only honest curiosity.

He looked at her for a moment, then quietly said, "There are some men we simply do not need in this world."

The butler hove in sight, all but babbling in consternation. Dalziel turned to deal with him. Christian rose and went to assist.

Tristan and Gervase got to their feet.

Phoebe set down her cup and looked at Deverell.

He met her eyes and held out his hand. "Come—I'll take you home."

They traveled the short distance in a hackney, not a suitable venue in which to broach the subject of Phoebe's vow. As soon as they were alone, in suitable surroundings—she was determined on that.

They walked into the Park Street house to discover Edith, Audrey, and Loftus in the drawing room, all waiting, agog, to hear that she was safe. Of course, once assured that was indeed so, they demanded to know all the rest.

Deverell suggested, and Phoebe concurred, that Skinner, Fergus, and Grainger, who Deverell had sent earlier from the club to reassure Edith, be summoned so all involved could hear their tale.

They told it as concisely as they could, but Edith, Audrey, and even Loftus had questions, wanting to know every little detail. Phoebe inwardly railed at the delay but accepted that they needed to be reassured. She and Deverell held nothing back; quite aside from all those present having a right to know, the scandal of Lord Lowther's suicide would be all over town come morning.

But at last they reached the end of the story. While Audrey and Edith exclaimed over Lowther, Deverell moved to Phoebe's side and took her arm. Bending his head, he murmured, "You're flagging—exhausted. You need to retire."

She blinked up at him, then realized. "Oh—yes." Turning to the others, she repeated his words, adding her own emphasis and letting her shoulders droop.

"Of course, dear—you must go up and rest. Don't let us keep you." Edith beamed at her—at them.

Audrey waved a dismissal. "We'll catch up with you tomorrow."

"I'll see you to the stairs." To the others, Deverell said, "I need to get on." To where he didn't say.

Phoebe turned to Skinner and Fergus. "Please take word to Emmeline and Birtles. I don't want them worrying unnecessarily."

"Aye." Fergus glanced at Skinner. "We'll get around there right away."

"And you"—Deverell looked at Grainger—"can hie back to the club and tell Gasthorpe what's happened. I have no idea when Crowhurst will get back tonight—it might be late." He said nothing about his own return.

Grainger beamed and snapped a jaunty salute. "Yes, sir." He turned and followed Skinner and Fergus through the door.

Phoebe followed more slowly, Deverell by her side. They paused in the hall. Deverell closed the drawing room door, waited until the other three had disappeared behind the green baize door, then he reached for Phoebe's hand; she gripped his. "Come on."

Hand in hand, they slipped up the stairs.

To her room.

At last! Phoebe led the way in, sweeping through the door Deverell set wide and on to the clear area before one window. Skinner had left a lamp burning, shedding sufficient light for her purpose. Marshaling her thoughts, she swung around to pace—and found he'd shut the door and was half-way across the room, advancing on her.

Her wits leapt to attention. Halting, she pointed at him. "Stop!"

He blinked, slowed, and did, leaving five feet of space between them. The look on his face as he searched hers plainly stated he had no idea what was going on. What she was thinking. If she was thinking or if she was panicking . . .

She waved her hands as if to erase his thoughts. "I need to talk to you—and I can't even *think* if you're too close." His wary tension evaporated; she glimpsed a fleeting quirk of his lips before he schooled his expression to attentive interest. She frowned at him. "Just stay where you are, and listen."

His lips set; his wariness hadn't entirely left him.

She drew breath, clasped her hands before her, and faced him squarely. "I know that when we first met, all those weeks ago at Cranbrook Manor, you had it in mind that I might make a suitable bride for you. You need to marry—that is beyond question—not just for an heir, but because of the many social obligations that now fall to you as Paignton, obligations no bachelor could easily fulfill."

She paused, then inclined her head. "So you have good reasons to hunt for a wife—indeed, it's incumbent on you to do so." She hesitated, searching his eyes, wondering if she dared put her suppositions into words . . . his steady, unwavering green gaze as always reassured her. Gave her the strength to say, "I . . . got the impression, all those weeks ago, that you seriously considered making me an offer, that you might well have done so if I hadn't made it plain that I was uninterested in marriage." Hesitating for only a heartbeat, she clasped her hands more tightly and lifted her chin. "Was that so?"

A moment passed while he searched her eyes, then he nodded. Briefly. "Yes."

Relief of the sweetest kind washed through her. "Good. Because what I wanted to tell you is that I've changed my mind." She held his gaze. "I'm no longer uninterested in marriage."

He stared at her for a strangely dizzying moment, then something changed. Some shift in the atmosphere, some cosmic realignment—some sudden and glorious upwelling of joy.

His features eased; he stepped forward.

"No—*wait!*" She held up a hand. "You have to hear me out. It's important—I'm not the sort of lady who changes her mind, not about things like that."

"Phoebe—"

"No!" She folded her arms, held his gaze. "I'm determined to say this—you have to listen."

Her chin had set in that determinedly stubborn way Deverell now knew very well. He was too relieved, too overjoyed to deny her anything—even an unnecessary delay at a moment like this. Although it was difficult to remain three feet from her and not close the distance, inclining his head, he acquiesced, inviting her to continue.

With something very like a warning frown, she went on, "I didn't know before, when I decided against marriage, what a marriage between people like us, you and me, might be like. I didn't even know men like you existed—there aren't that many of you around, you know. My views had been formed from what I knew then, what I knew of gentlemen then, and as you know that wasn't favorable."

She paused, her eyes on his, then simply said, "You changed my perceptions. You opened my eyes."

He nearly moved, but her eyes—violet blue and intense, colored by her emotions—held him.

"Not because of who you are, but because of *what* you are—the sort of man you are." Frowning, she tilted her head. "You're different, unconventional—you don't react as others would, as they do. Working with you, alongside you on the agency's business, I saw that every day. More than anything else it was what you did, your actions, that simply wouldn't let my preconceived notions stand. You forced me to rethink, to reform my views—so that you would fit, so that I could understand you." Her lips quirked as she straightened her head. "There aren't many who could have accomplished that."

She glanced past him, around, then brought her gaze, direct, open and serious, back to his face. "We're well matched here, in the bedchamber, but that alone would never have induced me to change my mind. But you and I, we're well matched in *all* spheres—in our interest in the agency, in going about in the ton, in the way we deal with society in general. It's as if our lives were created to be complementary—as if they were meant to interlock into one.

"But"—she drew in a long breath and raised her head—"there's one truth that has to be stated, that's at the heart of this, of me and you and what might be. What changed my mind about marriage—with you and only you—was that you always, in whatever sphere, allowed me to be me. Allowed me the freedom to be me. When I think of you, I don't think 'husband'—I think 'partner.' Our relationship isn't, and could never be, that of a conventional husband and wife of our class—it's been, from inception to now, something more akin to the notion of helpmates, a working partnership."

Her eyes locked on his. "And that's what I want—a partnership with you. For life. I believe it would be in both our best interests to marry, but I could never be a conventional wife—I know myself well enough to know that as truth and accept it. In the normal way of things, that would bar me from marriage—the usual sort of marriage among our class. However, with you . . . you're strong enough, unconventional and different enough to accept a different role, a different relationship, to live it, make it work so that I can be your wife."

She paused, then simply said, "The question is: Will you? Will you take my hand and be my partner in life?"

He held her gaze, saw the tension that held her, the emotion glinting in her eyes. Understood, now, why she'd insisted on speaking.

He stepped closer. "Give me your hand."

She did. He closed his fingers around hers and drew in a deep breath. In that instant knew that all he wanted and needed in life would be his.

When he hesitated, she shifted, with a hint of waspishness combined with uncertainty prodded, "Well?"

He smiled. Lifting her hand to his lips, he kissed her fingers. And spoke equally honestly. "I love you."

She hadn't said those words, but he didn't care. She could dress her feelings in whatever guise she chose, whatever logical arguments, but he could see the truth shining in her eyes. Holding her gaze, he kissed her fingers again. "Beyond all recall, beyond distraction."

He drew her nearer, bent his head, found her lips and covered them—drew her slowly, savoring every long-drawn second, into his arms, into a kiss that deepened and broadened and drew them both under.

She followed freely as always, without reservation. It would be so easy to accept all she offered and in return give her the simple "yes" she'd asked for . . . he drew her deeper into his arms, deeper into the kiss, for long moments let desire whirl while passion hovered in the wings . . . then with a sigh he drew back.

Breaking the kiss, he lifted his head. Looked down at her face as she blinked and struggled to refocus her eyes and her wits. Unwilling to release her, to forgo the feeling of her body supple and giving in his arms, the warmth of her against him, he waited patiently until she did, until he could hold her gaze and her attention.

"You have no idea," he said, "how much I would prefer to simply say, 'Yes, I'll be your partner, in anything and every-thing 'til death us do part,' to leave it at that and sweep you into my arms, into your bed and make love to you for the rest of the night—and thereafter for the rest of my life. I'd ex-pected to have to convince *you*—it would be so easy to say yes and have done. *But . . .*" Holding her gaze, he drew in a breath. "That wouldn't be fair—not to you, not to me, and most especially not to what's come to be, to what's grown between us."

He paused, then went on, "You're correct in saying that that isn't the norm, the customary mild affection between husband and wife. That it's something deeper and stronger, infinitely more demanding, commensurately more reward-ing. That it's something more, not less, and that we should embrace it, shield and honor it. In that vein . . . you spoke of the reasons why I need to wed, and you were right. But there's another reason—the reason I have to marry you, and only you."

Her eyes shone as if stars swam in them as she searched his face. "What?"

"I didn't even realize, not until I met you—not until you focused my attention and drew me into your life—that what I was missing, had been missing since I resigned my commis-sion, was a purpose in life, put simply, a reason for living."

She frowned, trying to see. "What of your position, your estates?"

Smiling a touch ruefully, he shook his head. "My fortune and estates I manage with ease—too easily. They're no challenge. The social obligations that I struggle to meet I see as an imposition—they'll never engage me, never excite me." He paused, then admitted, "Before I met you, I was restless, disengaged. In the way that matters most to a man like me, I had nothing to do. Nothing to engage my wits, nothing to challenge me. Nothing to build my life around, no commitment to set at its center."

Raising a hand, he brushed a heavy lock back from her cheek, let his fingers lightly caress."You've just offered me everything I need for a fulfilling life—a partnership with you. Yes, it'll be different—novel, challenging, never dull. Just the agency itself holds boundless possibilities—combining our forces, we'll be able to do much more while still keeping to your original, necessary, and wise charter. And that's not even the half of what you've offered me. A family, a partnership, a marriage with a difference, an intriguing future. A new, challenging, unconventional commission I can accept and commit the rest of my life to."

He looked into her eyes, violet-blue, shimmering. And quietly said, "If I understand anything, I understand that now—I need a purpose, and for that I need you.

"I need to be your husband, I need you as my wife—I need to have you at the center of my life. So yes, I accept your offer—I'll be your partner in life. We'll marry and make of our lives what we choose—husband and wife, partners and lovers."

The words had come readily, although they felt like a surrender, not to her but to what held them, to what had grown and twined about them and now linked them beyond parting. What would always be there, in every glance, every touch.

She felt it, too, valued it as he did; that truth shone clear in her lustrous eyes. She smiled, joy and more blossoming—along with a hint of his own ruefulness. "You are in so many ways what I thought I would never want—too strong, too powerful, dangerous, forceful, ruthless—the list goes on and on. But you've convinced me that instead you're *precisely* what I want, that to be your wife will be all and everything I'll ever want."

Smiling mistily, she shook her head. "I don't understand that, I'll admit. All I know is that I'll never be happy—never be as happy as I might be—unless I'm with you. Unless I'm yours."

Pushing her hands up over his shoulders, she wound her arms about his neck. His arms closing around her, he let her draw his head down, let her kiss him—let her take the lead and take him to her bed.

Let her take him into her arms, into her body.

Phoebe felt her heart swell, fuller, more joyous than it had ever been as he rose above her, her dark and dangerous lover, steely muscles gilded by candlelight as they shifted and flexed as he loved her.

As she loved him. Closing her eyes, she twined her fingers with his, clutched tight as the fiery tide rose and caught them. Whirled them from this world and consumed them.

They'd said all they needed to say, opened their hearts, confessed all their hopes and dreams, and found themselves in agreement, in complete and utterly blissful accord. As the night closed around them, they explored and discovered that with admission, acceptance, and commitment new landscapes appeared, walls they hadn't known existed dissolving to reveal a prize beyond price.

The ultimate reward.

The freedom to be themselves without restriction, to

know and share without reservation. To take their partnership to new heights.

To love and be loved.

To complete and utter distraction.

To complete and absolute satisfaction.

Epilogue

"There you are, my boy!" Edith Balmain smiled at Malcolm Sinclair as he followed Deverell into Edith's drawing room.

Deverell watched Sinclair return Edith's greeting with a gentle smile. He bowed over her hand, then she waved him to sit in the armchair facing hers.

Edith looked at Deverell; he nodded and, as arranged, retreated to the other end of the room, to lounge against the wall beside a window. And watch.

He'd agreed to fetch Sinclair, whom Edith apparently knew. She'd refused to tell him, or Phoebe, Audrey, or anyone else why she needed to speak with the young man, only saying it was a personal matter and avoiding all discussion.

None of them—except perhaps Edith—knew what to

make of Sinclair. On the night Lowther had taken Dalziel's advice and put one of his precious pistols to his head, Christian had eventually run Sinclair to earth in White's. When informed of his guardian's demise, Sinclair had blinked, then commented rather vaguely that he supposed that was the end of it.

When questioned as to his meaning, he'd claimed he'd been referring to his wardship, to being under Lowther's thumb, but Christian hadn't been convinced.

That morning had been the first time Deverell had met Sinclair. His reading of the young man tallied with Christian's. Lowther had said he was "bright enough," but that was far short of the mark. Sinclair was sharply intelligent, yet it was a detached, strangely disconnected intelligence the like of which Deverell hadn't encountered before. It, and Sinclair, seemed to have no focus, or none that Deverell could discern.

Sinclair seemed harmless enough; certainly he gave not the slightest sign of any leaning toward violence. Although well set-up, handsome in a still developing way, fashionably if rather somberly dressed, he projected very little physical presence. Tallish, with a lean figure still filling out, light hazel eyes, pleasing features, and shiny, fairish-brown hair, he would doubtless be a target in the coming years for the matchmakers. Especially now he'd come into his inheritance.

It seemed odd that Lowther hadn't pilfered the boy's money, but other than a few hundred pounds, the estate had been intact when, two days earlier, on his twenty-first birthday, Sinclair had taken possession under the terms of his father's will.

Lowther had had no heirs, and although little would be left after his creditors were paid, what little there was would also pass to Sinclair. He was now a very wealthy young man.

Deverell shifted and fixed his eyes on Edith's lips, tuned his ears to her words. He hadn't made any commitment not to eavesdrop; although he knew Edith had assumed the distance would mean he couldn't hear, his hearing was acute, especially when coupled with his eyesight, and given his and Christian's uneasiness about Sinclair, he felt justified in listening.

Sinclair was facing Edith; Deverell couldn't make out his words. But he could follow Edith as she came to the end of the usual platitudes and observances, and got down to business.

Dressed in various shades of soft pink, she appeared utterly harmless and inconsequential, something she definitely was not. He remembered that the first time he'd seen her, he'd recognized an observant nature he wouldn't have willingly challenged. Meeting an observer like her in a French salon had at one time been his worst nightmare.

Edith's bird-bright gaze was now resting on Sinclair.

"I've heard, of course, that you were involved in Lowther's dastardly scheme, but that the authorities have accepted that you acted solely under Lowther's orders and as his ward are therefore materially absolved of blame." She paused, then went on, "Of course, the authorities didn't know Lowther well, nor do they know you well. I, on the other hand, knew Lowther quite well at one time, and while I wouldn't claim to know you, yourself, I knew your parents, not just your mother but your father, too, very well indeed."

Edith paused, her gaze steady on Sinclair. "So I thought, my boy, that it's time we had a talk."

Edith waited, but Sinclair made no response. Lifting her teacup, she sipped. Sinclair had taken a cup but hadn't drunk; as Deverell watched, he slowly laid the cup and saucer aside on a table to his right.

The movement caught Deverell's attention, set his

instincts quivering. It was not just graceful but controlled—too controlled. Oh, yes, Sinclair was far more than he seemed. Had he forgotten Deverell was watching? Or had he not realized how revealing such minor honest gestures could be?

Given Sinclair's age, Deverell suspected the latter. Given Sinclair's intelligence, he felt sure of it.

Balancing her cup on her saucer, Edith continued. She was no longer looking at Sinclair. "Lowther was always a weak man. His weakness—his coldness, his lack of proper feeling—was what he had in common with your father. It was what made them such close friends. But while Lowther was clever enough, your father was brilliant." She glanced at Sinclair. "Everyone who met him knew it—the depth and breadth of his mind was undeniable.

"Unfortunately, however, he had no real ability to connect with the world beyond his intellect. He had no notion of other people, or society in general, no empathy whatever. He was the third son of a viscount yet had not the faintest concept of morals, ethics, or even propriety. He could speak nine languages fluently but couldn't comprehend that the world was real and did not revolve about him. Lowther, as I said, was similar, although he hid it far better. Your father, however—for him his salvation came in the form of your mother.

"She was his anchor, his link with the world. He would listen to her, and because he truly loved her—and for no other reason at all—he would do what she asked, to please her. Despite his flaws, he was generous in his love and totally committed to her. Together, with her acting as his conscience, he became for a brief time the brilliant scholar and philosopher he should have been."

Edith paused; her voice lowered and Deverell had to strain his ears. "There was, of course, a price, and in some ways that price was your isolation. Your mother never meant to neglect you, but your father's demands on her time and attention were constant and unceasing, so you were—in hindsight most unwisely—left much to yourself. And then they were gone—the brief flash ended with a carriage accident, and unhappily you were left to Lowther's care."

She looked directly at Sinclair. "Many of us tried to look in on you at first, but with your father's death Lowther became even more cold and distant, and less amenable to society's pressures. So you grew up alone with him your only guide. Looking back, that was something we—those of us who knew your parents—never should have allowed. But we never saw you, not since you were six, so didn't realize . . ."

Edith paused, then set aside cup and saucer and faced Sinclair. "I'm one of the few still alive who knew both your parents well. You're brilliant like your father—oh, you needn't try to hide it, and it's far too late to deny it—it shines in your eyes for any who know the signs to see. Knowing that, knowing Lowther and his limitations . . . well, my boy, it's hard to imagine he was the one who thought up the recent scheme, and not you. Regardless, I'm quite sure you have enough of your mother in you that it wasn't you who set the scheme in motion—that *was* Lowther—but the scheme I've heard described has the stamp of your mind on it, not his."

There was not a sound in the room; at the other end, Deverell stood transfixed.

"As matters stand," Edith continued, "the authorities have been lenient over your involvement. They've given you a chance—one I hope you see for what it is. Listen to me, Malcolm, for I've seen your kind before and few others ever have. You need to control the products of your intellect. You will always see opportunity and possibility where others see none, but too often your schemes will ride roughshod over the rights and indeed the lives of others. Unlike your father, you will see that—but like him, you won't really care. You will very likely not indulge in such schemes yourself—you have no pressing reason to—but you will be tempted, as you were with Lowther, to let others try them, if for no other reason than to see if they work."

Sinclair's stillness, complete and absolute, his attention locked on Edith, proved beyond doubt the acuity of Edith's words.

Studying Sinclair's face, Edith nodded. "Yes, I can see that in you, too. So consider this a warning—in all likelihood it will be the only one you'll ever receive. Stay on the straight and narrow. You're stronger than your father—you recognize right from wrong. Don't let your brilliance seduce you into letting the schemes your brain devises become reality, thus harming others, albeit at arm's length. Just because blame can never be sheeted home to you does *not* absolve you of it."

Edith sat back, eyes on Sinclair's face. After a moment, she said, "There's nothing more I can say, for you understand me perfectly. When next temptation comes your way, let it pass by."

A long moment passed in which neither Sinclair nor Edith moved, then she said, "Thank you for coming. Paignton will see you out."

Sinclair rose, as did Edith.

To Deverell's surprise, Sinclair hesitated, then bowed—gracefully, without the assumed awkwardness of youth. "Ma'am."

He turned and started toward Deverell, who strolled to wait by the door.

Deverell watched Sinclair draw nearer, saw the softening of his face as his youthful, vague, rather diffident mask slid back into place. His stride changed, too, less confident, more hesitant.

By the time Sinclair reached him, there was no hint of the dangerous man he knew Edith had faced.

Before the door, Sinclair paused and glanced back. Edith had risen and walked to her writing desk before the window; as they watched, she picked up her diary—a slim volume clasped between engraved silver plates with a large cabuchon amethyst adorning the front cover—then sat and, opening the diary, holding back a page, she reached for her pen.

Turning, Sinclair nodded vaguely in Deverell's direction. Without meeting his eyes, he allowed Deverell to show him out of the house.

Deverell spoke with Christian, then consulted with Dalziel, but they concluded that the official stance on Malcolm Sinclair was correct. Edith's conjecture that the scheme was the fruit of Sinclair's brain was hardly proof, and even she felt certain it had been Lowther, and not Sinclair, who had put it into action. Indeed, Lowther himself had confirmed Sinclair's lackey status.

"The man may have criminal ideas," Dalziel said, "but that's no crime."

"Just as long as he does nothing to convert theory into practice." Deverell met Dalziel's, then Christian's, eyes. They needed no words to know what each of them was thinking.

Malcolm Sinclair would bear watching.

Paignton Hall, Devon
Three weeks later

*T*hey were married in the chapel of his castle—an ancient place encapsulated within a much more modern structure.

Phoebe was thrilled and fascinated with her new and

fancifully different home, with the surrounding countryside, so lush and verdant, with the seas that sometimes thundered and at other times shushed so peacefully into the cove beneath her window.

Today the seas were peaceful, the sun beaming down as she and Deverell, arm in arm, wended their way through the huge crowd gathered to celebrate their wedding.

Everyone was there; she and Deverell had agreed to have their banns read and give everyone the three weeks to prepare and journey down to the hall. She'd convinced Emmeline and Birtles to close the agency for a few days and enjoy the castle's hospitality. They'd managed to bring Scatcher with them; he was wandering the old bailey, now an expanse of lawn on which they were all gathered, gazing in amazement at the surrounding castle walls.

Phoebe glanced around, too, but at the crowd, noting the many large gentlemen—the Bastion Club members and various others—present. Many were powerful, forceful men, ruthless when necessary, dangerous when crossed, and not one of them would she not trust with her honor, with her life.

For years she'd imagined such gentlemen didn't exist; now they surrounded her. Glancing at the one on whose arm she was strolling, she smiled to herself and leaned lightly, fleetingly, against him.

He looked at her but only smiled.

They stopped beside Jack, Lord Hendon, another of those large and powerful gentlemen. Kit, his beautiful wife, beside him, smiled delightedly and touched cheeks with Phoebe. Although older than Phoebe, she was of like mind in many ways and, as Phoebe now was, was included in that highly select group, the wives of the gentlemen of the Bastion Club, Jack being an unofficial club member.

Jack shook hands with Deverell.

When he turned to Phoebe, she stretched up and bussed his cheek. "Thank you for your help."

Jack grinned. "My pleasure." He glanced at Deverell. "Any time you want to stop a slaving ship, I'm your man."

Two days after Lowther had shot himself, they'd trapped the white slavers on the docks and rescued all the abducted girls. The men on the ship had hoisted sail and tried to slip away, but had found their way blockaded, not just by the water police in their rowing boats but by two large ships of the Hendon line, fully manned with cannons deployed.

"Have you settled all the girls yet?" Kit asked. "I sent Emmeline two more names I think would be suitable for some of your clients."

"Thank you." Phoebe pressed Kit's hand. "With all of you—and your friends, too—assisting, we've been able to place all the kidnapped girls, as well as a number who wanted to change households."

Her "little crusade" had grown; Deverell had remarked it was well on the way to becoming a secret cause célèbre, at least among a certain section of the ton.

"Indeed." Kit's eyes twinkled as she reclaimed her husband's arm. "And with the continued success of the gentlemen of the Bastion Club in finding suitable brides, there'll be positions aplenty for nannies and children's maids all too soon."

Phoebe blushed. She was grateful when Deverell excused them and guided her on; she hadn't told anyone their news yet—only him. "Do you think she guessed?"

In light of Kit's knowing smile, Deverell thought it very likely. He shrugged. "Everyone will know soon enough."

He looked down at Phoebe, at her bright eyes, at the garnet glints glowing in her rich, dark red hair. "Once you give me leave, I fully intend to shout it from the rooftops." Everything he could have asked from life he now had, all he wanted from life he now possessed.

Phoebe chuckled and let him lead her on to where Audrey and Loftus sat with Edith in the shade of one of the old towers. They chatted for some minutes. While Phoebe spoke with Edith and Loftus, Audrey stood; moving to Deverell's other side, she leaned on his arm.

He arched a brow at her.

"You're now the head of the family, so I thought I should warn you—I'm about to cause a scandal."

He raised both brows. "Oh?"

Audrey nodded, the peacock feather in her turban bobbing wildly. "I'm going to marry Loftus." Head high, she met his eyes. "Are you going to disown me?"

"Of course not." He'd guessed, and approved; Loftus provided the perfect foil for Audrey's flamboyant eccentricity, and having helped him to his own thoroughly suitable bride, it seemed entirely right that she should, through that, find her own happiness.

She considered him, then smiled softly. "Your father would have, you know."

Closing his hand over hers on his sleeve, he gently squeezed. "Thanks to you, I'm not my father."

Just as well; if he had been, he'd never have had the sense to pursue, let alone marry, an unconventional female like Phoebe.

And what a shame that would have been.

Last night, she'd found him in the library reading a book on India. After having him describe various castes and practices, she'd declared she was a maharani and he her pleasure slave; she'd ordered him to her bedchamber, there to fulfill her every wish, her every desire.

He was looking forward to discovering what unconventional tack she would lead him on tonight, their wedding night. He felt sure she'd have some novel idea, and if by chance she didn't, he had quite a few ideas of his own.

Alicia, Tony's wife, waylaid them, then carried Phoebe off to talk with the other wives—the increasing band of Bastion Club matriarchs-in-the-making. Knowing what was good for him, he yielded her up with good grace and took himself off to join his colleagues in the shadow of one wall.

Christian raised his glass to him as he came up. "I notice our dear ex-commander is as usual absent."

"Of course." Deverell glanced over the sea of heads. "We received the usual expression of regret."

"One day," Charles St. Austell predicted, "one of us is going to stumble across him in his true guise—I just hope it's me."

Tristan frowned. "Speaking of guises, one thing that puzzles me—I assume you noticed that your man Montague recognized him, and so did Lowther."

"So?" Tony Blake arched a brow. "We know he's one of us, almost certainly a son of the nobility."

Jack Warnefleet snorted softly. "Half the old biddies seem to know who he is—they just won't tell us."

"That's just *it,*" Tristan said. "They *all* know him—who he really is—but none of them, not *one,* uses his real name. They all refer to him as Dalziel. Why? For what possible reason would the entire ton—all the grande dames and peers—collude in such a thing, a noble gentleman—we all know he's that—not using his real name?"

They all blinked.

Eventually Gervase voiced the one reason that had popped into all their heads. "Scandal. For some reason he's debarred from using, or refuses to now use, his family name."

Deverell frowned, then glanced at Christian. "He's older

than us, isn't he?" Christian was the oldest of them by a year or so.

Christian grimaced. "I've never been sure, but yes, I think he is older than I am by a year, perhaps two."

"So it's possible," Charles concluded, "that there was some ungodly scandal in the years before any of us went up to town—in the years while we were at Oxford busy doing other things."

They all nodded.

"And of course none of us can remember it," Deverell said, "because we never heard of it, never knew of it in the first place."

A silence fell in which they all rapidly canvassed their sources, then Tony sighed. "It won't do us a bit of good, you know. All those who know his name also know the reason he doesn't use it, and for whatever reason, they have all accepted—every last one—that it's better if he's known as Dalziel, with that reason why wiped from collective memory."

Charles grimaced and sipped. "That must have been quite a scandal."

No one argued.

"So Royce whoever-he-is remains an enigma, at least for now." Gervase turned to Deverell and held out his hand. "I've got to get on—I'm expected at Crowhurst tonight."

Charles raised his brows. "Why the rush?" He waggled his brows. "Is there some particular someone waiting?"

They all noticed that the smile Gervase returned was somewhat tight. "Nothing as interesting, unfortunately. Family business calls, and I can't afford to let it drift."

Charles opened his mouth, then shut it.

Gervase made his farewells, then unobtrusively tacked through the crowd, heading for the archway and the stables beyond.

Deverell glanced at Charles. "What were you about to say?"

His gaze on Gervase's back, Charles replied, "Have any of you noticed how often he's called away, back to Crowhurst, on family business?"

Jack Warnefleet frowned. "Now you mention it, yes. He's hardly spent any time in town at all, although I know he intended to."

Christian cleared his throat. "According to Gasthorpe, it really is family business. Every time Gervase gets up to town, it's only a matter of days, apparently, before some missive arrives and he has to return."

They all stared after Gervase until he passed under the archway and out of sight.

"I wonder," Deverell said, "what's going on at Crowhurst."

THE SIXTH BASTION CLUB NOVEL

tells the tale of Gervase Tregarth, Earl of Crowhurst, who, far from having found a suitable bride, has barely had a chance to enter London's ballrooms. Family matters keep hauling him back to Crowhurst until his temper snaps and he declares he'll marry the first eligible lady who crosses his path. As matters transpire, that proves to be an exceedingly reckless, and exceptionally challenging, vow.

FROM AVON BOOKS, FALL 2007.

In the Meantime . . .

STEPHANIE LAURENS'S CYNSTER NOVELS
continue with

What Price Love?
coming in paperback from Avon Books
in February 2007.

Following is an excerpt from What Price Love?, *which is the story of Dillon Caxton, Flick Cynster's cousin and Demon Cynster's protégé, and the lady who captures his heart.*

The next Cynster Novel,

The Taste of Innocence
will be released in hardcover
from William Morrow, March 2007.

*R*eturning his gaze to her, he smiled. "Your name, Miss . . . ?"

Apparently at ease in the straight-backed chair, comfortably padded with arms on which she'd rested hers, she smiled back. "Dalling. Miss Dalling. I confess I've no real idea of, nor interest in, racing or racehorses, but I was hoping to view this register one hears so much about. The doorman gave me to understand that you are the guardian of this famous tome. I'd imagined it was on public display, like the *Births and Deaths Register*, but apparently that's not the case."

She had a melodic, almost hypnotic voice, not so much sirenlike as that of a storyteller, luring you to believe, to accept, and respond.

Dillon fought the compulsion, forced himself to listen dispassionately, sought, found and clung to his usual aloof distance. Although uttered as statements, he sensed her sentences were questions. "The register you're referring to is known as the *Breeding Register,* and no, it's not a public document. It's an archive of the Jockey Club. In effect, it's a listing of the horses approved to run on those racetracks overseen by the club."

She was drinking in his every word. "I see. So . . . if one wished to verify that a particular horse was approved to race on such tracks, one would consult the *Breeding Register.*"

Another question parading as a statement. "Yes."

"So it *is* possible to view the *Breeding Register.*"

"No." He smiled, deliberately a touch patronizingly, when she frowned. "If you wish to know if a particular horse is approved to race, you need to apply for the information."

"Apply?"

At last a straight, unadorned question; he let his smile grow more intent. "You fill out a form, and one of the register clerks will provide you with the required information."

She looked disgusted. "A form." She flicked the fingers of one hand. "I suppose this is England, after all."

He made no reply. When it became clear he wasn't going to rise to that bait, she tried another tack.

She leaned forward, just a little. Confidingly fixed her big green eyes on his face, simultaneously drawing attention to her really quite impressive breasts, not overly large yet on her slight frame deliciously tempting.

Having already taken stock, he managed to keep his gaze steady on her face.

She smiled slightly, invitingly. "Surely you could allow me to view the register—just a glance."

Her emerald eyes held his; he fell under her spell. Again. That voice, not sultry but something even more deeply stirring, threatened, again, to draw him under; he had to fight to shake free of the mesmerizing effect.

Suppressing his frown took yet more effort. "No." He

shifted, and softened the edict. "That's not possible, I'm afraid."

She frowned, the expression entirely genuine. "Why not? I just want to look."

"Why? What's the nature of your interest in the *Breeding Register*, Miss Dalling? No, wait." He let his eyes harden, let his deepening suspicions show. "You're already told us you have no real interest in such things. Why, then, is viewing the register so important to you?"

She held his gaze unwaveringly. A moment ticked by, then she sighed and, still entirely relaxed, leaned back in the chair. "It's for my aunt."

When he looked his surprise, she airily waved. "She's eccentric. Her latest passion is racehorses—that's why we're here. She's curious about every little thing to do with horse racing. She stumbled on mention of this register somewhere, and now nothing will do but for her to know all about it."

She heaved an artistic sigh. "I didn't think those here would appreciate a fluttery, dotty old dear haunting your foyer, so I came." Fixing her disturbing green eyes on him, she went on, "And that's why I would like to take a look at this *Breeding Register.* Just a peek."

That last was said almost tauntingly. Dillon considered how to reply.

He could walk over to the bookcase, retrieve the current volume of the register, and lay it on the desk before her. Caution argued against showing her where the register was, even what it looked like. He could tell her what information was included in each register entry, but even that might be tempting fate in the guise of someone allied with those planning substitutions. That risk was too serious to ignore.

Perhaps he should call her bluff and suggest she bring her aunt into his office, but no matter how intently he searched her eyes, he couldn't be sure she was lying about her aunt. It was possible her tale, fanciful though it was, was the unvarnished truth. That might result in him breaking the until-now-inviolate rule that no one but he and the register clerks were ever allowed to view the *Breeding Register* for some fussy old dear.

Who could *not* be counted on not to spread the word.

"I'm afraid, Miss Dalling, that all I can tell you is that the entries in the register comprise a listing of licenses granted to individual horses to race under Jockey Club rules." He spread his hands in commiseration. "That's really all I'm at liberty to divulge."

Her green eyes had grown crystalline, hard. "How very mysterious."

He smiled faintly. "You have to allow us our secrets."

The distance between them was too great for him to be sure, but he thought her eyes snapped. For an instant, the outcome hung in the balance—whether she would retreat, or try some other, possibly more high-handed means of persuasion—but then she sighed again, lifted her reticule from her lap, and smoothly rose.

Dillon rose, too, surprised by a very real impulse to do something to prolong her visit. But then, rounding the desk, he drew close enough to see the expression in her eyes. There was temper there—an Irish temper to match her accent. It was presently leashed, but she was definitely irritated and annoyed with him.

Because she hadn't been able to bend him to her will.

He felt his lips curve, saw annoyance coalesce and intensify in her eyes. She really ought to have known just by looking that he wasn't likely to fall victim to her charms.

Manifold and very real though they were.

"Thank you for your time, Mr. Caxton." Her tone was cold, a shivery coolness, the most her soft brogue would allow. "I'll inform my aunt that she'll have to live with her questions unanswered."

"I'm sorry to have to disappoint an old lady, however . . ." He shrugged lightly. "Rules are rules, and there for a good reason."

He watched for her reaction, for some sign, however slight, of comprehension, but she merely raised her brows in patent disbelief and, with every indication of miffed disappointment, turned away.

"I'll see you to the front door." He went with her to the door of his room, opened it.

"No need." Briefly, she met his eyes as she swept past him. "I'm sure I can find my way."

"Nevertheless." He followed her into the corridor.

The rigidity of her spine declared she was offended he hadn't trusted her to go straight back to the front foyer if left to herself. But they both knew she wouldn't have, that if he'd set her free she'd have roamed, trusting her beauty to extract her from any difficulty should she be caught where she shouldn't be.

She didn't look back when she reached the foyer and sailed on toward the front door. "Good-bye, Mr. Caxton."

The cool words drifted over her shoulder. Halting in the mouth of the corridor, he watched the doorman, still bedazzled, leap to swing open the portal. She stepped through, disappearing into the bright sunshine; the doors swung shut, and he could see her no more.